PENGUIN BOOKS

THE IDIOT

Elif Batuman is the author of *The Possessed: Adventures with Russian Books and the People Who Read Them* and lives in New York City.

* * *

Praise for Elif Batuman's *The Idiot*

"Batuman's novel is roaringly funny. It is also intellectually subtle, surprising, and enlightening. . . . Batuman has written a romantic comedy about the romance of language, a metacomic novel of ideas, and an adventure in grammar. *The Idiot* is an epic tale of words and the people who love them and live by them."   —*The New York Review of Books*

"Masterly funny debut novel . . . Erudite but never pretentious, *The Idiot* will make you crave more books by Batuman."   —*Vanity Fair*

"Not since Don Quixote has a quest for love gone so hilariously and poignantly awry. In spare, unforgettable prose, Batuman the traveler (to Harvard, to mysterious Hungary) recreates for the reader the psychic state of being a child entering language. We marvel and tremble with her at the impossibility and mysterious necessity for human connection that both makes life worthwhile and yet so often strands us all in torment. This book is a bold, unforgettable, un-put-downable read by a new master stylist. Best novel I've read in years."
—Mary Karr, author of *The Art of Memoir*, *Lit*, and *The Liars' Club*

"There is more oxygen, more life in this book, than in a shelf of its peers. And in the way of the best characters, Batuman's creations are not bound by the book that created them. They seem released into the world. Long after I finished *The Idiot*, I looked at every lanky girl with her nose in a book on the subway and thought: Selin."
—*The New York Times Book Review*

"Easily the funniest book I've read this year."   —*GQ*

"I'm not Turkish, I don't have a Serbian best friend, I'm not in love with a Hungarian, I don't go to Harvard. Or do I? For one wonderful week, I got to be this worldly and brilliant, this young and clumsy and in love. *The Idiot* is a hilariously mundane immersion into a world that has never before received the Nineteenth Century Novel treatment. An addictive, sprawling epic; I wolfed it down."
—Miranda July, author of *The First Bad Man* and *It Chooses You*

"Batuman's brainy novel is leavened with humor and a heroine incapable of artifice." —*People*

"Elif Batuman's novel not only captures the storms and mysteries and comedies of youth but, in its wonderfully sensitive portrait of a young woman adventuring across languages and cultures, it brilliantly draws to our attention a modern politics of friendship. This is a remarkable book."
—Joseph O'Neill, author of *The Dog* and *Netherland*

"Batuman has won a *Paris Review* Terry Southern Prize for humor, and her book is consistently hilarious. If this is a sentimental education, it's one leavened by a great deal of mordant and delightful humor. . . . At once a cutting satire of academia, a fresh take on the epistolary novel, a poignant bildungsroman, and compelling travel literature, *The Idiot* is also a touching and spirited portrait of the artist as a hugely appealing young woman." —*The Boston Globe*

"Elif Batuman surely has one of the best senses of humor in American letters. The pleasure she takes in observing the eccentricities of each of her characters makes for a really refreshing and unique bildungsroman: one more fascinated with what's going on around and outside the bewildered protagonist, than what's going on inside her."
—Sheila Heti, author of *How Should a Person Be?* and *Ticknor*

"No one writes funnier or more stylishly about higher education. Nothing written about grad school is as entertaining as her 2010 collection of dispatches from Stanford's comparative-literature department, *The Possessed*, and her studied satire of Harvard in *The Idiot* is nearly its equal."
—*The Village Voice*

"Batuman wittily and wisely captures the tribulations of a shy, cerebral teenager struggling with love, friendship, and whether to take psycholinguistics or philosophy of language. . . . Batuman's writing is funny and deadpan, and Selin's observations tease out many relatable human quandaries surrounding friendship, social niceties, and first love. The result: a novel that may not keep readers up late turning pages feverishly, but that will quietly amuse and provoke thought."

—*The Huffington Post*

"*The Idiot* is an impressive debut with a ridiculous amount of charm and a protagonist so relatable she's almost impossible to forget."

—The A.V. Club

"*The Idiot* is wonderful. Batuman, a staff writer at *The New Yorker* and the author of the sparkling autobiographical essay collection *The Possessed* (2010), has brave and original ideas about what a 'novel' might mean and no qualms about flouting literary convention. She is endlessly beguiled by the possibilities and shortcomings of language. . . . It is a pleasure to watch Batuman render this process with the wit, sensitivity, and relish of someone who's successfully emerged on the other side of it. For all of her fascination with linguistic puzzle boxes, the author tempers her protagonist's intellectual vertigo with maturity and common sense."   —*Slate*

"Beautifully written first novel . . . Batuman, a staff writer for *The New Yorker*, has an extraordinarily deft touch when it comes to sketching character. . . . The novel fairly brims with provocative ideas about language, literature, and culture."   —Associated Press

"A vibrant novel of ideas . . . Like her essays, Batuman's bildungsroman is a succession of droll misadventures built around chance encounters, peculiar conversations, and sharp-eyed observations. Both on campus and abroad, she brings the ever-fresh perspective of a perpetual stranger in a strange land. Her deceptively simple declarative sentences are underpinned by a poker-faced sense of absurdity and humor so dry it calls for olives."   —*San Francisco Chronicle*

"Batuman's sardonic wit makes for a delectable unfolding of Selin's experience of love, life, and language."   —BBC.com

"Charming, hilarious, and wise debut novel . . . Batuman titled the book *The Idiot* (after Dostoevsky's famous novel), but it isn't an excoriation of its heroine. Instead, it's a fond reflection. Oh, you poor, silly idiot, she seems to be saying. *The Idiot*, a novel of innocence and experience, is infused with the generous attitude that Dag Hammarskjöld expressed in his memoir *Markings*, 'For all that has been, Thank you. For all that is to come, Yes!'"
—*The Dallas Morning News*

"*The Idiot* is half *The Education of Henry Adams* and half *Innocents Abroad*. Twain would have savored Selin's first international trip to Paris, Hungary, and Turkey. . . . Our first footsteps into adulthood are often memorable. Taking them in Selin's shoes is an entertaining, intellectual journey not to be missed."
—*Shelf Awareness*

"Selin is entrancing—so smart, so clueless, so funny—and Batuman's exceptional discernment, comedic brilliance, and soulful inquisitiveness generate a charmingly incisive and resonant tale of the messy forging of a self."
—*Booklist* (starred review)

"Wonderful first novel . . . Batuman updates the grand tour travelogue just as she does the epistolary novel and the novel of ideas, in prose as deceptively light as it is ambitious. One character wonders whether it's possible 'to be sincere without sounding pretentious,' and this long-awaited and engrossing novel delivers a resounding yes."
—*Publishers Weekly* (starred review)

"Selin is delightful company. She's smart enough to know the ways in which she is dumb, and her off-kilter relationship to the world around her is revelatory and, often, mordantly hilarious. Readers who are willing to travel with Selin at her own contemplative pace will be grateful that they did. Self-aware, cerebral, and delightful."
—*Kirkus Reviews* (starred review)

The Idiot

Elif Batuman

PENGUIN BOOKS

PENGUIN BOOKS
An imprint of Penguin Random House LLC
375 Hudson Street
New York, New York 10014
penguin.com

First published in the United States of America by Penguin Press,
an imprint of Penguin Random House LLC, 2017
Published in Penguin Books 2018

Excerpt from *In Search of Lost Time, Volume II: Within a Budding Grove*
by Marcel Proust, translated by C. K. Scott Moncrieff and Terence
Kilmartin, revised by D. J. Enright (Modern Library, 1992).

Excerpt from "The Darling" from *The Comic Stories* by Anton Chekhov,
translated by Harvey Pitcher (Ivan R. Dee, Publisher, 1999).

ISBN 9781594205613 (hardcover)
ISBN 9780143111061 (paperback)
ISBN 9781101622513 (ebook)
ISBN 9780735223875 (international edition)

Printed in the United States of America
3   5   7   9   10   8   6   4   2

Designed by Amanda Dewey

But the characteristic feature of the ridiculous age I was going through—awkward indeed but by no means infertile—is that we do not consult our intelligence and that the most trivial attributes of other people seem to us to form an inseparable part of their personality. In a world thronged with monsters and with gods, we know little peace of mind. There is hardly a single action we perform in that phase which we would not give anything, in later life, to be able to annul. Whereas what we ought to regret is that we no longer possess the spontaneity which made us perform them. In later life we look at things in a more practical way, in full conformity with the rest of society, but adolescence is the only period in which we learn anything.

MARCEL PROUST, *In Search of Lost Time,*
Volume II: Within a Budding Grove

Part One

FALL

I didn't know what email was until I got to college. I had heard of email, and knew that in some sense I would "have" it. "You'll be so fancy," said my mother's sister, who had married a computer scientist, "sending your e, mails." She emphasized the "e" and paused before "mail."

That summer, I heard email mentioned with increasing frequency. "Things are changing so fast," my father said. "Today at work I surfed the World Wide Web. One second, I was in the Metropolitan Museum of Art. One second later, I was in Anıtkabir." Anıtkabir, Atatürk's mausoleum, was located in Ankara. I had no idea what my father was talking about, but I knew there was no meaningful sense in which he had been "in" Ankara that day, so I didn't really pay attention.

On the first day of college, I stood in line behind a folding table and eventually received an email address and temporary password. The "address" had my last name in it—Karadağ, but all lowercase, and without the Turkish ğ, which was silent. From an early age I had understood that a silent g was funny. "The g is silent," I would say in a weary voice, and it was always hilarious. I didn't understand how the email address was an address, or what it was short for. "What do we do with this, hang ourselves?" I asked, holding up the Ethernet cable.

"You plug it into the wall," said the girl behind the table.

Insofar as I'd had any idea about it at all, I had imagined that email would resemble faxing, and would involve a printer. But there was no printer. There was another world. You could access it from certain computers, which were scattered throughout the ordinary landscape, and looked no different from regular computers. Always there, unchanged, in a configuration nobody else could see, was a glowing list of messages from all the people you knew, and from people you didn't know, all in the same letters, like the universal handwriting of thought or of the world. Some messages were formally epistolary, with "Dear" and "Sincerely"; others telegraphic, all in lowercase with missing punctuation, like they were being beamed straight from people's brains. And each message contained the one that had come before, so your own words came back to you—all the words you threw out, they came back. It was like the story of your relations with others, the story of the intersection of your life with other lives, was constantly being recorded and updated, and you could check it at any time.

You had to wait in a lot of lines and collect a lot of printed materials, mostly instructions: how to respond to sexual harassment, report an eating disorder, register for student loans. They showed you a video about a recent college graduate who broke his leg and defaulted on his student loans, proving that the budget he drew up was no good: a good budget makes provisions for debilitating injury. The bank was a real bonanza, as far as lines and printed materials were concerned. They gave you a free dictionary. The dictionary didn't include "ratatouille" or "Tasmanian devil."

On the staircase approaching my room, I could hear tuneless singing and the slap of plastic slippers. My new roommate, Hannah, was standing on a chair, taping a sign that read HANNAH PARK'S DESK over her desk, chanting monotonously along with Blues Traveler on her Discman. When I came in, she turned in a pantomime of surprise, pitching to and fro, then jumped noisily to the floor and took off her headphones.

"Have you considered mime as a career?" I asked.

"*Mime?* No, my dear, I'm afraid my parents sent me to Harvard to become a surgeon, not a mime." She blew her nose loudly. "Hey—*my* bank didn't give me a dictionary!"

"It doesn't have 'Tasmanian devil,'" I said.

She took the dictionary from my hands, rifling the pages. "It has plenty of words."

I told her she could have it. She put it on the shelf next to the dictionary she had gotten in high school, for being the valedictorian. "They look good together," she said. I asked if her other dictionary had "Tasmanian devil." It didn't. "Isn't the Tasmanian devil a cartoon character?" she asked, looking suspicious. I showed her the page in my other dictionary that had not just "Tasmanian devil," but also "Tasmanian wolf," with a picture of the wolf glancing, a bit sadly, over its left shoulder.

Hannah stood very close to me and stared at the page. Then she looked right and left and whispered hotly in my ear, "That music has been playing all day long."

"What music?"

"Shhh—stand absolutely still."

We stood absolutely still. Faint romantic strings drifted from under the door of our other roommate, Angela.

"It's the sound track for *Legends of the Fall,*" whispered Hannah. "She's been playing it all morning, since I got up. She's just been sitting in there with the door shut, playing the tape over and over again. I knocked and asked her to turn it down but you can still hear it. I had to listen to my Discman to drown her out."

"It's not that loud," I said.

"But it's just weird that she sits there like that."

Angela had gotten to our three-person, two-bedroom suite at seven the previous morning and taken the single bedroom, leaving

Hannah and me to share the one with bunk beds. When I got there in the evening, I found Hannah storming around in a fury, moving furniture, sneezing, and shouting about Angela. "I never even saw her!" Hannah yelled from under her desk. She suddenly succeeded in detaching two things she had been pulling at, and banged her head. "OWW!" she yelled. She crawled out and pointed wrathfully at Angela's desk. "These books? They're fake!" She seized what looked like a stack of four leather-bound volumes, one with THE HOLY BIBLE printed on the spine, shook it under my nose, and slammed it down again. It was a wooden box. "What's even in there?" She knocked on the Bible. "Her last testament?"

"Hannah, please be gentle with other people's property," said a soft voice, and I noticed two small Koreans, evidently Hannah's parents, sitting in the window seat.

Angela came in. She had a sweet expression and was black, and was wearing a Harvard windbreaker and a Harvard backpack. Hannah immediately confronted her about the single room.

"Hmm, yeah," Angela said. "It's just I got here really early and I had so many suitcases."

"I kind of noticed the suitcases," said Hannah. She flung open the door to Angela's room. A yellowed cloth and a garland of cloth roses had been draped over the one tiny window, and in the murk stood four or five human-sized suitcases.

I said maybe we could each have the single room for a third of the year, with Angela going first. Angela's mother came in, dragging another suitcase. She stood in the doorway to Angela's room. "It is what it is," she said.

Hannah's father stood up and took out a camera. "First college roommates! That's an important relationship!" he said. He took several pictures of Hannah and me but none of Angela.

. . .

Hannah bought a refrigerator for the common room. She said I could use it if I bought something for the room, too, like a poster. I asked what kind of poster she had in mind.

"Psychedelic," she said.

I didn't know what a psychedelic poster was, so she showed me her psychedelic notebook. It had a fluorescent tie-dyed spiral, with purple lizards walking around the spiral and disappearing into the center.

"What if they don't have that?" I asked.

"Then a photograph of Albert Einstein," she said decisively, as if it were the obvious next choice.

"Albert Einstein?"

"Yeah, one of those black-and-white pictures. You know: Einstein."

The campus bookstore turned out to have a huge selection of Albert Einstein posters. There was Einstein at a blackboard, Einstein in a car, Einstein sticking out his tongue, Einstein smoking a pipe. I didn't totally understand why we had to have an image of Einstein on the wall. But it was better than buying my own refrigerator.

The poster I got was no better or worse than the other Einstein posters in any way that I could see, but Hannah seemed to dislike it. "Hmm," she said. "I think it'll look good there." She pointed to the space over my bookshelf.

"But then *you* can't see it."

"That's okay. It goes best there."

From that day on, everyone who happened by our room—neighbors wanting to borrow stuff, residential computer staff, student council candidates, all kinds of people to whom my small enthusiasms should have been a source of little or no concern—went out of their way to disabuse me of my great admiration for Albert Einstein. Einstein had invented the atomic bomb, abused dogs, neglected his children. "There were many greater geniuses than Einstein," said a Bulgarian freshman who had stopped by to borrow my copy of Dostoevsky's *The*

Double. "Alfred Nobel hated mathematics and didn't give the Nobel Prize to any mathematicians. There were many who were more deserving."

"Oh." I handed him the book. "Well, see you around."

"Thanks," he said, glaring at the poster. "This is the man who beats his wife, forces her to solve his mathematical problems, to do the dirty work, and he denies her credit. And you put his picture on your wall."

"Listen, leave me out of this," I said. "It's not really my poster. It's a complicated situation."

He wasn't listening. "Einstein in this country is synonymous with genius, while many greater geniuses aren't famous at all. Why is this? I am asking you."

I sighed. "Maybe it's because he's really the best, and even jealous mudslingers can't hide his star quality," I said. "Nietzsche would say that such a great genius is *entitled* to beat his wife."

That shut him up. After he left, I thought about taking down the poster. I wanted to be a courageous person, uncowed by other people's dumb opinions. But what was the dumb opinion: thinking Einstein was so great, or thinking he was the worst? In the end, I left the poster up.

Hannah snored. Everything in the room that wasn't a solid block of wood—the windowpanes, the bed girders, the mattress springs, my rib cage—vibrated in sympathy. It did no good to wake her up or roll her over. She just started again a minute later. If she was asleep, I was by definition awake, and vice versa.

I convinced Hannah that she had obstructive sleep apnea, which was depriving her brain cells of oxygen and compromising her chances of getting into a top-ten medical school. She went to the campus health center and came back with a box of adhesive strips that were supposed to prevent snoring by sticking to your nose. A photograph on the box showed a man and a woman gazing into the distance, wearing matching plastic nose strips, a breeze ruffling the woman's hair.

Hannah pulled her nose up from the side, and I smoothed the strip in place with my thumbs. Her face felt so small and doll-like that I felt a wave of tenderness toward her. Then she started yelling about something, and the feeling passed. The nose strips actually worked, but they gave Hannah sinus headaches, so she stopped using them.

In the long days that stretched between even longer nights, I stumbled from room to room taking placement tests. You had to sit in a basement writing essays about whether it was better to be a Renaissance person or a specialist. There was a quantitative reasoning test full of melancholy word problems—"The graph models the hypothetical mass in grams of a broiler chicken up to eighty weeks of age"—and every evening was some big meeting where you sat on the floor and learned that you were now a little fish in a big sea, and were urged to view this circumstance as an exhilarating challenge rather than a source of anxiety. I tried not to give too much weight to the thing about the fish, but after a while it started to get me down anyway. It was hard to feel cheerful when someone kept telling you you were a little fish in a big sea.

My academic adviser, Carol, had a British accent and worked at the Office of Information Technology. Twenty years ago, in the 1970s, she had received a master's degree from Harvard in Old Norse. I knew that the Office of Information Technology was where you mailed your telephone bill each month. Other than that, its sphere of activity was mysterious. How was Old Norse involved? On the subject of her work, Carol said only, "I wear many hats."

Hannah and I both caught a terrible cold. We took turns buying cold medicine and knocked it back like shots from the little plastic cup.

When it came time to choose classes, everyone said it was of utmost importance to apply to freshman seminars, because otherwise it could be years before you had a chance to work with senior faculty. I applied to three literature seminars and got called in for one interview. I reported to the top floor of a cold white building, where I shivered for twenty minutes on a leather sofa under a skylight wondering if I was in the right place. There were some strange newspapers on the coffee table. That was the first time I saw the *Times Literary Supplement*. I couldn't understand anything in the *Times Literary Supplement*.

A door opened and the professor called me in. He extended his hand—an enormous hand on an incredibly skinny, pale wrist, further dwarfed by a gigantic overcoat.

"I don't think I should shake your hand," I said. "I have this cold." Then I had a violent fit of sneezing. The professor looked startled, but recovered quickly. "Gesundheit," he said urbanely. "I'm sorry you aren't feeling well. These first days of college can be rough on the immune system."

"So I'm learning," I said.

"Well, that's what it's all about," he said. "Learning! Ha, ha."

"Ha, ha," I said.

"Well, let's get down to business. From your application, you seem to be very creative. I enjoyed your creative application essay. My only concern is that you realize this seminar is an academic class, not a creative class."

"Right," I said, nodding energetically and trying to determine whether any of the rectangles in my peripheral vision was a box of tissues. Unfortunately, they were all books. The professor was talking about the differences between creative and academic writing. I kept nodding. I was thinking about the structural equivalences between a tissue box and a book: both consisted of slips of white paper in a cardboard case; yet—and this was ironic—there was very little functional equivalence, especially if the book wasn't yours. These were the kinds of things I thought about all the time, even though they were neither pleasant nor useful. I had no idea what you were supposed to be thinking about.

"Do you think," the professor was saying, "that you could spend two hours reading the same passage, the same sentence, even the same word? Do you think you might find it tedious, or boring?"

Because my ability to spend hours staring at a single word had rarely been encouraged in the past, I pretended to have to think it over. "No," I said finally.

The professor nodded, frowning thoughtfully and narrowing his eyes. I understood with a sinking feeling that I was supposed to keep talking. "I *like* words," I elaborated. "They don't bore me at all." Then I sneezed five times.

I didn't get in. I got called to only one other interview, for Form in the Nonfiction Film: a seminar I had applied to because my mother, who had always wanted to be an actress, had lately joined a screen-writing class and now wanted to make a documentary about the lives of foreign medical graduates in America—about people who hadn't passed the medical board exams and ended up driving taxis or working in drugstores, and about people like my mother who passed the boards and became research faculty at second-tier schools, where they kept getting scooped by people at Johns Hopkins and Harvard. My mother had often expressed the hope and belief that I would help her make this documentary.

The film professor had an even worse cold than I did. It felt magical, like a gift. We met in a basement room full of flickering blue screens. I told him about my mother, and we both sneezed continually. That was the only freshman seminar I got into.

I went to the snack counter in the student center to buy a Diet Coke. The guy in front of me in line was taking forever to order. First he wanted iced tea, but there wasn't any.

"Do you have lemonade?" he asked.

"Lemonade, I have in the can and the bottle."

"Is it the same brand in the can and the bottle?"

"The bottle is Snapple. The can is, uh, Country Time."

"I'd like the bottle of lemonade, and an apple Danish."

"I'm out of the apple. I got cheese and raspberry."

"Oh. Do you have baked potato chips?"

"You mean the kind that's baked?"

It was the world's most boring conversation, but somehow I couldn't stop listening. It went on like that until finally the guy had paid for his Snapple lemonade and blueberry muffin and turned to leave. "Sorry for taking so long," he said. He was really good-looking.

"That's okay," I said.

He smiled, started to walk away, but hesitated. "Selin?"

"Ralph!" I exclaimed, realizing that he was this guy I knew, Ralph.

Ralph and I had met the previous summer at a program for high school juniors where you spent five weeks in a house in New Jersey studying the interdisciplinary history of the Northern European Renaissance. The thing that had brought us together was how the art history teacher mentioned the Doge of Venice, whom she called simply "the Doge," in every lecture, regardless of subject. She could be talking about the daily lives of burghers in Delft and somehow the Doge would come into it. Nobody else seemed to notice this, or to think it was funny.

We sat together with our drinks and his muffin. There was something dreamlike about our conversation, because I found that I couldn't quite remember how well we had known each other last summer. I remembered that I had admired him, because he was so good at imitating people. Also, I found that I now somehow knew a lot of information about his five aunts—more than one would know about someone who wasn't a friend. At the same time, Ralph was somehow categorized in my mind as the kind of person I would never truly be friends with, because he was so handsome, and so good at relating to adults. He was what my mother called, in Turkish, a "family boy": clean-cut, well-spoken, the type who didn't mind wearing a suit or talking to his parents' friends. My mother had really liked Ralph.

Ralph and I talked about our freshman seminar interviews. He had interviewed for a seminar with a Nobel Prize–winning physicist who hadn't asked a single question and just made Ralph wash some lab equipment. The equipment might have been a gamma ray detector.

I applied for a class called Constructed Worlds, in the studio art department. I met the instructor, a visiting artist from New York, in a studio full of empty white tables, bringing my high school art portfolio. The visiting artist squinted at my face.

"So how old are you anyway?" he asked.

"Eighteen."

"Oh, for Christ's sake. This isn't a freshman class."

"Oh. Should I leave?"

"No, don't be ridiculous. Let's take a look at your work." He was still looking at me, not the portfolio. "Eighteen," he repeated, shaking his head. "When I was your age I was dropping acid and cutting high school. I was working summers in a fish factory in Secaucus. Secaucus, New Jersey." He looked at me disapprovingly, as though I were somehow behind schedule.

"Maybe that's what I'll be doing when I'm *your* age," I suggested.

"Yeah, right." He snorted and put on a pair of glasses. "Well, let's see what we've got here." He stared at the pictures in silence. I looked out the window at two squirrels running up a tree. One squirrel lost its grip and fell, crashing through the layers of foliage. This was something I had never seen before.

"Well, look," said the visiting artist finally. "Your composition in the drawings is . . . okay. I can be honest with you, right? But these paintings seem to me . . . sort of little-girlish? Do you see what I'm saying?"

I looked at the pictures he had spread out on the table. It wasn't that I couldn't see what he meant. "The thing is," I said, "it wasn't so long ago that I was a little girl."

He laughed. "True enough, true enough. Well, I'll make my decision this weekend. You'll be hearing from me. Or maybe you won't."

Hannah was applying to be a campus tour guide. I heard her in the shower in the morning, reciting Harvard trivia in an enchanting voice. Later, when she didn't get the job and stopped reciting the trivia, I found that I somehow missed it.

I went with Angela to an introductory meeting at the Harvard student newspaper, where a young man with sideburns told us repeatedly, in the most aggressive manner, that the Harvard student newspaper was his life. "It's my *life*," he kept saying with a venomous expression. Angela and I exchanged glances.

On Sunday evening the phone rang. It was the visiting artist. "Your essay was somewhat interesting," he said. "Most of the essays were actually incredibly . . . boring? So, in fact, I'll be happy to have you in my class."

"Oh," I said. "Okay."

"Is that a yes?"

"Sorry?"

"Are you accepting?"

"Can I think about it?"

"Can you think about it? I mean, not really. I have a lot of other applicants I can call," he said. "So are you in or are you out?"

"I guess I'm in."

"Good. See you Thursday."

I auditioned for the college orchestra. The conductor's office was a hexagonal room with a bay window, a grand piano, and shelves full of books: orchestral scores, encyclopedias, volumes of music history and criticism. I had never seen a music person with so many books. I played the sonata I had prepared. My hands didn't shake, the room had great acoustics, and the conductor's expression was kind and attentive.

"That was lovely," he said, with some special emphasis I couldn't interpret. "Just very, very nice."

"Thanks," I said. The following Monday, I went back to the music building to look at the seating chart. My name wasn't there, not even in the second violins, nowhere. I could feel my face change. I tried to control it, but I could feel it wasn't working. I knew that everyone and his cousin at Harvard played the violin, it was practically mandatory, and there was no way they could all fit in a single orchestra—the stage would collapse. Still, I had never seriously considered that I might not get in.

I didn't have a religion, and I didn't do team sports, and for a long time orchestra had been the only place where I felt like part of something bigger than I was, where I was able to strive and at the same time to forget myself. The loss of that feeling was extremely painful. It would have been bad enough to be someplace where there were no orchestras, but it was even worse to know that there was one, and lots of people were in it—just not me. I dreamed about it almost every night.

I wasn't taking private lessons anymore—I didn't know any teachers in Boston, and I didn't want to ask my parents for more money. For the first few months, I still practiced every day, alone, in the basement, but it began to feel like a sad, weird activity, disconnected from the rest of human enterprise. Soon just the smell of the violin—the glue or the wood or whatever it was that smelled like that when you opened the case—made me feel melancholy. I still sometimes woke up on Saturdays, the day I used to go to music school, feeling excited to go and play; then I would remember how matters stood.

It was hard to decide on a literature class. Everything the professors said seemed to be somehow beside the point. You wanted to know why Anna had to die, and instead they told you that nineteenth-century Russian landowners felt conflicted about whether they were really a part of Europe. The implication was that it was somehow naïve to want to talk about anything interesting, or to think that you would ever know anything important.

I wasn't interested in society, or ancient people's money troubles. I wanted to know what books really meant. That was how my mother and I had always talked about literature. "I need you to read this, too," she would say, handing me a *New Yorker* story in which an unhappily married man had to get a rabies shot, "so you can tell me what it really means." She believed, and I did, too, that every story had a central meaning. You could get that meaning, or you could miss it completely.

I went to Linguistics 101, to see what linguistics was about. It was about how language was a biological faculty, hardwired into the brain—infinite, regenerative, never the same twice. The highest law, higher than Holy Scripture, was "the intuition of a native speaker," a law you couldn't find in any grammar book or program into any computer. Maybe that was what I wanted to learn. Whenever my mother and I were talking about a book and I thought of something that she hadn't thought of, she would look at me and say admiringly, "*You* really speak English."

The linguistics professor, a gentle phonetician with a mild speech impediment, specialized in Turkic tribal dialects. Sometimes he would give examples from Turkish to show how different morphology could be in non-Indo-European languages, and then he would smile at me and say, "I know we have some Turkish speakers here." Once, in the hallway before class, he told me about his work on regional consonantal variations of the names for some kind of a fire pit that Turkic people dug somewhere.

I ended up taking a literature class, too, about the nineteenth-century novel and the city in Russia, England, and France. The professor often talked about the inadequacy of published translations, reading us passages from novels in French and Russian, to show how bad the translations were. I didn't understand anything he said in French or Russian, so I preferred the translations.

The worst part of the literature class came at the end when the professor answered questions. No matter how dumb and obvious the questions were, he never seemed to understand them. "I'm not quite sure I see what you're asking," he would say. "If, however, what you mean to say is this other thing . . ." Then he would talk about the other thing, which usually wasn't interesting, either. Often one or more students would insist on trying to convey the original question, waving their arms and making other gestures, until the professor's face became a mask of annoyance and he suggested that, out of consideration for the rest of the class, the discussion be continued during his office hours. This breakdown of communication was very depressing to me.

You were only supposed to take four classes, but when I found out they didn't charge extra for five, I signed up for beginning Russian.

The teacher, Barbara, a graduate student from East Germany— she specifically said "East Germany"—told us about Russian names and patronymics. Since her father's name was Dieter, her full Russian name would have been Barbara Dietrevna. "But Barbara Dietrevna doesn't really sound Russian," she said, "so I call myself Varvara Dmitrievna—as if my father's name were Dmitri."

We all had to have Russian names, too, though we didn't need patronymics, because we weren't figures of authority. Greg became Grisha, Katie became Katya. There were two foreign students whose names didn't change—Ivan from Hungary and Svetlana from Yugoslavia. Svetlana asked if she could change her name to Zinaida, but Varvara said that Svetlana was already such a good Russian name. My name, on the other hand, though lovely, didn't end with an -*a* or a -*ya*, which would cause complications when we learned cases. Varvara said I could choose any Russian name I wanted. Suddenly I couldn't think of any. "Maybe *I* could be Zinaida," I suggested.

Svetlana turned in her seat and stared into my face. "That is so unfair," she told me. "You're a perfect Zinaida."

It somehow seemed to me that Varvara didn't want anyone to be called Zinaida, so I looked at the page of Russian names, and chose Sonya.

"Hey, Sonya, what a drag," Svetlana told me sympathetically in the elevator afterward. "I think you're much more like a Zinaida. Too bad *Varvara Dmitrievna* is such a zealous Slavophile."

"You guys were really torturing her with that Zinaida business," said Ivan, the Hungarian, who was unusually, almost unreasonably tall. We turned to look up at him. "I felt really bad," he continued. "I thought she was going to destroy herself. That it would be too much for her German sense of order." Nobody said anything for the rest of the elevator ride.

Ivan's comment about the "German sense of order" was my first introduction to this stereotype. It made me remember a joke I had never understood in *Anna Karenina*, when Oblonsky says, of the German clockmaker, "The German has been wound up for life to wind up clocks." Were Germans supposed to be particularly ordered and machinelike? Was it possible that Germans really *were* ordered and machinelike? Varvara was always early to class, and always dressed the same, in a white blouse and a narrow dark skirt. Her tote bag always contained the same three vocabulary items: a Stolichnaya bottle, a lemon, and a red rubber mouse, like the contents of some depressing refrigerator.

Russian met every day, and quickly started to feel internalized and routine and serious, even though what we were learning were things that tiny children knew if they had been born in Russia. Once a week, we had a conversation class with an actual Russian person, Irina Niko-laevna, who had been a drama teacher in Petersburg when it was still Leningrad. She always came running in a minute or two late, talking nonstop in Russian in a lively and emotional way. Everyone reacted differently to being spoken to in a language they didn't understand. Katya got quiet and scared. Ivan leaned forward with an amused ex-pression. Grisha narrowed his eyes and nodded in a manner suggest-ing the dawn of comprehension. Boris, a bearded doctoral student, rifled guiltily through his notes like someone having a nightmare that he was already supposed to speak Russian. Only Svetlana understood almost everything, because Serbo-Croatian was so similar.

The Boston T was completely different from the New York subway—the lines named after colors, the cars so clean and small, like toys. And yet it wasn't a toy, grown men used it, with serious expressions on their faces. The Red Line went in two directions: Alewife and Brain-tree. Such names were unheard of in New Jersey, where everything was called Ridgefield, Glen Ridge, Ridgewood, or Woodbridge.

Ralph and I went to a pastry shop he knew in the North End.

They sold cannoli like phone receivers, Noël logs like logs, elephant-ear cookies. Ralph ordered a lobster tail. I had a slab of German chocolate cake the size of a child's tombstone.

Ralph was doing premed and taking classes in art history, but thought he might major in government. Most government majors belonged to a social type known as "gov jocks." It wasn't clear to me what was going to happen to them after college. Were they going to be our rulers? Would Ralph become one of them? Was he one, somehow, already? Surely he was too funny, and not interested enough in war. But he did have a certain all-American quality, a kind of clean-cut broad-shoulderedness, as well as a powerful obsession with the Kennedys. He imitated them all the time, Jack and Jackie, with their slow, goofy 1960s voices.

"I've so enjoyed campaigning, Mrs. Kennedy," he said, looking in the distance with a startled, stymied expression. Ralph had already applied for an internship at the JFK Presidential Library.

Constructed Worlds met on Thursdays, for one hour before lunch and three hours after. Before lunch, the visiting artist, Gary, gave a lecture with slides while pacing around the room and giving decreasingly genial instructions to his TA, a silent Gothic-looking person called Rebecca.

On the first day, we looked at pictures of genre scenes. In one painting, shirtless muscular men were planing a floor. In another, gleaners stooped over a yellow field. Then came a film still of people in evening dress sitting in a theater box, followed by a cartoonish drawing of a party full of grotesque men and women leering over cocktail glasses.

"How *well* do you know this party?" Gary exhaled, bouncing on the balls of his feet. "You look at it and think: I *know* that scene. I've been to that exact fucking cocktail party. And if you haven't yet, you will—I guarantee it, you'll find yourself there someday. Because you all want to succeed, and that's the only way to do it. . . . *Selin* doesn't believe me, but she will someday."

I jumped. The cocktail party was reproduced in miniature in Gary's eyeglasses. "Oh no, I believe you," I said.

Gary chuckled. "Is that sincerity or what? Well I hope you do believe me, because someday you're going to know that scene by heart. You're going to know what every last one of them is saying and eating and thinking." He said it like it was a curse. "Power, sex, sex *as* power. It's all right there." He tapped the bilious face of a man who was holding a martini glass in one hand and playing the piano with the other. I decided that Gary was wrong, that I was definitely not going to know that man. He would probably be dead by the time I even turned drinking age.

The next slide showed a color photograph of a woman applying lipstick at a vanity table. The photograph had been taken from behind, but her face was visible in the mirror.

"Putting on the face: preparing the self for display, for a party or a performance," Gary chanted. "Look at her expression. *Look* at it. Does she look happy?"

There was a long silence. "No," intoned one student—a skinny junior with a shaved head, whose name either was or sounded like "Ham."

"Thank you. She does *not* look happy. I count this as a genre scene rather than a portrait, because what we see is the generic situation: what is at stake in the invention of the self."

The next slide was an etching of a theater from the perspective of the stage, showing the unpainted backs of the scenery, the silhouettes of three actors, and, beyond the footlights, a big black space.

"Artifice," Gary blurted, like someone having a seizure. "Frames. Who selects what we see?" He started talking about how museums, which we thought of as the gateway to art, were actually the main agents of hiding art from the public. Every museum owned ten, twenty, a hundred times as many paintings as were ever seen on display. The curator was like the superego, burying 99 percent of thoughts in the dark behind a door marked PRIVATE. The curator had the power to make or break the artist—to keep someone *sup*-pressed or *re*-pressed for a lifetime. As he spoke, Gary seemed to grow increasingly angry and agitated.

"You have Harvard ID cards. That ID card will open doors for you. Why don't you use it? Why don't you go to the museums, to the Fogg Museum, the Museum of Comparative Zoology, the Glass Flowers gallery, and demand to see what they aren't showing you? They have to show you once you have the card. They have to let you in, you know."

"Let's do it!" called Ham.

"You want to? You really want to?" said Gary.

It was time to break for lunch. After we got back, we were going to go to the museums and demand to see the things they weren't showing us.

I was the only freshman in the class, so I went by myself to the freshman cafeteria. Portraits of old men hung on the dark paneled walls. The ceiling was so high you could barely see it, though with effort you could make out some pale specks, apparently pats of butter that had been flicked up there in the 1920s by high-spirited undergraduates. I thought they sounded like assholes. What light there was came from a few high small windows and several massive chandeliers with antlers on them. Whenever a lightbulb burned out, a handyman had to climb up a two-story ladder and bat at the antlers, ducking to avoid being gouged, until he could reach the right socket.

Exiting the lunch line with a falafel sandwich, I noticed Svetlana from Russian sitting alone near a window, with an open spiral notebook.

"Sonya, hi!" she called. "I've been meaning to talk to you. You're taking linguistics, right?"

"How did you know?" I pulled out the chair across from her.

"I shopped the class last week. I saw you there."

"I didn't see you."

"I got there early. I noticed you when you came in. You're very remarkable-looking, you know. I mean that literally. Of course you're very tall, but it's not just your height." I was in fact the tallest living member of my family, male or female. My cousins said it was because I had grown up eating rich American foods and leading a life of leisure. "Your face is very unusual. You know that I, too, was flirting with the idea of linguistics. How is it?"

"It's okay," I said. I told her about the fire pits that the Turkic people dug, about how vowels changed over time and geography.

"That's *interesting*." She placed an almost voracious emphasis on the word "interesting." "I'm sure it's much more *interesting* than Psych 101, but you see it's inevitable really that I should take psychology, since my father is an analyst. A Jungian, a real big shot. He founded the only serious journal of psychoanalysis in Serbia. Then two of his patients became opposition leaders and the party started harassing my dad. To get the transcripts. Of course, they had it in for him anyway."

I thought this over, while trying to make the falafel stay in the sandwich. "Did they get the transcripts?"

"Nope—there weren't any. My father has a photographic memory, he never writes anything down. I'm just the opposite, a real graphomaniac. It's pretty sad, really. I mean, look at all the notes I've taken, and it's only the second week of school." Svetlana flipped through her notebook, displaying many pages covered on both sides in tiny, curly handwriting. She picked up her fork and judiciously composed a forkful of salad.

"Soldiers searched our apartment," she said, "looking for the imaginary transcripts. They came in uniforms with guns at eleven at night and trashed the place—even my room and my sisters' and brother's rooms. They took all our toys out of the box and threw them on the floor. I had a new *doll*, and the *doll* broke."

"That's terrible," I said.

"It was supposed to say 'Mama' when you pulled a string," she said. "When they threw it on the floor it kept saying 'Mama' until they kicked it. In my father's office they ripped the pages out of books, scattered every single sheet of paper, tore up the wall. In the bathroom they pried out all the tiles. In the kitchen they dumped all the flour and sugar and tea from the cans, looking for tapes. My little brother bit one of them and they hit him in the mouth. They took every single cassette. They took all my U2 albums. I cried and cried. And my mother was so angry at my father." Svetlana sighed. "I can't believe this," she said. "This is the first real conversation we're having and already I'm burdening you with my emotional baggage. Enough—tell me about yourself. Are you going to major in linguistics?"

"I haven't decided yet. I might do art."

"Oh, you're an artist? My mother is an artist. Well, she used to be. Then she was an architect, and then a designer, and now she's crazy and basically unemployed. But here I go again with my family. Are you taking any art classes now?"

I told her about Constructed Worlds, about how museums hid things from people, and how the class seemed to be planning some kind of heist.

"I would never have the nerve to take a class like that," she said. "I'm very traditional, academically—another legacy from my father. Basically when I was five he told me all the books to read, and I've been reading them ever since. You must think I'm so boring."

"Do you want to become an analyst, too?"

"No, I want to study Joseph Brodsky. That's why I'm taking Russian. I have some bad news, by the way—we're not going to be in the same class anymore. I had to transfer into another section because of my psych lab."

"That's too bad."

"I know—I really liked having it first thing in the morning. But don't worry, I think we live in the same building. Matthews, right? I'm on the fourth floor. I think we'll end up seeing a lot of each other." I felt moved and flattered by how sure she sounded. I wrote her phone number on my hand, while she wrote mine in her daily planner. Already I was the impetuous one in our friendship—the one who cared less about tradition and personal safety, who evaluted every situation from scratch, as if it had arisen for the first time—while Svetlana was the one who subscribed to rules and systems, who wrote things in the designated spaces, and saw herself as the inheritor of centuries of human history and responsibilities. Already we were comparing to see whose way of doing things was better. But it wasn't a competition so much as an experiment, because neither of us was capable of acting differently, and each viewed the other with an admiration that was inseparable from pity.

In the second half of Constructed Worlds, we went to the Museum of Natural History, where we saw a brace of pheasants that had belonged to George Washington, a turtle collected by Thoreau, and "about a million ants," described as "E. O. Wilson's favorites." I was impressed that E. O. Wilson had been able to identify, in this world of seemingly infinite ants, his one million favorites. We saw what was believed to be the largest skull of a living crocodile species in any collection. When they cut open the crocodile's stomach, they found a horse and 150 pounds of rocks.

After an hour of bugging the people at the front desk and standing around while people made phone calls, we got someone to show us the back room, where they kept things that weren't on display. There was a New Zealand diorama—a plaster meadow littered with decrepit stuffed sheep, as well as an emu and a kiwi bird—that had become infested with moths. "We've mostly been disinfecting, and patching up with acrylic," a museum employee told us.

"Acrylic? Why don't you use wool?" asked Gary.

"Mm, we tried wool first, but acrylic holds better."

"Do you see?" Gary demanded, turning to the class. "Do you see the artifice?"

We saw a lot of broken plaster Native Americans. School groups often tried to fight them.

"So this is what the curators are hiding from us," Ham remarked of a bison that had stuffing pouring out of its guts.

Gary laughed mirthlessly. "You think it's really any different at the Whitney or the Met? Let me tell you, kid, it's all blood and guts in the back room, in one form or another."

Ralph's roommate's name was Ira, which was short for Iron Dog. He was Native American and actually did a lot of ironing, early in the morning. Other than that he was the perfect roommate: gentle, polite, with an older girlfriend at the law school, so he was almost never home, really only coming in at dawn sometimes to iron his shirts.

One evening when Ira was at the law school, I went over to Ralph's room to study. Ralph was reading the *Federalist Papers*. I was reading "Nina in Siberia," a Russian text written specially for beginning students. The first part was called "The Letter."

1. The Letter

Ivan's father opened the door. "Who's there?"

"Good morning, Alexei Alexeich," said Nina. "Is Ivan at home?"

Ivan's father didn't answer. He just stood there and looked at her.

"Excuse me," said Nina, and repeated her question. "Is Ivan at home?"

"Why did we never understand him?" asked Ivan's father, very slowly.

"Excuse me, but I don't understand you," said Nina. "Where is Ivan?"

"God alone knows," said Ivan's father. He sighed. "You know where his room is. There, on the table, is a letter."

In Ivan's room, something was not quite right. The window was open. The chair lay on the floor. Nina's photograph lay on the table. The frame was broken.

"My photograph!" Nina picked up the letter, opened it, and read.

Nina!
When you receive this letter, I will be in Siberia. I'm dropping my dissertation, because particle physics no longer interests me. I will live and work in Novosibirsk, on the collective farm "Siberian Spark," where my uncle lives. I think it will be better this way. I know that you will understand me. Please forget me. I will never forget you.

Your Ivan

Nina looked at Ivan's father. "What is this?" she asked. "Is it a joke? I know Ivan, and I know he wants to finish his dissertation. How can he drop physics? He writes that I will understand him, but I don't understand."

Ivan's father read the letter, too. "Yes," he said.

"Do you think he wrote this letter seriously?"

"Only God knows."

"But if Ivan is really in Siberia, we must find him."

Ivan's father looked at her.

"Don't you want to find your son?" asked Nina.

Ivan's father was silent.

"Goodbye," said Nina.

Ivan's father did not reply.

The story was ingeniously written, using only the grammar that we had learned so far. Because we hadn't learned the dative case, Ivan's father, instead of handing the letter *to* Nina, had to say, "There, on the table, is a letter." Because we hadn't learned the verbs of motion, nobody said outright, "Ivan went to Siberia." Instead, Ivan wrote, "When you receive this letter, I will be in Siberia."

The story had a stilted feel, and yet while you were reading you felt totally inside its world, a world where reality mirrored the grammar constraints, and what Slavic 101 couldn't name didn't exist. There was no "went" or "sent," no intention or causality—just unexplained appearances and disappearances.

I found myself reading and rereading Ivan's letter as if he'd written it to me, trying to figure out where he was and whether he cared about me or not.

For the nonfiction film seminar, we watched *Man of Aran*, a silent movie from the 1930s, set on an Irish island. First, a woman rocked a baby in a cradle. This went on for a long time. Next, a man harpooned a whale and then scraped something with a knife. The intertitle read: "Making soap." Finally, the man and woman dug in the ground with sticks: "The people of Aran must farm for potatoes in the inhospitable soil."

Never in my life had I seen such a boring movie. I chewed nine consecutive sticks of gum, to remind myself I was still alive. The boy in front of me fell asleep and started to snore. The professor didn't notice because he himself had left after the first half hour. "I've already seen this film several times," he said.

In class the professor told us that, by the time of the film's making, fifty years had passed since the people of Aran had stopped harpooning whales. To capture the ancient practice on film, the director had imported a harpoon from the British Museum and instructed the islanders in its use. Knowing this, the professor asked, could we rightly classify the film as nonfiction? We had to debate this question for an hour. I couldn't believe it. *That* was the difference between fiction and nonfiction? That was something you were supposed to care about? I was more concerned by the question of whether the professor was kind or not, whether he liked us. "It's so interesting how you think there is, or should be, a right or a wrong answer," he said to one student in a gentle voice. At the end of class, another student said he had to miss next week's meeting to visit his brother in Prague.

"I guess I can't try to tape-record it, can I?" the boy asked.

"That would be completely worthless," said the professor in a friendly tone. "Don't you think?"

On Thursday, I got to Russian conversation class early. Only Ivan was there. He was reading a novel with a foreign title and a familiar cover: the illustration showed two hands tossing a bowler hat in the air.

"Is that *The Unbearable Lightness of Being?*" I asked.

He lowered the book. "How did you know?"

"It has the same cover in English."

"Oh. I thought maybe you knew how to read Hungarian." He asked if I had liked the book in English. I wondered whether to lie.

"No," I said. "Maybe I should read it again."

"Uh-huh," Ivan said. "So that's how it works for you?"

"How what works?"

"You read a book and don't like it, and then you read it again?"

Gradually the other students trickled in, followed by the teacher, Irina, who had a whole Central American village sewn to her sweater: tiny doll-women with yarn hair, donkeys with yarn manes, and cacti with spines made of yellow thread. She didn't dye her hair, which she wore in a snow-white French twist, and her dark, bright eyes had a burning expression that looked like it hadn't changed since she was a little girl.

She immediately started issuing directions that nobody could understand, telling some people to sit and others to stand. Eventually we understood that we were supposed to take turns reenacting the beginning of "Nina in Siberia." The girls were Nina, and the boys were Ivan's father.

I was paired with Boris, the one who always looked like he was in a waking nightmare—he turned out to be learning Russian in order to do archival research about pogroms. He didn't know any of his lines. We were standing there and he was supposed to say, "Why did we never understand him?"

"Tell me about Ivan," I prompted. "Did we understand him?"

"Oh, Ivan," he said. "Oh, my son."

Next I had to repeat the scenario with Ivan, who knew everything and said everything. He had studied Russian for a year as a child, behind the Iron Curtain. Later I remembered saying, "So you think he wrote this letter seriously?" He was supposed to say, "Only God knows." But what he said was: "Yes, I think it's serious."

For linguistics homework, I had to interview two native English speakers from different regions about how they used the words "dinner" and "supper." Hannah, who had grown up in St. Louis, thought supper was later and more formal. Angela, who had grown up in Philadelphia, thought that dinner was when everyone dressed up and ate with their family.

"We totally don't say that," Hannah said.

"What do you call a big formal meal on a weekend?"

"I don't know. A feast."

Feast, I wrote. "No, not 'feast,'" Hannah said. "Put 'banquet.'"

Angela and Hannah got into an argument about which was more formal, Thanksgiving dinner or the Last Supper. They debated the difference between supper and a snack. Hannah said it depended on whether the food was hot or cold.

"Not in my opinion," Angela said. "In my opinion"—she said it as if it were a book she could consult—"supper means you're sitting down and relaxing. If you eat standing up in a hurry, you're just having a snack."

"Even if you're eating lasagna?"

"I don't eat lasagna."

"You know what I mean."

"If you eat it standing up in between two classes, it's a snack."

"That's just to get *pity*," Hannah said, after a pause. "That's just so you can say later, 'Oh, I didn't have time for supper today because I was working. All *I* had was a snack.' What *is* it already?" she yelled. "Somebody's been knocking outside for like ten minutes."

The door opened and Svetlana came in. "Are you guys asleep?"

"No, I was just going out," I told her. "Thanks for helping me with the assignment," I told Hannah and Angela. That was the best thing about college: it was so easy to leave. You could be in the place where you lived, having an argument that you had basically started, and then you could just say, "See you later," and go somewhere else.

As I was putting on my jacket, I glanced around the room, trying to see it through Svetlana's eyes. The walls were still almost completely bare, except for the Einstein poster, Angela's Harvard pennant, and some certificates that Hannah had printed out on her computer. She had printed out a "procrastination award" and awarded it to herself. She had given me a "best roommate award," which was sad, both because Hannah wanted so much to be loved, and because this award was partly an insult to Angela. I didn't hang it up.

Svetlana wanted us to write and illustrate a story full of depravity and decadence. We went to CVS and bought construction paper, glue, markers, and a copy of *Vogue*. "Also I think my roommate has laryngitis," Svetlana said, tossing a box of medicinal tea into our basket. "Either that or she just doesn't want to talk to us. But she has to learn to be socially functional."

Everything Svetlana said left a strong impression on me: her certainty that she wanted to write a book about depraved people, her clear notion of how her roommate should behave, and the idea of a tea that made people socially functional.

We got in line to pay. When I took out my combination keychain/ wallet, Svetlana touched my hand and said she would get it. "My family has a lot of money," she said. I didn't understand what she meant. Didn't we all have a lot of money? I counted out the change for exactly half of everything, except the laryngitis tea. "If you say so, but you're being crazy," Svetlana said, pocketing the money and paying with a credit card.

Svetlana's common room had a Moroccan carpet, two big red beanbags, an R.E.M. poster, a Klimt poster, an Ansel Adams poster, and shelves full of expensive-looking museum catalogs and art books. A few potted trees stood by the window, and one of the three desks was almost completely covered with smaller plants: pale clammed-up buds, lurid green mosses, and inscrutable succulents in little plastic tubs.

One of the skinniest girls I had seen in my life was sitting on the floor with a soldering iron. She was Svetlana's roommate Valerie, and she was building a radio.

"How's Fern doing?" Svetlana asked her.

"The same." Valerie shrugged toward one of the bedrooms. I made out a military sleeping bag on the top bunk, with a mop of curly hair sticking out the top.

"Fern? Are you awake?" called Svetlana. The mop nodded. "I brought you some tea. You really can't go around not talking when you don't feel like it." She filled a white electric kettle, and poured a bag of powdered tea into a plastic mug shaped like a pineapple. "Fern, this is my friend Selin."

"Hi," I called.

There was no response.

"She says she can't talk," Svetlana told me. "She's a botanist, her name is Fernanda so of course her nickname is Fern. It suits her because ferns are so mysterious and sort of elusive, and they can survive anywhere. You know there are ferns that are older than dinosaurs, hundreds of millions of years old. Some of them don't need soil to grow. In Slavic folklore, if you find a fern seed it makes you invisible. Of course ferns don't actually have seeds." She didn't lower her voice, though Fern was just a few feet away in the next room. She poured the boiling water into the cup and stirred it with a cafeteria spoon.

"That smells awful," Valerie said. "Poor Fern."

Svetlana carried the cup into the bedroom and held it up to the top bunk. The lumpy sleeping bag changed shape, revealing a round face with huge eyes.

"Thanks," said Fern, not sounding particularly grateful.

"Drink up," said Svetlana neutrally, and rejoined me in the common room. "Let's go in my room so we don't bug Valerie."

Svetlana's bedroom was brightly lit, with a lava lamp, a stereo system, a bookshelf crammed with books and CDs, and an Edward Gorey poster that showed a lot of Victorian children dying terrible deaths. A plush armadillo sat on the bed. I asked Svetlana how she and her roommates had decided who got the single room, and whether they were going to rotate. She sighed. "It's embarrassing: Val and Fern *wanted* to rotate, but I said it would be too much of a pain and convinced them to draw straws instead. Then, wouldn't you know it, *I* drew the single, as if I'd planned it. Honestly, though, sometimes I think it's worked out for the best. Valerie's so nice that she doesn't seem to care whether she has her own room, and Fern isn't as private as you might think. She actually needs a lot of attention and stability, so Val is the ideal roommate for her. And now this is going to sound terrible, but in a way I think I'm more complicated than they are. Some people are just more complicated than others. Don't you think so?"

"I guess," I said.

"And privacy is more important to them." Svetlana proceeded to describe her roommates' family backgrounds, like they were characters in a novel. Fern's parents had wanted her to work at their store rather than go to Harvard, even though she had a full scholarship. Her father wasn't supposed to call her, but he did anyway sometimes, and asked for money, which she earned by working as a dishwasher in Mather, where the athletes lived, so they ate huge amounts of food and did disgusting things like mix ketchup and applesauce that the work-study students had to clean up.

Valerie was the world's most easygoing person but was sensitive about her brother, who was only two years older than her but already a graduate student in math. He had solved some problem of cryptography at fifteen and been recruited by the CIA.

"You can imagine how hard it is," Svetlana said. "Valerie is supersmart, but because she's not a prodigy in any particular field, she just doesn't know what to do with herself. Math would mean competing with her brother. On the other hand, she feels like math is the only rigorous discipline—the only thing worth studying. How can she differentiate herself from her brother if she can measure herself only by his standards?

"Now she's in an honors physics class that only the most advanced freshmen take. Out of the top twenty-five students in the whole freshman class, she's maybe one of the top three, but instead of feeling good about it she's embarrassed to even be in the same league as everyone else. Because when her brother was a freshman, he was taking graduate classes."

The book Svetlana wanted to write together was about the sexual initiation of a failed Russian car thief in Paris. His name was Igor and he was represented by a guy sitting on a rock in a cologne ad in *Vogue*. Svetlana cut out his figure, glued it to a piece of paper, and drew the rest of the scene with great assurance, barely hesitating over any detail.

"I draw like a kindergartner, so don't laugh at me," she said. Igor was sitting under a bare hanging bulb, on a bare mattress. His feet were soaking in a tub next to an ashtray, a rotary phone, and some empty bottles. Through a door behind him, you could see a chain-flush toilet with the seat up.

Igor was feeling blue, Svetlana wrote. *For two weeks he'd been living on mustard sandwiches. He stole the mustard off the table of a café.*

"Wow," I said. "And in this condition he's going to have a sexual initiation?"

Svetlana nodded. "These things happen when you least expect it." *That night he had smoked his last cigarette and finished the last bottle of vodka that his ex-girlfriend had left at his place,* she added to the story.

"He had a girlfriend?"

"Yeah, but for some reason she refused to have sex with him. Then she left. She had been Igor's only friend in Paris, and now she was gone. So when the phone rang that night, he was sure it was a wrong number. But he picked up anyway."

The caller, a mysterious girl, told Igor to meet her at the Zodiac Club. Igor went to the Zodiac Club, sat at the bar, and ordered a beer. There was only one girl there, drinking a green cocktail and paying no mind to Igor. Igor waited awhile, but nobody else came. So he asked the girl to dance.

But she said she couldn't dance with anyone, because she was Hitler's daughter.

At eleven-thirty, as abruptly as she had appeared at my room, Svetlana said she had to go to bed. "I'm kind of strict about sleep," she said, standing up.

Back in the common room, Valerie's radio was producing static. It was really working.

"Well, it's about time," she said. "I've been here since ten in the morning." She did something with a wire and caught a human voice out of the air. "I am most certainly *not* ashamed of the Gospels," the voice said.

The Constructed Worlds syllabus was a list of Gary's favorite books and movies, without any due dates or assignments. We were just supposed to read books, watch movies, and discuss them in class. The discussions were never that great, because everyone chose different books and movies.

"Do I really have to give you assignments, like children?" Gary demanded, when it turned out that yet again no two people had read or watched any of the same things. "Fine. You all have to read *Against Nature*."

At first I was excited about *Against Nature*, because Gary said it was about a man who decided to live according to aesthetic rather than moral principles, and that was something Svetlana had recently said about me: that I lived by aesthetic principles, whereas she, who had been raised on Western philosophy, was doomed to live boringly by ethical principles. It had never occurred to me to think of aesthetics and ethics as opposites. I thought ethics *were* aesthetic. "Ethics" meant the golden rule, which was basically an aesthetic rule. That's why it was called "golden," like the golden ratio.

"Isn't that why you don't cheat or steal—because it's ugly?" I said.

Svetlana said she had never met anyone with such a strong aesthetic sensibility.

I thought maybe *Against Nature* would be a book about someone who viewed things the way I did—someone trying to live a life unmarred by laziness, cowardice, and conformity. I was wrong; it was more a book about interior decoration. In his free moments from plumbing the subrational depths of upholstery, the main character devoted himself to the preparation of all-black meals, to hanging out with a jewel-encrusted tortoise, and thinking thoughts like, "All is syphilis." How was *that* an aesthetic life?

In literature class, we learned about Balzac. Unlike Dickens, to whom he was sometimes compared, Balzac didn't care for or about children, and was essentially unhumorous. Children weren't important to him at all—they barely figured in his world. His attitude toward them was dismissive, even contemptuous; and though he could certainly be witty, he wasn't what you would really call funny, not like Dickens was. As the professor spoke, I became aware of a slight sense of injury. It seemed to me that Balzac's attitude toward *me* would have been dismissive and contemptuous. It wasn't that I was a child exactly, but I didn't really have a history as anything else. At the same time, it was exciting to think that there was a universe—"a *monde*," the professor kept calling it, annoyingly—that was completely other from everything I had been and done, up to now.

2. The Telephone Number

Nina thought about Ivan all week.

In a physics lecture: "Does Ivan not love me?"

On the tram: "Why Siberia? Why did he say nothing?"

In the laboratory: "Soon he'll call and explain everything."

Two weeks passed. Ivan didn't call. Nina read and reread his letter.

Again, Nina knocked on the door of Ivan's apartment. For a long time there was no answer. Finally, Ivan's father said, "Who is there?"

"It's me. It's Nina again."

Ivan's father slowly opened the door.

"Alexei Alexeich, I must find Ivan," Nina said. "Where do you think he is? Do you think he could be with his mother?"

Ivan's father sighed. "In the letter, he says he is with my brother."

"Would you call your brother and ask him if it's true?"

"Impossible," said Ivan's father.

"Please, Alexei Alexeich. I need your help."

Slowly, he took a pen and paper and wrote a number. "Here's his number," he said. "Please don't come here again."

Nina took the number and put it in her bag. "Thank you," she said.

For a long time after she left, Alexei Alexeich stood and looked out the window. "Again my brother!" he thought, bitterly. "First, my wife. Now, my son . . ."

At home, Nina called the number that Ivan's father had given her.

A woman's voice could be heard. "Laboratory of Cosmology and Elementary Particle Physics."

Nina was very surprised, and said nothing.

"Hello? Hello?" said the woman. "Is anyone there?"

"Excuse me," said Nina. "Isn't this the collective farm 'Siberian Spark'?"

"No. This is the Laboratory of Cosmology and Elementary

Particle Physics, at the Novosibirsk Scientific Center, in the Siberian Division of the Russian Academy of Sciences."

"I'm looking for Ivan Alexeich Bazhanov, a young physicist. Does he work at your laboratory?"

There was a pause. "The name isn't familiar," the woman said. She hung up without saying goodbye.

Ralph and I were reading in his room. He was reading *The Canterbury Tales*. For some reason, he was under tremendous pressure to finish *The Canterbury Tales* in that particular sitting. I read the second part of the story about Nina. Afterward, we went to the video store to rent a movie. It was late, and everything we wanted to see was out. Eventually we chose a foreign film called *The Gift*. The case had a photograph of a gift-wrapped woman, her face hidden by a scarf, a big red bow tied over her arms: "The touching story of an incapacitated wife who gives her husband the one anniversary gift he never expected—the gift of another woman!"

We went back to campus and found an empty room with a VCR player in the basement. The movie turned out to be a caustic invective against the British health-care system from the perspective of an aging blue-collar couple in Yorkshire. The wife was wheelchair-bound because of a "mistake under the surgeon's knife." For two and a half hours the husband wheeled her through mud to various doctors, while she made wisecracks that we couldn't understand, because of her accent. The anniversary gift was a metal back brace. There was no other woman.

Svetlana and I took the T to Brookline to visit a Russian grocery store that rented out videos. The tracks ran along the middle of a two-way street lined by endlessly recurring churches, graveyards, hospitals, and

schools: institutions of which Boston seemed to have an infinite supply. Svetlana was telling me about a dream she had that she went to
Taco Bell and had to eat a burrito made of human flesh.

"I knew my father would be angry if I ate it, but also that he
secretly wanted me to," Svetlana shouted, to be heard over the train.
"Okay, so the burrito is obviously a phallus, a *human* phallus: it's simultaneously taboo, like cannibalism, and yet it's something that has
to enter your body. I guess I think my father has ambiguous feelings
about my sexuality."

I nodded, glancing around the train car. A 100 percent impassive
old woman with a shawl over her head was glaring at the floor.

"Sometimes I wonder about the man I'll eventually lose my vir-
ginity to," Svetlana continued. "I'm pretty sure it'll happen in college.
I've had relationships that were intellectually erotic but nothing ever
happened physically. In a lot of ways I feel like a sexual bomb waiting
to explode.

"My roommates are so different—Fern thinks if she has sex in
college, it'll mean something went wrong. Whereas I think if I *don't*
have sex in college, something will have gone wrong. With Valerie,
she's so easygoing you never know what she's thinking. How about
you, are you planning to have sex in college?"

"I don't know," I said. "I never really thought about it."

"I have," Svetlana said. "I look at strangers' faces while I'm walking down the street and wonder: Is he the one? I wonder whether I've
seen him yet, whether I've read his name printed somewhere, maybe on
some list or directory. He must exist *somewhere*—he can't not have
been born yet. So where is he? Where's this thing that's going to go
inside my body? You never wonder that?"

I had often flipped through a calendar wondering on which of the
366 days (counting February 29) I would die, but it had never once
occurred to me to wonder whether I had already met the first person
I would have sex with.

We got off at Euclid Circle. There was no circle—just a concrete platform with a pay phone and a sign that read EUCLID CIRCLE. I thought
Euclid would have been mad. "That's so typical of your attitude,"
Svetlana said. "You always think everyone is angry. Try to have some
perspective. It's over two thousand years after his death, he's in Boston
for the first time, they've named something after him—why should
his first reaction be to get pissed off?"

Bells rang when we opened the shop door, and then the smell of
salami and smoked fish hit us in the face like a curtain. Two clerks,
one fat and one thin, stood behind a glass counter.

"Hello," Svetlana said in Russian.

"'Hello,'" said the clerks, somehow making it sound ironic.

It was interesting to see so many Russian things: hard and soft
cheeses, red and black caviar, stuffed cabbage, bliny, piroshki, pickled
mushrooms, pickled herrings, a muddy tank of carp that were alive,
but perhaps only barely, and a barrel full of challenging-looking rect-
angular sweets, in wrappers printed with sentimental Cyrillic writing
and pictures of squirrels. There was a whole aisle in the dry-goods
section devoted to Turkish products: Koska halvah, Tat pepper paste,
Tamek rose-petal jam and canned grape leaves, and Eti biscuits. Eti
meant Hittite—there had been a commercial when I was little with
children chanting, "Hittite, Hittite, Hittite." The Hittites had been
beloved by all Turkish children, because Atatürk said the Turks were
descended from them and that's why it was okay for Anatolia to be
the Turkish homeland. It had to do with the Fourteen Points—with
the right to national self-determination.

It turned out that Svetlana knew all these brands, because they
had had them in Belgrade, and that the words for eggplant, bean,
chickpea, and sour cherry were the same in Serbo-Croatian as in
Turkish. "It stands to reason," she said, "since the Turks occupied

Serbia for practically four hundred years." I nodded as if I knew what she was talking about.

Svetlana bought half a kilogram of loose tea and asked in exaggeratedly correct Russian if it was true that the store loaned videotapes. One of the clerks handed her a binder with a list of titles. Svetlana flipped through the plastic-encased pages way faster than I could follow, picking out a Soviet comedy about a car insurance agent. The skinny clerk went to get the tape. The fat clerk asked her to write her name and address in a register. "Should I write in English . . . or in Russian?" asked Svetlana.

"As you like, it doesn't matter," replied the clerk. "Are you here from Russia?"

"No, I'm not Russian."

"Not Russian? How do you speak perfect Russian?"

"I don't speak perfect Russian. I can say very little. I'm taking a class in Russian language at the university."

"To me, it sounds perfect. And I'm, well, Russian."

"You see, the thing is that, by nationality, I'm a Serb."

"Aha," said the fat clerk.

"What is she?" asked the skinny clerk, returning with the tape.

"A *Serb*," said the fat clerk.

"Aha," said the skinny clerk.

On the train back, Svetlana told me about a Serbian movie director who had been friends with her father in Belgrade. The director's wife, an actress, had gone to Paris to make a movie with a young French director. The French director had died tragically, by falling off a barstool. "They say it might have been suicide," Svetlana said.

By the time we got back to campus at ten, I felt wiped out and speechless. Cut open my head, I felt, and you would find, as in the stomach of the world's largest crocodile, a horse and 150 pounds of rocks. I opened my notebook. *He died by falling off a barstool,* I wrote. *It might have been suicide.*

The phone rang—it was Ralph. He had gotten the internship at the Kennedy Library. It was a real internship, open to juniors, seniors, and even graduate students, and they had chosen Ralph. He would be working in the archival division, classifying materials and entering their information into a database.

To celebrate, we went to the basement of the Garage, where a small elderly Asian man sold frozen yogurt until late into the night.

"I'm thinking about espresso," Ralph said, "but part of me also really wants to try blackberry."

"Couldn't you get both?" I asked.

"Oh, that would be too much."

"You get one and I'll get the other and we can share."

"But I don't want to impose."

We got one of each. They tasted the same.

Ralph had brought me a book, a 1980s pocket paperback. It was the autobiography of Oleg Cassini, a Russian aristocrat who fled the revolution in 1918 and ended up in America and became Jackie's official fashion designer.

Jackie Kennedy's people first contacted Oleg Cassini in December 1960, when he was on vacation in Florida. He was told to report to the Georgetown University Hospital, where Jackie had just delivered her son John Jr.

On the plane, Cassini thought and thought about Jackie—about her hieroglyphic body and sphinxlike nature—then began to sketch. At her hospital bed, he showed her A-line dresses inspired by the simple lines of ancient Egyptian art. The pillbox was based on Nefertiti's hat. No other designer had designed a whole line just for Jackie. Cassini got the job: exclusive couturier to the First Lady. She always withheld a tiny part of herself, and still bought dresses from Balenciaga.

· · ·

In linguistics class, we learned about people who had lost the ability to combine morphemes, after having their brains perforated by iron poles. Apparently there were several such people, who got iron poles stuck in their heads and lived to tell the tale—albeit without morphemes. By studying where the poles were, and what morphemes got lost, you could figure out where the morphemes were stored.

We learned about the different ways Noam Chomsky was right and B. F. Skinner was wrong. Skinner overestimated how close humans were to animals, and then he underestimated the animals. The man didn't understand birdsong.

We learned that, because language was a universal human instinct, no human was bad at grammar—not even toddlers or black people. That's what the book said: you might think that toddlers and black people had no grammar, but if you analyzed their utterances, they were actually following grammatical rules so sophisticated that they couldn't be programmed into any computer.

We learned about the Sapir-Whorf hypothesis, which said that the language you spoke affected how you processed reality. We learned that it was wrong. Whorf, a fire inspector—they always called him a fire inspector—believed that Hopi people perceived time differently than we did, because their verbs didn't have tenses. He said Hopis didn't see two days as two different things, but rather as one thing that happened twice. It turned out he was somehow wrong about that— about the Hopis.

The Chomskians viewed the Sapir-Whorf hypothesis as the vilest slander—not just incorrect, but hateful, like saying that different races had different IQs. Because all languages were equally complex and identically expressive of reality, differences in grammar couldn't possibly correspond to different ways of thinking. "Thought and language are not the sssame thing," the professor said, whistling faintly, which he did only at emotional moments. He said the Sapir-Whorf hypothesis was inconsistent with "the tip of the tongue syndrome." They really called it a *syndrome*. It was when a word was on the tip of your tongue.

In my heart, I knew that Whorf was right. I knew I thought differently in Turkish and in English—not because thought and language were the same, but because different languages forced you to think about different things. Turkish, for example, had a suffix, -*mış*, that you put on verbs to report anything you didn't witness personally. You were always stating your degree of subjectivity. You were always thinking about it, every time you opened your mouth.

The suffix -*mış* had no exact English equivalent. It could be translated as "it seems" or "I heard" or "apparently." I associated it with Dilek, my cousin on my father's side—tiny, skinny, dark-complexioned Dilek, who was my age but so much smaller. "You complained-*mış* to your mother," Dilek would tell me in her quiet, precise voice. "The dog scared-*mış* you." "You told-*mış* your parents that if Aunt Hülya came to America, she could live in your garage." When you heard -*mış*, you knew that you had been invoked in your absence—not just you but your hypocrisy, cowardice, and lack of generosity. Every time I heard it, I felt caught out. I *was* scared of the dogs. I did complain to my mother, often. The -*mış* tense was one of the things I complained to my mother *about*. My mother thought it was funny.

In Russian class we learned the verb "to like" and talked about what kind of films we liked. I said I liked documentaries. Varvara seemed skeptical. "You don't find them boring?"

I looked at the table. Was it so obvious?

Ivan said he liked movies by Fellini. Varvara said that then he liked Italian films. I didn't know anything about Fellini; my mental image was of a human-sized cat.

The Harvard Film Archive had a Fellini retrospective. I decided to go, because Fellini was also on Gary's syllabus. It seemed weird that Gary and Ivan had the same favorite director. Gary's favorite movie was *La Dolce Vita*, and Ivan's was *La Strada*. Svetlana came with me to *La Dolce Vita*. "You talk of nothing but the kitchen and the bedroom!" Marcello Mastroianni shouted at his fiancée. He rejected her maternal, smothering love, preferring to meet glamorous foreign women at parties. In *La Strada*, there were no parties, and no one was glamorous. Giulietta Masina was in love with the strongman. The strongman told her that she was less like a woman than like an artichoke.

Svetlana took private French lessons from a grad student named Anouk. Every week, she wrote an essay about love, in French, and emailed it to Anouk, and they would meet at the Café Gato Rojo to discuss it together. Svetlana often recounted her essay to me when we were running together. Svetlana had no difficulty talking and running at the same time; she seemed able to keep it up indefinitely.

"For today," she was saying, "I wrote about how you can make absolutely anybody fall in love with you if you really try."

"But that's just not true," I said.

"Why not?"

"How could I make a Zulu chief fall in love with me?"

"Well, of course you would need geographic and linguistic *access*, Selin." We were jogging side by side along Oxford Street. I briefly dropped behind to let by a woman with a stroller. Svetlana had written about whether love was a game you could get infinitely good at, like in French novels—whether it was a matter of playing your cards right—or whether it existed between certain people in some kind of current and you just had to tap into it.

"So you think it's about playing your cards right?" I said.

"Pretty depressing, huh? Sometimes I think there could be two kinds of love. There could be one rare kind that just naturally exists between certain people. Then there's the more common kind that's constructed."

It was a mystery to me how Svetlana generated so many opinions. Any piece of information seemed to produce an opinion on contact. Meanwhile, I went from class to class, read hundreds, thousands of pages of the distilled ideas of the great thinkers of human history, and nothing happened. In high school I had been full of opinions, but high school had been like prison, with constant opposition and obstacles. Once the obstacles were gone, meaning seemed to vanish, too. It was just like Chekhov said, in "The Darling":

> She saw objects round her and understood everything that was going on, but she could not form opinions about anything and did not know what to talk about. How awful it is not to have an opinion! You see a bottle, for example, standing there, or the rain falling, or a peasant going along in his cart, but what the bottle or rain or peasant are for, what sense they make, you can't say and couldn't say, even if they offered you a thousand rubles.

Every now and then, a book had something like that in it, and it was some comfort. But it wasn't quite the same thing as having an opinion.

We rounded the T station in Porter Square. Below us, on the other side of a chain-link fence, train tracks and wet gravel gleamed under pink lights. There was a DUNKIN' DONUTS sign and a big clock. Someone somewhere was asking for money.

"Is it okay if I ask you a personal question?" asked Svetlana.

"Okay," I said.

"Are you dating someone now?"

"No."

"So who's the guy I always see you with? You know who I mean. Your height, brown hair, clean-cut, very American."

"Oh, Ralph. We're friends from high school."

"I couldn't tell from your body language—first I thought you were involved, then I thought you weren't. Did you used to go out or something?"

"No."

"Really? Why not? He's handsome."

"I don't know," I said. "Actually, I think he might be gay."

"Why do you think that?"

"He's really interested in Jackie Kennedy."

"Hmm. That's *interesting*." Svetlana said that she had a gay friend in the Serbo-Croatian Club, and that she had thought a lot about Jackie Kennedy, Maria Callas, and Marilyn Monroe—about how they were performers, aesthetic beings, close to powerful men, and unhappy.

The next day when Ralph and I were having dinner, Svetlana came to our table. "Mind if I join? I'm not interrupting anything?"

"Sure," Ralph said. Svetlana plunked down her tray and told us about Valerie's friendship with a deaf girl called Patience from her physics class. "I don't think Val even likes her that much, but you can't exactly diss a deaf person called Patience. But it is so exhausting to hang out with her! Okay, she can read *lips* but you have to be standing right in front of her and speaking distinctly, and meanwhile you have to worry about not looking patronizing. With some people, she can't understand at all, so Valerie translates. Valerie makes all her phone calls, too. It's very stressful for her. I don't know how long it can go on.

"As for Fern, she has a rash on her neck because of her biochem midterm. She always gets a rash, but this time it's more like hives, all down her back. It's pretty gross, so I won't go into details while you're eating. Naturally, she refuses to see a doctor. Hi, I'm Svetlana, you must be Ralph. I would shake your hand but I think I'm getting Fern's cold. That's the other thing—she has a cold. Sorry I'm talking so much. It's just such a relief to not have to worry about lip-reading."

After dinner, we ended up going to see Fellini's *Casanova* at the film archive. The path was too narrow for us all to walk together, so I walked with Ralph, and we talked about how Jackie hadn't wanted to read Casanova's memoirs because she thought he was a rogue, but Cassini had convinced her, and then she had written him a charming thank-you note.

After a while I felt worried about leaving Svetlana alone, so I let Ralph walk ahead. "I definitely see what you mean, about how he might be gay," Svetlana said. Dread shot through my chest. The feeling of having betrayed someone was just as bad as the feeling of being betrayed. It was worse.

"Svetlana!"

"What? He can't hear me, don't be paranoid."

Nothing about Ralph's back indicated that he had or had not heard her.

How could I have talked about him to Svetlana—how could I have given her any information about him at all? It occurred to me how sorry I would be if even Hannah heard the way I talked about her sometimes. How were you supposed to talk about people?

Casanova seemed somehow vindictive, as if Fellini were jealous of Casanova for having so much sex and was trying to make him look stupid. I didn't understand why the women laughed so much.

3. Fate in Novosibirsk

"Excuse me—do you go to the collective farm 'Siberian Spark'?" Nina asked the bus driver. She was at the Novosibirsk airport.

"No," said the driver. "You need a taxi."

"You're going to the 'Siberian Spark'?" someone asked. Nina

turned and saw a young man with a suitcase. "I'm going that way, too," said the young man. "Let's go together."

"Okay," said Nina.

In the taxi, Nina took Ivan's letter from her physics book and reread it.

"Look," said the young man, pointing out the window. "Do you see those lights? That's the center of the city, where more than a million people live."

"Oh," said Nina.

The young man looked at her. "I notice you have a physics book. Are you a physicist?"

"Yes, I'm a graduate student."

"I'm also a graduate student. Let's get acquainted. My name is Leonid. I study at the Irkutsk Scientific Center."

"I am Nina," said Nina. "I study at Moscow State University."

"Goodness, a Muscovite! Why are you in Novosibirsk?"

"I am studying the question of the physics of the locomotion of reindeer," said Nina. This was a lie.

Leonid looked thoughtful.

Nina was silent.

"Ivan Alexeich Bazhanov?" repeated the directress of the "Siberian Spark." She looked in a big book. "There's no Bazhanov here. However, there is a Boyarsky, also Ivan Alexeich."

"Has he worked here for a long time?" Nina asked.

"No, not long. Only three weeks."

Nina's heart beat faster. Ivan had disappeared exactly three weeks ago! "I would like to meet him," Nina said.

"You can meet him at five o'clock," the directress promised. "But now he's at the experimental farm."

"What kind of work is done at the experimental farm?" asked Nina.

"Important questions are studied. For example, what is the best food for reindeer? Which foxes have the warmest fur? Unfortunately, visitors are forbidden."

"I understand," Nina said.

In fact, Nina didn't understand. Why was the study of reindeer food a secret? Was it possible that the "experimental farm" was actually a nuclear physics laboratory? Could Ivan be hiding there under a pseudonym?

. . .

"I told you it would happen," Angela was telling Hannah when I came in. They both turned to look at me.

"We've been robbed," Hannah said.

They had taken my peacoat, Angela's Harvard scarf, one of Hannah's plaid shirts—she said it was her favorite—and all of Hannah's socks. She had been sorting her socks in the window seat and someone had just taken them all.

"I told you guys to lock the door when you go out. I *told* you," said Angela.

"I went down the hall for five minutes! Anyway, I thought you were home. How was I supposed to know? Even when you *are* home you just sit in there with the door shut."

"So lock the door anyway!"

The stolen peacoat had originally belonged to my mother, who had worn it for many years until she finally bought a shearling coat. I had taken it from her closet when I was fifteen, and then when she had seen me wearing it she said I could keep it. I had loved that coat—its square shoulders, big buttons, and faint smell of perfume.

Ralph was the one I immediately wanted to tell about the coat, because I knew he would make me feel better. He said we should do a shopping trip. He needed some shirts anyway. We decided to go to Filene's Basement, which was said to be an important part of Boston life.

From the top of the escalator, all of Filene's was spread out below you, like some historical tapestry. Then you were in it. As far as the eye could see, shoppers were fighting over cashmere sweater sets, infants' party dresses, and pleated chinos, with a primal hostility that seemed to threaten the very bourgeois values embodied by those garments. A heap of thermal long underwear resembled a pile of souls torn from their bodies. Women were clawing through the piled souls, periodically holding one up in the air so it hung there all limp and abandoned.

It turned out that Ralph had really specific and detailed thoughts about women's clothes. "You could buy that and start carrying a *straw bag,*" he said of some kind of a tunic.

I found a bright red fitted leather jacket with a hood, marked down 75 percent, in what looked like my size, and fought my way over to a mirror that had only two women jockeying for position in front of it. Standing behind them, I tried to see how I looked in the jacket. It wasn't clear to me what good this did, since I had read in a scientific study that the majority of girls and young women didn't perceive themselves accurately when they looked in the mirror. In the end I bought a shapeless ankle-length black cloak that could cover anything. It reminded me of Gogol's overcoat.

The whole week was depressing. I spent nine hours of it shivering, wrapped in the Gogolian coat, through a nine-hour documentary about the Holocaust. At some point I thought I had grown a lump in my thigh, but it turned out to be a tangerine—it had fallen through a hole in the pocket and ended up trapped in the lining.

I am wishing for extreme efficiency of all your enzymatic pathways, excellent regulation of cytokine works, and high endorphins, my mother wrote in an email posted at two in the morning, to make me feel better about midterms.

It would be an act of immense kindness on your part if you called Aunt Berna in Izmir, she fell and hurt her foot. I will get so many brownie points. You can call after 1 p.m. but not much after cause it is her cocktail hour and will not make sense. My mother was finishing a grant application, which she was going to drive to the Upper West Side to make the deadline.

Angela was on a special midterm study schedule that involved having a really loud alarm clock going off every twenty minutes. She didn't go to bed until four-thirty, and even then the alarms kept going, she just slept through them. I dreamed that for every "quantity" that you thought, you had to "wake up" to a certain extent. "Waking up" meant something different in the dream.

The rain was constant, and almost horizontal, because of the wind. The umbrella became a sort of visual joke. The libraries started giving out plastic bags that said A WET BOOK IS NOT A DEAD DUCK on the side. These bags were supposed to encourage you not to throw out wet books.

Only one typographer in all of Paris could decipher Balzac's revised galley proofs.

I wrote a research paper about the Turkish suffix -miş. I learned from a book about comparative linguistics that it was called the inferential or evidential tense, and that similar structures existed in the languages of Estonia and Tibet. The Turkish inferential tense, I read, was used in various forms associated with oral transmission and hearsay: fairy tales, epics, jokes, and gossip. I recognized that this was true, but had never consciously grouped those forms together or tried to articulate what they had in common. In fact it was really hard to articulate what they had in common, even though it was easy to follow the rule.

One of the most common uses of the Turkish inferential, the book said, was in speaking to children. This, too, I remembered: "What seems to have happened to the doll?" The inferential tense allowed the speaker to assume the wonder and ignorance that children live in—that state when every piece of knowledge is basically hearsay.

There were things about -miş that I liked: it had a kind of built-in bewilderment, it was automatically funny. At the same time, it was a curse, condemning you to the awareness that everything you said was potentially encroaching on someone else's experience, that your own subjectivity was booby-trapped and set you up to have conflicting stories with others. It compromised and transformed everything you said. It actually changed what verb tense you used. And you couldn't escape. There was no way to go through life, in Turkish or any other language, making *only* factual statements about direct observations. You were forced to use -miş, just by the human condition—just by existing in relation to other people.

Over Thanksgiving, I went to New Orleans to visit my father. Things between us felt easier and more relaxed than they had in years. It seemed to me that this was partly because I was coming not from my mother's house but from Boston.

My stepmother, who was also Turkish but really adaptable to different environments, had made a turducken. My half-brother, who was five, still wasn't over Halloween. It was all he wanted to talk about. "What if they say 'trick-or-treat' and you say 'trick' and then your whole house flies away because it's a balloon?" he asked. We all thought it over.

"Well," my father said finally. "Then I suppose you'd have to join the ranks of the homeless."

· · ·

It was snowing when I got back to Boston. I didn't have a hat or gloves. The previous winter, I had had gloves. I couldn't remember what had happened to them. They were different from the gloves of two years ago.

In the train station, people were drinking coffee and reading newspapers. I felt glad to see that life was going on—actual life, where people were working and staying awake and trying to accomplish things, which was the point of coffee. There was a poem with that mood by Pasternak: "Don't sleep, don't sleep, artist." It sounded better in Russian, because the word for "artist" had three syllables, it was an amphibrach, like "spaghetti," or "appendix." Don't sleep, don't sleep, gorilla, I thought as I went down the elevator to the subway platform.

I was somehow especially moved by Boston on this arrival, by its particular atmosphere. Riding to Cambridge on the T, I kept mentally arranging and rearranging the names of the Boston transit stations.

Eliot, Holyoke, Copley Square,
Symphony, Wollaston, Hoosac Pier,
Marblehead, Maverick, Fenway Park,
Haymarket, Mattapan, Codman Yard,
Wonderland, Providence, Beacon Hill,
Watertown, Reservoir, Mystic Mall.

Harvard Square looked both new and familiar. I felt like I would have been able to tell just from looking that this configuration of buildings and streets was familiar and meaningful to lots of people, not just me. It was weird to visit a suburb that nobody else ever visited or went to, and then to return to these widely known halls and buildings where famous statesmen and writers and scientists had been coming for hundreds of years.

When I got to the dorm, someone was being carried off on a stretcher. It was Hannah. "Hey, Selin!" she called, waving. "Isn't this *funny?*"

"Please lie down," a paramedic said.

"I fell down the stairs! Can you believe it?" She lay back down before I could answer, and the paramedics resumed their course toward a parked ambulance.

Hannah spent the night in the infirmary. I slept for fourteen hours. The next day, I went to the Army Navy Store to buy gloves. The Army Navy glove rack was dominated by giant multicolored tasseled mittens from Central America. There were also a few pairs of beautiful leather gloves, but they were both too expensive and too small. I bought a pair of blue ski gloves, and went to look at the shoes. I had been wearing the same men's running sneakers all year. I wore a women's size twelve, which was almost impossible to find. At the Army Navy Store I found a pair of unisex lace-up shoes manufactured in Poland out of what looked like waterlogged cardboard. Very heavy, with bulbous toes and plastic stacked heels, they were without question the ugliest shoes I had ever seen, but they were cheap and they fit.

It was snowing again the next day. At breakfast, three different people complimented me on my shoes. It felt like a dream. In Russian class we had to say what we had done over Thanksgiving. Ivan had gone to Canada.

"Your hair looks different," Grisha told Varvara.

"Oh? I haven't had it cut."

He squinted at her. "I think it *grew.*"

We learned some irregular verbs, which Varvara didn't call irregular. She said their irregularity did, in fact, follow a pattern, though there were irregularities in the pattern.

After class I was walking to the art building, staring at my shoes, wondering if I could lose them somehow, when I heard a voice behind me. "Sonya!" It was Ivan, extending a floppy blue slipper. "You dropped it."

I realized it was one of my new ski gloves. "Oh, no," I said. "It means I'm already trying to lose them."

"You're trying? Is it difficult?"

"I have to do it subconsciously," I explained.

"Aha," he said. "Sorry I interfered with your plan."

"That's okay. I'll lose them later when you're not around."

"Just in case, next time you drop something, I won't pick it up."

When one-third of the school year had passed, I told Angela and Hannah that it was time to rotate rooms. Hannah didn't want to move her stuff, so I moved into the single. It took two days to get Angela to actually switch places with me. I felt sorry for her, but not sorry enough.

The final assignment for Constructed Worlds was to construct a world. I had decided to write and illustrate a story. Like all the stories I wrote at that time, it was based on an unusual atmosphere that had impressed me in real life. I thought that was the point of writing stories: to make up a chain of events that would somehow account for a certain mood—for how it came about and for what it led to.

The atmosphere I wanted to write about had arisen a few years earlier, when my mother and I had gone on vacation to Mexico. Something went wrong with the chartered bus that was supposed to take us back to the airport, and it left us instead in the pink-tiled courtyard of a strange hotel, where Albinoni's *Adagio* was playing on speakers, and something fell onto our arms, and we looked up and it was ashes. I was reading Camus's *The Plague*—that was my beach reading—and it seemed to me that we would always be there, in the pink courtyard, unable to leave.

I wanted to write a story that created just that mood—a pink hotel, Albinoni, ashes, and being unable to leave—in an exigent and dignified fashion. In real life, we had been in that courtyard only three hours. I was an American teenager, the world's least interesting and dignified kind of person, brought there by my mother. It was the very definition of a nonevent: some Americans had experienced a flight delay. In my story, the characters would be stuck there for a long time, for a real, legitimate reason—like a sickness. The hotel would be somewhere far away, like Japan. The hotel management would be sorry that Albinoni's *Adagio* was piped into the halls and lobby for such a long time, but it would be a deep-rooted technical problem and difficult to fix.

Although Constructed Worlds was listed in the catalog as a studio art class, Gary said that studio was a waste of class time. We would have to learn to make time for art, like real artists. We weren't allowed to use the school's art supplies. This, too, was like life.

I went to the art store to buy supplies. Everything was too expensive. I ended up at the office supply store. I bought two reams of bright pink computer paper, and used them to cover the walls, floor, and furniture of my new bedroom. That way, I could take photographs that would look as if they had been taken in a pink hotel. Anyone who spent any amount of time in my room ended up slightly nauseated, because of all the rubber cement. Svetlana said she couldn't imagine how I lived like I did. "You realize *you* are now a sick person in a pink hotel," she said.

4. A Laboratory Romance

A tall young man was waiting outside the office. Nina saw only his back, but she recognized him immediately. "Ivan!" she cried.

The man turned. He wasn't Ivan—at least not Nina's Ivan. "Excuse me," said Nina, becoming embarrassed. "I'm looking for my acquaintance Ivan Alexeich Bazhanov. But I see that you are not he."

He smiled. "No, I'm Ivan Alexeich Boyarsky. I have the same name and patronymic, but a different surname."

"I made a mistake," said Nina. "Forgive me. Goodbye."

"Where are you going?"

"To the Laboratory of Cosmology and Elementary Particle Physics in Novosibirsk."

"That's three kilometers away, and you have a suitcase," observed Ivan Boyarsky. "Let's drive in my tractor."

People in Siberia were kind.

Nina knocked on the door of Ivan's uncle's laboratory. The door was opened by . . . Leonid, the young man from the taxi!

"Nina? What happiness! But I don't understand. Why are you here?"

"I'm here because . . . because Professor Bazhanov is my relative," lied Nina. "And you, Leonid—why are you here?"

"I'm visiting this laboratory to study the electrical properties of permafrost."

"How interesting," said Nina. "Is Professor Bazhanov here?"

"No, right now everyone is at the ice camp."

"May I wait?"

"Of course. Please sit."

But Nina couldn't sit. She wandered around the room.

In the laboratory stood three desks. On the first desk stood a placard on which was written: A. A. BAZHANOV. That was Ivan's uncle. On the second desk stood a placard with a woman's name: G. P. USTINOVA. And on this Ustinova's desk stood a photograph of Ivan—Nina's own Ivan! When Nina read the placard on the

third desk, she could scarcely believe her eyes: I. A. BAZHANOV.
Those were Ivan's initials. And there on the desk lay Ivan's notebook! On the notebook lay a note:

> *Ivan,*
> *I was delayed at the observatory. Forgive me. I will look*
> *for you at the ice camp.*
> *Your Galya*

Your Galya? Nina had a bad feeling.

"Tell me, Leonid," she said. "Who is G. P. Ustinova?"

Leonid's face darkened. "Galina Petrovna is our geochemist,"
he said. "I used to know her quite well. You know, we have a
'laboratory romance': she just married Ivan Alexeich, who also
works here. There, on her desk, is his photograph."

"Oh!" Nina looked at the photograph of Ivan. "He's very
handsome. But excuse me, Leonid. I have to go."

"What? Don't you want to wait for your relative, Professor
Bazhanov?"

"Forgive me. I can't wait anymore. Please don't tell anybody
that I came here."

Before Leonid could say another word, Nina was gone.

. . .

Hi, Selin!

 I got your message about the Iranian flick, but it's already
7:00 p.m. Sigh. My weekend is going all right, except I feel
kind of sick and I have incredible mounds of reading that is
not getting done. And my tae kwon do promotion is
tomorrow. Yesterday I tried to do an artistic project, but it's
hard with the time pressure and with the lack of privacy. I
really like Val and Fern but I need to be alone when I'm

playing around with stuff. Anyway. I hope you're enjoying the movie and it didn't turn out to be about some Iranian potato farmers. Sorry I couldn't come.

Your Svetlana

P.S. By the way, I dreamed you and I were shooting paint bullets at each other from toy guns in the middle of Memorial Drive and we were having a great time.

Hey, Selin,

I heard that you dropped by—but I was soundly asleep. I've been sick, but now I'm sort of OK. Is there a showing of the movie anytime later than 7:30. If there isn't, I'll go at 7:30, but if there is, that would be better because I'm trying to get some reading accomplished.

Hmm, I see that you've been studying russkii. I'm impressed. Other than my Charlemagne reading, I'm done with work. Horaay! (Is that how you spell horaay or is it with two o's.) Anyway, I also see from this paper that you're about to get into trouble again for not going along with your linguistics book's ideas. Sigh . . . some things just don't change, huh?

Today I gave blood and during it I had this weird fantasy about being strangled with a tube full of blood, curving around like a viscious intestant. It really freaked me out. Who knows where your blood goes. My blood is going to be inside someone else's brain. The blood that fuels my thoughts will fuel someone else's. What a strange penetration. Anyway. I really wanted to chat with you, but I guess you're off doing who knows what kind of a wild beagle project in the cold, the dark, the rain . . .

Let me know about the movie times. I'll be in my room . . . reading . . .

Your Svetlana

Hi, Selin.

There is no way in hell that I am going to make the
movie tonight. I have 180 pp about the Carolingian
*Renaissance that I've got to read tonight and that is _not_*
happy. Sigh. Our cinematic plans just seem to be very ill-
fated, huh? And it's all my fault, too. I'm consumed by guilt—
something you're so familiar with (ha, ha). I'd say that we'll
go to the Gogol one on Friday but by now I've learned not to
promise anything.

This pink paper is pretty cool, by the way. I hope it's OK
if I use a piece for the lowly utilitarian purpose of writing you
this note. (I purposefully chose a piece with a tear in it.) Just
to keep you up-to-date on my dream life, I dreamed my sister
was in a yoga accident and someone said she looked like a
squirrel in a blender. Pretty weird, huh?

Oh, here you are, wearing a cool yellow sweater. I admire
your bright colors.

                                                      Svetlana

· · ·

I was running low on money so I applied for a job at the library. When
I told my mother about it, the phone went quiet for a long time, and
even before she started talking, I could tell she was furious. The reason *she* worked so hard was so that I could devote myself to my studies
and not worry about money; if I needed more money she would borrow more from her retirement and mail me a check, and if I really
wanted to feel useful to society, there was nothing like community
service. I was immediately embarrassed for having wanted more
money. Money for what—more ugly shoes, more depressing movies?

Out of guilt, the habit of listening to my mother, and an interest
in second-language acquisition, I signed up to teach ESL at an adult
education program in a housing project. It turned out that they al-

ready had enough ESL teachers and what they needed was people to
teach high school equivalency math. I wasn't particularly interested in
high school math acquisition, but nobody ever said we were put on
this earth for our own entertainment.

To get to the housing project, you took one of the medical school
shuttles to some part of the medical school, walked past about fifteen hospitals, and then literally crossed some railroad tracks. I had
never been to a housing project and had somehow expected it to look
makeshift or cobbled together, and there was something terrible in its
institutional solidity. You saw that the buildings had always been depressing, they were depressing in their design and construction, and
would continue to be depressing, perhaps for hundreds of years, until
something powerful knocked them down. Patches of overgrown grass
resembled a comb-over on the head of a bald person who didn't want
to see reality. Every surface was covered with graffiti. There was nothing colorful or playful about the graffiti—it was the same illegible
scrawl repeated over and over and over, like a nasty thought you can't
shake.

The classrooms were in a residential building with an abandoned
stove in the front yard. I went upstairs to the rooms set aside for the
adult education program. There was a "lobby" with a children's miniature table and chairs, even though there were no children in the
program. On the table were a sign-in sheet, a dead spider plant, and a
dead spider. On a shelf in the closet lay a stack of marbled composition
notebooks and a box of unsharpened Ticonderoga pencils.

My student, Linda, came ten minutes late. She was about my age,
thin, with lilac-colored metallic lipstick and matching nail polish. She
handed me a folded piece of paper. I unfolded it. It read: *Linda needs
help with fractions.*

We went into the smaller of the two classrooms, and sat at a folding picnic table. She showed me the page in the book she was supposed to learn. It was a chart, for generating fractions.

Numerator	Denominator	Fraction
1	2	½
1	3	⅓
1	4	¼

But it seemed like she had already learned the chart, because when I wrote in some more numerators and denominators, like 2 and 3, she was able to sit them on top of each other, like ⅔.

"That's exactly right," I said.

Linda sighed, and looked out the window. "I just don't see the point of this," she said. That was a feeling I felt really sympathetic to. I pushed aside the chart and tried to explain the point of fractions. I started by drawing a circle and telling her it was a pie. She looked annoyed. I remembered that the program director, a senior who had been working with underprivileged adults since he was in high school, had said that, if you were teaching math, it was always good to talk about money, because it showed that math was important in daily life. I turned to a new page in the composition book and explained that the one-numerator and four-denominator was just like a quarter, and four of them made a dollar, so it was useful to be able to divide something into parts and talk about the parts.

"You probably already think about fractions all the time," I said. "It's just a matter of learning the words."

Linda sighed again. "Maybe this is important to you," she said. "But to me it's just not important. I got way more important stuff to think about."

I nodded, while I thought about what to say. "The thing is," I said, "it's important to pass the GED test. You have to learn fractions to pass the test."

"Nuh-uh," she said. She was still looking out the window. I looked out the window, too. I saw a dumpster and some pigeons. It had started to rain.

"How do you mean, 'nuh-uh'?" I said.

"Nuh-uh," she repeated. "There's no pies on the test. The test is on what's in the book. The regular teacher doesn't talk about pie."

I thought it over. I thought about the test. I said I wouldn't talk about pie anymore, and we would just learn what the book said. I turned to the next page. "Now you are ready to reduce fractions," I read. "Instead of two-fourths, write: one half." There were no illustrations, or explanations, or anything to indicate why two-fourths was the same as one-half. Under "Practice Problems," there was a whole list of fractions to reduce. The thought of trying to explain how to reduce fractions without talking about pie or money was terribly daunting.

"Since you already learned that chart," I suggested, "maybe we should just call it a day."

Linda didn't say anything. I wondered if "call it a day" was an elitist expression that only rich people used.

"Maybe we should go home," I said. "Until next week."

She nodded, put the book in her handbag, and left.

"You know you don't actually have to defend fractions to her," Svetlana said. "They don't really want her to understand—they just want her to memorize the book."

I had come home to find Svetlana seated at my desk writing industriously on a sheet of pink paper. She didn't look up when I came in. Reading over her shoulder, I saw that what she was writing was a note to me to cancel our plan to watch *Battleship Potemkin*. Her left hand toyed with the necklace she was wearing: a string of heavy amber beads.

She signed her name with a fancy *S* and handed me the paper. "I wrote you a note," she said. Instead of going to the movie, we went to her room and sat on her bed, reading "Nina in Siberia." It was convenient to read with Svetlana, because she already knew all the vocabulary from Serbo-Croatian, so instead of looking in the glossary, I could just ask her.

The story was confusing and sad. Nina found out that Ivan was working in his uncle's lab and had married a geochemist. But you weren't sure about any of it because she didn't actually talk to him— she just saw his desk with a nameplate and a note from his wife.

"Who writes this stuff?" I asked. The cover of the workbook was blank; it just read *Russian Reader I.*

"Beats me," said Svetlana, turning to her psych textbook.

I picked up my 1,020-page Norton Critical *Bleak House,* which was as simultaneously absorbing and off-putting as someone else's incredibly long dream. For about the hundredth time I read the same sentence:

> Vholes finally adds, by way of rider to this declaration of his principles, that as Mr. Carstone is about to rejoin his regiment, perhaps Mr. C will favour him with an order on his agent for twenty pounds on that account.

Again and again Vholes finally added the rider about Mr. C and the money. Again and again, Mr. C, his agent, the twenty pounds on that account . . . maybe.

Svetlana was highlighting something about deindividuation, while her left hand played with the amber necklace.

"That's a beautiful necklace," I said.

"Hm?" she said. I decided I had to make her look up. "Your necklace," I said. "It's beautiful."

"Oh—this? It's a gift from my analyst."

When she mentioned her analyst, I knew I had won and she would talk to me instead of reading.

Her analyst had been to a conference in Moscow over Thanksgiving. It was his first trip to Eastern Europe and everything reminded him of Svetlana. He kept meeting other women called Svetlana, many of them also analysts, though one was a travel agent. At the amber jewelry counter, he had debated whether it was unprofessional to buy Svetlana a gift. He consulted one of his colleagues, a Russian Svetlana, who had come to help him choose a gift for his wife. The Russian Svetlana had encouraged him to follow his more generous impulse.

"It's not such a big deal," Svetlana said. "As he pointed out himself, the price of the necklace was only about one-fiftieth of what I've paid him in fees since September. It all comes out of my insurance anyway. In a way, this necklace is a gift from Blue Cross of Massachusetts."

I didn't want to go back to *Bleak House,* so I asked about her health insurance. As I was asking, I thought to myself, *Bleak House* is practically *about* boring paperwork, so why don't I just read it instead of asking Svetlana about *her* boring paperwork? Svetlana's eyes opened wide. She said that the insurance form had a space for the mental health diagnosis, and she had seen hers. It was a four-digit number, corresponding to an entry in the *DSM-IV.*

"Just think," she said, "four numbers. That's it—that's what ails you." She had asked her analyst to tell her what her numbers stood for, but he wouldn't. He said the words in the *DSM* didn't count; the words that counted were the ones spoken there in that room between the two of them. But Svetlana had used a mnemonic device to remember the four numbers, they were imprinted in her brain, and later she went to the science library and found the *DSM-IV.* "I went into the stacks and saw it there," she said. "Two big hardcover volumes on the shelf."

"And?"

"And—I didn't look. I left the library. I just wasn't interested anymore."

I started forgetting things I'd read. It started in Russian conversation class. I got there late, they were already reading aloud. Ivan pushed his copy of the book toward me and pointed to the passage. At the line where she looked out the window and thought about Leonid, Ivan leaned toward me and said, "It seems she's always thinking about men."

"Sorry?"

"First she thinks about Ivan. Then she thinks about Leonid. But always about men."

"Oh, right," I said. "Weird."

Ivan and I were supposed to act out a scene in Novosibirsk, a scene I had read and thought about, but suddenly I couldn't remember at all what I was supposed to say. Furthermore, I couldn't look it up because I had forgotten my book. I stood, filled with dread, remembering only that there was bad news for Nina.

"Ivan, stand here and wait for Sonya," said Irina. "Not like that—with your back turned. Sonya, approach Ivan. No, not like at a funeral—you're in a hurry. Like this." Ivan stood facing the window and Irina hastened toward him, looking first preoccupied and then delighted: "Ivan!"

I was horrified. I didn't remember any meeting between Nina and Ivan. How could I have forgotten about something like that?

Irina turned to me. "Now it's your turn, Sonya."

I, too, crossed the room and tried to look delighted. "Ivan!" I said.

Ivan turned. His expression looked totally blank. "Good day," he said.

"Ivan?" I said. "Is it really you?"

"I'm Ivan, yes. Have we met?"

"What do you mean, have we met? I thought we were friends."

"Sonya," said Irina reproachfully. "Did you do the homework?"

"I really did," I said. "But somehow I forgot what happens now."

She sighed. "Read it now and remind yourself. Quickly!"

Ivan handed me the book. As I read, it came back to me that this wasn't the right Ivan—it was another Ivan with almost the same name. What a stupid detail to put into the story, I thought.

"Oh, sorry," I said. "I'm looking for Ivan Bazhanov. But you're another Ivan."

"Yes, I'm Ivan Boyarsky," said Ivan. "We don't know each other."

"I made a mistake," I said. "Sorry. I have to go."

"Okay," he said. "I'll bring you in a tractor."

"Thank you," I said. "People in Siberia are so kind."

I really didn't want to go to Constructed Worlds, and then I saw a Red Cross sign and remembered how Svetlana had donated blood, and thought that if I did it too, I might miss part of class. I followed the signs to the mezzanine of the languages building, which had been divided into cubicles with blue plastic screens.

"Please sit still while I draw some blood," a nurse said in a toneless voice, standing up and walking toward me. She leaned in close, brushing against my hair, and I heard a snipping sound. "This is the new thing," she said. "To draw blood from the ear." The nurse showed me a blurry purple mimeographed map of the world and asked if I had been to any of the highlighted regions in the past two years. It wasn't a big map—all of Turkey was the size of a grape. The bottom part was highlighted.

"Is that like the whole south of Turkey?" I asked. The nurse said it was only southeastern Anatolia. I said I had been to south-central Anatolia. She said that wasn't medically important. Then she asked whether I had had intercourse with a man who had had sex with another man since 1977, or accepted drugs or money in exchange for sex, or given drugs or money in exchange for sex. "Let me stop you right there," I said. She looked at me expectantly. "I mean, I haven't had sex with anyone," I said.

She looked at me harder, over the edge of her glasses. "Have you had sex with anyone who had sex in exchange for drugs or money?"

Downstairs, blinds had been drawn over the plate-glass windows. I lay on a table. There was an index card taped to the ceiling: *Trivia*

Question: Does the earth spin clockwise or counterclockwise, from the perspective of the North Pole?

"Good veins," the nurse remarked.

"Oh, thanks," I said.

The pulse in my arm grew slower, my hands got cold. I thought about the mimeographed map, the map of Anatolia, and which way the Earth spun. I figured it out eventually because of the song where "beauty and the beast" rhymed with "rising in the east." A white kitelike shape approached. "Some people are just a little slow," a voice said.

Time seemed to grow soft and gooey. The boy at the next table, who had come after me, was led away. He had already filled up his bag of blood. See, heart? Do you see? Can you learn? What can you learn? I found myself thinking about Nina, who always thought about men, and then I thought about thinking about Ivan and felt my pulse speed up. Maybe I could accelerate the process that way.

"Is this your first time?" a woman asked.

"Yeah," I said.

"I could tell." I hadn't felt the needle when it was in my arm but I felt it when they took it out.

Linda was late to our second meeting. I sat in the child-sized chair and looked out the cracked window at the dumpster, which now had a sofa in it. When my legs got cramped, I got up and inspected the spider plant and threw the dead leaves into the wastebasket. Then I started pacing through the three rooms used by the adult education program: up through the dark hall, back through the two interconnected classrooms and the lobby. I repeated the circuit again and again, like a nagging thought.

After forty minutes, Linda showed up. We went into the smaller classroom and sat at the picnic table. She slumped into a chair as if she hadn't sat down in days. I asked what was new in the fraction book. She flipped through the pages with her silvery purple talons and handed it to me open to a lesson about turning "compound fractions" like 2½ into "top-heavy fractions" like 5⁄2.

I knew I shouldn't draw three pies. I thought about how wonderful it would be to be eating pie. I tried to think of the easiest way to memorize how to do the exercises. "This isn't too bad," I said. "You just multiply the bottom number by the left-hand number. Then just add the top number and you're done!"

There was a long silence. "I've got so much more important shit to be worrying about," Linda said. "You have no idea."

"I guess the GED is also important?" I said.

She stared at me. "Who *are* you? What you do all day? Is this your job?"

"I . . . I'm a student," I said. The program director had specifically told us never to mention that we went to Harvard, and to deny it if we were asked outright; but he hadn't said who we were supposed to say that we were.

"A *student?*" She looked amazed. "You study this shit?"

"Well, not this shit exactly. I study different things. But at one point I studied fractions, yeah."

She shook her head. "You see what I'm saying? I'm just too busy for this."

"I see what you're saying," I said. "But isn't it sort of a choice? If you don't want to come here, you don't have to. But if you *do* want to come, we have to learn fractions."

"A choice?" She snorted. "Nobody's making any choices around here. The regular teacher said I have to come."

She asked where Ethan was. Ethan was her other tutor. I told her that he came on Tuesdays. She asked why he couldn't come on Fridays. I said that was how it was.

She sighed. "At least he's no *student,*" she said, inaccurately.

I sighed, too. "Don't you have some homework we could go over?"

After a long pause, she pulled out a torn sheet of newsprint—addition problems with fractions. It was homework, and she had done it. I corrected it with a pencil while she stared out the window. She got four right out of ten. I returned the sheet and explained the mistakes. She didn't look at me or make any other sign of recognition. I wrote some new problems similar to the ones she had missed. "Want to work on those for the rest of the period?" I said.

She still didn't look at me, but after a minute she took the paper and started to add up the fractions. Now it was my turn to stare out the window. The scratching of the terrible pencil and the snapping of her chewing gum.

5. Work a Lot, Forget Everything

When Nina left the laboratory, the snow and sky were turning dark blue. In the distance shone the lights of the "Siberian Spark." She walked toward them, thinking about what to do. Should she go back to Moscow? But Moscow would only remind her of what she wanted to forget . . .

Nina knocked at the gate of the collective farm. She had a question for the directress. She wanted to work there for a few weeks.

The directress was very happy. "Hard workers are always welcome here," she said.

Nina worked a lot and barely thought—not about Ivan, not about physics. She had even lost her physics book. It didn't matter. She cared for the gentle reindeer and the lustrous foxes. What happiness to work a lot and forget everything!

Nina became friends with Ivan Boyarsky—Ivan-2, she called him—and with his beautiful Ukrainian wife, Ksenia. Sometimes Nina asked herself: What would have happened if Ivan-2 hadn't been married? Would she have fallen in love with him? Strange. Why were all the Ivans in the world married?

Weeks passed. It was New Year's. Nina, Ivan-2, Ksenia, the directress, and all the workers drank Soviet champagne. "Happy New Year!" they said to one another.

One dark winter evening, the directress said that Nina had a visitor.

"Who can it be?" thought Nina.

There at the office stood Leonid. In his hand was Nina's physics book.

"Leonid!" said Nina. "How did you find me?"

. . .

Svetlana had asked her psychiatrist how long until she would be cured. He said that was the wrong question. Apparently nobody was ever "cured." Then she asked him how long until she would be able to function normally, and he said two years. At first, she said, that seemed like forever, but when she thought about it more, it wasn't that long.

"What does 'functioning normally' mean?" I asked.

"Being able to face the past. Having a normal sex life. Not lying awake all night in fits of anxiety."

"Oh. Are most people able to face the past and have normal sex lives?"

"Yes, as a matter of fact, I think they are," she said. "Anyway, if anyone is, it should be me. Deep down I have a talent for well-being. I can feel it."

I nodded. I thought she had it, too, a talent for well-being.

We read in the student newspaper that an unclothed male freshman had jumped from a third-floor window in the psychology building. A snowbank had cushioned his fall and he was in the infirmary being treated for exposure. The paper didn't mention his name but by lunch all the freshmen knew it was some kid Ethan who lived in Pennypacker.

In a Dickens novel, I thought, the Ethan who jumped out the window would turn out to be the same Ethan who tutored Linda. But this was real life, so it was probably a different Ethan. Certainly there was no shortage of Ethans.

Nonetheless, after lunch, I got a phone call from the program director telling me to go in to cover for Linda's usual teacher, who was indisposed. I told him I had class. He explained that we had made a commitment to the students in this community, who were making sacrifices to change their lives. We also had to make sacrifices—we had to set an example for them, because they had been disappointed so many times in the past. Everything he was saying made sense, and yet it didn't seem fair that he was yelling at me. I wasn't even the one who had jumped out of the window.

Linda asked three times what had happened to Ethan. "He jumped out a window," I said finally. "But don't worry, he's fine."

"A window?" She turned and looked at the window, like maybe she was also thinking of jumping out.

Linda was supposed to learn how to subtract fractions. Why was subtraction always harder than addition?

Misty frozen rain was whirling around as I left the building and walked back to the shuttle stop. The shuttle was somewhat less overcrowded than usual. I didn't get a seat but I had enough room to take out my Walkman, and occasionally I could see between people's heads out the window, and this made me cheerful. It was weird what was enough to make you feel good or bad, even though your basic life circumstances were the same.

Things changed somehow, and I was on the floor, eye-to-eye with some boots and a foil wrapper containing a mollusk of chewed-up gum. My Walkman lay nearby—the door of the cassette player had opened, and the wheels were turning. A few other passengers had also fallen, as had a paper bag of oranges.

The shuttle had rear-ended a Mercedes. The driver of the Mercedes got out of his car and came to the window to yell at the shuttle driver. The shuttle driver got out of the shuttle, to yell better. Looking out the window, I saw we were almost at Central Square. I made my way to the front of the bus, climbed out the driver's door, and started walking back to school.

Soon the sleet turned to snow and became beautiful, and everything suddenly felt more important and meaningful. Dinner had ended an hour ago, so I stopped at a convenience store and bought a yogurt and a chocolate bar. Everything in the store seemed super-focused and clear: the soda fountain, the refrigerated shelves where the yogurts sat, the red light of the scanner.

The next day, I called the program director and said I wasn't going to tutor math anymore. "You have to remember," he said, "that not everyone is a Harvard student. You have to learn to see things from other people's point of view. An upper-class privileged white kid, younger than you, comes to where you live and tells you, basically, 'You need to know this and this and this, and then you can be part of my society.' Are you going to immediately give this kid your trust?"

I thought it over. "I don't know," I said, "but I'm done with GED. If you need any ESL teachers, let me know."

"Setting up a good rapport takes time," he said.

"I'm going to hang up the phone now," I said.

He sighed. "I'll be in touch about ESL."

I decided to join Svetlana's tae kwon do class. First we ran around in circles barefoot. I had forgotten about my ankles and feet. The studio had a glass wall overlooking the pool, where a scuba lesson was in session. How did all those people know that they wanted to know how to scuba dive?

A boy with a green belt stood with me in a corner and demonstrated the first "form": a series of dancelike motions that supposedly defended you against some theoretical assailant. I didn't understand how a dance like that could defend you, unless the attacker also knew the dance, but in that case why would he be using it to attack you?

At the end of class, everyone sat on the floor while the advanced students took turns breaking wooden boards. The two instructors—one extraordinarily tall, the other remarkably short—held up the boards. The most advanced student, a brown belt, went last. The tall instructor stacked several planks for him to break, instead of just one. Grinning, the brown belt performed a series of decorative moves, yelled, and struck the wood with his hand. Nothing happened. He turned red and struck the wood again. On the third strike, splintering was audible. The fourth brought the planks clattering to the floor, accompanied by loud cheers. Still red, the boy bowed to the instructors and sat back on the floor.

"There's still a few more boards here," said the tall instructor, scanning the class. "Svetlana. Do you feel ready?"

Svetlana flashed him a sheepish smile that I had never seen before and stepped to the front of the class, brushing off her legs. "I'm going to take a few practice kicks," she announced. With each kick, her heel tapped the board's exact center. Again and again she repeated the same motion.

"I think you got it, Svetlana," the instructor said, as her sturdy pink heel tapped the center of the plank.

"Now you all know about my obsessive tendencies," Svetlana said. She stepped back and took a deep breath. Her smile vanished. Her leg shot out like a piston and the board cracked in two.

. . .

One morning, on my way to a lecture on Balzac, it came to me with great clarity that there was no way that that guy, the professor, was going to tell me anything useful. No doubt he *knew* many useful things, but he wasn't going to say them; rather, he was going to tell us again that Balzac's Paris was extremely comprehensive.

I went instead to the undergraduate library, to the basement where government documents were stored. This was the only area where laptops were allowed, because the clicking of keys was upsetting to non-computer users. I opened the file called pinkhotel.doc and started to write.

Nothing good was happening in the pink hotel. It was in Tokyo. A family was supposed to stay there for two nights. The father, a film director, was going to shoot a nonfiction film on a nightingale farm in the countryside. The nightingales' nests were used to make a skin cream. After two nights in Tokyo, the father and his assistant left for the nightingale farm. But the mother got sick, so she and the two daughters couldn't leave. They had to stay in the hotel. The older daughter was in love with the father's assistant. The younger daughter was a pest. The story was called "The Pest"—it was sort of an allusion to *The Plague*. It was a really depressing story.

In the weeks before winter vacation, I went running every night, alone, by the river. Svetlana didn't like to run in the snow, and she thought it was dangerous by the river after dark. But, wearing layers and shock-protected shoes and headphones, I felt completely insulated and safe. Scenery flashed by as if behind glass. On one side of the path, light from the sodium lamps shone on the half-frozen river and reflected off the low clouds; on the other, headlights in glowing pairs expanded, expanded, and rushed past.

One night around eleven, a bicycle materialized out of the darkness. "Hi, Sonya!" called the rider, and when he was gone I realized he had been Ivan.

By the time I got back and took a shower it was past midnight, but I wasn't tired at all, it felt like two in the afternoon. I dried my hair, boiled a pot of water, steeped an envelope of "cranberry tea" from the cafeteria. I was listening to a tape from the dollar bin at Christie's, of Khachaturian's violin concerto, conducted by Aram Khachaturian. If you listened carefully you could hear someone, maybe Aram Khachaturian, coughing.

I read for a while. Things were going well with Nina for a change, and yet I didn't like it that Leonid turned out to have been Galina's ex. Why did Nina's rival's rejected boyfriend have to come into anything? Was that narrative economy, or was it a statement about the way of the world—about how the jilted had to suffice for one another?

At two a.m., I started cleaning up my room, even though it wasn't that messy. From Oleg Cassini's memoirs, which were under the bed, I learned that Cassini had also suffered from insomnia. One night, he woke from uneasy dreams with the opening of Dante's *Inferno* setting off "a clangorous tumult in [his] subconscious: *'Midway the journey of our life, I found myself in a dark forest.'*" When I read these terrible words, chills ran up my arms. I knew "midway the journey" was supposed to mean midlife crisis. But to me it seemed that one had *always* been midway the journey of our life, and would be maybe right up until the moment of death.

I woke up at 9:07. I stared at the clock, wondering whether to stay in bed, go to breakfast, or go late to Russian class. It was weird to think that everyone was there right now—that class was going on, with everyone in the room. Now it was 9:09.

A few minutes later, a gust of wind was blowing dry snowflakes off a branch and onto my cheek, which was still warm from the pillow. I got to class twenty minutes late. Only Ivan and Boris were there. Irina was happy I came—she always liked it better when the class wasn't all boys or all girls. She told me to stand with Ivan, and said she had an idea: Why didn't Ivan pretend to be Ivan in the story—Nina's Ivan? "You finally meet," she said. "In Siberia. Do you understand?"

We said we understood, and stood there looking at each other.

"Ivan," I said. "Finally, we meet."

"That's true," he said.

Then neither of us said anything.

"Ivan," said Irina. "Don't you have something to tell Nina?"

"Well," he said. He looked at the floor and then looked at me. Lines appeared on his forehead. "I have a wife," he said. "And it's not you."

I knew it wasn't real—I knew it was just a story. But my stomach sank, my breath caught in my throat, a wave of nausea rose in my chest. I realized I had been hoping to hear a justification—like that he was a spy, or was escaping from being framed for a crime he didn't commit. I had been hoping to hear his marriage was a sham.

I told myself that nothing had really happened. Even within the story, Nina had already known that Ivan was married. There hadn't been any news. Nothing had changed.

But at the end of class, I still felt slightly annoyed toward Ivan, the way you feel annoyed toward someone in real life after they say something mean to you in a dream. Instead of taking the stairs with him as usual, I took the elevator.

Over vacation, I went home to New Jersey. Everything was at once overwhelmingly the same and ever so slightly different. The Oliveri sisters' plaster donkey was still standing in the driveway under the willow tree, just a little smaller than it had been. Inside, the house was incredibly clean, like a crime scene. My mother had started hiring a cleaner. There was basmati rice in the cabinet—a thing I had never seen there before. Since I had left, my mother said, the water bill had gone down by 80 percent.

My mother invited some colleagues to dinner. There was some reason they had to be invited. She had planned the menu from *The New Basics Cookbook*. I was supposed to make the dessert, a raspberry angel food cake with raspberry amaretto sauce. I had never made an angel food cake before, and got really excited when it started to rise, but then I opened the oven too soon and it fell down in the middle, like a collapsing civilization.

My mother's colleagues were cartoonishly awful. It was hard to believe they were hematologists—the idea that they were supposed to make sick people feel better was comical. "Fifteen years from now, the department will be nothing but beige faces," declared the department head, who was wearing a bow tie. I burst out laughing. Everyone looked at me. "I just can't believe you just said that," I said. My mother brought out the cake, which was by then completely flat.

"I see you have a flat cake for us, is that on purpose?" one of the hematologists asked. My mother's boyfriend, Steve, said it was a Fallen Angel cake. We ate it with the raspberry sauce. It was good, if you thought of it as a sort of pancake.

Another evening, my mother and I watched *The Sound of Music*. Because of commercials, it took more than four hours. Julie Andrews sang about how she must have done something good in her youth or childhood, and my mother sang along. She said she had probably done something good in *my* childhood, because I had turned out so well.

I was interested when the nuns sang about solving a problem like Maria. It seemed that "Maria" was actually a problem they had—that it was a code word for something.

My mother was rereading *Anna Karenina*. She said that *Anna Karenina* was about how there were two kinds of men: men who liked women (Vronsky, Oblonsky) and men who didn't really like women

(Levin). Vronsky made Anna feel good about herself, at first, because he loved women so much, but he didn't love her in particular enough, so she had to kill herself. Levin, by contrast, was awkward, boring, and kind of a pain, seemingly more interested in agriculture than in Kitty, but in fact he was a more reliable partner, because in the bottom of his heart he didn't really like women. So Anna made the wrong choice and Kitty made the right choice. That was what my mother thought that *Anna Karenina* was about.

I took the train to New York and looked at the tree in Rockefeller Center: a thing that millions of other people had also seen, unlike the Oliveris' donkey. Then I saw some Soviet propaganda posters at the Museum of Modern Art. One poster, for a railway line called Turksib, showed some Turkic-looking guys' heads apparently getting run over by a train. I wondered which had been seen by more people in the history of time: the tree, or that poster.

Final exams were after the vacation instead of before. Anyone who was in a seminar or language class had to be back on campus for reading period, which started on January 2. My mother was full of outrage and pity that my vacation was so short, but I was mostly glad to go back.

The atmosphere on the train in early January was totally different than it had been in mid-December. In December the train had been full of students—students slumped in a fetal position, or cross-legged on the floor, students with all their accessories: sleeping bags, guitars, graphing calculators, sandwiches that were 99 percent lettuce, the Viking *Portable Jung*. I had listened to my Walkman while reading *Père Goriot*. *Père Goriot*'s previous owner, Brian Kennedy, had systematically underlined what seemed to be the most meaningless and disconnected sentences in the whole book. Thank God I wasn't in love with Brian Kennedy, and didn't feel any mania to decipher his thoughts.

In January the passengers were sparser, older, more sober. I thought about how the baby turned into an old man. That was the riddle of the sphinx. It certainly wasn't very challenging. In Connecticut, the flurries turned into snow, swiftly fluttering down and down, like the night watchman's eyelashes. I went to the café car, which had bigger windows. It smelled of coffee—of the striving toward consciousness. In one booth, a man in a suit was eating a Danish. In another, three girls were studying.

"Hey, Selin!" one girl said, and I realized she was Svetlana, sitting with Fern and Valerie. Seeing them together like that, I was struck by how much larger Svetlana's head was than her roommates'. It really was strange that some people were physically larger than others. Svetlana said she usually took the shuttle back, but Logan was snowed in. Apparently the shuttle was an airplane. "Now I think I'll always take the train, it's so peaceful," she said. "It's embarrassing, but I'm terrified of flying, even for just an hour."

We talked about what we had to do over reading period. Svetlana and I had Russian class, while Valerie had a physics seminar—the one where the Nobelist made you clean lab equipment. "It's so unfair," she said cheerfully. "My brother has a whole month off, and I have to go back the day after New Year's to pour acid on used-up cathodes, just because the professor is too cheap to buy new cathodes."

"He makes them use carcinogenic solvents," Svetlana said.

"They aren't *proven* to be carcinogenic," said Valerie.

Fern was taking only lecture and lab classes, and said she was coming back mostly to look after the plants. "I guess I don't enjoy being at home all that much," she added.

Dusk was falling in Boston, which lay under eight inches of snow. We made a series of bad decisions, taking the subway instead of a cab, then riding for several stops toward Braintree instead of Alewife.

"North Quincy," said a digital voice as the doors opened onto glittering blackness.

"Isn't that in the opposite direction?" asked Valerie.

We all looked out the open door. The door closed. "Next stop, Wollaston," said the robot.

In Wollaston it took us a long time to find the stairs to the opposite platform. Svetlana had two big duffel bags in addition to her suitcase. "I don't know why I brought all this stuff," she sighed. Valerie and I dragged the heaviest bag up the stairs.

Campus felt deserted. Half the lights were out in the cafeteria, and there was only one line open, serving spaghetti and canned peaches. Our voices were tiny in the near-empty hall.

My room was incredibly quiet—you could hear the snow falling. Angela was still home with her family, and Hannah was stuck in St. Louis because of the snow. She emailed me about it frequently, sometimes in verse. I wrote back some verses, too.

Russian started the next morning. Ivan wasn't there. We had to talk about our vacations.

I tried to work in the dorm, but it was too quiet. Every time I looked up, Einstein seemed to be looking back at me in an expectant way, as if to say, *Now what?*

Eventually I went to the library and sat at a fifth-floor window overlooking the Hong Kong Lounge, a windowless structure that played a big role in Hannah's imagination. "Guess what it means if you order a *red egg roll*," she often said. Next to the Hong Kong was a Baskin-Robbins, dark except for the glow from the freezers. They closed early in the winter.

The fifth floor of the library was so empty that, even though computers weren't normally allowed, I took mine out and started to write about the people in the pink hotel.

Looking out the window, I noticed that there were two people in the closed Baskin-Robbins. All around them, chairs lay on the tables, legs up. One of the people was either very fat, or wearing a big coat.

At two in the morning the library closed and I walked home through the fresh snow. The clouds had cleared, revealing the stars. Light from even a nearby star was four years old by the time it reached your eyes. Where would I be in four years? *Simple: where you are. In four years I'll have reached you.*

I couldn't sleep. I read until five. At eight-thirty I went to Russian. Ivan still wasn't there.

The airport opened and Hannah came back. She was so happy. She said that at her house you had to be quiet and always wear socks because the carpets were all white, and because her older brother was mentally disabled. I had never thought about Hannah's home life or wondered why exactly she had to make so much noise.

6. The Power of Connections

Nina was outside with the reindeer. Suddenly, she saw a man walking quickly toward her across the tundra.

"Nina?" said the man.

"Professor Reznikov!" exclaimed Nina, recognizing her professor from Moscow.

"What happiness! Do you know, Nina, I was thinking about you! You see, I'm in Novosibirsk to visit Professor Bazhanov. He and I are working on a revolutionary experiment with scientists in Irkutsk, and we need a new assistant."

"An assistant?" repeated Nina.

"Nina, I will be honest. I hear that you have been having some problems in your personal life. But I hope you haven't dropped physics. I know you are talented and will be a good physicist. Will you be our assistant in Irkutsk?"

"With pleasure," Nina told Professor Reznikov.

As a farewell gift, the workers at the farm gave Nina a fur hat. Nina promised to write letters and they promised to answer.

. . .

Leonid and Nina drove to the airport. Leonid flew directly to Irkutsk. But Nina returned to Moscow first, to arrange her affairs.
Her father was overjoyed to see that she was safe, and to learn she
had found new, interesting work in Siberia. After one week, Nina
flew to Irkutsk.

Nina looked out the window of the airplane. "Siberia, again,"
she thought. She thought about the new life that would begin
here.

. . .

On Thursday morning before Russian conversation class, I stopped by
the CVS to pick up the photographs of the pink hotel. I was still trying to get the envelope open as I walked into the classroom. Even
without looking up I could tell that Ivan was there.

It turned out we were having a spoken exam. Two professors had
come to listen to us, and there was a tape recorder. We each had to say
our first and last names into the microphone—our real names, so they
could record our grades.

"Ivan Varga," Ivan said loudly into the microphone, and passed it
to me. I hadn't known his surname before.

We had to act out the beginning of "Nina in Siberia," explaining our actions and thoughts aloud, using the maximum number of
grammatical structures. I hadn't prepared at all, but felt incredibly,
unprecedentedly fluent. "Now I have to talk to Ivan's father," I said.
"Great. He doesn't like me. He's never liked me. I know just what he'll
say, in a gloomy voice: 'God alone knows.' Oh, that's how it always is
with me."

The professors laughed. I realized that everyone in the room was
sympathetic with Nina, with her objective situation, which was so
abnormal and so bad. Within the world of the story, nobody men-

tioned or acknowledged that things were abnormal, and so one tended to accept them unquestioningly. But if you pointed out the abnormality—if you could just state it factually—people in the real world would recognize it and laugh.

I found myself remembering the day in kindergarten when the teachers showed us *Dumbo,* and I realized for the first time that all the kids in the class, even the bullies, rooted for Dumbo, *against* Dumbo's tormentors. Invariably they laughed and cheered, both when Dumbo succeeded and when bad things happened to his enemies. But they're *you,* I thought to myself. How did they not know? They didn't know. It was astounding, an astounding truth. *Everyone thought they were Dumbo.*

Again and again I saw the phenomenon repeated. The meanest girls, the ones who started secret clubs to ostracize the poorly dressed, delighted to see Cinderella triumph over her stepsisters. They rejoiced when the prince kissed her. Evidently, they not only saw themselves as noble and good, but also wanted to love and be loved. Maybe not by anyone and everyone, the way I wanted to be loved. But, for the right person, they were prepared to form a relation based on mutual kindness. This meant that the Disney portrayal of bullies wasn't accurate, because the Disney bullies realized they were evil, prided themselves on it, and loved nobody.

In Constructed Worlds, we took turns presenting our constructed worlds. Ham brought in a fleet of tiny lead humanoid monsters, which he arranged on a table in some chesslike configuration that symbolized a turn in the tide of a long war they had been having. Each race or army had its own characteristics, such as life span, superpowers, and weaknesses. Some shot webs out of their legs like spiders. Others were incapable of pain. Still others were actually plants. It wasn't clear whether this counted as a superpower or a weakness.

One student had constructed a world that was just *Star Wars.* It was completely identical to *Star Wars*, only all the characters had old Welsh names.

Another student had made watercolor illustrations to accompany a story written by his girlfriend. We weren't allowed to see the story, because the girlfriend was really shy and lived in Minnesota, but it appeared to be about a half-naked girl who lived alone on a beach. One watercolor, captioned "I wish you could take me along," showed the girl on her knees in the sand, gazing up at some birds. In another, she was tying palm leaves to her arms ("They looked just like feathers"). A third showed her lying in a heap at the foot of a cliff.

Kevin and Sandy, Chinese American identical twins who were doing premed, each did a series of dark, expressionistic woodcut prints. Kevin's were illustrations of *Against Nature*, and included a view from below of the jewel-encrusted tortoise crawling in front of a fireplace, casting a huge shadow on an Oriental carpet.

Sandy's prints were all of churches. "What's the story here, what's the world?" Gary asked. Sandy said the story was that the churches were in Hungary. That was their world. Gary said it wasn't enough narrative to just be in Hungary. He said that wasn't actually a narrative. Sandy said he would add some narrative before the next class.

Ruby, a broad-shouldered half-Chinese girl from Arkansas, had made a video called *A Bone to Pick*. It opened with Ruby standing in a kitchen holding a big papier-mâché bone. "I found a bone, Dad, so who could I pick it with if not with you?" she said slowly. She had an amazing face, with a droopy unsmiling mouth and asymmetrical bangs.

The next shot showed a small Asian man in a yellow shirt, in poor focus, standing in front of a building. He seemed to be smiling and shaking his head.

"Is it a wishbone, Dad?" Ruby asked. "Should I have it looked at by a doctor? A paleontologist?"

Ruby explained afterward that the video was about her anger toward her father. "In an ideal world," she said, "my dad would have gotten on a plane and, you know, actually participated in something I care about. But of course he's too much of an asshole. Anyway, one day I found this old guy walking around Central Square, who *looked* kind of like my dad. My friend who helped me with the filming wasn't around, so I had to tape that part myself. I was pissed off at first because the guy refused to talk. I gave him ten bucks to read the lines I wrote and he just stood there shaking his head and smiling. Then I realized it was actually really symbolic of my relationship with my father, and that made it a stronger video."

I was supposed to meet Ralph for dinner. I got to the cafeteria early and stopped at the computer terminal. I had one new email. It said to chip in two dollars for someone's birthday cake. I still had time to kill, so I pressed *C* to start a new message and then, just to see what happened, I typed Varga into the recipient box. Magically, the email address appeared, and the full name: Ivan Varga. That was Ivan.

I thought a moment and started to type.

> Ivan!
> When you receive this letter, I will be in Siberia. I'm quitting college, because questions of articulatory phonetics no longer interest me. I will live and work in Novosibirsk on the collective farm Siberian Spark. I know that you will understand me and that it will be better this way. I will never forget you.
>
> Yours,
> Selin (Sonya)

Dinner was navy bean soup in bread bowls. "I don't think Lucky Charms *work*," said Ralph, pouring himself some Lucky Charms from the cereal dispenser.

. . .

Svetlana and I had planned to go to tae kwon do, but she didn't come to the meeting place. I thought about not going, but that would mean I usually went only because Svetlana did, as opposed to out of some pure, disinterested interest in tae kwon do. In fact I had no such interest, but I knew it was wrong to do things just because other people did. Other people couldn't be the reason why you did anything.

More than half the students were still on vacation. I was the only beginner. While everyone else practiced their forms with the short instructor, I went to a side room with the tall instructor, William, to learn about kicking.

William explained that a lot of people thought the roundhouse kick was in the knee, but actually it was in the hip. "I want you to really think about your hip," he said. I said I would, but it was difficult to think about anything when the room was so small and his body was so large, the long, heavy, dark-haired arms and legs inadequately covered by the white uniform. When his huge long bare foot shot out to kick the bag, I felt I should avert my eyes—though I also felt I should pay attention, because he seemed genuinely concerned that I learn how to do a roundhouse kick.

"More pivot in the hip," he said. He made a motion as if to correct the position of my hip, but without touching me. That was the philosophy of tae kwon do: full power and no contact. "I want you to imagine you're at one on a unit circle," he said. "Your hip is the sine and your knee is the cosine. The cosine is stable at one, like your knee. To make a big difference in the cosine, you have to do some crazy thing that let's not even think about, you'd hurt yourself. But a teeny little difference in the sine, and you're really *cruising* around that circle. See what I'm saying?"

. . .

I went to Svetlana's room after class. She was sitting on the floor looking pink and inflamed, holding the beige desk phone in her lap.

"You didn't hear?" she said, raising her streaming eyes. "Joseph
Brodsky died."

The news had reached her that morning, and already her subconscious had had time to incorporate it into a dream, because she'd taken
a nap after lunch. She dreamed they were sitting cross-legged near the
fountain outside the Science Center, she and Brodsky and some others, in a circle, passing some kernels of corn from palm to palm. There
was a faint ringing noise and the sky was the color of ash. The fountain had dried up. They were praying for rain. The sky was darkening,
but the storm didn't come—instead it was a solar eclipse.

I picked up a book that lay facedown on the floor—*КУРАНИИ*.
That was *To Urania*, in Russian. I opened a page at random. I
recognized approximately one word in each line: "here," "your,"
"probably."

I went back to my room and sat at my desk to check email. When
I saw Ivan's name in the in-box, I felt a jolt and realized I had been
hoping all day that he would write to me. The subject line was: Siberia.
I read the message several times. I couldn't seem to understand what
it was about. The individual words and even the sentences made sense,
sort of, but taken together, they seemed to have been written in some
other language.

Dear Selin, Sonya—I had a strange dream, the message began. The
dream was about the Yenisei River. Now I know you are there. I know
you will cheat on me with my future girlfriend's exboyfriend. However, I will
forgive you. Without you I would not have found Barbara, the perfect teacher-
machine.

Ivan asked if I could tell him the plot of *Goodbye, Summer*. That
was a BBC "soap opera" made for beginning Russian students. We
were supposed to have been watching it all semester. It was going to
be on the exam. If you would tell me about it, I would forgive you for Siberia,

the 150 years of Turkish invasion of Hungary, and, moreover, the horrible books about it which we had to read in school.

I had never heard of any Ottoman invasion of Hungary. As a child, I had been told that the Turks and Hungarians were related, that the Huns were Turkic, that both peoples had migrated west from the Altai and spoke similar languages. I had an Uncle Attila—it was a common Turkish name. But in Ivan's world, our ancestors had been enemies.

I felt dizzy from the sense of intimacy and remoteness. Everything he said came from so thoroughly outside myself. I wouldn't have been able to invent or guess any of it. He had told me a dream. He had typed: I know you will cheat on me. He said he would forgive me, twice. I hadn't done anything against him, but the thought that I had, or would, was somehow exciting. I wanted to write back right away, but he had waited a whole day, so I knew I had to wait at least that long.

Svetlana and I were passing through the weight-lifting room on the way to the lockers. "I mentioned to William how freaked out you were when he started talking to you about trigonometry," she was saying. "It won't happen again." I felt betrayed, and then I realized that Svetlana must have a thing for William. At that moment, I saw that Ivan was in the room, sitting at a machine, pulling an iron bar attached to a cord. On the other side of a pulley, stacked weights seamlessly rose and fell. Ivan stood and released the bar, and the weights dropped with a muffled clank. It was a low-ceilinged basement and he couldn't stand up all the way. He turned like maybe he had seen us, but I wasn't sure. I thought about whether to say hello, but by then we were at the lockers.

Dear Ivan, I typed. When I woke up, in Siberia, I felt so homesick. I thought the feeling might go away during the day. It didn't go away. I said I had left Siberia and come back. Part of me thought that nothing would be here anymore—that I would come up the escalator and there would be only snow. Instead I found brick walls, Balzac, frozen yogurt, alveolar fricatives, everything just the way I left it. I felt a great need to tell him how I was surrounded, overwhelmed, by things of unknown or dubious meaning, things that weren't commensurate to me in any way.

I started to summarize the plot of *Goodbye, Summer*. It was a long story and, as I wrote, I could tell that I was losing some kind of political capital. I deleted what I had written and typed instead: Sure, I can tell you the story. Now he would have to ask me again.

Before the exam, Svetlana and I met for breakfast. "You look as if someone died," she said.

"I didn't sleep well," I said.

"Don't tell me you're nervous," Svetlana said.

"Whenever I'm worried about anything," said this guy Ben, "I like to think about China. China has a population of like two billion people, and not one of them even remotely cares about whatever you think is so important." I acknowledged that this was a great comfort.

Svetlana liked to get everywhere early and we were among the first people in the examination room—a sun-drenched historic hall with oak pews. I sat near the end of one pew, and Svetlana sat in the row ahead and turned to face me. We were talking about whether Svetlana should attend the Brodsky memorial ceremony at Mount Holyoke. At some point she trailed off, looking up at something behind me.

"Sonya," Ivan said. "Can you really tell me the story of the BBC?"

I told him the story, starting from when Olga forgot her textbook in Victor's taxi. As the hall grew noisier, Ivan stepped in closer and leaned toward me. Soon he was crouched at my feet, holding the back of my seat for balance, frowning at the floor.

I got to the part where they both married other people, just as the proctor came in. "And that's the end," I said.

"You're my savior," Ivan said, meeting my eyes, and went to find a seat.

"Who was that?" Svetlana asked.

"Ivan, remember? We all used to be in the same class."

"I don't remember him at all. I don't see how I could have forgotten someone like that," she said. "Why didn't he just watch the thing himself?"

"I guess he was busy."

"He must have a very rich inner life," Svetlana said. I laughed. She wasn't laughing. "You really don't see anything strange about him? The way he looked at you—like he was trying to look *into* you. Didn't it make you uncomfortable? It made *me* uncomfortable."

It didn't make me uncomfortable.

Ivan wrote an email with the subject line: Lenin. He said that the Russians were thinking of removing Lenin from the tomb in the Red Square. Ivan would feel somehow lonely without him. Lenin had always been present—Lenin, like the picture on my wall, wrote Mayakovsky in their fourth-grade reader, but they didn't learn anything about why he committed suicide.

After 1990 all the Lenin monuments in Budapest were rounded up and deposited in a park outside the city limits. There they formed a wonderful community: much nicer than they ever imagined communism to be. Lenin greeted Lenin in front of another Lenin, while a proletarian— they called him the cloak-room sculpture—ran behind him with a banner: You have left your sweater, sir. The giant smiling Lenin who stood in the back had been defaced by vandals in the early eighties. Don't smile, Ilych, you know how it works: in 150 years we became no Turks, the vandals had written. The rhyme was better in Hungarian.

Another Lenin statue, a gift from the Soviet people, had been damaged on the train from Moscow. The top of his head fell off and got lost. Hungarian sculptors hastily made Lenin a hat, carved from the finest marble. At the magnificent ceremony during which the statue was unveiled, it became apparent that Lenin had two hats: one on his head, and one in his hands.

I read the message over and over. I wasn't sure why he had written it, but I could see that it had taken a long time, and that he was trying to be delightful. I kept thinking about the Lenins in the park, in a configuration that nobody had ever intended, but which was maybe somehow the true realization of communism. The writing style felt playful, but also serious. It was serious that Mayakovsky had killed himself.

My sleep life went totally off course. I seemed always to be thinking about the wrong things. Every night I went to bed around midnight, closed my eyes, thought a lot of jumbled thoughts, turned the lights back on, and read until four.

Because I wanted to understand Ivan better, I read *The Book of Laughter and Forgetting*. The very first thing in the book was a hat-related anecdote about the absurdity of Communist rule. Apparently the Communists had erased some guy from a photograph, but they had forgotten to erase his hat. I thought for hours about this hat. I knew it was connected somehow with the hat on the Lenin monument in Hungary. But how? It just seemed to sit there: this surplus hat.

Svetlana and I went to see *Three Songs about Lenin* at the Film Archive. In the third song, Lenin died. The whole end of the movie was just people crying: old people, young people, children; Russians, Tatars, Central Asians; at factories, in fields, at his funeral. There was a cut from dead Lenin in his coffin, to old Lenin smiling into the sun, and you could see all the difference between death and life. It had never occurred to me how many people had actually loved Lenin, really loved him with emotional love.

Svetlana said that when she was in the first grade, kids would torture each other in the playground by asking, "Who do you love more, Comrade Tito or your own mother?"

On the last day of Constructed Worlds, Gary helped us arrange our finished projects in an exhibition gallery.

Sandy, whose Hungarian churches had needed more narrative, had brought six new woodcuts of the same Hungarian churches—this time with pigs on the front steps. He said the pigs had run away from the neighboring farm.

Gary laid all the prints faceup on a table, then turned a few of them over to show us how different the remaining pictures looked, depending on how many were visible, and which ones. They really did look different. It was inspirational to see that Gary was actually good at something. We all agreed on the four prints that looked the best together. They weren't the four best individual prints—they were the four with the most tension. One had no pigs; the other three had pigs. We tried hanging them in different configurations. Everything turned out to be something you could change and manipulate. Ruby's TV stand looked best near the fake encyclopedia that a computer-science major made. The Hungarian churches looked best in a row, but the scenes from *Against Nature* looked better in a grid.

I had brought in twelve photographs of the pink hotel, and the class chose six of them to display. It was funny to see which ones everyone hated. One picture showed a guy from down the hall standing with a suitcase. Everyone unanimously hated the guy and his suitcase. They liked the pictures with Hannah, and the pictures with no people. We hung the six photographs in a row. Printouts of the story were stacked on a pillar under the photographs. I had chosen a ten-point font, both to conserve paper and to discourage people from reading the story, which I didn't think they would enjoy. Even though I had a deep conviction that I was good at writing, and that in some way I already *was* a writer, this conviction was completely independent of my having ever written anything, or being able to imagine ever writing anything, that I thought anyone would like to read.

When Hannah saw the printouts, she couldn't get over how many pages I had written, especially in such a small font. She was sure nobody else in the whole school was capable of writing such long and detailed stories, and urged me to enter the undergraduate fiction contest.

"Did you remember to enter the contest?" she asked, the next day.

"I couldn't find the building," I said.

Hannah, who knew the campus map by heart, walked me to the small wooden house where the literary magazine had its office. She watched me drop off a printout of the story, with my name and number on a separate piece of paper.

Exams ended. It was time to forget all the phonetic symbols, Russian verbs, and nineteenth-century plots. During the few days' vacation before the new term, Svetlana's mother came to visit. She slept in Svetlana's bedroom, and Svetlana stayed with me—she couldn't stay in her own common room, because Fern was growing a delicate plant that had to have a bright light shining on it all night.

Svetlana's mother took me and Svetlana to lunch at a French-Cambodian restaurant.

"Selin, this is my mom, Sasha," Svetlana said. "Mom, this is my friend Selin."

Svetlana's mother stared at me. "Darling," she rasped, "don't you have another coat?"

I was wearing the ankle-length Gogolian garment from Filene's. When I explained that my peacoat had been stolen, Svetlana's mother looked stricken. "Stolen? My God! Svetlana, you must have an old jacket you could give to Selin. Maybe your purple ski jacket? It's still at home. I can mail it to you."

"Mom, that jacket is two years old. The arms are short on *me*. It would never fit Selin."

"Oh. Yes, it's true, Selin, you're bigger than Svetlana. It's a pity."

"I like Selin's coat," said Svetlana.

"Oh, me too, don't misunderstand, it's . . . elegant. Maybe too elegant—maybe just a tiny bit ridiculous. But of course you must wear it until you can get another. You must not freeze to death."

A clay pot was brought to the table, with something sputtering wrathfully inside in coconut milk. Svetlana's mother reminisced about her favorite childhood holiday. "We would go to the—what's the word? Where they are dead. Cemetery, cemetery. The Turkish cemetery. And we would dance on their graves. There would be a band, oh, not large, maybe five or six musicians, and many flowers, and the girls wore the most beautiful silk dresses. Red, yellow, white, all different colors. It was a beautiful holiday."

"Mom," Svetlana said, "that's not an appropriate story to tell my Turkish friends."

"Don't be ridiculous. It was a very sweet, innocent holiday, full of dancing and flowers. Selin won't be offended. The Turks were a powerful, well-respected enemy."

"Like the Serbs in Bosnia?" said Svetlana.

"What does that have to do with anything?"

"I just can't believe you're talking about the Turks, as if it's the greatest thing in the world to be a Serb right now."

"It's no different to be a Serb than anyone else. I am not the one doing this ethnic cleansing. I personally wish the Bosnians nothing but the best. I wish the Turks nothing but the best also. I was only mentioning a memory from my happy childhood, so why must we always have these political conversations? Let's be frivolous." She turned to me abruptly. "Do you wax your eyebrows? Surely you must pluck them, with tweezers. No? They have such an interesting shape. It doesn't quite look natural. Of course, you don't *need* to do anything with your eyebrows. Well, maybe you could just clean them up a little bit, right here, but it's not a crisis. Not like Svetlana, who won't do anything with hers, and they make her look so angry."

"I *am* angry, Mom. It's not my eyebrows."

"Yes I know, darling, you keep saying that. But they give you a *sullen* look, like a sulky little boy. You would be so much more attractive without it. Don't you think, Selin?"

I knew the look she meant, it was at a certain angle when she looked down, and it was dear to me. "I like Svetlana's eyebrows," I said.

"Ah!" She sighed. "You girls are so young."

"I don't feel young," Svetlana said. "This day has aged me a thousand years. You cannot imagine, Selin, what a tiring day this has been. Arguing endlessly since seven in the morning about how Sasha fucked up my childhood."

"Well, you know darling, it wasn't arguing, since I agree with you completely. I was monstrous. Monstrous. But what's the point of dwelling on all that now? Who cares? Now we can move on. Am I correct?"

Svetlana didn't say anything but seemed to simmer almost audibly like the coconut milk in the little pot.

"You turned out great," I said, and put my hand on hers. "I mean, just look at you!"

"That is not the point!" exclaimed Svetlana's mother, rapping the table with her ring. "Even if she was monstrous, we'd simply have to work with what we had. There would be no point *arguing*."

SPRING

On the first day of the semester, we learned some irregular Russian nouns that looked feminine but took masculine case endings. They were good nouns: "calendar," "dictionary," "briefcase," "bear." Ivan came late, and sat directly behind me. In his physical presence it was impossible to believe that he had written me those emails.

Because we were sitting close to each other, Ivan and I ended up being partners in a drill on the instrumental case. You had to ask each other what you wanted to "become" after the university. Whatever that thing was, it had to go in the instrumental case. Ivan said he wanted to become a mathematician. I said I wanted to become a writer.

"What do you want to write? Histories, essays, poems?"

"No, novels."

"Interesting," said Ivan. "In my opinion, you can write a good novel."

"Thanks," I said. "In my opinion, you can become a good mathematician."

"Really? How do you know?"

"I don't know. I'm polite."

"Aha, I see."

That seemed to do it for our conversation. I looked around at the rest of the class. They were all still talking, laboriously, like seals.

"Where do you want to live after the university?" I asked, though it wasn't part of the exercise, and didn't use the instrumental case.

"After the university here?" Ivan pointed at the floor. "Here, at Harvard?"

"After the university, here at Harvard."

"I want to live in Berkeley."

I tried to remember what Berkeley was. "In . . . California?"

Ivan nodded. "I want to go to graduate school at Berkeley in California."

I had never been to or thought about California.

Varvara handed out the last installment of "Nina in Siberia." It used all six grammatical cases. Ivan and I took the stairs together.

"What are you going to do now?" he asked. It sounded existential.

"I don't know," I said, trying to keep up.

He slowed down. "Are you going to a class?"

"Not for another hour," I said. "What are *you* going to do now?"

He hesitated for a fraction of a second. "I'm going to a class."

"Oh."

"I don't really want to go."

So don't go, I tried to say. He held the door for me—a heavy fire door. I didn't like to walk ahead of him. I didn't like him to leave my field of vision, and I didn't like that he could see my back. I went through the door. We said goodbye and I went to the student center, where I bought a coffee and sat down to read about Nina.

7. *The Eclipse*

That spring, there was a solar eclipse. Nina and Leonid went to a conference in the city of Ulan-Ude, in the Buryat Republic in Eastern Siberia: the best place in the world to observe the eclipse.

Nina's presentation was a great success. Everyone agreed that it was "the latest word in physics." Afterward, there was a big dinner. The physicists ate sturgeon, drank vodka, chatted, and told anecdotes until late at night.

"Good evening," said a stranger. Nina and Leonid turned and saw—a shaman. "For only two rubles, I will tell your fortune," said the shaman.

Leonid gave the shaman two rubles. The shaman looked for a long time at Nina's palm. "You're starting a new life," he said finally. "It seems to me you will be married soon."

Leonid gave the shaman five more rubles.

The next morning, Nina woke at dawn and dressed in her warmest clothes. She put on her fur hat from the "Siberian Spark." She and Leonid went to the observation site. There were many physicists there.

Suddenly Nina heard a familiar voice. "Nina!"

She turned and saw Ivan.

"Nina," Ivan said. "Congratulations on yesterday's brilliant presentation. How glad I am to see you! Tell me, how is life?"

"Ivan!" said Nina. "Life is very good."

"Hello, Ivan," said Leonid.

"Hello, Leonid," said Ivan.

The three students fell silent.

"Nina. Leonid. Listen," Ivan said finally. "I want you to finally know the truth about me. In Moscow, Nina was my friend, and I thought that I loved her. But last summer I met Galina and fell in love. Galina lived in Siberia and planned to marry Leonid. I lived in Moscow and planned to marry Nina. Galina and I simply decided to forget about each other. But then I received a letter from my uncle. He invited me to work in his laboratory in Novosibirsk. I understood then: this was fate."

"Fate?" repeated Nina.

"I decided to go to Novosibirsk, but I was afraid to tell you, Nina. Somehow it seemed to me that you would understand that everything was over between us. Later, when I learned that you had come to Siberia, I understood how stupid and cowardly I had been. I started to write you a letter, but I couldn't find the words. Nina, forgive me if you can."

"Forgive you, Ivan?" said Nina. "But I'm grateful to you! If you had stayed in Moscow, I wouldn't have come to Siberia. If I hadn't come to Siberia, I wouldn't have met Leonid."

"Kids!" someone shouted. "The eclipse is starting!"

Gradually, the sun became a smaller and smaller crescent. The moon's shadow swallowed nearly the entire sky. The many-colored corona grew brighter and brighter. At first Nina and Leonid took turns looking through their solar telescope. But then they looked into each other's eyes.

I read the last installment with a sinking feeling. Everything about it rang false: the shaman's prophecy, Ivan's explanation, and especially the "happy" ending. Why did Nina have to look into Leonid's eyes, instead of into the telescope? How did Leonid solve anything? Why did every story have to end with marriage? You expected that from *Bleak House,* or even from *Crime and Punishment.* But "Nina in Siberia" had seemed different. Of everything I had read that semester, it alone had seemed to speak to me directly, to promise to reveal something about the relationship between language and the world. For the mystery to be tied up so glibly, for everyone to be paired off and extinguished that way, felt like a terrible betrayal.

Caught up in Nina's story, I missed the beginning of the next class I was shopping: a seminar on the Spanish avant-garde. I found a seat

just as the professor was sliding a cassette into the video player. The
tape was cued up to a shot of a cloud bisecting the moon, followed, a
moment later, by a razor blade bisecting a woman's eyeball.

The professor stopped the tape and flipped on the lights. Just from
looking at his ravaged, lined face, I thought, you could somehow see
that he wasn't American.

"This," said the professor, "is the problem with Buñuel. Why exactly does he show us a moon, and then an eye? Two unrelated images.
Why does he juxtapose them?" He looked around the table. Nobody
said anything.

"Exactly," he said. "There is no answer, because this is surrealism.
We can suggest many interpretations, but we can prove nothing, and
we will never have an answer. Let us think for a moment of Freud. I
have read Freud's *Interpretation of Dreams*, and I found it extremely
unsatisfying. In this book, for example, Freud interprets a dream. I
read his interpretation. I think, Yes, this is possible. Maybe his interpretation is correct. But how can he prove it? He cannot prove it. For
this reason, discussion is endless, and it is useless. We encounter this
infinite uselessness also in our attempts to interpret Buñuel."

I looked around the table. The other students were either nodding
or taking notes. Nobody else seemed to find it appalling or shameful
that a literature professor should stand up in front of a classroom and
say that interpretation was infinitely useless.

"We just saw a shocking scene," the professor continued. "In this
scene, an eyeball is cut open. Of course, when he was filming, Buñuel
didn't really use a woman's eye. He used a cow's eye."

The boy next to me seemed to undergo some kind of spasm and
scribbled something in his notebook. I glanced at the page. In jerky
handwriting he had written: *Cow's eye.*

"However," the professor continued, "even if Buñuel himself didn't
really perform such an act of human violence, film itself was already a
new and violent medium. Film is a medium that fragments and dis-

members the human body. We see the actor's head but we don't see his body. It's as if he has been decapitated. Yet he does not appear to be dead. He is talking, and moving, like a live person. What a paradox! In Buñuel's time, viewers would stand up and look under the screen, trying to find the rest of the body. Never before had people seen a human body fragmented in this way, and this was already a terrible shock for them."

When he called film a "paradox" I felt a wave of almost physical pain. "What about portraits?" I blurted.

The professor turned in my direction and fixed his ravaged gaze on my face. "Portraits?"

"In a portrait you just see someone's head, without their body. But people don't assume that the person in the portrait has been decapitated."

"Ah—the bust," he said. "I think that you are referring to Greek and Roman busts, no? For example, a bust of Aphrodite. Yet often what we see in a museum presented to us as a bust is actually the head of a statue that has been broken off from the body, because of some accident. The Greeks and Romans would have been horrified to see a disembodied head in that way."

I considered this. "What about coins? Didn't coins just show a ruler's head, without his body?"

"Naturally," the professor said wearily, "coins are very old, and we could discuss this if we wanted. My point is that film was a revolutionary medium."

I was impressed by that rhetorical turn: now *I* looked like an asshole, because it was like I was saying that film wasn't a revolutionary medium.

In the end I signed up for a different Spanish film seminar, taught in Spanish, by an adjunct instructor. The adjunct instructor also said stupid things, but they were in Spanish, so you learned more. I was the only person in the class who wasn't a heritage speaker, so I talked the slowest and had the worst accent. I had studied Spanish in high school because my father, a leftist, said it was important to know the language of the working classes. I liked Spanish—I liked how the donkey had a place in the national literature—and I liked the idea of watching Spanish movies in Spanish, of learning about a different world in the language it had been thought up in.

Ivan didn't write back to me on the day I had predicted. Again and again I checked my email, and he always hadn't written. When his name finally appeared in those green letters on the black screen, I felt amazement and fear, partly because I had stopped thinking he would write, and partly because the subject line said, in Turkish: Don't be ridiculous!

Dear Sonya, Ivan began. I was "domuzuna calismak" in the library on my philosophy paper when I found this dictionary. In Turkish, *domuzuna çalışmak* meant working to your pig. It wasn't anything anyone ever said, or ever would say. Probably he had meant to say "working like a pig." Nobody would have said that, either. The pig wasn't much talked about in Turkish culture, and definitely wasn't known for its hard work; that would have been the donkey. Still, I thought it was wonderful that Ivan had decided to read a Turkish-English dictionary, and that he had brought to it such a unique perspective.

Turkish, he said, was the only language that could express that there was indeed not much difference between a latrine and Ivan's paternal aunt. It was full of Hungarian words, like for handcuffs and beard: Compared to Turkish, all Western European languages are just "garb." For weeks, just thinking about that line could make me laugh aloud. *Garbi* was Turkish for Western, related to *garip* (alone, stranger, strange). But "garb" was also like "garble" and "garbage," and it was

also just weird clothing, and I thought he was right. All those Western languages *were* garb.

I wanted to know how it was going to turn out, like flipping ahead in
a book. I didn't even know what kind of story it was, or what kind of
role I was supposed to be playing. Which of us was taking it more
seriously? Didn't that have to be me, because I was younger, and also
because I was the girl? On the other hand, I thought that there was a
way in which I was lighter than he was—that there was a serious
heaviness about him that was foreign to me, and that I rejected.

I won four pounds of cashews in a raffle. For a couple of days I skipped
lunch and dinner and just ate cashews. Every night I read until four,
then slept until the alarm went off at eight. After morning classes, I
slept some more and then went to more classes. The days took on a lurid,
nightmarish quality, like they were all part of some long unbroken
thing, and even though it was disorienting and gave me a constant headache, it was also exhilarating, and I didn't really want it to end or change.

At four o'clock one morning when I still couldn't sleep, I got up
and wrote Ivan a long email about how much I believed in the Sapir-
Whorf hypothesis, even though the Chomskians were so dismissive of
Whorf and called him a fire prevention engineer.

It was during his work for the Hartford Fire Insurance Company
that Whorf developed a deep mistrust of language, of its unseen
structures, which seemed always to be causing fires. In one factory, he
found two rooms with oil drums. In one room the drums were "full";
in the other, "empty." Workers were less careful around the "empty"
drums, which in fact contained gas vapors; there were more vapors in
that room than in the one with the "full" drums, and workers would

go in there and light cigarettes and burst into flames. What had started the fire? Wasn't it the binaries that were built into our language? What if our language had a different concept of "empty," or no concept of "empty"? What was an "empty" oil drum?

Having hit Send, I walked to the snow-covered river, sat on a bench, and ate cashews. The sky looked like a load of glowing grayish laundry that someone had washed with a red shirt.

I began to feel that I was living two lives: one consisting of emails with Ivan, the other consisting of school. Once, a few hours after getting an email from him, I ran into Ivan on the street. I knew he had seen me, but he acted as if he hadn't. He just kept walking and didn't say anything.

Later I was walking to the gym with Svetlana and we passed a guy I knew from linguistics class. "Hey Selin, how's it going," he said. I paused to reply. Svetlana also had to stop walking, and so did the guy. None of us could go until I said something. But I thought and I thought, and couldn't think of what to say. After what felt like hours, I just gave up and started walking again.

"What was that all about?" asked Svetlana. "Who *was* that?"

"Nothing. Nobody."

"Why wouldn't you talk to him?"

"I couldn't think of an answer."

Svetlana stared at me. "'How's it going' isn't a question. It's not like he actually cares how it's going."

"I know," I said miserably.

"I get that you despise convention, but you shouldn't let it get to the point that you're incapable of saying, 'Fine, thanks,' just because it isn't an original, brilliant utterance. You can't be unconventional in *every* aspect of life. People will get the wrong idea."

I nodded. It was true that I wanted to be unconventional and say meaningful things. At the same time, I felt very strongly that the problem was bigger than that. Something basic about language had started to escape me.

I thought I could fix it by taking classes. I signed up for a seminar on the philosophy of language. The point of the seminar turned out to be to come up with a theory such that, if a Martian read it, the Martian would understand what it is that we know when we know a language.

To cover all the bases, I also signed up for a class on psycholinguistics, which had a prerequisite in neural networking. In addition to not having taken it, I also didn't know what neural networking was. For some reason, this didn't really bother me, or seem like a problem. The handsome Italian professor wore the most elegant suits I had ever seen, in the most subtle colors—gray with a hint of smoky blue so elusive that you had to keep looking to be sure you hadn't imagined it. The class met on the tenth floor of the psychology building, most of which was devoted to an institute for bat study and smelled accordingly. It was total sensory discord to see the handsome professor in his elegant suits stepping out of the elevator into the hall of stinky bats.

Ivan started writing emails about fate and freedom. He seemed really worried about the possibility that we might not have free will. Lucretius and quantum theory came into it. The way I felt—and at no time more than when I was looking at the green cursor on the black screen, trying to compose an email to Ivan—I had nothing *but* free will. The thought that it might be limited in some way made me feel only relief.

My friend/ex-math teacher Tomi, who has been teaching for 20 years, says he can tell for most kids what the rest of their life will look like.

There are exceptions, like with Freud who could not analyze certain
people. I am afraid to ask him about myself. On the other hand, I am
on the boundary of being a scientist, and so far the only scientific
explanation for free will is that it is an illusion. I don't like that.

. . .

In the bookstore, waiting for Svetlana to finish comparing different
editions of *Beowulf*, I started flipping through Nabokov's *Lectures
on Literature*, and my attention was caught by a passage about math.
According to Nabokov, when ancient people first invented arithmetic,
it was an artificial system designed to impose order on the world.
Over the course of centuries, as the system grew more and more intricate, "mathematics transcended their initial condition and became
as it were a natural part of the world to which they had been merely
applied. . . . The whole world gradually turned out to be based on
numbers, and nobody seems to have been surprised at the queer fact
of the outer network becoming an inner skeleton."

Suddenly, all kinds of things I had learned in school seemed to
fit together. Could it be true, what Nabokov said—that the abstract
calculations had come first, and only later turned out to describe reality? Hadn't the Greeks come up with the ellipse from doing solid
geometry, from slicing up imaginary cones, and then centuries later,
the ellipse turned out to describe the exact shape of planetary orbits?
Hadn't ancient people invented trigonometry, centuries before anyone knew that sound waves were shaped like sine waves? Fibonacci
came up with the Fibonacci sequence just from adding up numbers,
and then its ratio turned out to be encoded in the seed spirals on a
sunflower. What if math turned out to explain how everything
worked—not just physics but everything? Could that be what Ivan
was studying?

· · ·

I went with Hannah to her Multivariable Calculus class. It was required for premeds. The instructor was a shaggy barrel-chested undergraduate wearing a bright green jogging suit. He started to talk, loudly. I couldn't understand a word he said. It wasn't because of the subject matter; rather, it was impossible to pick out a single recognizable syllable.

In the hall after class, Hannah and her premed friends were joking about how they would sabotage someone called Daniel who always broke the curve. Daniel was standing right there, smiling modestly.

"Could you guys understand anything that guy said?" I asked during a pause in the conversation.

One of the premed students, a beautiful girl with eyebrows like two wispy feathers high above her eyes, glanced over at me. "No, nobody can understand him," she said. They all started talking about how they would set off a smoke bomb in Daniel's dorm on the night before the exam.

I went to the first meeting of the only math class in the course catalog that wasn't required for premeds and didn't have any prerequisites. It was called Sets, Groups, and Topology: "an introduction to rigorous mathematics, axioms, and proofs, via topics such as set theory, symmetry groups, and low-dimensional topology." The chairs weren't in rows so much as in a big crowd. I recognized Ralph's roommate Ira and sat near him. More and more people kept coming in and sitting on the floor. It became very hot. A bearded man came in. He surveyed the room with melancholy eyes. "I am Pal Tamas," he said. "This is my Hungarian name. That is why I speak with this accent. In English, I am Tamas Pal. Soon my assistant will come with the syllabus."

I wasn't even surprised when the assistant turned out to be Ivan. I could see that he saw me, too, but we didn't smile or wave. He started handing out the syllabus, which was still hot from the photocopier and contained unexpected diacritics. Tamas Pal turned out to be "Tamás Pál," and Ivan turned out to be "Iván." The subject for the first week was "Continuity, Connectedness, and Compactness." When I tuned in, Tamás Pál was talking about how it was impossible to trisect an angle.

"This is probably counterintuitive," he said.

I couldn't imagine what it would mean for an angle to be impossible to trisect. If a thing existed, couldn't you cut it in three? The professor started sketching diagrams and equations on the board. I copied everything in my notebook. Ivan was sitting on the floor, leaning against the wall. There was a ragged spot in his jeans just below the knee. It made a much stronger impression on me than the proof about angles.

I decided not to attend the second meeting of Sets, Groups, and Topology. Instead, I went to the science library to read a journal article about linguistic priming. Apparently if you had just seen a picture of an elephant it made you faster at recognizing the word "giraffe." A picture of a train would help you recognize the word "trail," and a picture of a pail would help you recognize "pale." Didn't the trains and pails prove that people thought differently in different languages? As I kept reading, I myself became less and less able to perform simple word recognition tasks. I increasingly didn't know what to do with myself. This not-knowing was physically painful, like sleeplessness.

I went to the math class.

The professor was talking about set theory. "Consider the set of people in this room," he said. "There are about forty members. Now let us choose a subset within this set. Let's say: the people who know each other. Most of us are still strangers to each other, but not all of us. For example, I know *Iván*." He pronounced it in a really specific way, stressing the first syllable.

"I don't know how many other members belong to this subset of people who know each other, but my guess would be ten or fifteen. So I will draw some connectives, like this." He drew a bunch of dots on the board and connected some of them, like constellations. Were Ivan and I among the connected ones—the subset of people who knew each other? What was it to know each other?

In the evening, Svetlana showed me how to play squash. I had never been in a squash court before. Inside the blindingly white cube, our sneakers squeaked and Svetlana's voice sounded strangely removed, as if over a telephone. The blue rubber ball was so small, so fast and crazy. To think this world was too deterministic for some people!

I remembered as we were walking back from the courts that Ivan was teaching a section for the math class at nine. An enormous moon hung over the sports center. I probably wouldn't go to the section. I went home, took a shower, and got dressed. When I looked at my watch, it was exactly ten to nine.

I went to the Science Center. I couldn't find the room, which was in the five hundreds. There was no fifth floor in the elevator—the buttons skipped from three to six. I got in the elevator anyway and rode to the eleventh floor and back, as if the fifth floor might suddenly appear. Back on the ground floor, the doors opened. Ira stepped inside. "There's no fifth floor," I said.

"Hey," he said, and stepped into the elevator. "Are you going up?"

"Well, that's the thing," I said.

Ira pressed the button for the third floor. It turned out you had to get out of the elevator and cross a metal walkway that stretched across an atrium. A big messy garden was hanging over the atrium, in a shallow tray held up by chains. It was like in Babylon, back when everyone spoke the same language. On the other side of the atrium was a flight of stairs that went to the fifth floor.

The classroom was almost as bright as the squash court. To see Ivan standing in front of a blackboard was somehow terribly embarrassing. And yet, you were supposed to look at him—that's why he was there. He looked so tall and almost puppetlike as he paced back and forth, wrote on the board, and flung out his arm to point at what he had written. His shirt had come untucked at the side. He was working really hard. He used the word "suffer" three times. I couldn't remember any other instructor mentioning suffering even once all year.

I looked around the room at the other students. Ira was wearing glasses and looking straight ahead. Two guys in puffy jackets and giant sneakers were slouched all the way down in their seats, moving chairs around with their feet. A girl with a black miniskirt, bright red lipstick, and messy hair was nodding, a smile fixed on her face.

Ivan was talking about closed sets, open sets, odd numbers, even numbers, and days of the week. There were points that were really close to closed sets, there were points closest to the closed set. There was a kind of set that was open and closed at the same time. There was a proof that said there was a set such that it didn't contain certain of its own elements.

"I'm a really bad artist," Ivan said, drawing a picture of a house. He gave the house a chimney, and drew smoke coming out of the chimney. The smoke looked like barbed wire. He was drawing so much smoke! A big cloud, big as the whole house. What was going on in there?

Ivan drew a circle around the house. "The house is inside the world," he said. "You can be inside the house or outside the house, but you can't leave the world."

"Is there smoke in the house? If it's not suffocating, I will stay indoors; if it proves too much, I'll leave. Always remember—the door is open." That's what Epictetus said about suicide.

Next to the house, Ivan drew a stick figure. The head was level with the chimney. In Turkish, if you said, "her head hasn't reached the chimney yet," it meant she was still young enough to get married.

"Is he outside or inside?" said Ivan. "You see, he's outside the house, but inside the world."

At the end of class, I left immediately, before the clock finished striking ten. Inside the world, yes—but at least outside that room!

February rolled around. The philosophy professor's unwavering concern for Martians came to strike me as eccentric, even troubling. For the benefit of the Martians, we spent hours trying to put things like metaphor and malapropism into logic notation. Under what conditions would it be true that "Kenji placed a flag on the pinochle of Mt. Fuji"? (None! None! Under no conditions!)

It turned out that the theory of meaning that would work best for the Martians was a "theory of truth" that gave the truth conditions for every sentence. The solution would look like a series of propositions having the form, "'Snow is white' is true iff snow is white." The professor wrote this sentence on the board during nearly every class. Outside the window, snow piled deeper and deeper.

In Russian class, nobody cared about truth conditions. We *all* said, "I have five brothers."

I dreamed that Ivan said to identify a point that was really close to the set from Tuesday to Friday. To get the right answer, you had to have a fake Rolex, where the second hand ticked, unlike on a real Rolex, where it swept. On a fake Rolex, the answer was "23:59:59 on Sapir," because Sapir was the word for Monday, at least in the first two weeks of the month; in the latter two weeks, the first weekday was called "Whorf." It was important not to regard "Sapir" and "Whorf" as just two synonyms for Monday, because a day's placement within a month affected its essence.

Dear Selin, Ivan wrote.

Would you trade wine and cheese for vodka and pickles? Why does a Greek hero have to fight his fate? Are dice a lethal weapon? Is there any way to escape the triviality-dungeon of conversations? Why did you stop coming to math?

. . .

I wrote to Ivan about my dream. He replied that if I gave math a chance, I would see that it was a small and private world: just you and the reasons—no masculine bullies, with their calendars and dictionaries. I remembered then the Russian words for calendar and dictionary, the way they looked feminine but were actually masculine, and I thought he was right: that was what my dream had been about.

The thing with the Rolexes is amazing, amazing, Ivan wrote. Light, he said, seemed to sweep, but quantum theory said it ticked. Waves were the combination of sweeping and ticking. Could true sweeping ever happen on this Earth of ours? Maybe one could do sweeping math, or sweeping sex. Sweeping was beautiful, but powerless. Energy came from ticking—the capacity for rapid change. Immortality was sweeping. Lives coming and going, generations, years, minutes, seconds: all are on the fake Rolex.

On Valentine's Day, Hannah forwarded me a chain email: Forward this to five people, or your heart will be broken in the next twenty-four hours. It didn't promise anything good if you did forward it—just that if you didn't, your heart would be broken. This has been proven to work. 300 happy couples have broken up within twenty-four hours of deleting this message. What kind of person would write a letter like that?

I went to dinner at the cafeteria with Ralph. It was fajita night. In line, I made up a poem about decision making. "Your choice in tortilla, be it corn, wheat, or flour, / Can alter the wind, fifty-two miles per hour." There were boxes of "conversation hearts" everywhere, with their ominous gnomic sayings. ASK ME, NO WAY, I DO, WHO ME? Later, I was eating carrot sticks and Ralph said I reminded him of a horse.

"Are you mad at me for something?" I asked.

"No, why would you say that?" Ralph said.

Ivan wrote to me about clowns. He said that we had forgotten the clowns, who now performed only in prisons and insane asylums. The implication was that this was a bad thing.

I wrote to Ivan about a movie I'd seen in Spanish class, about an old man whose friends all rode around town in motorized wheelchairs. The old man dreamed of becoming a paralytic, so he too could ride in a wheelchair. There were a lot of farm animals roaming in the streets, representing the chaos of the *franquista* period.

Ivan stopped coming to Russian class. He took longer each time to write back to me. One day at four in the morning he sent a really long message about alcoholism and vertigo. I found it in the student center with Svetlana.

"Who wrote you the monster email?" she asked, looking over my shoulder.

"Nobody," I said, and closed the message. But she had seen his name. She said Ivan's last name was an anagram for one of the Serbo-Croatian words for the devil: "You know, like *vrag*, the Enemy." I was mad and said that "Svetlana" had "Satan" in it, too.

. . .

I read Ivan's messages over and over, thinking about what they meant. I felt ashamed, but why? Why was it more honorable to reread and interpret a novel like *Lost Illusions* than to reread and interpret some email from Ivan? Was it because Ivan wasn't as good a writer as Balzac? (But I thought Ivan *was* a good writer.) Was it because Balzac's novels had been read and analyzed by hundreds of professors, so that reading and interpreting Balzac was like participating in a conversation with all these professors, and was therefore a higher and more meaningful activity than reading an email only I could see? But the fact that the email had been written specifically to me, in response to things I had said, made it *literally* a conversation, in the way that Balzac's novels—written for a general audience, ultimately in order to turn a profit for the printing industry—were not; and so wasn't what I was doing in a way more authentic, and more human?

The adult education program assigned me an ESL student, Joaquín, a Dominican plumber with white hair, tinted glasses, and ramrod-straight posture. He came right on time and greeted me warmly in Spanish. I smiled but didn't reply. With ESL students, we had been told to pretend not only that we didn't go to Harvard but that we didn't know any Spanish. We were just supposed to have dropped out of the sky, Martian-style.

"How are you today?" I asked.

His face lit up. "Joaquín," he replied.

"Not *who* are you—*how* are you."

He beamed.

I drew three faces on the blackboard: one smiling, one with a straight mouth, and one frowning. "How are you?" I asked. Then I pointed in turn at the faces. "I'm great," I said. "I'm so-so. I'm terrible."

"*Sí,*" said Joaquín.

"How *are* you? Are you *great?*" I tapped the smiling face.

He squinted, took off his glasses, and put them on again. "I," he said, then pointed from himself to the board. "I. Joaquín."

"It means *cómo está,*" I said finally.

"*Ah, cómo está?*" Joaquín repeated, beaming more widely. "*Bien, bien. Pues, sabe, estoy un poco enfermo.*" It turned out Joaquín had come to America to have a specialist treat his diabetes-related eyesight problems. His son lived in Boston with his wife, who was a nice girl but careless. Joaquín asked where I was from, what kind of a name Selin was, what my parents did, whether I was a student. I answered everything in English first, but then also in Spanish. "You're a good girl," he said. "Your parents must be very proud."

The next week, I was supposed to get him to say what color things were. There was a worksheet. He was supposed to say that the paper was white, the pen was blue, and the board was black.

"The paper is white," I said, holding up a paper.

He nodded. "*El papel es blanco,*" he said.

"Right, so repeat after me. The paper is white."

"*Papel, es, blanco,*" he said, with a serious expression like mine.

"No, repeat the words *I'm* saying," I said. "The paper is white."

After twenty minutes he could say, "Papel iss blonk." He said it with an expression of great patience and kindness. We moved on to "The pen is blue." We started with "*El bolígrafo es azul,*" and eventually got to "Ball iss zool." Then our time was up.

Whether because the shuttle had a particularly high ceiling, or because the passengers that day were unusually short, large numbers of people seemed unable to reach the handrails. With every sharp movement, people stumbled into each other and someone ended up in someone else's lap.

Clinging to the handrail, I felt overwhelmed by fatigue. What was
I doing? For whose benefit? Who would understand what Joaquín
meant by "Papel iss blonk," let alone "Ball iss zool"? That wasn't English. It was some kind of creole. No—a pidgin. If we had children
and they grew up talking like that, they would add more grammar
and *then* it would be a creole. It wasn't even a creole.

Back at our room, I took a Snackwell low-fat brownie, Hannah's least
favorite snack, from a care package her mother had sent her, and ate it
in front of the computer. I found an email in Turkish from someone
called Yıldırım Özguven, sent from a German university address. It
didn't say much, just that it had been a long time since we had been
in touch, and he wished me success in my studies. I didn't know anyone called Yıldırım Özguven, a name meaning "Thunderbolt Self-
Confidence." I thought about it for a long time and I was absolutely
positive he was a stranger. Probably he had looked in the Harvard
directory for girls with Turkish names and, drawing on the hereditary
self-confidence his family was known for, had written me that stupid
note. The more I thought about it, the angrier I got. How could this
guy be so presumptuous? How dare he assume that I knew his "garb"?
Why did that keep happening to me?

Gradually this anger settled upon its secret, rightful object: Ivan.
What gave him the right to sit down at three or four in the morning
and write whatever came into his head, about clowns or vertigo, and
then *send* it to me? I took a shower and, though it was barely nine-
thirty, crawled into bed and fell immediately into troubled sleep.

At two-thirty I was wide awake. I knew there was no way I would fall
back asleep, not for hours. I put on sweatpants and went downstairs to
the computer room. The only light came from the Coke machine and

the "Flying Through Space" screensaver. I put six dimes in the machine and a can tumbled out like a body falling down the stairs. The Diet Coke was cold and spiky against my warm pink throat. I could feel my eyes clearing. I sat at one of the computers. Dear Ivan, I typed.

> I have been teaching ESL for community service. Instead of
> "The paper is white," this guy says "Papel iss blonk." I understand,
> because I was there when he invented it. But as far as teaching
> English goes, I've failed. I am now the interpreter of a language that
> only he and I can understand. It makes me so tired, even angry. Why
> should *I* have to figure it out? Why don't any messages come to me
> clearly?
>
>   I don't understand what you wrote about alcohol. Is it about
> alcohol? Or about the other disgusting things that might not seem
> disgusting, once the desire to experiment takes over? How can
> vertigo be the desire to fall and not the fear? Why not just jump?
> I don't understand why you told me these things.
>
>   I do want to understand you.

When I woke up again, it was snowing. I had slept through Russian. It was time for the philosophy of language. The same pale words, *"Snow is white" is true iff snow is white,* were written on the board for about the hundredth time. The class mechanically turned to look out the window.

I thought about Ivan and felt regret and shame. I shouldn't have told him that I wanted to understand him. I shouldn't have wanted to understand him.

A student asking a question was sitting in an amazing posture: legs crossed at both the knee and the ankle, arms intertwined, elbows on the desk, fingers knit together, like his whole organic being aspired to be a French cruller.

"I mean," he was saying, "if you look at that whole ontological *crisis* group in Pittsburgh . . ."

Some students laughed. Didn't they see? Everyone wanted what they couldn't have. Even this young fellow, bright, witty, everything going for him, wanted to be a cruller. Well, of *course* the flip side of desire was fear.

At three in the morning, I logged on and typed finger varga. I had never before been able to bring myself to use the Unix command "finger," because it sounded so disgusting, and also the thing it did was shameful—it showed you when and where another user had last logged in. A couple of seconds passed, and then the computer said: On since 02:43:10. It made me feel peaceful to see that he was online. I went to sleep and dreamed about a tremendously urbane guy called Phil Lang, who had lustrous hair and didn't like me. It turned out he was the philosophy of language.

·   ·   ·

Dear Selin,

There is this text editor, emacs. To exit, you have to press Ctrl-x and then quickly Ctrl-c. If you accidentally get into it, you can't get out until you learn Ctrl-x-ctrl-c. Of course, you can ask help—Ctrl-h, easy—and another Ctrl-h tells you how to use the help. But then help fills up your screen and stays there. You could search help for "kill buffer" to hide help, but first you have to search help for how to search help. Finally, your friend tells you to print help. Then you get a 10-page single-spaced printout with two columns labeled KEY— BINDING. On the left, you have the combination of keys (Ctrl-ctrl, etc.). On the right, the "bindings": cut-kill-region, kill-sentence, even transpose-sexpr.

This guy, emacs, knows a lot, but you have to learn his (her?)

secret language. Some say that Microsoft Word is for kids, but emacs—it's the God; the screen shakes under the keystrokes. Once you learn the key-bindings, you are fine. I am getting better, and I am afraid. What if everything I can learn in emacs is limited by 300 or so valid keystrokes? Do I still want to learn it then?

There is this thing with talking, you know.

I had been skimming through the message about the text editor, but at the line about talking, I came up short. I couldn't believe it was there. I read it again and again. You asked me a real question now and that is stepping over some boundary. He said he was glad, because he had wanted to talk to me in his own voice, but had been afraid to trivialize our conversation, for reasons that, written here, would themselves trivialize it. If he met me in the street now, he would say hi and keep going, because—it feels right this way (I refuted all my rational arguments), because spoken language is so demystified, so simplistic, a trap. I would have to just say some of the keys of the few available bindings . . .

I worried increasingly that I was the victim of some elaborate hoax. What if Ivan had concocted this whole pretentious correspondence, just to see how far I would go? I'm glad you're finally talking to me directly, he wrote, in the middle of a flowery paragraph about how he wouldn't talk to me if he saw me in the street. But what exactly was the con? The message had been posted at five-thirty, and Ivan had been logged on since two forty-five. Those were important, delicate hours. People didn't give them up so easily. Why would anyone go through so much inconvenience just to mystify me? The idea flashed across my mind that it might be revenge, maybe not even conscious, for . . . But that seemed too nonsensical to contemplate. In the end, I thought, I had no choice but to assume he was being sincere. If it turned out he wasn't, then so much the worse for him.

. . .

Winter drew to a close. Gray dull snowbanks began melting to reveal all kinds of half-frozen garbage. The air smelled of dirt. You were always tripping over dead birds. Daffodils came up, just in time to be crippled by a late snowfall, which turned immediately into slush.

Joaquín was late to our third meeting. I sat at the table and wrote some things I had been thinking about in a spiral notebook. I consulted my watch. Twenty minutes had passed. Joaquín had been punctual the last two times, so I started to feel worried. I found a list with the names and contact information for all the students. There was only one Joaquín but there was no phone number, just a street address.

A couple of days later, the office called and said that Joaquín wouldn't be coming in anymore. He had had eye surgery and now he was blind.

At the two-thirds mark of the school year, Hannah said she didn't want the single room. She said she didn't much like being alone, and was ceding her rights to Angela. So Angela moved back into the single and I moved back in with Hannah.

My high school friend Hema mailed me a mixtape with a song by They Might Be Giants. There was a part where the guy warbled in his weird characteristic tone, at once plaintive, cheerful, and resigned:

No one knows these things but me and him,
So I'm writing everything down in a spiral notebook.

Again and again I listened to these lines, marveling at how accurately they described my life situation.

I missed so many Russian classes that I got a letter from the Freshman Dean's Office saying that I needed a signed letter from the instructor if I wanted to stay in the class. I went to Varvara's office hours. She signed the letter right away and said I shouldn't worry about the dean, but she had been noticing I hadn't been myself this semester, and I might get a B.

"Is it because of your roommates?" she asked. I had forgotten that I had talked in class about my roommates. "I know that can be difficult," she said. "I had to switch roommates in my first year at university." I wondered for the first time whether she had gone to the university in East Germany, and what she had been like when she was a freshman.

I told her that things were going better with my roommates. She asked if there was anything else I wanted to talk about. She looked so kind and earnest, with her big gentle eyes and square jaw.

"Do you think the name Sonya is bad luck?" I blurted.

"How do you mean?"

"In *Uncle Vanya*, and in *Crime and Punishment*. Even in *War and Peace*, she's pathetic, she's . . ." I hesitated, not wanting to say the phrase Tolstoy had used, which was "sterile flower."

"She doesn't get the man," said Varvara. I saw surprise and compassion in her eyes and sensed, with a flash of dread, that she knew what I was talking about.

Ivan and I had settled into a rhythm: he would take a week to write to me, and then I would force myself to wait a week before writing back.

This already felt like a huge waste of time. Then eight days went by and he didn't write, and then it was ten days, and I was sure he was never going to write to me again, and I was in despair. Finally he sent a message. The subject line said crazy, which I found encouraging because that was how I felt. But when I opened the email, it was only one line: My thesis is due in two weeks—I will write to you then.

In Spanish class we watched an angry movie in Basque and a sad movie in Galician. The teacher explained in a matter-of-fact voice that the landscape of Galicia was unbearably beautiful, that it always rained, there were castles and petroglyphs and dolmens and the coast was pure stone like Ireland's. Introspective, resigned, and melancholy, the people answered one question with another in a singsong, and played "primitive bagpipes" called *gaita galega*. Their language contained eight falling and rising diphthongs: *ai, au, eu, ei, oi, ui, ou,* and *iu*. The "Galician trinity" was cow, tree, sea; the Galician himself was a tree with wings: despite roots he flew away.

"Snow in springtime, what is this?" the Italian psycholinguist demanded in a tone that clearly signified charm and humor, but which to me seemed, like nearly everything he said, pregnant with the unspeakable sadness of the world. "Why is nobody capable of really enjoying a leisurely lunch?"

In philosophy class, we talked about the problems we would have on Mars—the language problems. Supposing we went to Mars and the Martians said "gavagai" every time a rabbit ran by; we would have no way of knowing whether "gavagai" referred to rabbits, to running, or to a kind of fly that lived in rabbits' ears. I found this incredibly depressing—both the obstacles to understanding and the rabbits with flies in their ears.

Late one night Ralph called and asked if I was busy. We went to Pizzeria Uno. "I don't even know how to talk about it," Ralph said, and ordered bruschetta. I didn't know what bruschetta was.

Ralph told a long story about Cody, a guy who lived in his hallway, and whom Ralph and I had both found annoying on previous occasions. I couldn't figure out why he was talking about Cody, and when he would start talking about whatever the real problem was. First Cody had loaned Ralph a book about Auden. Ralph had then read a *New Yorker* article about Stephen Spender that had to do with something in the book, so he photocopied it and left it in Cody's door basket. Later Cody said something interesting about the article and Ralph thought that maybe Cody wasn't so bad. But then Cody berated him about some kind of lamp and put his hand on Ralph's waist. That was it—that was the whole story. At first, I thought it was Cody's strange comments about the lamp that had upset Ralph, but it wasn't. It was that Cody thought Ralph was gay.

"What could have given him that impression?" Ralph said. "Was it because of Stephen Spender?"

"Maybe it was that," I said, wondering who Stephen Spender was.

"Did *you* ever think anything like that about me?"

"Oh, Ralph." I touched his shoulder, wondering what was the right thing to say. I said that probably Cody's actions were less a reflection of how Cody thought Ralph felt, and more a reflection of the fact that he, Cody, thought Ralph was funny and handsome and lovable, which Ralph was.

"And anyway," I said after a moment. "I mean—that wouldn't be the end of the world. You wouldn't be like Cody, like weird about lamps. You would still be yourself." He looked up from his half–iced tea half-lemonade with an expression I had never seen before.

Ralph and I went to the student center to study for midterms. He was reading an econ textbook and I was studying psycholinguistics. Every time I looked up, I caught the eye of Ham from Constructed Worlds, who was sitting at a nearby table with three other guys.

After a few minutes, Ham came to our table.

"You seem pretty interested by that book," he said. "What's it about?"

I tipped it up to show the cover, which was purple and said LANGUAGE in big white letters.

"Man, do I hate language," Ham said. "If I had it my way, we would all just grunt."

"If we all did that, the grunting would become a language."

"Not the way I would do it."

"Really," I said.

In reply he made some kind of noise.

I went home for spring break. My mother and I stayed up late talking. When I woke up the next day she had gone to work. I went running, but not for long, because the batteries in my Walkman started to die. "No one knows these things but hiiim and meee," droned a hideous distorted version of They Might Be Giants. I headed home. Mrs. Oliveri was wandering around the driveway wearing a yellow cardigan. I had never had that much to talk about with Mrs. Oliveri, who was ninety-eight. My first thought was that I could probably get into the house without her noticing, but then I felt guilty for thinking that and called out a greeting. She didn't seem to hear. "Hi!" I called twice more, loudly. She still didn't answer. Apparently she didn't want to trivialize our relationship with spoken language. I walked right up in front of her. "Hi!" I said.

"Oh, hi! Where'd you come from? I didn't see you!" She looked up at the sky. I said I had come from the driveway. She just couldn't believe it. "From there? There? But I didn't see you!" She said it was so good to see me. Then she said, "Oh, I love you!" and patted me on the arm. I was really confused; she had never said she loved me before. I patted her arm too, and said it was really good to see her. When I went inside to take a shower and looked in the mirror, I was surprised by how radiant my own face looked.

When my mother came home, she explained that Mrs. Oliveri had had a stroke. She was mad at the other Mrs. Oliveri, because she had charged her ten dollars for being late with rent. Just then the doorbell rang. It was Mrs. Oliveri—the one who hadn't had a stroke. She was carrying a cake. My mother made a funny face. "Well, thank you," she said. "Would you like to come in?" The cake turned out to be made almost entirely of frosting.

My mother said that something had to be done about my hair. Over the weekend she took me to her stylist in New York. There was another snowstorm, although immediately after, the sun came out and it was almost sixty degrees, so the snow melted. Nothing was real anymore; everything was over. The hairdresser, Gerard, had sideburns, a pin-striped vest, and a vivacious laugh. He said he liked how my hair didn't just lie there. "It retaliates, it bounces back. That's what I like. I bet it's like the person who wears it. I bet you don't just *lie* there."

I felt so dispirited. What were you supposed to do, other than lie there? What did my hair know that I didn't? Also, why was a gay man telling me his hypotheses about my sexual performance? None of it made sense. Gerard kept complaining about the music. He said they had really good music, like Santana, but instead they kept playing Chris Isaak. My hair ended up really short.

. . .

I went back to school the Saturday before classes resumed. The train was nearly empty. The conductor recited the names of the stops in Connecticut with weary incredulity, as if he couldn't believe how many there were. "*South* Saybrook. Saybrook *Race*track. *Say*brook. *Old* Saybrook. *North* Saybrook. Saybrook *Falls.*"

When I got back, Ivan still hadn't written. I called Ralph but there wasn't any answer. Then Svetlana called. We spent that evening and the whole next day together, walking down Mass Ave and across the bridge to Boston. We stopped at Tower Records, then walked up Newbury Street. We came to a bead store. Svetlana didn't think there was anything embarrassing about going to a bead store in Beacon Hill and spending almost twenty dollars on beads.

Back in Svetlana's room, we listened to the CDs she had bought— Joni Mitchell's *Blue* and Bach's *St. Matthew Passion*—and made necklaces, periodically holding up the strands and comparing them. Svetlana explained how her necklace was characteristic of her and mine was characteristic of me, and I thought about how probably, as long as civilization had existed, women had been threading beads onto strings or reeds or whatever. Then I wondered whether it had always been women. Maybe in ancient times men had been into beads. Today, though, it was hard to imagine boys sitting around on beanbags, listening to Joni Mitchell, holding necklaces against each other's necks, and talking about Svetlana's sister. Some part of me worried that this was why women would never amount to anything, that we were somehow holding ourselves back.

Over the break, Svetlana had visited her sister at art school. She had found her sitting cross-legged on her bed in a minuscule dorm room, sipping the same cup of lukewarm coffee she had been reheating in the microwave every two hours, building an artichoke out of tiny sticks. The artichoke was a requirement for all the art school first-years. The previous week everyone had had to make a shoe out of wire.

Sasha, their mother, wanted to send the sister to a Russian healer, a man who painted mystical paintings of the night sky. One of his paintings hung in her, Sasha's, bedroom. It showed a lone balalaika sailing past a harvest moon.

Back in my room, the only new email was from my mother, and had the subject line: ant invasion.

> I had to do a mini extermination. I decided to throw out neighbors' cake which must have chagrined the ants, but they are no longer either.

In the morning when I saw Ivan's name in the in-box I almost started to cry. It reminded me of a kind of torture I had read about where afterward the captors returned your senses to you one by one, and you felt so grateful that you told them everything.

The sun, Ivan wrote, was going to rise. Outside his window, a traffic light oscillated between red and green. Occasionally, now, a car would drive by. In Russian you could describe that car, and other cars, with prefixed verbs of motion: what insignificant subtleties! Ivan had just finished grading the homework for my would-have-been classmates; his train to Yale left in an hour. Tomorrow was California. Now the sun was up and he hadn't gotten anywhere. Fortune presents gifts not according to the book.

I could see it all so clearly—the traffic light changing all night for nobody's benefit, the first cars passing by as the sky grew light—and

I was overcome by the sense of how much more there was in his life than in mine, by the things to do and distances to travel, while I never had done anything or gone anywhere, and never would. All I had ever done was visit my parents all the time—first one parent and then the other, with no sign of it ever stopping. Worse yet, I knew I had no one to blame but myself. If my mother told me not to do something, I didn't do it. Everyone's mother told them not to do things, but I was the only one who listened. The eternal pauper in the great market-place of ideas and of the world, I had nothing to teach anyone. I didn't have anything anyone wanted. I reread Ivan's email and looked in the face of this terrible indignity.

. . . .

Dear Ivan,

My break was bullshit. I don't know what anything means. I have this book that says LANGUAGE on the cover and it isn't teaching me anything. I think the problem goes really deep down. The oil-drum is empty, so you throw in a cigarette. The whole thing bursts into flames.

I don't understand anything that happens, or how. I don't understand why it will trivialize these letters to say hi, or to actually talk to each other. You say you're not in the mood for insignificant subtleties. But insignificant subtleties are the only difference between something special, and a huge pile of garbage floating through space. I'm not making that up. People discovered it in the nineteenth century.

I think I'm falling in love with you. Every day it's harder for me to see the common denominator, to understand what counts as a thing. All the categories that make up a dog—they go blurry and dissolve, I can't tell what anything is anymore. Chills go up the backs of my arms and songs go around in my head. "[If I Must Be Put to Death, Let It Be] by Your Aristocratic Little Hand."

Your Sonya

It was late when I sent the email. Afterward I went running by the river. Everything looked fanatically crisp, both more and less real than usual. The ground was there every time. I didn't ever want to stop running. I didn't want to go on to the next thing, or the one after that.

Back at the dorm I took a shower, logged onto Unix, and did "finger" to see where Ivan was. He was online, on a server called neptune .caltech.edu.

I got out a book and started to read. The book seemed to involve Spain in some way. Every five minutes I checked to see Ivan's online status. Sometimes he had been idle for a minute or two; then he became active again. I tried to imagine him there in California, where it was three hours in the past, typing on a computer called Neptune, pausing for a minute or two, and then typing again.

At 2:40 a.m., he sent me an email. I read it through twice. I didn't understand every word, but my body knew it wasn't good news. There were individual lines that made my heart soar, but underneath it the base, the floor, was sickening.

I read the message a third time.

Dear Sonya, it began. There is so much I want to write to you. Ivan was sitting in a tiny room at Caltech. I was describing something like the vertigo of "falling out of language." He felt it, too. His favorite thing about math was that the relationship between thinking and writing was so direct—you wrote math just the way you thought it.

When I write to you, I feel something similar, as if my thoughts and moods are directly in the keystrokes. I don't know why I want this, because clearly it is really hard to understand. I understand maybe one-third of what you write, and probably vice versa.

On the other hand, from the third that I do understand, I get
more of You than I could ever get from anything down-to-earth and
crystal-clear, like an explanation or an essay. Whatever you write
with so much care and intensity has an image of You in it. That's why
I fear the triviality of conversations. What if I want to get to You to
the same degree as through these letters—and I find out that I can't?
Of course, it's just a fear. We could try it anyway. We could walk
and walk, and talk only if something comes up.

Toward the end, he turned to the subject of love, which he said
was so complicated that he couldn't write a single meaningful sentence about it. I have been through a lot of things in the past two years, and
my thoughts about love have changed. I have a girlfriend whom I only sometimes love. I do think about you a lot. My love for you is for the person writing
your letters.

It took a lot of effort to assimilate the meaning of those sentences—
to push them through my brain. I felt every level, graphemic, morpho-
logical, and semantic, and they all hurt. He said "my love for you"—and
then he said it was for someone else, for the person writing my letters.
He went on about the tremendous value of these letters that were
really hard to understand; and the difficulty of understanding seemed
to be precisely what was the most valuable to him.

The fourth time I read the email, I stopped at the sentence about
his girlfriend. Was it possible that *that* was the most important sentence? But to me, the idea of the girlfriend didn't carry that same
feeling of direness as the feeling that he didn't actually want to know
me, or know anything, he just wanted to guess and wonder and disappear.

Well—at least I knew, now. I wouldn't write to him anymore, there
wasn't any point. We had done it already, and I didn't have anything
else to say, and anyway he didn't have time. I shut down the computer
and went to bed.

· · ·

When I woke up, a song was playing in the hallway about how there was an ordinary world somewhere that some guy had to find. I went out to brush my teeth. Hannah was at her computer.

"Hey," she said. "Have you had breakfast yet?"

We went to breakfast. It was almost eleven and the ice cream was already out for lunch. Hannah dug into a big bowl of strawberry ice cream, while relating an incredibly detailed dream she'd had about the television show *Friends*. I mechanically chewed some cereal and sipped black coffee.

Girl Scouts had gotten into the cafeteria. I hadn't seen a child in months. Two of them came to our table. "*Wouldn't* you like to buy some cookies?" asked the one with the most hair. I bought two boxes of Thin Mints and gave one to Hannah. "I took a brownie from your care package," I said.

"That's fine! They're for sharing." She beamed. Any token of friendship made her so happy.

I had been a Girl Scout once, or rather a Brownie. One afternoon I had taken a rake from the garage and raked old Mrs. Emmett's yard, to try to get a badge for good deeds. Old Mrs. Emmett reported me to the police for trespassing, and because she said I had poisoned her dog. I hadn't even known she had a dog. Well, she did—a poisoned dog.

When the time came to sell cookies, my mother, to whom few things could have been more shameful than the idea of my going door-to-door trying to sell anything, sold all the cookies herself, to her own mother. Ten years later, when I was visiting my grandmother in Ankara, I found them in the pantry: thirty unopened boxes of Girl Scout cookies.

"Why didn't you eat your cookies?" I asked.

"Oh, they're cookies? I thought they were candles," said my grandmother.

"Is something the matter?" asked Hannah. "You're not your usual cheerful self."

"I'm feeling kind of down," I said.

"Did something happen?"

"I like someone who doesn't like me," I said. I had thought of it as an approximation, but once I said it, it felt like the truth.

I finally went to visit Ralph at the JFK Library. I caught a shuttle from a gray deserted T station, surrounded by howling winds. I was the only passenger. The driver ignored all the other stops and careened straight to the library: a concrete and glass structure reminiscent of both a tombstone and a spaceship. I waited for Ralph in a bleak pavilion overlooking the ocean. I kept saying, "Oh, no," while snapping and unsnapping my jacket sleeve. Ralph and I laughed when we saw each other. We walked through a simulation of the 1960 Democratic National Convention and saw the pink coat—"radioactive pink," John Kenneth Galbraith called it—that Cassini made for Jackie to meet Jawaharlal Nehru in. It had a Nehru collar and a matching hat. When Jackie wore it, a Delhi paper likened her to Durga, Goddess of Power.

The next morning, I found an email from Ivan with the subject line: Where are you? He said he needed to hear me. He tended to think he had a lot to say, but first he had to know what I thought. He was at Caltech now, with his high school friend Imre. A Russian statistician, whose facial expression resembled that of a lion tamer who had put his head in the lion's mouth for only one second and then immediately taken it out again, had lectured Ivan and Imre for an hour about his work. The whole time, Ivan had been thinking about what to write to me.

Ivan had drunk some apple wine with Imre, so he could talk about me. If you wanted to talk to Imre about anything, without it turning into a competition, you had to give him wine first. But so much wine was not enough. They found another bottle, but no corkscrew. Ivan knew a trick from his father: you wrapped the bottle in a towel and banged it against a wall. Instead of a towel, they used Imre's sweater. Instead of a wall, they used a modernistic fountain. The bottle smashed into pieces.

Ivan and Imre walked three kilometers to buy more wine, drank it, and went back to the department to do email. In the computer room, Imre dropped the bottle and the rest of the wine spilled everywhere, seeping out into the hallway. The men's room was out of paper towels. While they were mopping the hall with paper towels from the women's room, a German number theorist turned up and started talking to them about his work. Now Imre was waiting at the fountain. Ivan had promised to go with him to Universal Studios—he had figured out a way to get in without paying the thirty-five-dollar entrance fee. He wanted to write to me more in-depth, but he couldn't until he heard my voice.

I turned off the computer and went to Copley Plaza with Ralph, to help him buy suspenders. I had trouble with the revolving doors. I kept thinking about how, if someone said to pay thirty-five dollars, or to use a corkscrew, I didn't try to outsmart them. How would I get anywhere in life? How could anyone ever be interested in me?

Passing the women's perfume, cosmetics, handbags, and sunglasses, we took an escalator down to the men's department. The men's department made no sense, the way nothing seemed designed to surprise or delight you, and everything looked the same. How could anyone choose between so many gray jackets? But I kept touching the broad solid shoulders and, even though there was something ridiculous about their sobriety and self-importance, I felt a wave of longing.

The suspenders had to go with khaki pants, a navy jacket, and a burgundy tie. It was hard to hold the three colors in mind at the same time. We both liked red suspenders, but not with a burgundy tie. Like a fool, I asked Ralph the color of his shoes.

"Black," he said.

"Black shoes, navy jacket," I mused. We looked at each other with identical stricken expressions: "Brown shoes." We went to the shoe department. That was the beginning of the end, not just because shoe shopping was always sad—what was "Cinderella," if not an allegory for the fundamental unhappiness of shoe shopping?—but because the shoes were past the pajamas and underwear. The pajamas were where we really lost everything—our sense of purpose and of who we were. The shoes had at least been related to the suspenders. Here, colors were irrelevant—or not irrelevant, but bearing different meanings. There were boxers printed in red, NO NO NO, with green glow-in-the-dark letters that spelled YES YES YES.

Another day passed. Ivan's computer log-ons migrated from Caltech to UCSD, then UCLA. Time and again I tried to write to him, but was paralyzed by the thought that anything now depended on what move I made. Wasn't that what he himself had said: that there was something he wanted to tell me, but only if I said the right thing first?

I couldn't work or sleep. I didn't understand what the point of anything was, or what was supposed to happen. I was writing all the time, either in the spiral notebook or on the laptop, as close as I could to nonstop, often noting down what time it was, because I wanted to feel that I had all the time accounted for. Of course, it wasn't possible to account for all the time. By the time you had written down what time it was, it was already later than it had been.

I wanted to tell someone what was happening, but I didn't know how or who. I couldn't tell Svetlana; she would talk about Satan, or say I should forget about Ivan because he had a girlfriend. But what if

there was some other connection to be made there—what if that
wasn't the only thing in the world? I told an abridged version to my
mother. I could hear that it didn't make sense. As a story, it didn't
make sense. I couldn't talk. I couldn't read.

I made an appointment with a counselor at the undergraduate health
clinic. In the waiting room I picked up a pamphlet titled *Facts and
Myths About Acid Indigestion* because I usually enjoyed myths, but
these were lousy. "Peppermints are good for acid indigestion." A nurse
said something that was almost definitely supposed to be my name. I
followed her to a door with a brass plate that read CHILD AND ADO-
LESCENT PSYCHOLOGY. Inside, a white-haired man with a pink face sat
behind a desk surrounded by wooden blocks and plastic pigs. There
were no other animals—just pigs. Ivan had mentioned pigs in his
emails, several times. Was there something about pigs that I didn't
know?

"Please, have a seat," said the child and adolescent psychologist, gesturing toward a range of chairs, some child-sized, others, I
supposed, adolescent-sized. I sat in one of the larger chairs and told
him everything. I told him about the sleeping and the talking and the
reading, about the exchange of emails, about my confession and Ivan's
reply. It took a long time.

"How did you respond when he told you about his girlfriend?" the
psychologist asked.

"I didn't write back," I said.

He nodded vigorously. "Then what did this fellow do?"

"He wrote to me again. He said that he had more things to say to
me, but he had to hear my voice first."

"Meaning that he wanted to speak to you on the telephone?"

"Excuse me?"

"He had to hear your voice, meaning that he was going to call you?"

"Oh—I think he was just asking me to write back. I think when he said 'voice' it was, um, metaphoric."

"I see. Your *writing* voice."

I was embarrassed almost beyond speech by the phrase "writing voice." "Yeh," I managed.

"Have you spoken on the phone with him since he left?"

"I've never spoken to him on the phone at all."

"What? Not even once?"

"No."

"How about that! So you've never heard *his* voice, either. Except, of course, his writing voice."

"Well, we've spoken together in class, and sometimes a little bit afterward."

"That's right, you had that class together. In Russian. But other than that?"

I shook my head. "Just the, um, writing voice."

"How about that," he said again. "What will you do now? He wrote you a second email. Are you going to reply?"

"I don't know," I said. "I want to, but I don't know how. I don't know what's a good thing to say and what's a bad thing."

The psychologist leaned back in his chair. There was a long silence. "You know, Selin," he said. "I don't like the sound of this at all."

I was surprised—I hadn't known he was supposed to like or not like the sound of things. "No?" I said.

"No," he said. "This whole thing reminds me of the Unabomber."

"The Unabomber?"

"The Unabomber."

"Why?"

"I don't know. I just keep thinking about the Unabomber."

"Because he was a math major?"

"Oh, that's interesting. I wasn't thinking about that." He jotted something on a notepad. "I was thinking about computers, that this is all about power and computers. That's where the power is, in the computers."

"Oh," I said.

"You're at a very vulnerable point in your life. You've left home for the first time, you're feeling challenged and overwhelmed by your schoolwork. And this computer fellow, he's where—in California?"

"Yeah. He's visiting graduate schools."

"He has a girlfriend, he's graduating, he's going to California. This is not a fellow who's going to be there for you. Not in the short run, and not in the long run. From what you've described, it sounds as if he barely exists at all. He's just a voice from behind a computer. Who knows who or what is behind there—behind the computer? He obviously enjoys hiding. And you, too, are hiding behind the computer. This is perfectly understandable. Human beings, all of us, hate to take risks. We *all* want to hide. And thanks to this *e-mail*"—he said it like it was a word I had made up—"thanks to this *e-mail*, you can have a completely idealized relationship. You risk nothing. Behind your computer screen, you're completely safe. Now, here's something I'd like you to think about. You don't actually know a thing about this fellow, do you? It's possible he doesn't even exist."

"Excuse me?"

"This person you've been telling me about. It's possible he doesn't exist at all."

I could feel the fabric of reality crumbling around me. I looked closely at the pink face of the child and adolescent psychologist. He didn't seem to be joking, or speaking metaphorically. "We were in the same class, for a semester," I said slowly. "I saw him almost every day. We spoke to each other. I—my memory is pretty clear on this." As I spoke I became more confident. "I really do think he exists. I mean, I'm not a hundred percent sure, but I'm not a hundred percent sure I'm sitting here talking to you, either, you know?"

"But you and I are sitting face-to-face. We're real people. He isn't operating on the level of a real person. He isn't a real person to you. If he was a real person, you would have all kinds of opportunities to see the flaws in the situation—or to see that, as far as you're concerned, he *isn't really there*. Instead, because he exists as a series of messages, he's *always* there, every time you turn on the computer. I bet you read those messages over and over, am I right?"

"Yes."

"Of course you do. And he's the ideal companion, because you get to fill in the blanks. Now I'm going to ask you a question and I want you to just think about it for a moment." He paused. "What if this computer fellow had . . . bad breath?"

"Excuse me?"

"Just think about it for a moment."

I thought about it. "I'm sorry, I don't think I understand the question."

"What if you got to know this fellow, in person, and he turned out to have bad breath?"

I thought some more. "Well, I guess if it turned out that way, then I would have to take some kind of action at that point," I said. "But until then, there doesn't seem to be much point in worrying about it."

"Exactly! Because he's not a real person, you don't have to worry about it. Do you see what I'm saying? He looks like an ideal person, but the real person behind that mask could have all kinds of problems."

"Oh—like bad breath."

"Exactly."

"Look," I said. "I don't want to sound like, 'I'm so cerebral I wouldn't care what kind of breath he had,' but I just feel like we could work around it somehow. It's so rare in the world to meet somebody you connect to. Most people are so awful. In the big picture, bad breath just seems relatively manageable. Like it seems like there are a lot of products designed for that. As opposed to making a person seem interesting and meaningful."

The psychologist tapped his index fingers together. "I'm interested in your comment that most people are 'so awful.' What makes most people awful?"

I told him my theory. Most people, the minute they met you, were sizing you up for some competition for resources. It was as if everyone lived in fear of a shipwreck, where only so many people would fit on the lifeboat, and they were constantly trying to stake out their property and identify dispensable people—people they could get rid of. That was how Hannah was—she wanted to make an alliance with me against Angela. "Everyone is trying to reassure themselves: *I'm* not going to get knocked off the boat, *they* are. They're always separating people into two groups, allies and dispensable people."

"Do you see yourself as one of the dispensable people?"

"The point is I don't want to get involved in that question, and it's *all* most people want to talk about. The number of people who want to understand what you're like instead of trying to figure out whether you get to stay on the boat—it's really limited."

"Selin, what I'm hearing is a very simple, very natural thing: fear of competition and fear of rejection by your peers. Obviously you were extremely successful in high school. Then you come to Harvard, and here's sixteen hundred kids your age who are every bit as successful as you—some of them maybe even more so. In every conversation with your peers, you find a subtext of competition. You worry that now you won't make the grade, you'll be rejected.

"I'm afraid our time is up, but I think this was a productive meeting. I'm hearing a lot of contradictory emotions from you. It seems to me that your sense of other people's awfulness might be compensating for your own sense of inferiority and fear of rejection. You rationalize the rejection of your peers by telling yourself it comes from other people's deficiencies rather than your own. *They* can't understand your philosophy or your ideas.

"All of this leaves you terribly lonely and isolated, which I think explains your susceptibility to this computer fellow. He seems to be offering you just what you want: a noninterpersonal interpersonal relationship. With him, you don't have to worry about whose side of the room the extension cord is on. But that's because it isn't a real intimate relationship. Real life is about discussing these things and coming to terms with them. This explains your anxiety, your sense that you're going to make some kind of mistake.

"What I want to help you to understand in the next few weeks is that real intimacy is a place where there are no mistakes, at least not in the sense you feel. You don't just blow everything with one wrong move. A friendship is a space where you're supported and free to *make* mistakes. I think when you reach this understanding a lot of things are going to feel better for you."

There didn't seem to be anything to say in response to this, so I just nodded and put on my jacket. He said the whole mental health department was moving to a new building soon. He drew a map of the old and new buildings on the back of his card and handed it to me. I put it in my pocket, but I knew I wasn't going to use it.

Light rain was falling outside. I didn't have an umbrella. Dread gripped my stomach. I had betrayed Ivan by talking about him—by causing a stranger to call him "this computer fellow" and to compare him with the Unabomber. Thanks to me, there now existed in the world some neural representation of "this computer fellow." I had the irrational fear that Ivan would find out about it, or that he somehow already knew.

I tried to comfort myself with the reflection that Ivan had, after all, also talked about me, and that whatever his friend Imre thought about me was probably no less stupid than whatever the psychologist thought about Ivan. This thought did not raise my spirits.

· · ·

Dear Ivan,

Your message wasn't easy for me to understand. I guess I'm too used
to thinking of words as a means to an end. Words create a mood, but
they aren't the mood itself. I definitely agree that some moods can't
be conveyed by clear and logical language, or by essays. Essays can
be such a pain! Basically, the reader isn't on your side, so you can't
leave out any of the logical steps. And sometimes when a connection
is delicate, the steps take too long to spell out—it just isn't possible,
by the time you get to the end of the steps, the mood is lost.

In that sense, it's better to write a letter to a friend. You can get
away with more. You can make bigger jumps. Of course, there's
always a chance that she (he?) can't follow you. I think about that all
the time. When is a mood no longer worth the confusion? What's the
right proportion?

I never thought to differentiate between you and the person who
writes your letters. But I think I see your point. I send you an email:
how do you know who wrote it? It could be anyone. There's no way
for me to convince you. I say, "It's me!"; you say: "Who's 'me'?"

Wouldn't it be amazing if it turned out that we both had
ghostwriters? Just imagine them taking a long walk together,
walking and walking, and talking only if something came up . . .

· · ·

Ivan appeared at redwood.stanford.edu, then kepler.berkeley.edu.

Svetlana and I went jogging. She kept saying how free she felt in
shorts—she had Naired her legs for the first time. She talked about a
poem she had written, in which she dropped her laptop in the rain
and swallowed the universe. She was worried that "swallowing the

universe" sounded pretentious, because the sensation she was trying to describe was really similar to the sensation of swallowing an entire hard-boiled egg. Should she just say she had swallowed a whole egg, and leave the universe out of it? But the egg *felt* like the whole universe. "It's so hard to be sincere without sounding pretentious," she said. "I mean, what are you supposed to do if you really happen to feel like you've swallowed the universe? Not say so?"

"I've been wondering that, too," I said. In the end, I thought she should just say she felt like she had swallowed the universe, unless it was really *exactly* the same feeling as having swallowed a hard-boiled egg, because in that case it was probably better to err on the side of caution.

"I guess," she said.

Ivan sent an email. It was a sort of prose poem about stars and hell. It was really about those things. Sometimes I made jokes, to myself, about stars and hell. There was nobody else to tell them to.

The adult education program assigned me a new student. The form read only "Dinah, algebra, Thursday 7 p.m."

Dinah was about my mother's age and wore, on the bosom of her flower-printed dress, a large button displaying a slightly blurry snapshot of a black boy getting up from a desk, looking over his shoulder. Dinah herself kept sitting down and standing up again, taking things out of a big red tote bag. She told me that the boy in the photo was her son, Albert, who had passed away in January at age eighteen. I, too, was eighteen. How could she not be wondering, as I myself was now, why I was alive and sitting in a room with her, while her son no longer existed?

"I'm so sorry," I said.

"Thank you, honey," she said. "These things happen for a reason. But I don't know the reason. That's why I'm back in school."

"It's wonderful that you're doing that," I said, because I still believed in school.

"It sure is, honey. After all, what do I have to do all day? So now I'm going to college! The thing is, I just don't know about this algebra." She sighed. "I go to the class. I don't understand. So, I *don't* go to the class. I *still* don't understand. Inside or outside of that class, I don't understand a word that man says. Ascending other, descending other—it just doesn't mean anything to me."

By this time she had produced from her tote bag and set on the table three bags of pink yarn, three loose cigarettes, a gold lighter, a spiral notebook, an algebra text, two broken pencils, and a picture frame decorated with a yellow ribbon and a sprig of some leafy plant. The picture frame contained a larger print of the same photograph of her son.

Having arranged these items in a row, Dinah adjusted her chair and opened her notebook. "Okay," she said. "Now, the first thing I want you to explain to me is the Other."

"The Other," I repeated, to buy time. I was pretty sure that the Other was a French construct having something to do with either sex or colonialism.

"That's right. The Descending Other."

"Hmm," I said. "Could it be you're thinking of descending *order?*"

Dinah stared at me, then slapped the table and shook her head. "That's it, that's exactly it! Do you see what I'm telling you? I don't understand a thing that man says! I don't even understand the *words* he says. So first off what I want you to explain to me is this descending other. I mean order. Ha! Ha! I said 'other' again! Will you listen to me?" She picked up a cigarette and started twirling it between her fingers.

"Descending order is just when you start with the biggest number and go down to the smallest number," I said. "In order. Like, that's the *kind* of order they're in. So let's say you have some numbers, like one, nine, and three. And you want to put them in descending order. That would be, nine, three, one."

"Okay okay, wait a second. How do you get the three and the one from the nine?"

"Well, I just sort of made them up. As an example of some numbers."

She looked at me for a second. "You know what, honey?" she said. "You're going to have to excuse me. I think I need a cigarette. No, you don't get up. You stay here. I'll be back in five minutes."

"Excuse me?"

"Now, don't you worry about me. Because I'm here. I'm not going anywhere, nooooo, sir, I'm here." She picked up her lighter.

"Okay, but where are you going?"

"I just—I'm *here*, honey, that's all that counts," she said, and went out the door.

I looked at the three bags of pink yarn. Then I got up and looked out the window. Some kind of slush was falling out of the sky and piling up on the ground. It reminded me of stars and hell.

The next afternoon in the library, I picked up Pablo Neruda's "Ode to the Atom" and started to read. There were words I didn't know, but I didn't slow down. I just guessed the meaning and kept going, and I saw then that Ivan was right: it was exciting not to understand.

The atom was seduced by the army—by a military man. *Tiny little star, buried in metal*, the military man said, or seemed to say. *I will unchain you, you will see the light of day. You are a Greek god, come lie on my fingernail. I will guard you in my jacket like a North American pill.*

The atom heard the army, and came out, and was unleashed. It became rabid luminosity. It assassinated germs and impeded corollas, and in Hiroshima the birds dropped like charred pears from the sky. Finally, the poet beseeched the atom to go back into the ground. "Oh, *chispa loca*," he said. "Oh crazy spark." *Bury yourself back in your blanket of minerals, return to blind rock, collaborate with agriculture, and in place of these mortal ashes of your mask take on the noble something of the other thing, abandon your rebellion for cereal and your unchained magnetism for peace between men, so that your luminous something won't be a hell but rather happiness, hope, contribution to the earth.*

The thing that struck me was how the poem was all about stars and hell. As I had this thought, I looked out the window and saw that it was snowing again, even though it was April—and then suddenly the wind changed and the snow started gusting *upward*, back into the sky. I had to tell these things to Ivan.

I realized, as I was writing to him, that my favorite parts of the poem were the beginning and the middle—the seduction of the atom. The end was also beautifully written, but I didn't like it as much. I told Ivan it reminded me of the rhyme my grandfather used to recite when I had a stomachache: "To the mountains, to the stones, to the birds, to the wolves, let Selin's stomachache go, let it go."

> Things just aren't that easy in real life. You can't just tell an ache: "Go back into the rock." Moreover, I think "peace" is misleading. It can't possibly be the same thing as cereal.

. . .

When I woke up in the morning, I found Ivan's reply.

> Dear Sonya,
> I was going to write to you that there is no snow in Berkeley, but in fact there is no snow here either, and everything else is in order, below my window the traffic light changes back and forth, like my

heart. Now I have fifteen hours to decide where to spend the next
four years—New Haven or California.

   Your atom, I think it will never go back to peace, to cereal or
rocks or anything like that. Once it has been seduced there is no
way back, the way is always ahead, and it is so much harder after
the passage from innocence. But it does not work to pretend to
be innocent anymore. That seduced atom has energies that seduce
people, and these rarely get lost.

   From your message, I figured out what happened: the snow fell
the wrong way (up), slowly, until it all disappeared. This is fine if the
fresh grass does not hide back in the earth, and what comes is Hello
Spring, not Goodbye Summer. Not that again.

                                                        Your Vanya

The things kept accumulating—the stars, the atoms, the pigs, and the
cereal. It was decreasingly possible to imagine explaining it all to anyone. Whoever it was would jump out a window from boredom. And
yet here *I* was, watching the accumulation in real time, and not only
was I not bored, but it was all I could think about. This discrepancy
seemed to set up an unbridgeable gap between me and the rest of the
world.

   I went running and thought about whether Ivan was saying that
I was the atom, the crazy spark—the one that now had the energies to
seduce people. Was he calling me, or sending me away? On the one
hand, he was saying it wouldn't work to go back into the ground. On
the other hand, when he talked about the way ahead being harder,
that sounded like something I had to do by myself.

The phone rang. It was the editor of the literary magazine. I had won
first prize in the fiction contest. The editor said that nobody on the

fiction board knew me or had heard anything about me, and they had debated whether I was a boy or a girl. "*I* thought you were a girl," she said. "I mean a woman." All the winning entries would be published in the spring issue of the magazine. My entry was longer than the stories they usually published, and they had talked about making cuts, but they couldn't figure out what to cut, so they were just going to run the whole thing in an extra-small typeface. The editor, Helen, told me the date of the cocktail reception where the winners would read from their entries. I would get a fifty-dollar gift certificate from Words-Worth Books.

"Okay," I said, writing down the date.

"Are you . . . excited at all?" she asked.

"Definitely," I said. "I'm super-excited. Thank you."

Dread clenched my stomach. I liked that I had won a contest and that they had thought I was a boy, and I was glad about the fifty dollars. But I didn't want my story to be published, or to read from it. I didn't want anyone to think I thought it was good.

I took my only pair of dress shoes to the shoe repair shop. They had come apart at the toe. The heels weren't looking so great, either. The shoe repairperson glanced at the shoes without touching them. "Sweetie," he said. "You need new shoes."

I went to several shoe stores and asked to see whatever they had in women's size eleven. Nobody made women's shoes in twelve. Almost nobody made eleven, either. Sometimes the salespeople would admit outright that their largest size was ten. Other times they brought shoes in European size forty-one and said they were U.S. eleven. This was untrue; a European forty-one was an American ten. The shoe would physically not fit on my foot, and still the salesman—it was only men who did this—would jam in the shoehorn: "It's an eleven, you asked for an eleven, it's your size."

. . .

Ivan sent me a long message, even though it wasn't his turn. The beginning was a sci-fi meditation about a boy in a desert with some light green melodies floating through something. The boy turned into green vapor and wanted to break apart, or come together, it wasn't clear which. This went on for a considerable time. Then the subject changed. I summon you words, o my stars, condensation of matter, he wrote:

> You are the second stage of creation. You fill the empty space and the desert. You may be a means to an end, but that end is the beginning of everything. Without you, there is nothing—no soil for creation.
>
> You're right about the poet—and how right you are. Poets are liars, obsessed with cereal. They try to hammer the atom back to Fruit Loops, life back to paradise, and love back to nonexistent simplicity. You're right—they shouldn't do that. It isn't possible, and they shouldn't pretend.

This email filled me with unmixed joy. It was what I had been waiting for him to say—that you couldn't go backward from love, and that he was calling me, that I should go. I felt a kind of peace and relief I had never felt before. Nothing about the birds falling out of the sky like charred pears seemed like a dangerous omen to me, and I wrote back with an open and light heart: Are you busy tomorrow afternoon, or Thursday? I'm free after two. I hit Ctrl-S. It felt like a dream. It was even more like a dream when he wrote back, in Russian: We'll see each other tomorrow, 3, Wid. steps.

I knew that Wid. had to be Widener, the library, and yet at the same time it seemed that this wasn't something I actually knew—that I was only guessing.

. . .

At breakfast in the cafeteria, a guy I knew slightly invited me to opening night at the repertory theater that same evening. He said it would
be a huge favor, because he was in love with the sound engineer.
Nothing he was saying made sense. It felt insane to make a plan to do
something *after* I was going to meet with Ivan—like making plans for
after my own death. I said I would go.

On the library steps, a group of boys in red tracksuits were posing
while a girl in an identical tracksuit took their photograph. A skinny
guy hauling a huge tote bag full of books resembled the boa constric-
tor digesting an elephant. Two girls in headscarves were descending
toward me; as they passed I heard one of them say to the other in
Turkish, "You didn't forget your glasses, did you?"

Ivan was there already—he was sitting at the very top. I waved,
but he was staring fixedly at a lecture hall across the yard. I started
to climb the steps, first one by one, then two at a time. There were
only about a thousand of them. I looked up to see how close I was.
Ivan had stood up and was skipping down toward me. We both half
raised our arms in salute. Then he was very close up—closer to me,
it seemed, than he had ever been. We walked down the steps in silence.

"You sat so near the top," I said.

"I'm sorry?"

"You sat so near the top."

"Near the what?"

"The top. Of the steps."

"Oh, the top. Sorry. I was hiding."

"Hiding?" I repeated.

"Oh, not from you, of course! From my roommate. He's really curious about you. I showed him something you wrote and he liked it, and now he wants to see you. But I don't want him to, so I've been avoiding him all day."

I felt like I had swallowed a hard-boiled egg. He had shown his roommate something I'd written? How? Had he forwarded him the email, or let him read it over his shoulder? And now this roommate was at large? I glanced around. I saw: a church, a dog, a tree. Everything looked strangely isolated, as if each item in the landscape had been purchased separately from a catalog.

"Don't worry," Ivan said, "I probably lost him by now. He almost definitely just went home."

We left campus and turned onto one of the side streets leading to the river. It seemed to me that I had never before been on this particular street, and had never seen the basement café located underneath a store selling mirrors. We sat at a table under a yellow umbrella in the little brick courtyard, which was crammed between the mirror store and an iron fence. Ivan was facing the street, and I was facing a window full of mirrors.

I had never actually been to a café—not the kind in a basement where people went to drink espresso-based drinks. I read the menu over and over, like a test I hadn't studied for.

"What is this Sanka?" demanded Ivan. "I always wonder this. No matter where you go, it's always the cheapest thing on the menu. It sounds to me somehow Eastern European. What do you think it could be?"

"Decaffeinated instant coffee," I said.

He blinked. "I'm sorry, what?"

"It's a brand of instant coffee. Like Nescafé, only decaf."

"Decaffeinated Nescafé? But that sounds totally useless." He slowly started to nod. "Aha, okay, I get it—it's some kind of useless crap, so they give it an Eastern European name."

The waiter came to take our order. Why were we here, why was he bringing us things? I ordered iced coffee. Ivan ordered peppermint tea. It came in a pot.

"So," Ivan said, pouring tea through a strainer. "Did you prepare?"

"For what?" I took a sip of iced coffee. It tasted different than I had imagined.

"For this."

"There was preparation? Did *you* prepare?"

"Oh, I'm never prepared. My roommate, on the other hand, is completely different, very anal. He asked what I had prepared to say to you, and when I said, 'Nothing,' he was horrified. 'Oh, no, you have to tell her something nice.' He gave me a poem to read you, can you believe it? Obviously he had written it himself—it was an incredibly shitty poem. The first line ended with "I," the second line with "sigh," the third line with "die." I told him, 'Look, I'm not going to subject Selin to the poem you wrote. Make one of *your* friends listen to it.' But he kept denying that he wrote it! 'No, no, no, I didn't write it. *Yeats* wrote it.' Yeats, can you imagine?"

"Oh, Yeats," I said.

"But I found out later that he was telling the truth. He showed me in a book. The poem is really by Yeats!" He laughed and laughed.

I was laughing, too, because the way he did it was contagious. Yeats? What was he talking about?

"How is your coffee?" Ivan asked.

"I think it's okay," I said. "I think I don't like iced coffee."

"Would you like to order something else?"

"Oh, no thanks."

"Oh, you ordered it on purpose? I see. I did that in Frankfurt when I didn't have any money. I'd always order Guinness, because it's cheap and I don't like it, so each glass lasted me a really long time and they couldn't kick me out of the bar."

"They'll never be able to kick me out of here," I agreed sadly.

. . . .

"Radu, my roommate?" Ivan said.

"Yes?"

"He's really desperate for a girlfriend."

"Oh?"

"It's gotten really bad. He's even hitting on freshmen."

"Really," I said, feeling slightly insulted.

"He follows them around, he spies on them."

"Do they get mad?"

"I don't know," he said. "Maybe they think it's funny."

"Maybe," I said doubtfully.

"Radu is Romanian. Last summer he was working in Washington, but he was in love with a girl back in Romania."

"Oh."

"She was in Romania, and Radu sent her a postcard every day. And in these postcards, he gradually revealed more and more of his feelings toward her. He was very careful to make a gradual transition—so she wouldn't get scared."

"Did it work?"

"No," he said, starting to laugh, "because she was in Berlin! He sent the cards to her family house in Bucharest, where nobody was there but her grandmother. The grandmother received every day a postcard from Radu in Washington!"

"Oh no! Couldn't she have forwarded them?"

"She was an eighty-year-old grandmother! Was she supposed to go to the post office every day for Radu's sake?"

"I guess not."

"Of course not. She just waited for her granddaughter to come back in September, and then she handed her the postcards all at once, in a plastic bag." He seemed particularly impressed by the plastic bag, and indeed a moment later he repeated this detail. "Ninety postcards in a plastic bag."

"That's terrible," I said, though I was laughing again, too.

"What's so terrible? The girl got the cards in the end. Her grandmother could have just thrown them out. He was lucky."

"No he wasn't!" I said. "They must have seemed so boring and repetitive, when she read them all in a row like that. One day at a time it would be much less boring."

"Hmm," said Ivan. "You've got a point. Reading ninety cards in one day is different from reading one card per day for ninety days." He leaned back in his chair and stared into space, apparently satisfied with the conclusion we had reached.

"So what happened in the end?" I asked.

"Hmm?"

"With your roommate and the girl."

"Oh—nothing."

"Nothing?"

"Well, they met, they took a long walk, there was some kind of a river, or maybe it was a moon. I forget the details. Then she said to him, 'Radu. Do you know how to make somebody fall in love with you, if they aren't already?'" He paused and looked at me. "Do you know the answer?"

"How to make someone fall in love with you?" I flushed. "No."

He was already laughing—it almost prevented him from uttering the joke. "'You have to improve your soul.' That's what she told Radu. Ha! Ha!"

I suddenly became unable to laugh. "Improve your soul," I repeated, and I felt my voice shake. "I'll try to remember."

Ivan stopped laughing. "I didn't mean that," he said.

But it was no use. Everything he said seemed to reach me so directly—everything, starting with Radu and his postcards, seemed to bear some bad omen. I could barely speak, and he kept up the whole conversation all by himself. He said funny, surprising, and charming things, all of which distressed me deeply. He said that when he was home in Hungary he felt that he would have to entertain his parents and his sisters and take them out; two years ago they had all gone to Florence in his mother's very small Mazda, him and his mother and his sister and his friend Imre, and they had lived in that car for three days. All that time he had been taking some kind of class, there in the car, to fulfill his Social Analysis requirement. Harvard had given him core credit for driving around Italy with four people in his mother's tiny Mazda.

"You're always sad when you leave Rome," he said at some point. "You're always depressed until you go back."

He talked about learning to ride a motorcycle, about getting the license. His youngest sister had visited him and they took road trips to New York and to Annapolis. His sister wasn't supposed to mention the motorcycle to their parents, only then she did. But she went back before he did, so she was the only one who got a hard time. Periodically Ivan would say I should talk more and keep him from bullshitting. It wasn't clear to me in what sense he meant "bullshit." I had the uneasy feeling I was being warned about something. I said no, it was interesting. He said he just didn't want to feel that he was telling me all this bullshit.

He talked about his Czech dentist, how she came to Budapest and he was excited to show her around, except that she came with her grouchy husband, who didn't like anything. The figure of the dentist's grouchy husband seemed to hold some dire portent.

When the waiter brought the bill, I reached for my combination keychain/wallet.

"You didn't honestly think I was going to let you pay for this, did you?" said Ivan. He had a men's leather wallet. We left and started walking. We ended up at a bridge to the Business School. Ivan said there was a church there, or a garden, something we looked for but never found.

"There are two bridges you can take," he said as we crossed over the highway.

"Oh," I said.

"This is the less romantic one."

We were walking on a winding asphalt path through manicured lawns. There were lots of shrubs and, here and there, a brick or stone building. People were playing Frisbee. At one point, in my alacrity to keep the right distance from Ivan, I stepped on a Scotch terrier. It yelped. I registered a woman's surprised expression. "I'm so sorry!" I exclaimed. We had passed before she had time to answer.

"You sounded really sorry, about that dog," said Ivan.

I tried not to look stricken.

"Do you like animals?" Ivan asked.

I thought about it. I had no idea if I liked animals. "I don't think so," I said.

"You don't?"

"Well, I always feel resentful that they don't really like me. But I'm still sorry to step on them."

"Animals don't like you? Why not?"

"Well, I mean they can't *really* like you—like a person can."

"Aha. You can't forgive them for not being people."

"I used to have a dog, and I had a recurring nightmare that he could talk, all along. He said, 'All you do is patronize me, you talk to me like an idiot, you give me a stupid name.'"

"What was the dog's name?"

Before I could answer, Ivan pulled me by the elbow so I stumbled off the path, out of the way of a heavyset man who whizzed by on Rollerblades, brushing my arm. The man was wearing knee pads, elbow pads, and a helmet. Just ahead of us he hit a small bump in the asphalt, wobbled, and regained his balance.

"Ah, I was really hoping he would fall," Ivan said. "I would have laughed a lot."

I felt utterly crushed. How could he *want* to see somebody fall? Was that why he had agreed to see me? As we walked on, I stared at my feet, pondering the likelihood that I would misstep. I noticed that

Ivan was also regarding my feet with a preoccupied expression. But when our eyes met, he smiled. "Cool shoes," he said.

We walked to the river, to the edge of a highway, and came to a supermarket and went inside. It was so strange to see normal people buying groceries. There was a promotion on strawberries. Boxes of strawberries had been stacked into a castlelike formation, flanked by cans of whipped cream.

"I wonder what we could do with that," Ivan said, somehow almost angrily, looking at the whipped cream. I felt my face flush. We decided to buy some strawberries. In the checkout line, we both noticed a magazine called *Self*. Ivan said he didn't think they could tell him anything he didn't already know.

We were walking on some sort of highway, alongside multiple lanes of whooshing cars and trucks. We came upon a grassy island in the road. There were some chairs on the grass, and a rusty shovel, like props in some depressing play.

"Maybe this is where we should sit," Ivan said.

We sat on the chairs and opened the box of strawberries. I took a strawberry. I saw now that it was covered with dirt. We didn't have any water, so I brushed it off as best I could with my hand and ate it. It was crunchy with dirt. I took another. It looked just as dirty as the first. I held it for a long time. Ivan was talking about his friends who were going to visit him that evening: a high school friend and his girlfriend, who was in a wheelchair. Apparently this friend dated only disabled women. He had started with one disabled woman, and then started dating her friend, and then a third unrelated woman—all three of them in wheelchairs. They were all really cool girls. Cars roared past, a few feet from our faces. Each contained some person or persons. None of those people had to sit on these chairs like we did. Then again, maybe they were going somewhere even worse.

Ivan and I both stared at the strawberry I was holding.

"I can't," I said.

He nodded. "We'll have to bury it." He stood, picked up the rusty shovel, and stepped on the blade to penetrate the hard earth. He dug a small hole and we put in the strawberry.

"This is the best place for it," I said.

"I know," Ivan said. "Should we just bury all of them?"

We buried all the strawberries and resumed our walk.

Several times I tried to talk, so he wouldn't have to do it all himself. The words were always wrong. I said someone was die-hard, and he thought I was saying something about their heart. I described someone else as "starting to crack."

"Crack?"

"Like fall apart. This perfect—she starts out all perfect and then suddenly starts getting upset at all these little things." I sounded like the aphasics in our linguistics textbook: "Write, writed, not today, but yesterday."

Ivan asked what I was doing over the summer. I didn't know. He seemed surprised and somehow displeased. "You should try to go somewhere," he said. He said I should apply to *Let's Go*, the student budget travel guidebook series. If they chose you as a writer, you could go for the summer to any country in the world.

Ivan was going home to Hungary for seven weeks, and then to Japan with Radu for a math conference. He said mathematicians never got any vacation so they were always having conferences, for example in Honolulu. He talked about mathematicians as if they were somehow fundamentally different from other people. The conference was on environmental science, a subject about which Ivan knew nothing. But his thesis was on random walks so he made up a story about the random walks of foxes and rabbits, and the environmental scientists believed him and bought him a plane ticket to Tokyo.

I had the uncanny sensation that this conversation had been prefigured by the story of Nina: Nina, who had pretended to study the locomotion of reindeer, and whom physics kept pushing east.

At some point in our conversation, Ivan mentioned that strawberries grew on trees. I said I thought they grew on little plants close to the ground. No, he said—trees.

"Okay," I said. I knew that in my life I had seen strawberries growing, on plants, but this didn't seem like irrefutable proof that they didn't grow on trees.

"You're easy to convince," he said.

We walked for three hours. On the way back we got lost and had to climb down a steep hill. I really didn't want to climb down the hill. I actually walked into a tree and then stayed there for a minute.

"What are you doing?" Ivan asked.

"I don't know," I said.

He nodded. He said there were lots of possible ways down the hill, but probably the best way was one where you didn't have to go through a tree. Then he started talking about the execution of Ceaușescu and his wife.

Ivan's dorm room was in the corner of the eleventh floor of a concrete tower overlooking the river. The room was completely enclosed by windows, it was twilight, and being there felt like floating in a blue box. Bicycles and sculls streamed by far below with their blinking lights, like a galaxy. I saw the traffic light Ivan had written about— the one that kept changing all night like his heart. When we sat on the floor, I placed my hands next to me to feel less adrift. Ivan said that the reason his room was so clean was that he was loaning it to the friend whose girlfriend was in a wheelchair: the building had been built in the seventies and was not only riot-proof but also completely wheelchair-accessible. I hadn't asked why his room was so clean.

Ivan's computer was on. The sentence "What are the sparks?" was scrolling across the screen. He said it was to remind him of something, but he didn't remember what.

"I have the same lamp," I said, noticing his human-sized halogen lamp—the one they sold at the bookstore. Hannah and I had chipped in for it. I had never had a halogen lamp before, or seen one. I loved that lamp.

"Everyone has that lamp," Ivan said. He said he didn't like it, because he preferred for things to be unique, otherwise it was like eating at McDonald's when you could be eating at some random place. He didn't go to Baskin and Tombins, in fact he didn't even know what it was—was it ice cream?

"It's ice cream," I said.

Ivan described some of his friends. One explored caves. Another was Indian, and gay. "He's the most beautiful person I've ever seen in my life," Ivan said, and I felt a pang that took a moment to identify: So he's more beautiful than me. A third friend was a typical Jewish intellectual who idiosyncratically also did crew. I had only a distant idea what crew was, and no concept of what made it an idiosyncratic pursuit for a Jewish intellectual. Ivan was also friends with Rupert Murdoch's son, who dressed like a slob. Who was Rupert Murdoch? I knew I knew, but I couldn't remember. A famous foxhunter?

Ivan asked what kind of music I liked, and put a Vivaldi record on a record player.

"I haven't seen one of those since I was little," I said.

"Yeah," he sighed, "apparently now I have to show off to you my record player."

We listened to the whole record. Ivan's friends still hadn't arrived. Ivan asked if I wanted to get dinner.

The cafeteria was like a scene from a different movie—the hexagonal trays, the workers' paper hats, the air heavy with institutionalized chowder. I trailed behind Ivan. It was insane to me that he even ate every day, and that he was going to do it now.

I ate two forkfuls of rice. Ivan talked about the asparagus in Frankfurt. I peeled an orange, using a knife, the way my father did, so the peel all came off in one piece—the only trick I knew. Suddenly I remembered about the play.

"I have to go," I said.

"Right now?" Ivan looked at the scroll of orange peel and the un-eaten orange.

"I had a really nice time," I said. We looked at each other and I took my tray to the conveyor belt that went to the dishwashing room.

I ran to my dorm, changed into the only dress I owned, and ran back downstairs. The guy was at the door. I barely recognized him: in addition to being someone I hardly knew, he was now wearing a tux-edo. "I really owe you big time," he said, and launched into a long story that I couldn't follow about someone whose mother played the tuba.

The theater was concrete, chilly, with an echo, full of girls' self-important singsongy voices. There were boys there, too, but you mostly heard the girls. Where did they get so much confidence, so many opinions, such complicated dresses? Every dress was made with multi-ple fabrics, or had slits or straps or an asymmetrical skirt. One girl was wearing a fake, gauzy, see-through dress, with a whole other tiny dress, the real and concealing one, underneath. My dress was black jersey. I had bought it on sale at the Gap.

The curtain came up. A bare-legged girl was swinging on a swing. Speaking in a loud, knowing voice, she said witty and cynical things about some man.

Afterward there was a reception with champagne and strawber-ries. "These strawberries are *so clean*," I said. I wanted to tell the guy about the afternoon I had spent walking around a highway with Ivan, but didn't know how to bring it up. We talked briefly to the sound engineer, the one he had a crush on. We complimented her on the sound. There had been some loud atonal noises at different points during the play. "I think that went really well," the guy said excitedly, as she walked away.

He offered to walk me back to my dorm, but seemed relieved when I said I could get back by myself. The minute I was alone, I felt a hollow bereft feeling in my chest, and I realized that I missed Ivan. How could I miss him? I didn't even know him.

Here's what I learned about random walks: If you were standing at a tree and started taking steps in random directions, you would eventually end up back at that tree. It could take a really long time, during which you could get really far away—but if you kept it up for longer still, you would eventually get back there. *There it is again—that incredibly old tree.*

"Strawberries," I read in the *Encyclopædia Britannica*, "are low-growing herbaceous plants with a fibrous root system and a crown from which arise basal leaves."

The psycholinguistics professor was talking about his email correspondence with a colleague in Paris. Because UNIX didn't support diacritics, *á* became *a*, and so did *à*. "Are the 'invisible' diacritics still being processed?" he asked. "If so, how could we test whether this processing occurs on a graphemic or a phonemic level?"

Two grad students started to debate how to test where the processing was taking place. But I couldn't stop thinking about *á* and *à*—about Europe, where even the alphabet emitted exuberant sparks—about Ivan's mother's Mazda, and how you were always sad when you left Rome.

. . .

In Russian class we had to retell the plot of Lermontov's "The Fatal-
ist." The big question was whether our fate was written in the sky.
The story made no sense to me, and I didn't retell it well. I kept saying
"He threw himself onto the table," instead of "He threw the card onto
the table." There was a one-syllable difference. I said it wrong seven
times. Irina kept correcting me—she mimed someone throwing herself on the table so I would see my mistake. I didn't hear the difference
until the eighth time.

Hannah came with me to the reception at the literary magazine,
wearing penny loafers with white socks and a black blazer with shoulder pads. She was the only person I had told. She said when I was
famous she would tell everyone she had known me in freshman year.

Helen, the fiction editor, was petite and cute, with a down-to-
earth manner. I could see she wanted me to like her, and I did like her.
Without knowing how to demonstrate it through any speech act, I
towered over her mutely, trying to project goodwill.

The third-place fiction winner read from his story about a woman
who had night sweats and then found out her grandmother had been
in the Holocaust. The second-place winner read from an allegorical
text in which a man woke up one morning to find that his head had
been replaced by a gigantic butt. I understood right away that, although my story wasn't good, these were at least equally bad. This was
partly a relief, but not entirely. Why were we all so bad at writing
stories? When would we get better?

After the reading, someone put on an Ella Fitzgerald CD, and
Helen introduced me to the other editors. They were all witty and
urbane, somehow uniformly so—they all seemed to have the same
collectively self-deprecating sense of humor. The funniest and most

caustic guy, a poetry editor, was wearing a trench coat and sunglasses indoors. Helen said his name somehow ironically, as if he was some kind of celebrity. He briefly shook my hand before turning to say something funny to someone else.

There was only one editor I recognized, Lakshmi, who was also a freshman and lived in my building. All I knew about her was that she was beautiful, did drugs, spoke with a British accent, and had grown up in different foreign countries. She seemed really impressed that I had won this prize. "Still waters run deep," she kept saying. She was nice, but I felt relieved when she left to talk to a guy wearing a bandanna, leaving me free to sit on a sofa and look at people. As usual, the girls were more interesting to look at. The features editor had chestnut hair, mobile features, and a rich, drawling voice that seemed to go over more registers than most people's, like a clarinet. Then there was a girl whose slender neck, emerging from a collar edged with layered purple and black ruffles, clearly had no idea what ruffles were, or that they were there; it was just peacefully going about its business, holding up the Muppety head with the eyes and all that hair.

Helen handed me a plastic cup of red wine—my first glass of wine. It was completely different from how wine was when you took only a sip. It tasted completely different when you drank it in a quantity and swallowed it down.

When I got to our meeting the next afternoon, Dinah was already waiting in the classroom. "Hi, how are you, I'm fine but I didn't do my homework," she said, and put a textbook on the table. It read *Introductory Accounting.*

"Accounting?" I said.

"Oh, did I say 'accounting'?" she said. "I meant algebra. I mean— I forgot my book. Oh, Lord, I forgot my book!" She started hitting herself on the head.

"Please don't do that," I said. I found an algebra book in the supply closet, and asked her to check if there was anything in it similar to what she had been learning. She slowly turned the pages. "*This* is what I don't know," she said, stabbing a page with her finger. "This about the polynomials."

I was worried at first about explaining polynomials, but it went as smoothly as a dream; it was nothing like trying to tell Linda about fractions. Dinah understood right away the difference between binomials and trinomials, and coefficients and variables. I told her about "adding like terms." That took more time, but when she understood it, I felt really happy.

"Now I'm going to add up the ones that are alike," she said. "You hope!"

After she could add like terms, we started to simplify polynomial expressions. "Oh, I'm having a good time," she said. "See, this is what I didn't know, all this about polynomials. I never knew these polynomials could be fun."

I applied to *Let's Go*, the travel guidebook series that Ivan had told me about, to be a researcher-writer for Russia, Spain, or Latin America. The interview was conducted by three *Let's Go* editors. First they asked me to describe the Au Bon Pain in Harvard Square in the style of a *Let's Go* guidebook. I had never read a *Let's Go* guidebook.

"You can get a tuna sandwich for five dollars," I said. The editors exchanged glances.

"What do we miss out on if we don't hire you?" one girl asked.

I had never heard of such a question and felt a combination of shock and exasperation. Were they really going to make me pretend that I was doing *them* a favor? I said I was good at languages. The editor said right away that I hadn't studied Russian for long enough to go to Russia—you had to have had at least two years, ideally more.

You had to be able to bribe people. They said it would make more sense for me to go to Turkey, because it was such a popular vacation destination and because so few Harvard students spoke Turkish. But I had spent every summer of my life in Turkey, and wanted to go somewhere new. "What about Spain or Latin America?" I asked. They said the bar for Spanish was really high because a lot of applicants were native speakers.

"What if we were to ask you to describe this room, in Spanish, in the style of *Let's Go?*" one editor said. I looked around the room. It was a totally pointless room, containing nothing of interest. "*Una atmosfera antipática,*" I said. "*Mejor evitar.*"

The editors exchanged glances again. "We'll be in touch," the girl said.

When I told Svetlana about the interview, she said I had been crazy to apply—everyone who did *Let's Go* had a nervous breakdown. Specifically, the guy who had gone to Turkey the previous year, an American who spoke no Turkish, had first gotten severely beaten and then had a nervous breakdown. A prostitute had come to his hotel room in Konya and he had sent her away, but then later some guys came and beat him up. The whole episode had somehow been minutely documented in *Rolling Stone* magazine as part of some kind of exposé.

Over lunch, Lakshmi from the literary magazine told me about the preoccupying problem of her life. The preoccupying problem of her life was a boy. He was a senior, like Ivan. Lakshmi and I tried to discuss our shared plight, but the things that happened to us were so different that they barely seemed comparable or commensurable. Noor was from Trinidad and studied literature and economics. He was into theory. Every weekend, Lakshmi went out with him and his friends to clubs or raves—institutions I couldn't begin to imagine, architecturally or in any other way—where they did ecstasy and talked about post-colonialism and deconstruction. Sometimes Lakshmi would black out and wake up in Noor's bed, though nothing ever happened. "Nothing happened, of course," she would say, in a rueful tone that seemed to imply that this outcome was somehow to Noor's credit.

I could see that my stories made as little sense to Lakshmi as hers did to me. The emails, the walking around, the burial of strawberries. Lakshmi said that I must have been leaving something out.

Hannah and I were cleaning the room while listening to the radio. The DJ gave away a Butthole Surfers CD to the twenty-seventh caller, Mary from Dorchester, who shrieked orgasmically for fifteen seconds. Just then the phone started to ring. I knew it would be Ivan.

"Guess where I am," Ivan said.

"I don't know."

"I'm at your house."

"My *house?*"

"Your next year's house. You're supposed to be here."

It was true—the freshmen had just had a housing lottery and we were all supposed to be having brunch in our new dining halls, while the senior class had brunch in the freshman dining hall.

"I didn't go," I said.

"Yeah, I figured."

"What about you? Why aren't you at *your* brunch?"

"I hate stuff like that, where they try to make you feel nostalgic."

There was a pause.

"Well, it's a good thing I didn't go to your brunch to look for you, too. It would have been like 'The Gift of the Magi,'" I said. I was sorry as soon as I had said it.

"Like what?"

"Ah, never mind."

"The gift of the what?"

"The Magi—it's a story they make you read in American high schools."

"I don't know this story."

"Well, no, why would you."

"Why not? You mean, because I didn't go to an American high school?"

"Right."

"But *you* went to an American high school."

"True."

"So I can infer that you *do* know this story."

"Right again."

"Logical inference is something they teach you at Hungarian high schools."

"Lucky you," I said.

"Lucky me," he said. "So tell me the story."

I tried to think of something else I could say instead. I couldn't think of anything. "Once upon a time," I said, "there was a poor married couple. Even though they were incredibly poor, they each had one prize possession."

"Wait, I'm sorry, I didn't understand. They each had one what?"

"A *prize possession*. Something that was really valuable to them."

"Oh, a prize possession. Go on."

"The husband's prize possession was his gold watch, and the wife's prize possession was her beautiful long hair. These two things were a huge consolation for them. They might have been cold and starving, but at least they had this great watch and this amazing hair.

"Then it was Christmas, and they had to buy each other presents. They really—um. They really loved each other, and wanted to get each other amazing presents. But they didn't have any money. So the wife sold all her hair to a wig-maker, to buy the husband a chain for his beautiful watch. Meanwhile, the husband pawned his watch, to buy jeweled combs for the wife's beautiful hair."

"Uh-huh," said Ivan encouragingly.

"That's it. That's the end."

"What? The story is finished?"

"That's right."

"I don't think I understand."

"Well, it's ironic. The woman can't wear the combs, because she sold her hair, and the man can't use the chain, because he sold his watch."

"So these combs were something that the woman would wear? Like a decoration?"

"Right."

"Not something that she would use like a tool—for combing the hair?"

"No. At least, I don't think so. Anyway it doesn't matter, right? Because she doesn't have any hair anymore."

"I see," Ivan said, after a pause. "Now I understand your comparison. You're saying that if *you* went to the freshman cafeteria today to look for me, you would be as useless as *I* am now at Mather House looking for you. Furthermore, you would be as useless as a watch chain without a watch, or a comb without any hair. This situation reminds me of a Hungarian expression: 'As useless as a bald man's comb.'"

I said that was a good expression.

"You say it for something that's really useless," Ivan said.

The spring issue of the literary magazine came out. My story was printed right after the one about the guy whose head turned into a butt, on a page facing one of Sandy's woodcuts of a pig on the steps of a Hungarian church. After two pages you came to a poem about a waterfall that turned out to be about bulimia. The rest of my story was in the back, in tiny print. I was relieved, both that the text had been broken up and that the print was so small and dense, because it was almost physically impossible to read.

The next afternoon, I found an email from Ivan. He said that someone had stolen his copy of the literary magazine, so he wasn't sure yet, but he had heard that I had won the whole contest—that my story was right there, across from Sandy's pigs. It made me so happy, like only once before, he wrote. The other time had been when he was accepted to Harvard. That part of the email was in Russian.

Dinah came to our lesson almost an hour late, long past when I had stopped expecting her. I was just sitting there writing in my notebook.

"Oh, it's the lady of the hour," I said, because I was happy to see her and didn't know what to say, and this was something I had heard people say before.

"What lady—who?"

"Nothing, I don't know. It's just good to see you."

"Well, that's why I came," she said. "I didn't want to leave you here. I didn't want you to think I was gone."

We had to confront a problem we had previously managed to avoid: negative numbers. Dinah didn't understand negative numbers. I hadn't noticed for a while, because she was able to add negative numbers to positive numbers, but it turned out she had made up a rule: "Always subtract, then keep the sign of the biggest number." I told her that rule wouldn't work if you had to add a negative number to another negative number. She wasn't convinced. She seemed to think it wasn't relevant. And in fact there weren't any problems in the book about adding two negative numbers, so I stopped trying to explain it. But now the time had come to multiply negative and positive numbers, and here, too, Dinah wanted to keep the sign of the biggest number. It didn't prevent her from getting the right answer some-times. She correctly said that 2 times -5 was -10; on the other hand, she thought that -2 times -5 was -10. Also, she thought -5 was bigger than -2.

I told her that with multiplication it didn't matter which number was bigger. If there was an even number of negative signs, the product was positive; if there was an odd number, the product was negative.

"So odd numbers are always negative?"

"No," I said, feeling my pulse accelerate. "I'm sorry. Hang on, I'm going to think of a better way to explain it."

Once she saw I was agitated, Dinah grew calm and comforted me, just like my mother did. "Honey," she said, putting down her pencil, "don't you worry, we're going to get this right sooner or later." She pushed her notebook toward me. "Now you're going to write down exactly what you were just saying, with examples, and then I'm going to go home and look them over, okay? How does that sound?"

"It sounds good," I said, and started writing in her notebook.

"But don't forget to put in an example," she said, looking over my hand, "because I see all these words, 'coefficient,' 'variable,' I just go, shoo-eee, I don't know what that's all about." As I wrote in the ex-amples, she nodded. "That's what I'm saying," she said. "Now we're going to be just fine."

Ivan called at ten that night.

"Where are you?" I asked.

"I'm outside your house."

I looked out the window. He was standing under a streetlight at one of the emergency telephones. Those phones were a direct line to campus police—they didn't even have number pads. I had no idea how he had used one to reach my room.

I went downstairs. He seemed different from usual—more restless. "I think we need to get a drink," he said. He had said before that he thought drinking would help me. He said it would help with talking. This obsession with drinking was one of the things that had most surprised me about college. I had always looked down on alcohol, because my parents liked to drink at dinner and it always made them more annoying. I had known that alcohol was supposed to be a big part of college life and that some people would really care about it, but I hadn't realized it would be basically everyone, except the most humorless or childish people, and also some people who were religious. There didn't seem to be any way of not drinking without it being a statement.

"Fine," I said. "Let's get a drink."

Ivan took me to an upscale beer garden twinkling with white Christmas lights. The bouncer asked for our IDs. Ivan didn't seem to understand at first why we weren't being allowed in. He seemed to think we were somehow being discriminated against.

"I'm not twenty-one," I told him.

"*That's* the reason?"

"That's it, pal," said the bouncer.

We walked twenty minutes farther from campus to a crowded bar in a basement, where we came up against a warm wall of cigarette smoke, beery exhalations, and some kind of vaporous sawdust. Ivan found a table where people seemed to be thinking about leaving, a high table with stools, and loomed over them until they got up. "You can wait here," he said. "What do you want?"

"I don't know," I said. Ivan looked at me for a moment and then went to the bar.

All around, people were shouting, wearing T-shirts. Their backs seemed more numerous than their faces. I saw Ivan leaning over the bar and talking to the bartender, who had a pixie cut, laughing eyes, and dimples, though her mouth wasn't smiling. Ivan came back with two pint glasses of beer and handed me the paler one. The glass was heavy in my hand. It felt expensive and adult.

I didn't understand why we had to be there in that place. At the same time there was nowhere in the world that I would rather have been. I thought about what a special, unusual person Ivan was—how much more present and alive than other people, how he said and thought things that nobody else said or thought, and how ready he was to walk around with me for hours. All I had to do was write him an email, and then he walked around with me all day long. Who else in the world would do that?

"Health," Ivan said in Russian, and we clinked glasses.

The beer was cold and not especially unpleasant but I couldn't tell what the point of it was. Like the iced coffee, it was at once watery and bitter. Apparently that was desirable.

"Is it okay?" Ivan asked.

"I'm not sure," I said. He picked up my glass and took a sip. I looked at him closely. "It's beer," he said, shrugging. "Try this one." He pushed his glass toward me. I tried it. It tasted extremely similar to mine.

"Do you like mine better?" he asked. I shook my head. We traded back our glasses.

I wasn't sure I would be able to finish the beer. Swallowing became increasingly difficult. I thought I could feel my body swaying ever so slightly on the high barstool. I didn't find that talking was any easier. All around us people were laughing and roaring so loudly that we had to lean in close and shout past each other's ears. "Linger" by the Cranberries was playing in the background. "You've got me wrapped around your finger," the singer warbled over and over, in a girly, excessively beautiful voice. It felt ominous to me—the aestheticized girliness, infatuation, and weakness.

"Do you like the Cranberries?" Ivan asked.

"I don't really like this song," I said. "Do you?"

"I like it." He was pulling apart and counting a wad of fives and singles. "I have enough money for two more each."

I realized he meant two more beers. My heart sank. I had thought getting "a drink" meant you only had to have one drink.

"I can't," I said.

"Why not?"

"I have to get up early."

He stared at me. "It's not even eleven yet."

I felt so unhappy. I just didn't understand why we couldn't skip the part where I drank two more pints of beer. "Well, I don't want to *push* you," Ivan said, somehow ironically, as if alluding to the scenario known to us both in which boys pushed girls, and which was so obviously not what was going on. I was embarrassed, because I felt that, by refusing to drink—by being afraid to drink—I was implying that I thought that *was* what was going on, and that he was going to "take advantage of me," a phrase it was impossible to imagine without quotation marks.

"How about if I get one more and we share it?" Ivan said.

I said okay. He went to the bar. "Linger" ended and was succeeded by "Smells Like Teen Spirit," a song I liked because it seemed so companionable and free, and simultaneously negative and cheerful. Ivan came back with another pint. It was the slightly darker beer that he had been drinking. Perhaps for this reason, because it was his, and because we took turns picking up the glass, I liked it better. I took tiny sips, barely enough to swallow, and each time I felt the cold, unfamiliar flavor again, I thought about whether it was a reminder of something or a continuation, and whether it mattered how long you continued something that was temporary.

"Are you sure you wouldn't have another?" Ivan said when the pint was finished. I thought about it, but couldn't see how to back down from the stand I had somehow taken.

When I stood up, the room swayed and I immediately walked into a table. Ivan took my arm. I felt embarrassed for causing him trouble, but I also felt wronged, because it was his doing that I was causing trouble.

"I might be drunk," I said.

"I don't think it's possible to get drunk from one beer," he said.

My feelings were hurt. Did he think I was faking it? In the next moment I wondered: *Was* I faking it? Was I actually capable of walking in a straighter line than I had been? It seemed to me that when I concentrated, I was. My face grew hot. I walked very carefully in a straight line.

As we were heading down Mass Ave toward campus, a man stepped out of a doorway. "I'm selling books," he said. Instinctively I averted my eyes, picked up my pace, and changed course slightly to give him a wider berth—just as Ivan did the opposite, slowing down right in front of the man, looking right at him, right into his eyes. "Books, really?"

I was overcome by the sudden sense of Ivan's freedom. I realized for the first time that if you were a guy, if you were some tall guy who looked like Ivan, you could pretty much stop to look at anything you wanted, whenever you felt like it. And because I was walking with him now, for just this moment, I had a special dispensation, I could look at whatever he was looking at, too. So I, too, looked at the man— at the lines etched into his face, at his crafty and reproachful expression, at his cloudy eye and his piercing eye, overhung by a wilderness of eyebrows.

The man opened one flap of his trench coat. Strapped to the inside, contraband-style, was an array of paperbacks: *The Fountainhead, Dr. Atkins' Diet Revolution,* an introduction to the philosophy of Heidegger, *The Communist Manifesto,* a Dear Abby anthology, *The Seven Habits of Highly Effective People,* and a Spanish-English dictionary. The man looked awkwardly down over the titles, apparently deciding which one to offer Ivan. I wondered which it would be—what it was that he had noticed about him.

"I don't know if you're a Spanish speaker," the man said finally, pulling out the dictionary. He had noticed Ivan's foreignness.

"No. I'm not."

"Then you can *really* use this dictionary," the man said ingeniously. "It's only one dollar. See the price on the cover—fifteen dollars. In Canada, twenty-*one* dollars. Canada's just a few hours from here."

Ivan dug in the pocket of his jeans—an amazing sight, someone you're infatuated with trying to fish something out of a jeans pocket—and came up with fifteen cents.

"Every bit helps," said the man, filing the nickel and the dime away in separate pockets. He took out a bunch of postcards, the kind dispensed in restaurant toilets, and gave one to Ivan.

"Are you going to give it to your girlfriend?" he asked, looking from Ivan to me. "Why aren't you holding hands when you love each other?"

"Well," Ivan said. "Because there's a time and place for everything."

As we turned to walk away, some object came flying at us, toward Ivan's chest. He caught it with one hand. It was the Spanish dictionary. "You already bought it," called the man, who seemed related to Nina's shaman in Ulan-Ude.

Ivan asked if I needed a dictionary for my Spanish class. I told him I already had one. He crammed the dictionary into his jacket pocket. "Well, maybe I'll use it someday." I felt a wave of longing. Where would he use the dictionary, with whom?

The sidewalk got wider and I again had difficulty walking in a straight line. Ivan explained that all I had to do was keep a constant distance between myself and the wall. This struck me as indescribably funny. When I laughed, Ivan also laughed. We were at the campus gates now—we were really near my dorm. Ivan handed me the postcard. It showed an Eskimo drinking Evian water in an igloo. Etched on the back with a ballpoint pen were the words "You have a warm hart."

"Is it true?" asked Ivan.

"'Hart' spelled that way is an animal."

"What kind of an animal? Wait, I know. It's like a deer, isn't it? I've seen it in Shakespeare." Ivan was crazy about Shakespeare. Once when we were walking around somewhere he told me the whole plot of *Pericles, Prince of Tyre.* It took twenty minutes.

"A warm heart," repeated Ivan, holding my wrist. "I think it's probably true." I looked at him. He was smiling and looked gentle. What if he thought I was expecting something?

"I'd better go," I said.

"Right now?"

"Yeah."

"To do what? Sleep?"

"Yeah." I looked at him.

"Okay," he said.

I felt like I had won, and yet when I turned to go through the gate I also felt like something had been ripped out of my chest.

Hannah was at her computer. "Where have *you* been?" she asked.

"In a *bar*," I said. Her eyes widened. I told Hannah about the evening in a voice full of grief but without being able to convey what exactly had been grievous.

"Was it fun?" she asked.

"I don't know," I said. I really didn't know.

My clothes smelled like my aunts, the ones who still smoked. When I climbed up into the bunk and lay down, the room started spinning. It got worse when I closed my eyes. I tried opening my eyes and sitting up. Then I was less dizzy. But what was I going to do—sit there like that all night?

I forced myself to lie back down and keep my eyes closed, and soon I fell into a shallow sleep about Rupert Murdoch. When I woke up, the light outside had gone out—Hannah was snoring away under me. I was thirstier than I had ever been in my life. I found my mug in the dark, went down the hall to the bathroom, and ran the cold tap, thinking about my warm hart.

Svetlana and I watched a movie about Pablo Neruda's mailman. I had thought it might somehow resemble that poem about the atom, but it didn't. The night was humid and glutinous, and everyone's hair was wrecked. When I got back to the dorm, Angela, who usually stayed in her bedroom with the door closed, was sitting at her desk with a hand mirror and a wide-toothed comb.

"I don't know what to do," she said. There was a big wing of hair that kept floating up in front of her forehead, like a gigantic sandwich. She gave me some hairpins and asked me for help. I felt touched and tried to pin it down. But it was no use—the pins weren't strong enough.

My hair was like a loaf of bread *behind* my head, with a frizzy halo around my face.

I found a voice mail from Ivan, asking if I was free that evening. "Maybe you will call me back," he said. I thought about whether to call him. Angela asked if I thought she should use hair spray. I said I thought hair spray would just harden it the way it already was.

"Yeah . . ." she said. I could see she was going to use hair spray.

As she was shaking the can, the phone rang.

"Hello?" I said, my heart racing.

"Darling." It was my mother. She had just watched *The Wizard of Oz* and wanted to tell me how hilarious it was when the wizard floated away in a hot-air balloon, waving and shouting, "Goodbye, folks!" She said she had never noticed before how funny this was. The way she described it was really funny.

She asked what was new with me. I told her I had just gotten this message from Ivan and was trying to decide whether to call him, since it was now nearly eleven on a Friday, a time when nobody was home. She said that of course I should call him—that if he had asked me to call him he probably would be home. She sounded a little bit forlorn. Her boyfriend had just gone home—she had sent him away after *The Wizard of Oz*.

After we hung up, I dialed Ivan's number and got his machine. "I called but you weren't there," I said, and hung up.

I decided to take a shower. As I was looking for the towel, the phone rang. My heart sped up again. It was Ralph. He asked if I was up for a walk. He came over right away, clutching a videocassette in a plastic case. Even his neatly trimmed hair had turned puffy and untoward. He said he needed to return the cassette first, so we decided to walk to the video store.

In the hallway I started to lock the door, then remembered that Angela was in her bedroom. Ralph made a joke about the door—about how defiantly I had looked at it. We started laughing hysterically, because of the door and because of everyone's hair, when I turned and saw, to my horror, Ivan's hair rising up above the bannister, frizzed out of his head like a diabolical tent.

"Oh—hi," I said. I stopped laughing. "We were just returning Ralph's movie."

"Oh," Ivan said.

"I'm sorry—did you want to . . ." Ralph looked from me to Ivan.

"No, no, return your movie," Ivan said to Ralph. "Will you be around later?" he asked me.

"I'll call you when we get back," I told Ivan.

"You don't have to come," Ralph told me.

"No, we planned to go," I told Ralph.

The three of us headed down the stairs. Someone somewhere went out a fire door, triggering an alarm that sounded like the chirping of a million demented cicadas.

"So, you guys just watched a movie," Ivan shouted over the alarm.

"*Ralph* watched a movie," I said, at the same time that Ralph said, "*I* watched a movie."

But Ivan seemed determined to believe that Ralph and I had watched the movie together. "Did you guys fight over what to get?" he asked jocularly.

"I wasn't there," I said.

We went out the gates and started walking toward the square. Ralph and Ivan were talking about the housing lottery. Periodically I would step off the curb or trail behind them. It turned out that Ralph had been assigned to the same house that Ivan lived in, the twelve-story high-rise. Ivan started describing the view from different windows. He seemed to know the view from every window.

"Oh, good to know," Ralph kept saying.

We stopped at a red light. "I guess I'll go back and do some math," Ivan said darkly, and loped off into the night.

Ralph and I returned the movie, *Peter's Friends*. I had never seen Ralph hate a movie so much that he had to go out in the middle of the night to return it. We kept walking toward the river. It seemed like it was just starting to rain. The closer we got to the river, the more raindrops we felt—but then every time we headed back toward the square the raindrops would stop. We tried walking around the square for a while, but that was depressing, so we started to go back toward the park outside the school of government.

"It looks like we're going *back to the park*," we said, looking at the sky. It didn't rain. We got to the park. But what if it started to rain now?

"Should we turn back?" I said.

"I think we're turning back," Ralph said.

"Are we?"

"I think it's because we ran into your friend."

When he said that, I felt ashamed. "That's not true," I said. "Let's keep going."

We spent the next two hours doing the kinds of pointless things we always did. We walked back to the river, and when it did finally start raining, we ran into the lobby of the DoubleTree hotel and sat on the floor in the glass elevator and watched the rain. Sometimes someone called the elevator and it went up or down. Nobody seemed to mind us, or told us to leave. When the rain stopped, we went to Chili's and ordered an Awesome Blossom: a gigantic battered deep-fried onion cut into petals. We ate about a third of it. Then it became impossible to eat any more.

One of the most remarkable things about the giant sculpted deep-fried onion was its powerful resemblance to an artichoke. Ralph told me about the onion and artichoke theories of humanity, which he had learned in sociology class. According to the artichoke theory, man had some inner essence, or "heart"; according to the onion theory, once you had unwrapped all the layers of society off of man, there was nothing there. Seen from this perspective, the idea of an onion masquerading as an artichoke seemed sinister, even sociopathic. In later years, the Awesome Blossom became known to contain almost three thousand calories and was named the Worst Appetizer in America by *Men's Health*, at which point Chili's took it off the menu.

By the time I called Ivan, it was one in the morning.

"How sleepy are you?" he asked.

"Not very. How sleepy are you?"

"Not very." Ivan wanted to come back to my dorm—to see how I lived. I didn't want him to see how I lived, but there didn't seem to be any way to avoid it, and anyway what good would it do to hide?

I hung up the phone and looked in the mirror. Nothing I had done in the past two hours had had any kind of positive effect on my hair.

Ivan knocked on the door. His eyes wandered around the room, lingering on Albert Einstein. It seemed to me that he had some negative thoughts about Albert Einstein, but if so he kept them to himself.

Hannah came out of our bedroom yawning. Her hair looked flawless, as usual. "What's going on?" she said. She said she couldn't sleep. I knew it was a fake yawn, and it wasn't true she had been trying to sleep—she could *always* sleep. She introduced herself and started asking Ivan a billion questions. When she ran out of questions she started just listing the names of different math TAs and asking if he knew them.

"Was she the hypochondriac?" Ivan asked afterward. "I wanted to try to make her worry about the dampness, but I was afraid she might have been the wrong roommate."

"No, she's the hypochondriac. Our other roommate wouldn't have talked to you."

"She wouldn't have talked to me?"

"I mean, she's shy—she wouldn't have asked you questions."

"Oh, I see. I like being asked questions."

I nodded thoughtfully. "Why *is* that?"

After a moment Ivan burst out laughing, and I felt proud.

We walked to the river and sat on a bench. "It wasn't a good arrangement for you to call me," he said.

"Why not?"

"I wasn't able to work. I didn't get anything done."

I tried not to show how happy I felt when he said that.

"All the lights are pointing toward you," Ivan said, looking at the streetlights on the opposite bank, reflected in the river.

"Those ones over there are pointing toward you."

"Really?" he said. "Not to you, also?"

"No, to you."

"Well, you're right, I feel that they're pointing to me also."

I felt a wave of physical attraction toward him. He was sitting in an uncomfortable-looking position, leaning forward, with his legs pressed together and his arms crossed in his lap.

We sat there for a long time, wondering if it would rain again.

"How long do you think we've been sitting here?" Ivan said.

"A long time," I said. Near the riverbank, something stirred in the reeds. "What animal could that even be?"

"A fish," Ivan suggested.

"We could have been sitting here long enough for the fish to evolve."

"It's possible. By that point we would probably evolve, too. What would we evolve into?"

I felt my body tense up. "I don't know," I said.

It was three now, and too cold to stay on the bench. At the same time, it was also too cold to move. It felt almost as if, if we sat there longer, it might get warmer again—it might actually become earlier rather than later, and things might still turn out differently than they had.

We went to Ivan's room and listened to records, one after another. Each record was so particular and specific—almost arbitrary. What if a few notes were different? Would that make it better or worse?

Ivan slid toward the floor, hands clasped around his knees, and leaned his head back against the sofa. He watched the ceiling. The room grew lighter. I knew I shouldn't be staring at him like that, and turned to look out the window. That's what windows were for. The sky was mauve, and so were the concrete buildings. The brick buildings were a soft, glowy orange. The river was like an endless silver scroll.

I looked back at Ivan, to see if he was asleep. He was still looking at the ceiling, in a half-vigilant posture that seemed to say: *Don't worry about the ceiling—I've got it covered.*

I tried to analyze the feeling of fatigue. There was heaviness in the legs, a faint ache behind the forehead and in the eyes, and something in the shoulders. Everything sounded both loud and distant. I stood up. It felt like getting out of a car after a long drive. I placed my palm on the cold glass. In the empty intersection below, the red light turned green. The time on the clock radio was 6:26.

I had left a handprint on the glass. It overlapped with a clock tower. I wiped it with my sleeve and sat on the floor next to Ivan. I, too, leaned my head back and looked at the ceiling, at the corner where it met the two walls—a delta like the place where a woman's legs meet. I sat up. Ivan sat up. He stretched out his legs, took off his glasses, rubbed the bridge of his nose.

"Are you tired?" I asked.

"Nah, not really." He put his glasses back on. "I think my body has accepted the fact that the night is over and it didn't get to sleep. How about you?"

"My body accepts it, too."

"I'm starting to understand you better," he said. "You don't eat, you don't sleep, and you don't drink. Are you always like that, or just around me?"

I thought it over. "I eat and sleep more when you're not around."

"But no drinking."

"Actually when you're not around I get hammered every night. With my real friends."

"Really?"

"No."

He sighed. "I'm not saying we have to get hammered, just one or two drinks. I honestly think we could bypass a lot. I see you don't mind staying up all night—but alcohol is exactly the same. You just bypass the suffering. Otherwise it's really similar. You suddenly see connections that you missed before. Something breaks down. I don't know what to call it—those blocks, that obstruct a connection in your mind."

"Inhibitions," I said.

"Yes, exactly," he said. I felt my face flush. "I don't mean," he added, "that you never talk about sex, and then you get drunk and suddenly you can talk about sex."

"Right," I said.

Time passed. I was thinking about how much time we had, and how little, at the same time. At some point, Ivan asked if I liked doughnuts. This question struck me as absurd. The clock in the tower struck seven, then seven-fifteen. Ivan said we might as well get breakfast. We conducted ourselves through the riot-proof hallway to the elevator.

The pale morning air was incredibly fresh and eager to penetrate the lungs. We crossed the street to the cafeteria, which was empty except for one table where six guys in sports jerseys were sitting. You could see that they were talking loudly, yet the overall quiet was undisturbed, as if their conversation hovered just over their table, like in a comic strip.

Ivan took some of everything: scrambled eggs, a pancake, ham, fried potatoes. He filled two glasses with orange juice from the machine. I put Cheerios in a bowl, took a banana, and poured a cup of coffee. We sat down. I sliced the banana on a plate, then transferred the slices into the Cheerios.

"We have nothing to say," Ivan observed.

I nodded.

"We've exhausted each other. We've proved that we're both finite personalities." He sounded annoyed. "How long can we continue this? We make up something for each word, like a dictionary, then we repeat the words. But when the words are used up . . ."

I had no idea what he was trying to say. "*Language* is infinite," I ventured.

"There's a finite number of *words*," he said. "Just infinitely many combinations."

I told him that Chomsky said the number of words was also infinite. "Because you could have an antiaircraft missile, and then to fight it an anti–antiaircraft missile missile, and then an anti–anti–antiaircraft missile missile. Missile."

"Yes, okay. Maybe we can talk like that from now on."

"From 'from now on' on."

He didn't laugh.

I pushed the Cheerios around with my spoon. There was only one letter—*o*—but infinitely many combinations. Ivan moodily ate his eggs, pancake, ham, and potatoes, and drank the orange juice.

"Okay," he said, pushing back his chair. "I guess now you can go home and sleep or whatever. Whatever secret things you do when I'm not around."

"Oh," I said. "Okay. You can go do your secret things, too."

"Yeah, I have lots of secret things to do."

We threw out our trash, put the trays and plates on the conveyor belt, and went outside.

"See you later," I said.

"Yeah, eventually," he said. "You notice we're not very good at getting in touch."

"We'll get better," I said.

He frowned. "You can call me, too, you know. You don't have to wait for me to call."

"Okay," I said sadly: so, he wasn't going to call me. "I'll call you, next time."

"Good," he said, and turned back toward his building.

I tiptoed into the bedroom, hoping that Hannah wouldn't wake up. There was a rustling sound. I froze. Hannah sat up, yawned, and stretched elaborately. "Whoa—did you just come home?"

"Yeah."

"Where did you sleep?"

"I didn't sleep. I just sat in a room all night. So I'm kind of tired."

"Sounds like you need to get some rest," she said, jumping out of bed.

"That's the plan," I said, climbing from the top of the dresser to the upper bunk.

"Right *now?* You don't even want breakfast?"

"I already ate." I pulled the covers over my head. Hannah clopped around for a while, talking about her keys. Finally, she left. I lowered the bedcovers, took out my copy of *Little Dorrit*, and stared at the first page until I fell asleep.

I woke up at three. The cafeteria wouldn't open for another two hours. I went to the student center, where I bought a tuna sandwich on a baguette and gnawed on it for a while. The consumption of that baguette seemed to require some kind of ear muscles that I had lost during the two-million-year course of human evolution.

I found a book of fables and read two fables about harts. They both ended badly. In "The Hart in the Ox-Stall," the hart hid from the hunter in an ox-stall. The hunter noticed its antlers sticking out of the straw and killed it, proving that "nothing escapes the master's eye." In "The Hart and the Hunter," the hart deplored its legs for being less handsome than its antlers. Later, when it was running from a hunter on its legs, its antlers got tangled in a tree and it got killed. The moral was: "We often despise that which is most useful to us." In general, the hart's biggest problem was antlers. Or no, it wasn't antlers at all, it was hunters.

Svetlana turned twenty and had a party. I debated for a long time what to get her, settling in the end on a big bunch of sunflowers.

Their bigness didn't register with me at the florist's. The flowers actually seemed to grow as I walked back through the square until, by the time I got to her party, their bright yellow faces were almost the size of human faces. The idea of putting them in a vase was insane, like stuffing nine people into a vase. We ended up using someone's decorative plastic wastebasket. Fern filled it with water from the shower down the hall.

Most of the Serbo-Croatian Club was there—they had brought slivovitz. There was a lemon cake. All I could think about was that, the last time I had talked to Ivan, he had said he would try to call that night. The cake was better than it looked. I talked to six Orthodox Jewish guys who were going to be in Svetlana's rooming block next year. All were suffering from food poisoning. Because of a holiday, they had had to eat chicken soup that had been kept on a warm stove all night, just below boiling temperature. "It's the perfect way to grow bacteria," explained Jeremy, who studied microbiology. When I left, Svetlana was conversing animatedly in Serbo-Croatian with a guy wearing plastic-framed glasses. She sounded different when she spoke Serbo-Croatian, somehow lazier but at the same time more lively.

I had one new voice mail. It was from my mother, who described how, after months of work, her lab technician had slipped, fallen, and broken all the pipettes: "I think it was a Freudian slip."

I put down the phone. It started ringing again almost immediately. It was Ivan. He said that he was at the student center, so if I walked toward him and he walked toward me, we would meet in the middle. It seemed to me that there was more than one way to walk to the student center and that we could miss each other, but when I started walking, there was Ivan. He seemed excited. "I was just studying for the Shakespeare final with my girlfriend—well, now my ex-girlfriend," he said. My heart jumped. Did that mean he didn't have a girlfriend anymore? He said he had ended up just talking to his exgirlfriend about Shakespeare, and about the human condition, and about me, and she had brought up some interesting examples from Shakespeare, and they had talked about me and Shakespeare.

"You remind me a little bit of Shakespeare," he said. I looked at him. Was he drunk?

We went to his room, and he took out a cardboard box full of photographs. He showed me a picture of his first motorcycle, a Honda. I was troubled by the motorcycle. He felt to me increasingly like the parody of a love interest. Several pictures had been taken in Thailand. One showed Ivan standing next to an elephant. He and the elephant had almost exactly the same facial expression. In another, Ivan was standing in front of a Buddhist temple, facing the sun, with his mother and his sister, but the shadows were so dark that you couldn't make out their faces.

"Here's one of my ex-girlfriend," Ivan said. He showed me a picture of a slight girl with long reddish hair, wearing a tank top, a long skirt, and a backpack. I looked at the picture carefully, trying to figure out what made her a girlfriend. She was petite, curvy, and toughlooking, though her smile was open and almost childlike. There was a donkey in the picture. That couldn't be relevant. Or could it?

Ivan had taken a few photos out of the box and set them aside facedown, like cards that wouldn't be played until later. "These I don't want you to see," he explained, "because then you would know things about my life that I don't want you to know."

The openness with which he said this made me laugh. I didn't ask, or even wonder, what was in the pictures. The role of a suspicious woman seemed like a cliché having nothing to do with me or with the time that we lived in.

"In the second semester of my junior year I started having all these

complicated ideas about love," Ivan said. "I got a C-plus in a graduate math class. I never got a C in math before. I felt so terrible." He
stared into space, apparently transfixed with horror by the recollection
of the C-plus.

"There's something I want to tell you about," Ivan said, "but I don't
want you to feel pressured." He said that his friend Peter, who was
also Hungarian, and a graduate student in economics, ran a philan-
thropic program where he sent American university students to teach
English in Hungarian villages every summer. The teachers had to buy
their own plane tickets, but everything in the villages was paid for.
There was even a small stipend.

"There's one empty slot left," he said. "If you want it, you can
probably have it. I mean, Peter is my friend. And you even have experience teaching English."

I reflected back upon the three ESL lessons I had given Joaquín,
before he went blind.

"I guess that's technically true," I said.

"I'd be in Budapest, so we could see each other on the weekends,"
Ivan said. "But otherwise, I don't know what kind of place those
villages are. You'd be surrounded by goats. But you'd be in Europe."

I couldn't picture it—neither Europe nor the goats. Would they be
indoors? Ivan said I should think it over, and I pretended to think. But
there was nothing to think about. Teaching English in a Hungarian
village wasn't something I could weigh against anything else, because
I had no idea what it was, and even if I had, I didn't know what the
other possibilities were. Moreover, my policy at the time was that,
when confronted by two courses of action, one should always choose
the less conservative and more generous. I thought this was tanta-
mount to a moral obligation for anyone who had any advantages at all,
and especially for anyone who wanted to be a writer.

. . .

I met Ivan's friend Peter in the café of the Science Center. He was way more normal than I expected. His appearance, clothes, and manner of speaking all resembled those of other people. He talked about Ivan as if he and I were regular friends or acquaintances.

"Do you think you'll see Ivan tomorrow?" he asked.

He might as well have been asking if the interdimensional portal would be open. "I really couldn't say," I said.

Peter complimented my idiomatic English and asked how long I had been in America. "I've always lived here," I said.

"Always?" He looked startled, like maybe he thought that I meant since 1776.

"I mean, I was born here, and never left."

"Oh, that's funny. Ivan identified you as being Turkish."

"No, I'm from New Jersey."

"What exit?"

Peter had grown up in Queens with his mother, a dermatologist. Now he was getting a Ph.D. in economics and East Asian studies. The Hungarian village program was a first step in his plan to build a global network of not-for-profit schools to teach English and computer programming in the developing world. One had to start small, with what connections one had. The connections he had were with wonderful people in village governments in Hungary and Romania, and for three years now he had been sending Harvard students to their communities. Speaking in a measured, gentle voice, he described the importance of cultivating connections, the presence of good people everywhere, the need to identify people who weren't just good but who could make things happen, and the school system in Kyrgyzstan.

Peter gave me a leaflet describing the program. There was an application on the back, but he said I didn't have to fill it out because Ivan had written me such a glowing letter of recommendation.

He did? I almost said, but stopped myself.

"I trust Ivan," Peter said. "I trust his opinion of people."

Summer was in the air. Bright, hot, lazy, each new day seemed to hang suspended, like a big shimmering balloon, right in front of your face. As usual, I didn't have anything to wear. How was it I didn't have the right clothes for *any* weather? I cut the legs off of my older pair of jeans and dropped the amputated legs, two frayed graying cylinders, in the dumpster.

Wearing the cutoffs with a bright yellow polo shirt and my mother's oversized 1970s sunglasses, I walked across the quad to the philosophy building, where Peter was having an orientation meeting. Inscribed over the door in huge letters were the words: WHAT IS MAN THAT THOU ART MINDFUL OF HIM. I had seen this inscription countless times, without really thinking about it. It was a good question. What *was* man? It occurred to me that I could be less mindful of man, and I seemed to catch a glimpse of freedom.

There were six of us at the orientation, three girls and three boys. I was the only freshman. We played a mnemonic game to remember each other's names. Memorization was so weird—the way it consisted of attaching one thing to another thing, with no way to root anything in place. If you wanted to remember your keys, you could imagine them in an amphitheater, but nobody ever said how you were supposed to remember the amphitheater.

Looking compact, neat, and almost nautical in shorts and a faded blue and white T-shirt, Peter told us about the program. I had thought we would all be teaching together in one school, but it turned out that each of us would be in a different village, living with a different family. We would teach every day for three or four hours. The village schoolteachers would tell us what subjects they were studying and we would think of exercises and drills and games. Simon Says was a good game for parts of the body. Twenty Questions was good for vocabulary. Music was a good learning tool, especially the Beatles, because even the littlest kid could understand "I want to hold your ha-a-a-a-and." The most important thing was to be relaxed, patient, and playful.

In the afternoons, we would share American culture in a free-form way outside the classroom. Peter showed us some slides of previous participants sharing American culture. One guy was playing basketball with the children. He had brought the hoop from America and hammered it to a fence. Another guy was playing the guitar. He had taught the children Bruce Springsteen. After the slideshow, Peter said that one of last year's teachers had come to talk to us about his experiences. Last year's teacher walked in. It was Sandy from Constructed Worlds.

A fond smile hovered on Sandy's face as he recalled his time in the Hungarian village. There hadn't been electricity or hot water. The students had all been boys ages eight to fourteen. "They'll try to push you," he said.

"*You* really had some adventures," Peter said.

"The antlers," Peter and Sandy said in unison.

Sandy told us about the time when one of his students had taken down the antlers that hung for some reason on the schoolroom wall, and charged at Sandy with them. Sandy had climbed up on his desk and used his chair to try to defend himself without causing injury to either the boy or the antlers. Everyone laughed. I didn't think I would survive being chased with antlers.

During the lunch break, Sandy and I reminisced about Constructed Worlds and talked about Ivan—it turned out he and Sandy lived in the same dormitory. "Really interesting guy," Sandy said, seeming impressed that I was friends with him. I asked more about the antlers. He said the principal had made a big deal out of it, and that had made things worse. Whenever possible, the best course was to talk things through with the kids directly.

"You'll have a great time," he told me.

·   ·   ·

It was almost exam period, and right after that we would have to evacuate the dorms. Each day was hotter than the one before. Nobody had enough cardboard boxes. Some people acted as if it were really easy to get boxes for free and only an idiot would pay for boxes. I only found one free box. Fruit flies were living in the box. Ralph and I made a date to go buy boxes.

I called my mother and asked her if it was okay to go to the Hungarian countryside for five weeks to teach English. I explained that they would pay for everything except the plane ticket, and in August I could head straight from Budapest to Turkey, to meet her and my aunts—it wouldn't be that much more expensive to go to Budapest first.

"This is that Ivan's idea, isn't it?" she said. "Darling, is he a trustworthy person? Who else will be there?" I told her about Peter, how he had been doing this program for years, and was getting a Ph.D. in economics, and how his mother was a physician in Queens. It was the information about his mother that seemed to reassure her, especially when I told her that Peter had given us her phone number. He had specifically said that, although he was going to be in Mongolia for part of the summer, our parents could always find him by calling his mother in Queens.

"You really want to go?"

"Kind of, yeah."

"You really like this boy," she said, sounding so sad and affectionate that tears came to my eyes.

. . .

I wrote to Ivan on Friday morning, and thought he would call me either that evening or Saturday. He didn't. On Sunday, I studied Russian with Svetlana. Svetlana had made up a song to help memorize the declensions of irregular nouns. It was a doleful little tune, more of a chant really, with only two notes: "There are no citizens. There are no citizens. I see the citizen. I see the citizen."

Svetlana was way better than I was at memorizing. She accepted it in her heart as something necessary. Growing up in America, I had been taught to despise memorization, which was known as "rote memorization," or sometimes as "regurgitating facts." The teachers said that what they wanted was to teach us to think. They didn't want us to turn out like robots, like the Soviet and Japanese schoolchildren. That was the only reason Soviet and Japanese children did better than us on tests. It was because they didn't know how to think.

By high school, I sensed that the teachers weren't leveling with us. Our biology teacher would say: "I don't want you to memorize and regurgitate, I want you to understand the elegant logic of each mechanism." Nonetheless, on the test you had to draw a diagram of RNA transcription. When it came to science or history, reason got you only so far. Even if each step followed from the previous one, you still had to memorize the first step, and also the rule for how steps followed from each other. It wasn't as if there was only one way the world could have turned out. It wasn't like strawberries *had* to grow from bushes. There were lots of ways things could have turned out, and you had to memorize the particular one that was real.

Or . . . did you? *Was* there only one way the world could have turned out? If you were smart enough, could you deduce it? A tiny part of me held out the hope that you could. And that part was bad at learning Svetlana's song.

. . .

On Monday, my mother called. She asked about the weekend and about Ivan. I said I hadn't heard from him.

"Not all the weekend?" she asked. "Why? What was he doing?"

"I don't know," I said.

There was a pause. "Selin, are you being safe?"

I had a sinking feeling. "I'm trying," I said.

"I mean, are you using condoms?"

"What? No. I mean we're not having sex."

"You aren't?"

"No."

"Are you sure?"

"Yeah."

"Well, if you do, just make sure you use protection. Even in the Hungarian villages. It's really important."

After we hung up I felt sick. I realized I had been in despair for the past three days.

The phone rang. I would die if it wasn't him. That thought, I knew, was itself lethal. In the time it took to pick up the phone and say hello, I thought again and again: *What is man that thou art mindful of him. What is man that thou art mindful of him. What is man.*

"Selin," Ivan said. "Hey."

"So what have you been up to?" asked Ivan.

"Nothing. Writing this philosophy paper. What have you been up to?"

"Trying to figure out how to get my stuff to California and put it in storage, things like that."

"Oh, I know." I said it seemed very hard that every single thing in the room had to be either thrown out, or put into storage, or conveyed somehow to my mother's house.

"For you? Why is it hard for you? You're coming back next year. Put everything in storage here and go home."

I told him I didn't have a ride because my mother would be in Turkey, and I couldn't carry all my things myself on the train, so I was mailing stuff home. He asked if I was using the book rate, because that was the best deal. He said you could use the book rate for other things besides books—they didn't want you to do it, but you could. He had talked the woman at the post office into it. I felt tired and hopeless.

"So," Ivan said. "Do you want to go swimming?"

"Now?"

"Well, it's hot out, don't you think?"

"Yeah." It really was hot. He said we could meet at the freshman cafeteria at five and have dinner first. He asked if I was brave enough to ride on a motorcycle. I didn't think a motorcycle sounded scary. It was no antlers.

After we hung up, I paced around the room, thinking about the indignity of worrying about my bathing suit. It was my high school bathing suit. High school reminded me of Ralph, and how we were supposed to buy boxes. I called Ralph.

"I can't do the boxes," I said.

"Oh," he said. "No problem. How about dinner—not that, either?"

I had forgotten we had said anything about dinner.

From a distance I could see Ivan perched on a parapet, arms clasped around his knees. I had never noticed this parapet, let alone thought of sitting on it.

He jumped down when he saw me. He had a black laptop case slung across his chest. Whatever was in it was lighter than a laptop.

He asked if it was okay if we stopped at the express mailbox—he wanted to drop something off before the five-thirty pickup. We walked together down the stone steps.

The temperature had cooled in the past couple of hours. The sky was pale blue, there was no wind at all, and the air seemed to be exactly body temperature.

"There's my girlfriend," Ivan said, almost conversationally.

"Oh?" I said.

I looked around. I saw some trees, a road, two mailboxes, an old man walking a dog, a young man carrying a baby in a sling. The baby was dressed in pink, so that was a girl. But she was too young to be anyone's girlfriend. A girl with long frizzy hair spilling over a vinyl backpack was walking in our direction on the opposite side of the street. But she looked right at us with no change of expression and kept walking.

"This was bound to happen sometime," said Ivan. "Yooo," he called. I thought he was going to say "yoo-hoo," but it turned out to be "Eunice." "Yooonis!" he called. Nothing happened. He quickened his pace. I hung back. "*Hey*, Eunice," he said, in the same warm voice he used with me on the telephone. Only then did I notice a girl kneeling at the bike rack with her back toward us, unlocking a bicycle. She was wearing white jeans and a red-and-white-striped shirt, and her black hair was pulled back in a high ponytail that swayed from side to side.

The fourth time he called, she turned and stood up, brushing off her tiny hands. "Oh, hi," she said, barely audibly.

Ivan put an arm around her waist. She looked really small next to him. "This is my girlfriend, Eunice," he told me. "This is Selin, who I told you about," he told her.

"What?" she said.

"Selin," he repeated, "this is Selin."

"Nice to meet you," I said, extending my hand.

"Oh!" she said.

I briefly held a small, cold, unenthusiastic object.

"I talked to Vogel," the girl told Ivan, retrieving her hand.

"Oh, really?" said Ivan.

"They're giving me money, for the Chinese thing."

"What?"

"For the Chinese thing, they're giving me twenty-five hundred dollars. But I'm not sure if I should do it."

"Uh-huh."

"It's so boring."

"Yeah, you shouldn't be like that."

"What?"

"You shouldn't do those things that bore you."

"But I need the money."

They talked for a while about the twenty-five hundred dollars and the mysterious, boring Chinese thing that she didn't want to do.

"Can't you just take the money?" Ivan was saying.

"What?"

"Can't you take the money and not do it?"

"Of course not."

He shrugged. "Well, it's better than shoveling snow."

"I know," she said. She had a bright red mouth drawn with lipstick, slightly smaller than her actual mouth. Suddenly the image came into my mind of her putting on her lipstick in the morning while Ivan stood in the door and they talked about nothing, like they were doing now—about the trivial and contentious things that somehow made up the whole of life. Everything stopped. Space and time shut down, one dimension at a time, the sky collapsing from a dome to a plane, the plane collapsing into a line, and then there were no surroundings, there was nothing but forward, and then there wasn't even forward.

. . .

"We're going swimming!" Ivan was saying in a bright voice, like it was great news.

"What?" said Eunice.

"Selin and I are going swimming."

She frowned. "But the movie starts at nine-thirty."

Ivan frowned, too. "I know."

"So you should come by nine-twenty."

"Yeah, fine," he said. "We'd better go, then."

"See you."

She got on her bike and we kept walking. Ivan came to a stop in front of the self-service FedEx box and set down his laptop case in such a way that it would certainly fall into the gap between the box and the wall. He opened the drawer under the box, took out a form, and started filling it out.

Ivan's bag fell to the ground, following the dictates of fate. We both bent down. I was faster. I handed him the bag.

"Sorry," he said. "I mean, thanks."

I leaned against the wall and looked at the sky. A white line hung midair and the jet flew on. Ivan noisily crossed something out, then crumpled the paper into a ball. "This isn't the one I need," he said. He crumpled up two more forms before getting one right. He then destroyed an address label in the attempt to detach the backing, and had to fill out a new label.

I told him it was okay—we weren't in a hurry.

He glanced up at me and smiled. "It's the second time I'm mailing this stuff to this guy Or-chid," he said, pronouncing it with a soft *ch*. "He seems really incompetent. By now I have to FedEx it. I need the ticket soon, to get the Japanese visa."

I looked at the name on the invoice: Orchid Jones. "I think it's a she," I said.

"Really? Is Or-chid a girl's name?"

"Orchid, it's a flower."

"Oh, *orchids?* Those obscene flowers? Then I agree with you that Orchid Jones is probably a woman."

I watched him write a check for $689.92. He wrote in all capital letters, and the *I* arched back like an inverted *C.* He took out a credit card and started copying the number.

"I bought a return ticket directly from Tokyo to San Francisco," he said. "I'm not coming back here. I shipped my stuff to the math department in Berkeley. It's all sitting there, in some office. They're stuck with it all summer." The thought seemed to cheer him.

I tried to laugh, too. I picked up his wallet and looked at his school ID and driver's license. He wasn't smiling in either picture.

"Does it look like me?" he asked.

"What?" I said.

"Does it look like me? The picture?"

I said it did. I said that if I hadn't known better, I would have been completely taken in.

"What?" he said.

"If I didn't know better, I would have thought it was you."

"You would have thought it was me, in my own photograph?"

"Right."

He frowned. "So who do you think it is now?"

"Never mind," I said.

"Okay," he said, proceeding to drop his credit card. I let him pick it up himself.

In the cafeteria line I took a knife and fork. Ivan handed me another knife and another fork. I stared at the two knives and two forks. At the salad bar, Ivan put lettuce and tomatoes in a bowl and topped them with dressing. I also put some things in a bowl but at the end it wasn't a salad, it was just a lot of random things in a bowl. At the soda fountain, Diet Coke seethed over my wrist.

We found two empty seats at the opposite end of a table from four football players. The football players' trays resembled futuristic cities, with glasses of milk and Gatorade shooting out like white and fluorescent skyscrapers.

The cut corn on my plate reminded me of teeth. I kept thinking about the story by Poe about monomania, where the man has monomania, and it turns out to be about teeth.

"What are you thinking about?" Ivan asked.

"Teeth," I said.

He looked at my untouched tray. "Are your teeth bothering you?"

Ivan ate a hot meal, and then a bowl of Jell-O. He used a fork to eat the Jell-O. I didn't want to be the kind of person who lost her appetite over some guy, so I ate a few chickpeas. Then I thought, why should I be the kind of person who eats when she isn't hungry, just to prove some kind of point? I put down my fork.

"Where's all your stuff?" Ivan asked.

"My stuff?"

"For example, your bathing suit. I assume you were planning on wearing a bathing suit."

"I *am* wearing a bathing suit."

"Oh, under your clothes? Aha. But how about a towel?"

I had forgotten about a towel. He said I should go to my room and get one; he would get the bike and meet me at the gate.

Back in my room, I emptied out my backpack and threw in a beach towel and a plaid shirt. I looked around, wondering what else to bring. I saw Einstein. This reminded me to bring a hairbrush. I couldn't think of anything else, after the towel and the shirt and the brush.

As I approached the gate, I heard footsteps pounding behind me. I stepped aside. Something jumped and landed beside me.

"You walked right past me," Ivan said, out of breath. "I was yelling, I was calling your name."

I thought of how Eunice hadn't heard him, either. It wasn't his day for catching girls' attention.

The motorcycle was bright yellow. Ivan handed me a bike helmet. When I fumbled with the buckle, he took the helmet from my hands, tightened the strap, put it back on my head, and snapped the buckle under my chin. He put on his own helmet, which had a clear screen over the front, and showed me where to sit. He told me that I should hold on to him, that if we tilted to one side I shouldn't get worried or try to lean the other way, I should just do whatever he did.

"My main piece of advice," he repeated, "is to hold on to me really tightly. Then you won't fall off." I nodded. It hadn't occurred to me that one could fall off. I climbed up behind him, looking at the ground and hoping not to see anyone I knew.

The engine started and we pulled away from the curb. It was amazing to cover the same ground one usually traversed on foot, but with no effort, and so much faster.

"You should hold on to me tighter," Ivan said over his shoulder, picking up speed.

He was wearing a floppy dark orange shirt that I had often seen, without ever having thought that I might someday touch it. I placed my arms lightly around his waist, trying to minimize actual contact. The idea of holding on to him felt unthinkable and wrong, like picking up a wild animal.

After a while, though, the feeling of embarrassment was lost in the pure, primitive joy I felt at the sensation of so much speed. When Ivan merged onto the highway, accelerating into a higher gear, I couldn't help laughing. The wind was unbelievably strong and made me worry about my contact lenses, so I mostly looked down, watching the asphalt rush away beneath us, occasionally looking up to steal a glimpse of a hotel or a gas station. Whenever Ivan leaned back, our helmets clicked.

The first thing you saw at Walden Pond was a replica of the cabin Thoreau had lived in. Neither fully life-sized nor miniature, it was just a few degrees smaller than usual, like the petites section of a department store. Through the window, we looked at a petite pan sitting on a petite woodstove, a petite fishing pole, a petite chair at a petite table and, on the table, a petite lamp and a petite manuscript—presumably *Walden*, but a little bit smaller. "Thoreau was pretty short," Ivan said.

"Either that or he was too cheap to build a full-sized house."

The water was clear green, surrounded by wooded hills. On a sandy beach, small children were wading around in yellow inflatable wings while their mothers sunbathed. It was weird to think this scene was part of their childhoods. Ivan said he thought we could find somewhere less crowded. I followed him over a fence, where a sign said not to walk on the bank because it caused erosion. We climbed this bank into the woods and began to walk along a shelflike path cut in the hill.

"Hey, wait, you're American," Ivan said suddenly. "You must have read his book! So what's his story, this Thoreau?"

"I read it in high school. I don't remember it so well."

He laughed. "Because high school was such a long time ago for you."

"It was sophomore year of high school. That was three years ago!"

"Okay, okay. Did you like it when you read it three years ago?"

I hadn't found Thoreau to be the world's most likable character—the way he looked down on Emerson, and then used Emerson's money to build his cabin. "I remember he said the Egyptians wasted their time building the pyramids, because the pharaoh should have been thrown in the Nile like a dog," I said. "He said the Egyptian slaves should have been out sucking the marrow of life."

"Sorry, I didn't hear—what should they have been doing?"

"Sucking the marrow of life," I said loudly.

"Aha, okay. So he's some kind of a Communist. How did he end up here, at the pond?"

"He wanted to leave society and experience life firsthand, to build a house with his own hands. In the book he keeps listing the price of every nail and all his groceries, to prove how simple his needs are. Some lady tries to give him a mat, but he won't take it."

"I'm sorry, what was the woman wanting to give him?"

"A *mat*."

"A mat? Why did she want to give him a mat?"

"I don't know," I said. "I guess she felt sorry for him."

"Aha, okay. Go on. She wanted to give him a mat but he didn't want it."

"Right—he said it would have taken up too much space."

"Was it a big mat?"

"I don't know," I said. "I don't think so."

We came to a break in the trees, beyond which lay a smaller, completely empty beach covered with smooth pebbles. It looked so clean and clear and perfect, like a metaphor for something.

"Does this look like a good place?" asked Ivan.

"Yes," I said.

"Good. Let's change." Scrambling up the hillside, he disappeared into the woods. I climbed a short distance in a different direction. I sat on a rock and took off my shoes. For a while I held one shoe and stared into space. Then I took off my T-shirt and socks. Leaving the jeans on over my bathing suit, I edged down the hillside. Ivan came running down wearing denim cutoffs, his pants slung over his shoulder, and jumped from the bank onto the path.

We deposited our bags on the beach. I took off my jeans.

"I was wondering whether you would swim in your jeans," Ivan said.

We waded into the pond. Translucent minnows circled our ankles. They were so alive. It was almost pure life in those little bodies, there was so little room for anything else. The sun was low and there was a breeze. The water felt ice-cold. I felt paralyzed by the thought of going in. Then I resolved myself and dove under. I felt my skin tighten all over, and realized how infrequently one felt conscious of one's whole body at once, as a continuous surface.

"You should come in," I gasped, almost speechless with cold. "It's *wonderful.*"

Ivan looked really different without his glasses, with wet hair. I said it was like the first time you saw a fluffy dog after it was wet.

"So in your analogy I'm a fluffy dog?" he said.

"Yeah. Although I guess in most ways you're not really like a fluffy dog."

"I'm not like a fluffy dog? Now you will hurt my feelings."

We swam the breaststroke side by side toward the opposite shore, telling each other about how we had learned to swim: me at day camp in New Jersey, him with his parents at Lake Balaton. Ivan asked about day camp. He wanted to know what the deal was. I asked about Lake Balaton. He said his family used to go there every year but now it was too crowded. "Not like here," he said. "I bet right now there are about two people in this whole lake. Including us."

"Two people including us?"

"That's right."

The trees were etched with tremendous sharpness against the pearly, sooty clouds, and the water was so clear you could see the bottom. Ivan asked how deep I thought it was. He dove under and was gone for what felt like a long time.

"Did you touch it?" I asked.

"No."

He tried again, raising his arms above his head and plunging feet-first. I floated on my back and stared at the sky.

"Can you lie on your back and look at your toes?" asked Ivan from some unfathomable distance. I looked over. He was right next to me.

"I don't know," I said. "Not for very long."

"My father could. When I was a kid, he would lie on his back and stick his toes out and say, 'I bet you kids can't do this.' My sisters and I would try so hard, but he was right—we couldn't do it. He said it was because we weren't smart enough. I would get really mad." He laughed, then looked over at me. "Stop trying, it's impossible. It's just because he was so fat. That's how my father could do it."

We turned back toward the shore. A calm duck crossed our path, leaving a V-shaped wake. Ivan swam a few strokes right behind the duck. "Ehh," he said, sounding at once so human and so much like a duck that I couldn't help laughing. "That one duck in an empty lake—it looks like it's going to evolve into something."

I agreed that the duck had a pioneering look.

"Next would be us. What do you think *we* would evolve into?"

"I don't know," I said. I wondered why he kept asking that.

When we neared the shore, Ivan started swimming faster, right up to the edge of the water, then staggered out onto the beach. I slowed down and watched him. He reached for his bag, then seemed to change his mind and picked up mine instead, unzipped it, and took out my towel. It struck me as strange that he should have forgotten his own towel when he had remembered to remind me to bring mine. Also why would he *rush* out of the water like that and then take my towel? I reached the shallows and started to stand, but it was so cold that I went back in, to wait until he was done with the towel. Meanwhile, Ivan just stood there dripping, holding my towel. It was a beach towel with a design of big multicolored wristwatches.

There seemed to be nothing to do but to get out of the water. I swam in until the sand scraped my knees, then waded to the shore. I walked up to Ivan. He stepped behind me. I turned. His hand touched my shoulder. I moved aside. I realized he was trying to wrap my towel around my shoulders. In a panic, I turned to face him and took the towel from his hands.

"Thanks," I said.

"That's okay," he said. From his laptop bag he produced a blue bath towel and started to dry his back. I brushed my hair and wrung out the water. Ivan picked up his clothes. "Don't look," he said.

I turned. I could hear him unzipping his cutoffs. I waded into the water up to my ankles. My feet looked ghostly and white against the pebbles. A school of tiny fish, black this time, darted past like arrows in a siege.

"You're doing really well," Ivan said behind me.

I looked up at the opposite shore. "I'm doing well?"

"Yeah, you're doing way better than me."

At what? I tried to ask, but couldn't.

When I couldn't hear any more clothing sounds, I turned around, but, having received a brief impression of Ivan with only one leg in his jeans, faced front again. I couldn't get at my own clothes, since they were behind him. I adjusted the towel around my waist and looked at the sky.

"Do you need some help?" he asked after a moment.

I turned again. He was fully clothed. "I don't think so," I said, wondering why I would need help putting on my own clothes.

"You might need help holding up the towel," he said.

"Holding up the towel," I repeated. I deduced that he was proposing that I take off my bathing suit while he held up a towel as a screen. I tried to imagine it. Would he be holding the towel *around* me somehow, or only in front? Which way would I be facing? Which way would he be facing? What about the other directions? And what was the point, when there was nobody there besides him and the ducks?

I told him that I was just going to put my clothes on over my bathing suit.

"I don't think you should do that," he said, in such a definitive tone that I felt shocked.

"Excuse me?"

"It's wet, it's windy. You'll be cold."

I wondered why I felt so much resistance to letting him hold a towel in front of me while I took off my clothes. After all, *I* was the one with the crush. Later, when he was gone, wouldn't I wish to be back here again, just as we were now?

"Just think," he said. "What would your mother say?"

Tears welled to my eyes. My mother would be sorry for me.

"I mean—she wouldn't want you to catch a cold. Maybe she would be mad at me if she thought I made you catch a cold."

"I—" I tried to answer, but couldn't. I looked at the ground.

"Okay, okay, Selin, it's up to you," he said.

Silently I collected my jeans, T-shirt, and plaid shirt, and put them all on over my damp bathing suit. I sat on a log to put on my shoes. The sun broke through the clouds, staining them orange. It became a little warmer. We walked back to the entrance, so I could use the bathroom. A sign said not to flush paper towels down the toilet. The toilet was just a board with a hole in it—there wasn't any flush.

"Do you want to head back now?" Ivan asked, back outside.

"Do you have to head back?" I asked.

"Not right now. We have time to watch the sunset."

We climbed back over the fence and walked for a comically long period of time, without being able to find the sun. "Don't worry, we'll find it," said Ivan. "At the latest, by tomorrow morning."

I thought how wonderful it would be to walk around with him until the following morning. I really felt that way, even though he stressed me out so much, and all we ever did was mishear each other and say "What?" all the time. Just then the pond came into sight, and

suspended over it the quivering molten yolk of the sun. We sat on a
log and watched it sink toward the horizon.

"Did you know I brought you a book?" said Ivan.

"No."

He took a slim green library book out of his bag. It was fairy tales,
in Russian. The first tale was called "The Something Goat." Neither
of us knew what kind of goat it was. Clearly, there was no avoiding
goats. Leaning over the first page we established that a merchant had
three daughters. He built a new house. The eldest daughter went to
the house and something came to her. The youngest daughter also
went to the house. She was sad, Ivan said—pathetic.

"Pathetic?" I echoed. Ivan knew more Russian than I did now—he
had skipped a semester and started going to Slavic 102, because there
weren't enough students and otherwise it was going to be canceled.

Ivan nodded. "Maybe not pathetic exactly, but sort of pitiful."

It grew too dark to make out the print. Ivan said he thought the
Hungarian word for goat was borrowed from Turkish. The words
were indeed similar. Then we compared "grass" and "cow" and "pig."
They were different. "Apple" was the same, and so was "boot."

"How many words do you think we can come up with, if we keep
going?" asked Ivan.

"A lot, right? I mean, we know a lot of words."

"Well, we would count only the hits."

"Oh! Then I don't know."

We walked back to the parking lot. It was getting dark faster and
faster.

There was no self-serve island at the gas station, so we stopped at the
full-service one and got off the motorcycle. A skinny freckled boy
ambled toward us. Ivan was looking at the gas prices. The boy's eyes
met mine. I understood right away that he was the same age as me,

and I knew that he knew the same about me. Ivan unscrewed the gas cap. The boy unhooked the nozzle and handed it to him. We watched Ivan fill the tank.

"Cool bike," said the boy.

"Thanks."

"Yamaha?"

"Suzuki."

It said SUZUKI right on the tank.

"Huh." The boy took Ivan's money and sauntered back to the station building.

"That full service was amazing," Ivan observed, starting the ignition.

Back in Cambridge, the bank clock read 8:40. We went to Ivan's dining hall. The dining halls were open late for exam period. At a table near the door, two students were slumped over their books, either asleep or murdered. In a corner, a girl was staring at a stack of flash cards with incredible ferocity, as if she were going to eat them.

On a table near the hot-water machine lay the greater part of a wrecked cake, with still-legible cursive letters reading HAPPY BIRTHDAY, MAY BABIES! There was a basket of bananas next to the cake. We sat at a table with two cups of tea and some bananas. Ivan told a story about how he had been at a café in Budapest with his girlfriend and an arrogant waiter wouldn't let him, Ivan, order in Hungarian.

"He insisted on speaking to my girlfriend in English. He was so proud of his English. She couldn't understand a word he said, but still he wouldn't give up."

We sipped tea and looked out the window.

"One thing I don't get about you," Ivan said, "is to what extent you feel American or Turkish. How is it for you when you're in Turkey? Do you feel different?"

"I feel like a kid."

"Like a little girl, huh? It must be really terrible for you."

"I learned Turkish when I was three, so I don't know enough words. I can't talk about anything," I said. "How about you? Do you feel differently when you're in Hungary?"

Ivan pushed his paper cup in various directions, as if it were a king under check. He said that in Hungary people were more honest. If they thought you were doing something stupid, they let you know right away. Americans were polite and remote, as if there were bubbles separating everyone. "You can't tell if someone really likes you," he said. "You can't get close. There are all these blocks."

"Blocks," I echoed.

"I know that's the cliché about America: 'Oh, it's so impersonal! Oh, I feel like a number!' That's not what I mean. I'm not saying the Hungarian way is better. In general, I think isolation is a good thing. With most people I'm so thankful not to be really close to them. In Hungary they would immediately start to tell you all this shit." He paused, apparently thinking about different shit he had heard in Hungary. "Of course," he continued, "it's also possible to feel *too* protected. In Hungary I feel more vulnerable."

"I see," I said. "So here you feel more *in*vulnerable."

"Well, maybe it isn't so simple as that."

I finished my tea and put our two banana peels in the empty cup. Outside the window, the light turned green. A biker with a blinking taillight sped alongside the river. When I looked back at Ivan, he was looking at me. "I have to go," he said.

"Okay," I said. I felt certain that something was finally over, and I didn't feel badly about it—I felt relief. "Thanks," I said.

"What?"

"Thanks, for today. I had a nice time."

"Come on, Selin. I should thank *you*. *I* had a nice time." He pushed back his chair and stood up. "Now it's time for you to go home and take off that wet bathing suit."

We walked away from the river, past his parked motorcycle,

toward the yard. When we got to Quincy Street, Ivan turned left, while I continued straight. It was dark, and I lingered at the intersection a moment and watched him. He looked so free, walking slightly hunched over, his shirt flapping a little behind him. When I crossed the street by the bank, the clock read exactly 9:20.

The next day, Friday, felt like a new era. Hannah had exams all day so I sat in our common room, working on my philosophy paper about action sentences. Nobody knew how to put action sentences into logic notation. Donald Davidson thought the action was an invisible extra thing, hiding in the sentence. He thought you had to call it "*x*." I read and reread the examples.

I flew my spaceship to the Morning Star.
(∃ *x*) (Flew (I, my spaceship, *x*) & (to the Morning Star, *x*))

Did spaceships even work that way?
The phone kept ringing.
First, a guy from my philosophy class called to ask if I knew the article where P. F. Strawson said that the paraphrasability of singular terms didn't necessarily imply that you could eliminate singular terms from a language.
"I can picture it so clearly," he said. "It looks like a manuscript, like in Courier font. I can even picture the paragraph I want. It's on the lower left-hand corner of a left-hand page."
"If you can picture it that clearly, why can't you read the picture?"
"It doesn't work that way."
The minute I hung up, the phone started to ring again.
"Hello?" I said. I reminded myself that it couldn't be Ivan, because I knew Ivan wouldn't call me again.
"Oh, Oleg!"

"Ralph! How was chemistry?"

"Let's just say that on reflection, one wouldn't want to be a doctor anyway. It's so terribly middle-class."

"Totally. White coats before Memorial Day."

"I do like those jade green scrubs."

"Maybe something could be done with that, for afternoon wear."

"Shall we discuss the designs over dinner?"

"In an hour? I'm still writing this paper."

"The philosophy paper! One was so insensitive not to ask. How is the paper?"

"Well, it needs more words."

Five minutes after we hung up, the phone rang again. It was somebody called Jared calling to ask whether I would consider voting him onto some committee I had never heard of.

"I hear you," I said, and hung up. The phone started ringing again immediately.

"*What*," I said.

"Selin?" said my mother.

"Oh, sorry," I said. "I thought you were calling to ask me to vote you onto the Student Initiatives Committee."

"No, sweetie, I don't want to be on the Student Initiatives Committee. I was just thinking about you. I was wondering how your exams are going, and how things are with your Hungarian friend."

I told her a short version of what had happened the previous day. "I think we're not going to talk anymore," I said.

"What will you do when he calls you?"

"He's not going to call."

"Of course he will. Womanizers always call back. That's their best quality."

I didn't say anything. Womanizers?

"Sooner or later, you'll have to speak to him again, and if I were you,"

I would decide in advance what position to take. I mean, let's think about why he let this happen. Probably he just wanted to upset you."

"He wanted to make me *upset?*"

"He wanted proof that you care about him."

"But he already had proof."

"Well, maybe you should pay him the compliment of being upset and see what he does."

I tried to swallow away the lump in my throat. I heard some background noises on my mother's end of the phone. A metal drawer slid shut. "Yes, I did. You're absolutely right," my mother was saying. "I'll be there in a moment.

"I'm sorry, my sweet," she said, "somebody I need to talk to came into the lab. I'll call tomorrow. If I don't find you, you call."

"Okay."

"Promise?"

"I promise."

"Okay. Now, don't let any of this lower your mirth index. Think of Tamerlane."

My grandfather used to comfort my mother, during her childhood, by reminding her that they might have been related to Tamerlane.

"Okay," I said, though I had never seen how Tamerlane helped anything.

"Remember, you have the best heart and mind, and whatever you do is right. Bye-bye, my sweet. Don't forget the fruit group."

The phone started to ring. What if it *was* Ivan, and now I had to give him the compliment of being upset?

"Hello?"

"Hey," said Lakshmi. "What are you doing tonight?" Noor was DJ-ing for a hedge fund guy's birthday at a club in Boston. It sounded awful, but still better than sitting by the phone and pretending to write this paper and wondering whether Ivan would call, which was apparently what my dumb brain had lined up for me.

"I don't have an ID," I said.

Lakshmi said it wouldn't be a problem. She said it wasn't hard to get into these places—all you had to do was be an attractively dressed female.

"Oh," I said.

"What's the problem?" asked Lakshmi. "You're female. You can be attractively dressed. Isabelle is buying me some tequila, and I already have salt. I'll probably get depressed seeing Noor with other women, so then we can do tequila shots and unburden our souls. I'll finally learn all your secrets!"

"Great," I said, wondering what the salt was for.

After we hung up, I sat staring at Einstein for a few minutes, waiting to see if the telephone would ring. It didn't. I reread the last sentence I had written in my paper. It wasn't very clear. How could I capitalize on this unclearness to make my paper longer?

"In other words," I typed.

But the action sentences were really difficult to think about, and instead I found myself wondering about Eunice, what she studied, how old she was, whether she was also graduating, whether she was going to California. I minimized WordPerfect, opened Netscape, and searched the university directory for the first name "Eunice." There were eleven Eunices. All eleven seemed to have the power of making me feel bad.

Lakshmi was wearing a strappy black top, a leather skirt, and spike-heeled boots. Her glossy lips shone as bright and wet as her laughing black eyes, which were lined with kohl. She was so beautiful.

We waited for a long time at the gate for Isabelle, Noor's best friend, who was apparently French and super-hot and brilliant and so-phisticated, but also really sweet and protective. Finally Isabelle turned up, looking younger than I had imagined, wearing a fluffy white car-digan. She had been unable to bring the tequila.

"I feel *terrible*," she said, with a French accent.

"Don't worry about it," Lakshmi said. They kissed each other. Isa-belle hailed a cab to go to her mother's friend's gallery opening. As we walked to the T, Lakshmi spoke with despair about Isabelle's cardi-gan, about how smart it was, and how effortlessly Isabelle trod the fine line between sexy and angelic. A bearded self-deprecating man was singing folk songs near the station entrance. As we crossed the street I noticed Ivan and Eunice in the crowd of listeners. Ivan was holding his motorcycle helmet, and Eunice was holding the bike hel-met. They seemed completely absorbed. At the end of the song, they neither applauded nor made any move to leave.

"So," Lakshmi said at the subway platform. "How's your mys-tery man?"

"We actually just walked past him," I said. "He was with his girl-friend."

"What? Where?"

"Outside. They were listening to that guy with the guitar."

Lakshmi wanted to run upstairs and look, but she couldn't afford another T token—she was always short on pocket money. "I just can't believe he was actually there," she kept saying. "I can't believe he really exists. You never tell me anything about him."

Lakshmi always asked me questions about Ivan that I didn't know how to answer: how attractive was he, how smart, how well dressed, which movie actor he most closely resembled.

"He's really tall," I said.

"What a description, from a writer."

I told her he didn't remind me of any movie actor. "Isn't that the point of liking somebody?" I said. "They form their—"

"Their own type," Lakshmi chimed in. It was one of her manner-isms; she guessed what you were going to say and then said it with you. It didn't mean she agreed. "No, I don't think so," she said. "I think he has to fit a prototype. Love at first sight is possible only be-cause you recognize a type. You're already looking for him. You know, he's your father, your schoolmaster. He's someone you've seen before."

A train rumbled into the station, but it turned out to be going in the opposite direction.

"How about the girlfriend?" Lakshmi said. "Is *she* attractive? Is she well dressed?"

"I don't know."

"You must at least have an opinion."

"I know it's weird. But I honestly can't tell."

"In relative terms, is she more or less attractive than you?"

"That's the most depressing thing you could possibly say to me."

"I'm only trying to help you come up with a prognosis."

"I can give you a prognosis right now, in three letters," I said. "Bad. The prognosis is bad. It doesn't matter what I look like. I could look like Juliette Binoche, and it wouldn't make a difference."

"Juliette Binoche doesn't have a good body. Of course, she has an angelic face, but have you really looked at her legs?" Lakshmi paused. "I suppose what you mean is that it wouldn't make a difference if you were stunningly gorgeous." She started to laugh. "Why not? Because of your *insufferable personality?*"

We were both giggling about my insufferable personality when the train pulled in. The car was too crowded for us to talk. We just stood there clinging to the ceiling bar, swaying in our stupid shoes. The train emerged briefly from the tunnel and crossed a bridge. The glass turned from distorting mirrors into windows, and you could look out at the world—at stars, water, lights, boats.

Lakshmi had borrowed an ID from an Indian medical student named Denise. Five-foot-three and twenty-six years old, Denise bore little physical resemblence to Lakshmi, and almost none at all to me. Lakshmi showed Denise's ID to the bouncer. He waved her in. She slipped the ID into my hand from behind the velvet rope—I was supposed to walk around the block and come back in ten minutes. I went to a diner and ordered a coffee. A group of Pakistani guys was sitting at the next table. "Hey, are you Pakistani?" one of them asked.

"No," I said.

"Why are you lying? It's obvious."

"I'm not."

"Why are you ashamed to be Pakistani?"

"I'm Turkish," I said. "We look the same."

"Why are you saying that, why are you ashamed?"

I left the money on the table, went back to the club, and showed Denise's license. The bouncer waved me in.

The music was pulsing like a bodily function. I saw Noor right away at the turntables, wearing headphones. I knew from Lakshmi that he was extremely attractive and dressed really well. I looked at him and tried to understand what an attractive well-dressed man looked like. He had facial stubble and an earring.

Lakshmi's eyes were shining. She touched my waist and pointed out a guy and said that if I went over and flirted with him, he would give me some ecstasy. I looked at the guy. "I'm okay," I said.

Dance songs turned out to consist of one sentence repeated over and over. For example: "I miss you, like the deserts miss the rain." Why would a desert miss rain? Why wasn't it okay for a desert to be a desert, why couldn't anything just be what it was, why did it always have to be missing something?

Short aggressive men kept dancing up close to Lakshmi, who had found a way to incorporate rejection into her dancing, rolling her eyes and tossing her hair and angling her lovely shoulders away. Less frequently, one of the men would try to dance with me. I would nod in a businesslike manner and then turn away as if I had re-

membered something important I had to do. It went on and on, the
dancing. I kept wondering why we had to do it, and for how much
longer.

On Sunday night, the third night after our swimming excursion, I
found a voice mail from Ivan. He sounded the same as always. He said
he was calling to see how I was. I didn't know what to say to him. I
stopped answering the phone. He left messages again on Monday and
Tuesday. Tuesday was the last day of exams. I spent Wednesday with
my second cousin Murat, who was in Boston for an engineering conference. I showed him around campus, and he came over to my room
to help me carry some boxes to storage. As I was taping the boxes
closed, the phone started to ring.

"Aren't you going to answer that?" Murat asked, after the third
ring.

I let it ring two more times, then picked up.

"Selin, hey," said Ivan.

"Hey."

"What have you been up to?"

"Nothing."

"I thought you must be busy with something. I've called you a few
times. Maybe you got my messages."

I nodded. "Yeah," I said.

"You did?"

"Yeah."

"Well. I just thought it would be nice to see you. Do you have
plans this afternoon?"

"My cousin is here."

There was a pause. "Is everything okay?"

"Yeah. I just can't really talk now."

"I guess I'll let you go, then."

"Okay."

"Bye."

"Bye."

Murat and I had dinner at an Indian restaurant, and then he went back to his hotel and I came home and found Ivan's email. I started to cry as soon as I saw the subject line: byeselin.txt.

Dear Sonya, he wrote. I won't try to talk to you anymore. If there are misunderstandings you want to talk about, I'm ready to do it. If there are misunderstandings you don't want to deal with, that's fine, too. He had thought a lot, he said, about whether to keep meeting me. Lately, he was really into existentialism. The existentialists said you couldn't make decisions based on preexisting norms or codes, which were always too general for any given case. Rather, every decision you made created you. The decision (existence) comes first, and creates essence.

Ivan's decision to meet with me had created something that he thought was good. But he had always known it was harder for me. He had always tried to make sure that he didn't force me or pressure me to do anything. He hoped I was still going to Hungary, which was a big enough country for two people not to meet if they didn't want to. You should get over this Vanya, and these wild dreams of atoms, sparks, Rolexes, and everything else, he wrote in conclusion. Let it not create destruction, but growth and life for the future.

I started to walk around the room, dazed with pain. I had no idea what to do with myself. I couldn't imagine how I was going to dispose of my body in space and time, every minute of every day, for the rest of my life. I didn't understand how he was okay with never seeing me again, or why he was acting as if it were my idea, or whether I was supposed to not go to Hungary, or what I was supposed to do there without him. More painful and incomprehensible still, he had, with no warning and for no reason I could see, taken back what he had said about the atom—that it was allowed to come out and play, and be a crazy spark, and lie on his fingernail. He had called me, and now he was sending me into a rock, like my grandfather had sent a stomachache.

It seemed so impossible that for a moment I thought maybe I had imagined that he had said those things before. But I looked up his emails and they were right there, plain as day.

> I think your atom, it will never go back to peace, to cereal or rocks or
> anything like that. Once it has been seduced there is no way back.
>   That seduced atom has energies that seduce people, and these
> rarely get lost.
>   I summon you words, o my stars.
>   Without you there is nothing.

Then I reread what he had written now—that I had to get over the wild and crazy dreams, and abandon destruction, and build life for the future. He meant I had to go away, so *he* could build life for the future. He meant: disappear and become nothing. I couldn't wrap my head around such perfidy. There just seemed to be no reason for it.

I wrote back right away. I wrote terrible things—the worst things I could think of. I called him a movie director. At the end, I copy-pasted the lines he had written to me before, the lines that had moved me so much, and which he had now recanted so mystifyingly, and then I hit Ctrl-S. It was over.

Part Two

JUNE

The day after my nineteenth birthday, my mother drove me to the Pakistan Airlines annex at JFK: a narrow temporary building with dusty windows, shared by Air Poland. The Air Poland logo was a skinny, malnourished-looking birdlike creature. I kept misreading things. ONLY ENTRUST YOUR LUGGAGE TO UNINFORMED PORTERS. I saw Ivan everywhere. A tall angular woman with a briefcase, a worker's chrome ladder. Walking through security was like dying—the way you had to say goodbye to everyone, the way you became just your name on a paper and gave up your money and your watch and your shoes. "I'm so happy you're going to see Paris," my mother said, and I saw tears in her eyes. My mother had never been to Paris, but my grandmother had, as a young girl, and said it was the most beautiful place on Earth.

I was going to spend two weeks there with Svetlana and her high school friends Bill and Robin. The fourth member of their party, Fred, had unexpectedly gotten an internship at Merrill Lynch and Svetlana didn't want to be the third wheel. She said I was the only person who could be asked to fill in at such short notice—I was the only person she knew who did things like that. "You could be my

European traveling companion, like in a novel," she said. "Afterward you can go straight to Hungary." The plan had been for everyone to stay in Svetlana's aunt's apartment, across from the Musée d'Orsay. Fred's father, a currency trader, had booked four economy seats on the cheapest plane across the Atlantic: the first leg of a Pakistan Airlines flight to Islamabad. Svetlana transferred Fred's ticket to my name, and that was the end of it.

The flight was delayed two hours. I had never been unaccompanied in the international terminal before, and wandered around for a while reading my horoscope in magazines and looking in all the shops. Brookstone was selling a "quiet hair dryer" that let you hold a phone conversation while blow-drying your hair, without the other person knowing. Finally, when there didn't seem to be any point in putting it off any longer, I got on the moving walkway.

The gate was in its own glass-enclosed room with another round of security. Waiting at the metal detectors, I looked through the windows and scanned the crowd for Svetlana. I didn't see her. The one I saw was the Ivan look-alike—apparently, every room had one. This time he had a crew cut.

Once I passed through the security check, I saw Svetlana right away, sitting in a bank of orange swiveling chairs with a handsome all-American-looking couple.

"Selin!" she cried, throwing her arms around my neck and kissing my cheek.

"Selin!" mimicked Bill, and hugged and kissed me, too.

"I thought you wouldn't come," Svetlana said. "With you, I never know. We would hear from you weeks later, from Brazil. Bill and Robin kept pointing girls out and saying, 'That must be her'—and it would be some super-normal-looking girl with a ponytail and hiking boots."

. . .

Svetlana and I made our way to the bathroom, passing right behind the Ivan look-alike, who was waiting in some kind of line, talking to a girl with wispy blond hair.

We were so close that I could read the back of his T-shirt. It said HARVARD MATHEMATICS 1995–96, followed by several columns of names. Ivan's name, Ivan, was in the last column.

"Oh—hello," Svetlana said. "Ivan" didn't turn, but the girl did.

"Hey, Svetlana," she said slowly, as if figuring something out.

"Do you know my friend Selin? Selin, this is Emery. She does Russian, too." We shook hands. Emery had a pale face with a round pink spot on each cheek, and very blue eyes.

"Ivan" turned halfway toward us. Except for the crew cut, he really looked a lot like Ivan, even his earlobes. But Ivan had said he was going to Budapest after graduation, and graduation had been several days ago. Several days ago, he had traveled from Boston to Budapest. Therefore, he could not now be on a plane from New York to either Paris or Islamabad.

"We're going to the bathroom," Svetlana said.

"Oh," Emery said in the same pensive voice.

"I'm such a wreck. I can't even tell you," Svetlana told me, as soon as the bathroom door had closed behind us. In the past week since school had ended, Robin, one of Svetlana's oldest friends, had been out of town, and Bill, who was really competitive and with whom Svetlana had always had a sexually tense relationship, long before he and Robin had started dating, had come over every day to play chess with Svetlana's father and tennis with Svetlana. Svetlana stepped into a stall and I heard the bolt slide. Bill had said something really offensive to her, late at night, in a car. She repeated his terrible words to me from inside the stall.

The toilet emitted its death roar. Svetlana washed her hands and took three sheets of paper towel. "Sasha deals with him the best. 'Billy,' she says, 'you must stop at once this autoerotic babble.'" She carefully dried her hands and threw out the towels. "What do you think of Emery? For some reason she leaves a very strong impression on me. She looks exactly how I picture Nadja, André Breton's Nadja. I saw her once walking really slowly down Dunster Street in the pouring rain with no umbrella—gorgeous, completely drenched. Naturally, being me, I had a raincoat *and* an umbrella. I tried to hold the umbrella over her, but she kept stepping away. Her hair and clothes were streaming wet, plastered to her body, with those big blue eyes looking out from her thin face. That's when she told me she was coming to Paris."

When asked about her plans, Emery had simply said, in a contemplative tone, "I'm going to be walking some dogs." Svetlana had asked what kind of dogs. Emery replied, "I don't know—just some *doogs*."

I considered this. "What Russian class is she in?" I asked.

"She just finished 102. Why?"

"That's the class Ivan took," I said. "I kind of think that's him with her in line."

"In line *here*, at the airport? Ivan? But how could he have known you were going to be on this flight?"

"He couldn't. It must just be a coincidence. Or maybe it isn't even him."

"Couldn't he have found out somehow from the ticket office?"

I thought about it. "But the ticket wasn't even in my name until two days ago."

"That's true. It's enough to make you think he has supernatural powers. Why didn't you say anything when we walked past him?"

"I wasn't sure if it was him."

"Don't tell me you forgot what he looks like."

"Well, his hair was too short."

Svetlana shook her head. "I will never understand you. You realize hair can be cut, right? It doesn't fundamentally alter your identity?"

"But what if it isn't him?"

"Well, does it *look* like him? Except for the hair?"

I didn't answer right away. "Everybody looks like him," I said.

Svetlana rolled her eyes. "A seven-foot-tall Hungarian guy who stares at everyone like he's trying to see through their souls, and you think everyone looks like him. Okay, here's the plan. We're going to walk outside. I'm going to talk to Emery, and you're going to say hi to Ivan. If it's not him, all you have to say is, 'Sorry, I thought you were somebody else.' Simple, right?"

The next thing I knew, we were walking up to them. "So, Emery," Svetlana said. "Where in Paris are you going to stay?"

"I'm not sure."

I stood beside Ivan. "Hi," I said.

He didn't look at me. "Happy birthday," he said.

"I didn't recognize you because of your haircut," I said.

His gloom seemed to intensify. "That's why I got the haircut."

I thought that was funny, but he didn't laugh.

"I didn't know you were going to Paris," I said.

"I didn't know *you* were going to Paris," he said.

Then we stood there not saying anything.

"Well, see you later," I said.

"I guess so," he said.

"That wasn't so bad, was it?" asked Svetlana afterward.

"I don't know," I said. "He sounded angry."

"You always think everyone is angry. Come on, don't be morose." She put her arm around my shoulders. "I tried to find out the situation from Emery, but she doesn't know anything. She doesn't know why he's here. They just met by chance in the airport."

"She doesn't even know what dogs she's walking or where she's going to stay," I pointed out. "Why would she know *his* plans?"

"Well, I thought it would cheer you up that at least they're not going to Paris together. I mean—she is really beautiful."

We rejoined Robin and Bill. Bill kept asking questions. "*Who's* this guy? *What's* his name? That's his *name?* Selin *likes* him?" He turned to me. "Why do you look like that? You should be happy. A lot of things can happen in an airplane, at night, thirty thousand feet above the ocean."

Our seats were all in the back of the cabin, but down different aisles. Ivan was sitting in the emergency row next to a man in a suit. Our eyes met. I couldn't keep walking because a man was blocking the aisle trying to stuff a large quilt-wrapped object into the overhead bin. It was visibly clear to everyone, including the man, that the object was larger than the bin, but still the situation went on.

"I think we have to talk," Ivan said.

"I'm in 44K," I said.

Eventually, a flight attendant took the quilted object away from the man. I found my seat and started to read *Madame Bovary.*

"Selin!" I looked up. It was Svetlana, leading a grandfatherly Pakistani by the elbow.

"This gentleman has kindly agreed to switch seats with you," she said.

I didn't want to change seats. But the man was smiling and looked really proud of his good deed. I thanked him and followed Svetlana to the other side of the plane. Bill was on the aisle seat and I had the window, with Svetlana between us. For some reason, Robin was sitting directly ahead of Bill. They couldn't talk to or see each other.

Svetlana, who was afraid of flying, gripped Bill's and my hands. Some flight attendants came out and showed us how we could use our seat cushions to float around on the Atlantic Ocean. The engines started. A muezzin's call sounded and a praying man appeared on the movie screen, kneeling diagonally toward the ocean.

"Why are they showing that?" asked Svetlana.

"So if you die suddenly you won't go to hell," Bill said, incorrectly, raising his armrest. "Here, lean against me."

Svetlana closed her eyes, released my hand, and curled up against Bill. With an escalating, deafening roar, the plane finally lifted off.

Outside the window, the city lights grew tiny. It was exactly midnight. Then there was nothing below us but clouds. The person in front of me reclined his chair until he was lying in my lap. I felt almost tenderly toward him. Time passed. A flight attendant asked if we wanted the American or the Pakistani meal. I asked for the Pakistani meal.

"There isn't any," said the attendant. "Here's an American meal."

I opened the foil lid and looked at the American meal. I couldn't tell what it was. The man in the seat ahead of me started tossing and turning. His pillow fell into my dessert. The pink whipped foam formed meaningful-looking patterns on the white fabric. I saw a bird—that meant travel.

I turned on the light and tried to read *Madame Bovary*. One sentence made a particularly strong impression on me: "Often some prowling nocturnal animal, a hedgehog or a weasel, would rustle through the foliage, and occasionally they heard the sound of a ripe peach dropping from one of the trees along the wall." It reminded me of the video for "Human Behavior," where Björk was chased through the forest by a giant hedgehog.

Around two o'clock, Ivan appeared on the opposite side of the plane, peering at the row numbers. He stopped at 44. He was looking very closely at the grandfatherly Pakistani man in 44K.

I unbuckled my seat belt and stuffed *Madame Bovary* in the seat pocket. The way to the aisle was completely obstructed by the intertwined sleeping forms of Svetlana and Bill. Ivan had turned away from the Pakistani guy and was rubbing the back of his neck.

I waved, but he didn't see me. I flashed the overhead light on and off a few times. Finally, he walked over. "My friend switched my seat," I said. He glanced down at Svetlana. I tried to squeeze by without waking her, but her eyelids flew open and her eyes focused on Ivan.

"What?" she said.

"I'm sorry," I said. "I'm just trying to get out."

She turned her head to face me. "Oh," she said, and drew her knees up to let me pass.

Ivan and I walked around the plane, looking for somewhere to talk. There wasn't anywhere. We stopped outside the toilets, leaning on opposite walls.

"I thought you were home already," I said.

"You forget I had to graduate," he said. "I have a degree now."

I held out my hand. After a moment, he took it. I looked down. Was this really his hand—the hand that he wrote with, the hand he did everything with? How was it possible? Then I worried I had held his hand for too long, and let go.

"What have you been doing since graduation?"

"I had to get to New York," he said. "I rented a car. I almost stopped in New Jersey. I thought, Maybe I'll see what's going on with this place. But I wasn't on good terms with you." He met my eyes.

"I see," I said.

"So I went straight to New York. I played basketball with some Hungarians in Brooklyn. They were really Hungarian, even for Hungarians—they made me feel like an outsider. It was pretty boring. Also I don't like basketball. People always expect me to be good because I'm tall." He glanced at me. "Are you good at basketball?"

"No."

"Me neither."

There was a pause. I asked how long he would be in Paris. He didn't answer. "One day I almost got beat up," he said. "Downtown. I was buying a CD player for my little sister's birthday, and the guy was trying to rip me off. I tried to hit him, over the counter, and then he was going to jump over, but some other guy stopped it."

"When is your sister's birthday?"

"I just missed it," he said. "I really wanted to be there. I miss her birthday, every year."

"But you got the CD player in the end?"

He nodded. "I got one from somewhere else. It's underneath us." He pointed at the floor. "With my copy of the literary magazine."

"Will you be in Paris for long?" I asked.

He seemed not to hear. "Stuff like that can really bring out the sadist in you," he said. "I'm standing there thinking of all the different ways I'll rip out this guy's guts."

I fell silent. Why did he have a sadist in him? And why didn't he want to tell me how long he would be in Paris? I decided to try again. "How long will you be in Paris?" I asked.

"I don't know!" he said. "Three or four days. But aren't you supposed to be really pissed off at me? And I'm supposed to be really hurt—isn't that how it is?"

"What?"

"I'm supposed to be really hurt by your last email. And you're supposed to be really pissed off. You're not supposed to be making *small talk*." I knew "small talk" was a phrase he had learned from me. And I knew he was right—I was supposed to be mad. But I felt so happy to see him. It was impossible to hide how happy I felt, and even if it had been possible, I wouldn't have wanted to.

"I wasn't hurt," he said. "I was like, pfff . . ." He waved at the floor.

When he said that, *I* felt hurt for a moment. "Well, then what's the problem?" I said.

He sighed. "So you're not pissed off?"

"I guess not," I said.

"But you were, earlier."

I nodded.

A flight attendant bumped my shoe with a mop. "The restroom is empty," he said. "This is a waiting area for the restroom."

"Our seats aren't together," said Ivan. "We're standing here so we can talk."

"I ask you to return to your seat," said the attendant, raising his mop.

We walked along the shadowy aisles, among rows of sleeping blue bodies with gaping mouths. We stopped in an alcove in front of an emergency door. Ivan sat on the flat part of the door, where DO NOT SIT HERE was printed in red. I leaned on the wall, where it read DO NOT LEAN. On the movie screen, a tank blew up and a woman in fatigues dove into a ditch.

"Where are you going from Paris?" asked Ivan.

"What do you mean? Budapest."

"I remember that part," he said. "I meant before."

"Nowhere else—just Paris. Where are you going?"

"I think to Lake Geneva, to visit Tomi. He's in Montreux in the summer. His wife is Swiss." Something about how he said "his wife" sounded racy. "I'm already going to hitchhike to Budapest, so why not stop in Geneva? Maybe also in Venice."

I nodded. I had never heard of anyone hitchhiking anywhere as their first-choice mode of transportation. Ivan asked whether I was going to travel around Europe after I left Hungary.

"I'm going to Turkey," I said. I didn't really like to think about after I left.

"Oh, that's good. It's good that you're getting back to Turkey. I'll be in Tokyo then. I finally got my ticket. I really wanted a stopover in

Bangkok, and I finally managed it. I'll be there three days. I'm really happy to get back to Thailand."

I wondered what it was about different places that made him want to go there, or get there, or get back there, and why it was good that I was getting back to Turkey.

"What's Thailand like?" I asked.

"Hm? I didn't hear you."

"Never mind," I said, because I didn't actually care what Thailand was like.

"No, tell me."

"Nothing. I asked what Thailand is like. Dumb question."

"No, it's not dumb. Let me think," he said. "Thailand is really hot. They sell really good food on the street, that you aren't supposed to eat. One day I ate a lot of it anyway."

"What happened?"

"I got really sick."

There was a pause.

"Did you say something?" he asked.

"No."

"Oh. I thought you said something."

"It must have been the plane."

"Hm?"

"It must have been the plane that made a sound, and you thought it was me."

"Oh? You're pessimistic. I would think that by now I can tell you apart from an airplane. Are you comfortable standing like that?"

"No. Are you comfortable sitting like that?"

"No. Let's try that chair." He opened a fold-down chair that was strapped to the wall and sat on the right edge of the seat. I sat on the left edge. On the movie screen, the woman in camouflage was wading through mud. What made her so beautiful? Her cheekbones and throat and waist. Orange light flashed through the forest. The woman was flung against the wall of a trench.

"It's weird to see it without sound," I said.

"It doesn't look like we're missing that much," Ivan said.

A man appeared in the trench, also in fatigues. The woman turned to face him, lips parted. They kissed passionately, then moved apart, and their expressions turned grim. The man said something. The woman nodded tightly.

Our conversation turned to the subject of deafness. Ivan described to me a comedy sketch in which a deaf man invented a vibrating light-up headset to let him know when the telephone was ringing. The sketch ended with the phone ringing and the deaf man saying proudly, "Hello?"

I told him a Turkish joke about two deaf fishermen. "Are you going fishing?" the first fisherman asked. The second fisherman said, "No, I'm going fishing." Then the first fisherman said, "Oh— I thought you were going fishing."

Ivan told me a joke about a scientist who had a grant to study fleas. He would shout, "Jump," and measure how far the flea jumped. After a while it got boring because the flea always jumped the same distance, so he pulled off the flea's legs, one by one. The distance got shorter and shorter, until finally he had pulled off all six legs and the flea didn't jump at all. "If you remove six legs," the scientist concluded, "the flea cannot hear." I thought it was really funny.

"So, tell me about it," Ivan said.

"About what?"

"Tell me what you were angry about. Before, I mean—when you were angry."

I tried to think back to what I had been angry about—to what the first thing had been. "When we ran into your girlfriend, and you didn't call me afterward, it made me think that you did it on purpose—like you brought me there, and staged this meeting, to give me a message."

He nodded. "I thought about that a lot," he said. "Whether I did it on purpose."

"Really?"

"Yeah. My girlfriend and I had a fight when I went back. I was still wet, I didn't have time to take a shower. She asked where I'd been. I explained I was swimming. I had to tell her about you, how we had been meeting. I think she got jealous. She said, 'So what's going on, is she in love with you?' And I said, 'I think she used to be.' She said, 'Does she want anything from you?' I said, 'I don't think so, not anymore.'" He paused. "And then she asked me, 'Do *you* want anything from *her?*' I said, 'No, of course not!'"

Even before I had understood the words, I felt a blow. "I see."

He glanced at me. "I *had* to say no."

I nodded. "And then?"

"And then? And then she got really nasty. I said, 'You're being really nasty.' And then she stopped. And, well, if you see her at the airport, don't think I did it on purpose—because she's coming to meet me."

I wondered if I should ask him questions about his girlfriend. At that moment there was nothing I wanted to know. But I remembered how curious I had felt when I had looked for her name in the directory, and thought I should probably shore up some knowledge against the future time when I might feel like that again. "Did your girlfriend just graduate, too? Was she a senior?"

"What? No, she's a doctoral student—she just got her MA. You know, it's a coincidence—today is her birthday."

"How old is she?"

"Twenty-six."

"Twenty-*six?*"

"She's a little older than me," he said, sounding proud. "The guy she dated before me was a professor—he was ten years older than her."

"Wow," I said. That professor had been alive for almost twice as long as I had. What had happened to him? Instinctively I glanced around, as if he, too, might be on the plane.

"In the fall I'm going to Berkeley," Ivan continued, "and my girlfriend is staying at Harvard. So I don't know what's going to happen." I felt him looking at me. "I thought a lot about whether I was doing something wrong with you. I wanted to give you a chance to stop this whole thing, if you wanted. I guess you thought that was—what word did you say in your email? 'Presumptuous.'"

"For you to assume I'm so heartbroken," I said. "It *is* presumptuous."

"Yeah, I get it." He sighed. "My friend Imre said I was behaving really badly toward you. He said I was—what was it, it was a funny expression. *Leading you on.* He said I was *leading you on.*"

It felt like being hit again, this time in the stomach. Ivan was looking at me. With a sinking feeling, I realized he expected me to say something.

"And you, what do you think?" I said. "Do you think you're leading me on?"

"Well, I tried to explain to Imre that it's not like that, but he was really dismissive. He said I was starting to sound banal, and like a real asshole."

"But that doesn't matter, what your friend thinks. What do *you* think?"

"Well, obviously I hope I'm not being an asshole toward you. But I did worry that I'm leading you on, because of what you wrote to me when I was in California. When you wrote that letter to me—it was nice for me, I really liked it. I'm worried it's just good for my ego."

Ivan, Ivan. He got up in the morning, put on some clothes he got from somewhere, drank his orange juice, and went out into the world of chalkboards and motorcycles. He could be really arrogant some-

times. His jeans were always too short, and he thought clowns had
something complicated to teach us about human fallibility. And still
no waking moment went by that I didn't think of him—he was in the
background of everything I thought. My own perceptions were no
longer enough to constitute the physical world for me. Every sound,
every syllable that reached me, I wanted to filter through his consciousness. At a word from him I would have followed him anywhere,
right off the so-called Prudential Tower. A thousand glowing seat
belts appeared in the dark, and the floor began to shake.

A voice said we were passing through some turbulence and should
return to our seats, but nobody came to chase us out of the fold-down
chair. At first I liked the shaking, but as it grew more violent, I began
to feel smaller and smaller and loose in this world, like a ball in a lottery machine. I tried to hold on to a seat back, but I couldn't reach and
was sure I was going to fall.

I didn't fall. The plane tilted in the opposite direction, and then it
was Ivan who had to scramble to keep his balance, and then the plane
righted itself.

On the movie screen, the couple in camouflage leaped into a helicopter, and credits rolled over the helicopter. Then there was another
prayer call, and then the map came back on the screen. We were flying over Iceland. It was five in the morning, Boston time.

"Our usual hour," Ivan observed. "Aren't you sleepy?"

"No."

"How could I forget? You're never sleepy."

We sat for a minute in silence.

"I'm sorry," he said, "but I think I'm pretty useless."

"Useless?"

"I just think we should try to get some sleep. Even you."

Bill and Svetlana formed a continuous hulking mass, deaf as coral.
A cone of light hung over my empty seat.

Ivan cleared his throat. "You can get back in there," he said.

I held the back of Bill's seat, climbed onto his armrest, and stepped across his lap to Svetlana's armrest. In the process, I bumped Bill in the face with the seat of my jeans.

"Whatsthat!" he exclaimed.

"Sorry, sorry," I said. "Go back to sleep."

Svetlana opened one eye. "Bill woke up with your butt in his face!" She sighed. "That's so funny."

It was a beautiful morning in the sparkling, futuristic airport. I stood next to Ivan at the baggage carousel.

"Bonjour," he said.

"Hi," I said.

We stood watching the luggage pass us by like barrels in the river of time.

"I see my bag," he said. He didn't move. I wondered which bag was his. I tried to picture him carrying each of them. The one he claimed was a red internal-frame backpack, and then an Aiwa CD player in its box. He slung the backpack over his shoulder and tucked the box under his arm. "So," he said. "I'll see you in Budapest."

"So long," I said.

He turned and walked into the revolving doors. When the compartment reappeared, it was empty.

Seeing my own suitcase, I dragged it off the carousel and over to Svetlana, Bill, and Robin.

"You've got it really bad," Bill informed me. "Your whole expression changes when you look at him. You look scared to death."

"Don't worry." Robin patted my arm. "We're in the world's most beautiful city. You'll forget all about him."

Svetlana rolled her eyes. "Robin, you're the only person in the world who would have such a ridiculous idea, that beauty makes you forget about love."

Svetlana had four suitcases and we were among the last to exit customs. There was no sign of Ivan or his girlfriend. Emmanuel, a handsome middle-aged friend of Bill's father, picked us up in a mini-van. He didn't speak English. I was the only one who didn't speak French. I could tell that Bill's French wasn't great, and Svetlana's was really good.

Emmanuel left us at his daughter Jeanne's apartment in the Marais. We were going to spend a few days there, while Jeanne was in Brittany with her boyfriend, until Svetlana's aunt Bojana could fly over from Belgrade and let us into her place.

Robin and Bill took Jeanne's bedroom; Svetlana and I shared the futon in the living room. The futon was bright green, with a lemon-yellow quilt and orange cushions.

"I find this apartment very intimidating," Svetlana said. "Jeanne is only twenty but she already has a taste."

"What makes you think that?" Bill said. "The fact that she has a boyfriend and you don't?"

"That's not the point," Svetlana said.

While they were arguing, I lay on the futon and fell asleep. But Svetlana shook my arm and said we had to go out and get some sunlight, to regulate our biological clocks.

"You mean our *internal* clocks," said Bill. "Biological clock is what makes you start thinking about having a baby."

We trudged to the Tuileries park, sat on iron chaises-longues, and stared at the fountain, which was full of ducks. It seemed very remarkable that you could travel halfway around the world and still end up looking at some ducks.

"We have to stay awake," said Svetlana. "We have to think of some kind of narrative."

When we woke up, more than an hour later, Svetlana, Robin, and Bill had all gotten sunburned. My sunglasses had left big pale circles around my eyes.

We walked to Saint-Germain and ate omelets. The powerful watery mustard made you intensely aware of the area behind your nose. We spread it on the baguette they gave you for free, and ate it till tears ran down our faces.

There was no shower at Jeanne's apartment, just a bath. You dumped water on your head out of a metal pot.

Everyone else was asleep by eleven-thirty. I wandered around, looked at Jeanne's bookshelves, stood on the balcony, wondered who Boris Vian was, drank glasses of water, memorized the numbers one through twenty in *Teach Yourself Hungarian*, and started writing a letter to Ralph, who was interning for his congressman. *In Washington, I know, you will just be drinking your after-dinner coffee, and the summer light will continue for perhaps another two hours,* I wrote, in what was meant to be the voice of Oleg Cassini. *Frankly, my sangfroid has deserted me.*

I lay beside Svetlana on the futon and tugged at the free end of the quilt. She was bundled up as tightly as some kind of mollusk. After a while, I gave up and tried to sleep anyway. I couldn't sleep.

The closets contained many articles—liquor bottles, brandy snifters, cases of cigarettes, folding chairs, skis, tennis rackets, and a sewing machine, among others—but none that could be construed in even the broadest sense as a blanket.

I lay back down, tugged harder at the quilt, and eventually secured a section large enough to lie under. But the moment I relaxed my hold, Svetlana rolled away with a reproachful murmur and reabsorbed my gains. I started to feel really depressed. It was like she didn't even know me anymore. I wondered if Ivan was asleep. It was terrible to think that he was in this city, possibly very nearby, but I couldn't see him or talk to him because he didn't love me. I couldn't be with him for one minute, not even for the weird leftover hours that nobody else wanted, like from one to three a.m. on a Wednesday. There it sat on the desk, a few feet over my head, reflecting a streetlamp: the Parisian telephone, one of millions, on which Ivan would not call me.

I tried to think positive thoughts. Only one thought brought me comfort, and it was: *What is man.*

What is man that thou art mindful of him, I thought over and over, until the lump in my throat subsided.

I got up and rummaged in my suitcase—the lump momentarily resurged when I encountered the bag of Blow Pops I had bought, as instructed by Peter, to give as rewards to the Hungarian schoolchildren—until I found sweatpants, socks, a long-sleeved shirt, and a towel. I got dressed, lay down, draped the towel over my legs, and listened to a discount cassette of Brahms's four-handed piano compositions until I fell asleep.

When I woke up, the sun was blazing. Svetlana was gone. I was lying under the bath towel and the quilt. I followed the sound of voices into the kitchen.

"Hey, Selin," said Svetlana. "I tried to wake you up to ask what you wanted, but it was impossible. So I just got you a croissant." It bore no resemblance to any croissant I had ever seen in America. "I don't know if you're aware of it, but you have a very different personality when you're sleeping. In waking life you're Miss Easygoing, but at night you kept stealing the blanket. I pulled it back, and you were really aggressive."

The croissant was crisp and soft and flaky at the same time. Just biting it made you feel cared for.

The Louvre caused Svetlana terrible anxieties, which she was able to control by focusing monomaniacally on one painting per visit. In general we both thought you got more from staring at one picture for twenty minutes than from looking at twenty pictures for a minute each. For nearly half an hour, we stared at a tiny fifteenth-century illumination of a Madonna in a lime-green robe confronting a silver whale, apparently indoors. Svetlana said that she identified with that Madonna more than with any other woman in any other painting. She kept asking me what painting I identified with. I didn't identify with anyone in any paintings.

I finally identified with a painting in the Picasso Museum. Titled *Le Buffet de Vauvenargues*, it showed a gigantic black sideboard scribbled over with doors, drawers, pigeonholes, moldings, and curlicues. Two roughly sketched figures, one big and one small, flanked the sideboard. The sideboard was the thing between them.

Svetlana said I had to take a more proactive view of my personhood. She said it wasn't okay to identify with furniture. Indeed, Sartre had illustrated "bad faith" using the analogy of thinking of oneself as a chair—quite specifically, a chair. Objective claims could be made about a chair, but not about a person, because a person was in constant flux. I said the buffet was also in flux. I said its existence preceded its essence. Of all the museums we saw, I thought the Picasso Museum was the most interesting, because it was all about one person, and because it reminded me of Ivan. At the same time, if you looked at it a certain way it seemed like a monument to destroyed women—their ossified bodies and shattered psyches.

In Versailles we shuffled through room after room filled with gold and mirrors. After a while, the number of gold-encrusted rooms began to seem not just extravagant but actually insane.

We walked to Montmartre. The white dome of Sacré-Cœur, glimmering in the twilight, resembled a giant alien egg. Inside, women were weeping and lighting candles. No men were weeping—only women. Two tables away from us at the outdoor café, a small boy in an orange puffy vest was sobbing with no restraint. A man sat across from the boy, methodically eating an omelet.

At the Pompidou Center we saw an exhibit based on Georges Bataille's concept of "the formless." There was a Turkish film festival in the cinema downstairs. Svetlana and I ran into the screening room just as the lights were going down. The movie was in Turkish with French subtitles, so we could both understand, by different means. The whole action took place in a bar, with only two characters—the bartender and a man with an annoying smile fixed on his face. Sometimes, the man would dream about a woman, who would appear through a mist, dressed in pink. The rest of the time the man just talked to the bartender about God, wine, and love. Periodically, he asked if somebody called Mahmut Bey had arrived yet. The bartender always said no.

Near the end, the bartender asked who Mahmut Bey was. "Mahmut Bey is . . . coldness," said the man, through his annoying smile. "Mahmut Bey is wetness. Mahmut Bey is friendlessness, winelessness."

It was a truly terrible movie. Still, we were glad we had seen it, because of Mahmut Bey. We thought of him often after that.

"The boy who convinced you to go to Hungary, he must be very handsome," Svetlana's aunt Bojana told me. "You can find an excellent coffee in Budapest. I see that you are looking at my tea tray. Do you like it? It's quite a good tray. I will make it a gift to you. But not now—only when you get married."

We had left Jeanne's apartment, and were drinking tea in Bojana's cavernous penthouse. Robin and Bill were staying in the guest suite, while Svetlana and I were in the spare room, which had two futons, a silk carpet, and French windows that gave onto a long stone balcony facing the Musée d'Orsay. Hanging on one wall was a small oil painting of a beige man pushing a wheelbarrow.

"I have put you with the Goncharova," Bojana told us.

I didn't know who Goncharova was. Svetlana told me later that she was a Blue Rider and Pushkin's great-niece. The painting had been a gift from Bojana's husband. I asked what Bojana's husband was like. Svetlana said in a matter-of-fact tone that he spent most of his time in Stockholm with his other family. Bojana visited them every Christmas, bringing vitamins for the children. "She says they all look terribly anemic. They must take after their mother, because Uncle Gunnar is very robust. Well," Svetlana sighed, "it's time for the aunt-niece chat. I'll come get you for dinner."

I lay on one of the futons and flipped through a chess book I had borrowed from Bill in an attempt to make friends. There was a Hedge-hog Defense and a Budapest Gambit. From the chapter on computers I learned that the first chess-playing automaton, known as "the Turk," had been built in the 1760s by a Hungarian, Baron Wolfgang von Kempelen. Outfitted with a turban and mustache, the Turk could roll his eyes, bang his fist, and say, *"Échec."* He checkmated Benjamin Franklin in Paris and Frederick the Great in Prussia. I thought it was funny that the Turk said *échec,* because it sounded just like the Turkish word for donkey. Basically, the Turk had called Benjamin Franklin a donkey in Turkish.

After von Kempelen's death, the Turk was bought by Johann Maelzel, the inventor of Beethoven's ear trumpet. Maelzel sold it to Napoleon's stepson, then bought it back with an IOU, which he hadn't repaid by the time Napoleon's stepson died, so he fled to the United States. America's first chess club, in Philadelphia, was founded in honor of the Turk.

Edgar Allan Poe saw the Turk in Virginia, correctly guessed how it worked, and wrote an anonymous exposé about it in the *Southern Literary Messenger.* The Turk's moves were made by a "diminutive chess master" who hid under the table and followed the game upside down using magnets. According to the 1894 edition of the *Encyclopædia Britannica,* the first operator, the Polish patriot named Worousky, had escaped suspicion because, unbeknownst to the public, his legs were artificial: the real ones had been lost in a campaign.

On tour in Havana in 1837, Maelzel caught yellow fever. He died on the way back to New York, and was buried at sea near Charleston. The Turk was auctioned in Philadelphia for four hundred dollars and donated to the Chinese Museum, where it was destroyed in the fire of 1854.

"What are you reading?" Svetlana asked. I showed her the book. She skimmed the pages about the Turk. "I find this very sinister," she said. "I think you see yourself as an automaton in the hands of Ivan."

"But the Turk outlives everyone."

"Yeah, but then he burns up in that fire. It's like Mephistopheles's invention of Faust. Do you know, my mom thinks Ivan is the devil incarnate?"

"How does your mom know Ivan?"

"I told her on the phone about how he turned up on our flight to Paris. My mother is convinced that he did it on purpose—that he was pursuing you. She said, 'There's no doubt in my mind that he planned it. I can just see that poor Selin in this situation, pursued by the devil incarnate.'"

"That's crazy."

"Of course it's crazy," said Svetlana. "I never said my mother wasn't crazy. If it makes you feel any better, I just told the same story to Bojana, and she just thinks it's a terribly funny coincidence."

I felt a wave of nausea to realize that I had propagated these stories just by telling Svetlana what was going on—just because I had wanted to tell some other person the basic events of my own life.

Svetlana said that I thought of myself as a robot who could act only negatively. She said I had cynical ideas about language. "You think language is an end in itself. You don't believe it stands for anything. No, it's not that you don't believe—it's that you don't care. For you, language itself is a self-sufficient system."

"But it *is* a self-sufficient system."

"Do you see what you're saying? This is how you get yourself involved with the devil incarnate. Ivan sensed this attitude in you. He's cynical in the same way you are only more so, because of math. It's like you said: math is a language that started out so abstract, more abstract than words, and then suddenly it turned out to be the most real, the most physical thing there was. With math they built the atomic bomb. Suddenly this abstract language is leaving third-degree burns on your skin. Now there's this special language that can control everything, and manipulate everything, and if you're the elite who speaks it—*you* can control everything.

"Ivan wanted to try an experiment, a game. It would never have worked with someone different, on someone like me. But you, you're so disconnected from truth, you were so ready to jump into a reality the two of you made up, just through language. Naturally, it made him want to see how far he could go. You went further and further—and then something went wrong. It couldn't continue in the same way. It had to develop into something else—into sex, or something else. But for some reason, it didn't. The experiment didn't work. But by now you're so, so far from all the landmarks. You're just drifting in space."

"Sometimes I fantasize about being an analyst," Svetlana said, "but when I brought it up to my shrink, he said I'd be terrible. He said I'd never let the patient get a word in edgewise. I wonder if I should call my shrink. He's on vacation but he gave me his cell phone number. He said I could call collect. Is that odd? I might do it." She sat up. "Bojana really likes you, by the way. She told me to remind her to give you the silver tray when you get married."

"I wonder what makes her so sure I'll get married."

"Well, if you don't, then you don't get the tray," Svetlana pointed out. "I don't know if Robin gets a tray when she marries Bill. Bojana did admire how physically well-put-together Robin is, with her matching sandals and dress and necklaces. She said that Robin already has a woman's style, and that you have a bright, striking look, like a child's, but that I need to be completely revamped. Starting with my hair."

"Your hair?"

"Yeah, I have to go to her stylist and get a six-hundred-dollar haircut, and then we're going to a boutique where her friend Nika works so she can give me a clothes makeover. Then we have to have tea with Nika, who has a very attractive son. She keeps saying things like, 'Of course you aren't fat, but if you could only lose just five or ten pounds . . .' The fact that I used to be bulimic in high school is just not important to anyone in my family. When my own mother found out, she said, 'Goodness, don't torture yourself—there are pills for this.' And she gave me a bottle of diet pills."

As we were crossing the street, Svetlana pulled Bojana out of the path of a speeding moped.

"Thank you, darling," said Bojana.

"Just think how it would have looked in the papers," Svetlana said. "'Aunt Hit by Moped, Niece Avoids Haircut.'"

The waiter at the bistro seated us in the front window. Bojana put on her reading glasses and ordered a bottle of Merlot. The menu was a five-course prix fixe. Svetlana ordered for herself and Bojana. Robin

ordered for herself and Bill. I found some words that I thought I recognized in each course, and told them to the waiter, who went away.
The Merlot cascaded into our glasses with a throaty gurgling sound.

"Svetlana tells me you will be spending some time in Budapest,"
Bojana said. "It's a marvelous city. I spent a marvelous weekend there
when I was your age."

I told her I would be in Budapest only a couple of days before
heading to a small village to spread American culture.

"A small village?" Bojana set down her glass. "What on Earth do
Hungarians in a small village need with American culture?"

"I think it's related to globalization."

"For a month, you say? Five weeks? No no, darling—it's impossible. Go to Budapest, yes. Sit in a café and drink a really good cup of
coffee. You can find excellent coffee in Budapest. In a village, I can't
say. The coffee may be very bad. Go to your village, if you must, for
one week or ten days. Then hop on a train to Belgrade. You can stay
with me."

I felt touched. "You make it sound so simple."

"Of course it's simple. Buy a ticket and get on a train! Who can
force you to spend five weeks in a Hungarian village? I've never heard
of such a thing."

When our first courses arrived, I discovered that I had ordered a
cantaloupe filled with port. Everyone else had ordered asparagus. I
had no idea how to eat a cantaloupe filled with port. It was a whole
cantaloupe with just the very top cut off, filled to the brim. The patterns on the rind resembled ancient hieroglyphs.

"I have met some very attractive Hungarian men," Bojana said.
"Tall, attentive to women. I'm speaking about Budapest. In the villages, I can't say. They may be tall but I think you might get bored."

I saw I had been given a giant soupspoon. I dipped the edge of the
spoon into the melon, causing the trembling liquid to overflow.

"Selin already has a tall, attentive Hungarian," Svetlana said.

"Oh yes, Don Juan from the airplane! How could I forget? Maybe you will not be bored after all. The boy sounds like he could entertain you."

I said I was easy to entertain. Bojana said it was clear I had never spent five weeks in an Eastern European village.

"You don't know how miserable I was," Svetlana was telling Bojana. "I barely left the house except to go between the apartment and the Sorbonne. I was so petrified of those thin, well-dressed French women. I already feel like a lump without you tormenting me."

"All I want is to give you a gift, a new dress, maybe a haircut, something fun. Why is this torment? Maybe I suggested you lose five or ten pounds. Is that a crime? Me, I should lose *fifteen* pounds."

"You don't understand. When you were my age you were throwing parties for two hundred people, including Tsvetaeva's niece and half the Polish nobility. As you keep telling me."

Svetlana pushed back her chair. After a minute I followed her. The bathroom was up a narrow red spiral staircase. I went through the door marked DAMES.

"Don't be sad," I said. "Think of how you kicked a piece of wood in half."

There was a silence. "Like—a bulldozer!" Svetlana wailed from inside the stall.

The next morning, Svetlana went out with her aunt. It was the first time since the airplane that she and I had been apart for any length of time. I went to a newsstand and bought a map—*un plan,* as though you wanted to build Paris instead of walk in it—and a pack of Gitanes.

I didn't really smoke, I had done it maybe ten times before, mostly with Lakshmi, but the blue cardboard boxes were so beautiful, with the picture of the ghostly woman leaning into a cloud, and something about being alone made me want to mark the time in some way. Lighting a match felt exciting and a little bit dangerous, and when the flame came into contact with the paper, it made a sound like the needle coming down on a record player—like the music was about to start. Cigarettes never made me feel sick. I had grown up around smokers, and anyway I never inhaled too deeply.

I walked around all day. Around five I stopped at a café where I ate a smoked salmon sandwich and read two chapters in *Teach Yourself Hungarian*. I was increasingly struck by the similarities between Hungarian and Turkish—not the actual words, but the grammar. Both languages were agglutinative, meaning that the syntax was conveyed by strings of suffixes that were tacked onto the ends of words. Both had vowel harmony, and neither had grammatical gender. Both used a single word for "he" and "she": *ő* in Hungarian, *o* in Turkish.

At dusk I found myself in the Place de l'Opéra. Everything was lit up: Café Opéra, Métro Opéra, the Opéra itself, hulking cakelike in the middle. Rows of white taxis gleamed in the dark like the Cheshire Cat's grin.

"Excuse me," said an Asian woman, gently touching my arm. "I am looking for this building." She showed me a guidebook written in Japanese, open to a picture of the opera building.

"That's it," I said, pointing.

She thanked me and started taking photographs.

At first I thought it was weird that she hadn't recognized the building when it was standing right in front of her. Then I thought the weird thing was that anyone ever did recognize a giant domed green and gold building from a tiny flat gray picture.

· · ·

All the lights were on in Bojana's kitchen. Mozart's *Requiem* played at low volume on a tinny stereo. Svetlana was sitting with her back to the door. Her hair was layered in a way that brought out all the different shades of blond, like neatly composed tailfeathers. The haircut had taken almost two hours, which she had spent explaining in French to her aunt's stylist that external appearances are meaningless. The stylist had disagreed, maintaining that truth was beauty and beauty truth.

"Have a kumquat." Svetlana slid the bowl toward me. "I've been craving extreme sensations. I wonder if Bojana has any of that mustard."

In the brightly lit refrigerator, black champagne bottles lay on their bellies like black dogs with wire muzzles. Two oblong root vegetables gleamed palely through a plastic drawer. Then Svetlana opened the drawer and we saw that they weren't root vegetables at all, but enormous eggs. This was the kind of mystery we could talk about for hours. Were they goose eggs? Svetlana said the eggs could never have fit inside a goose, let alone come out. She thought they were ostrich eggs. But how had Bojana managed to acquire ostrich eggs during just nineteen hours in Paris?

Svetlana's new dress lay nestled in tissue in a striped shopping bag. It was black and trapezoidal—broad in the shoulders, tapering toward the legs.

"Nika picked it out," she said. "We'd been there for two hours. Bojana kept choosing these clingy little numbers, and then Nika would bring out something big and black, like, '*C'est sexy, mais c'est plus andro-gyne.*'" Svetlana replaced the dress in the bag. "Nika had changed. She was hysterical. In February she went back to Belgrade for the first time since the war, because her mother was sick. She stayed there until her mother died in April, and then came back to Paris like this. At one point she laughed so violently that she dislocated her jaw. You could see it was something that happened to her regularly. She was in a lot of pain, but we couldn't tell at first because her jaw was stuck in a laughing position. Fortunately she knew how to fix it by herself. It made a horrible noise. Bojana says that she needs to develop a more sober outlook."

Bojana had also bought Svetlana a womanly perfume, called Feminité du Bois. It was so woody and musky and strong that one spritz of it gave us both a headache. We opened the windows. It didn't help.

"Hey Svetlana," I said.

"What?" she said.

"'All is syphilis,'" I said, and we dissolved in laughter.

The next day, we all went together to La Villette. It was about to rain. Walking through the gardens, we came upon an orange metal sculpture with a bar on a pivot. Every time the wind gusted, the bar swayed and made a squeaking sound.

"What is that?" Robin asked.

"It's a modern-day sundial," said Bill. He said it worked by the Earth's magnetism.

"Oh, neat! So you can use it now, even when it's cloudy?"

Robin asked a lot of questions about the modern-day sundial. When Bill finally told her he had made it up, they had a huge fight.

The modern-day sundial swung and creaked, drawn by the magnetism of the Earth. Mahmut Bey was pulling it with his long friendless arm.

.   .   .

Leaving Robin and Bill to reconcile, Svetlana and I went to the English bookstore. Svetlana bought the collected works of Saki, and I bought *Dracula* and Flaubert's *Three Tales*. We spent the rest of the day on Bojana's enormous balcony eating cherries and reading.

Svetlana, who was good at reading aloud, read me Saki's story "Esmé." "All hunting stories are the same," it began. Esmé turned out to be a hyena.

One of the Flaubert stories, "The Legend of Saint Julian the Hospitaller," was also a hunting story. Julian was obsessed with hunting, and a stag told him he would kill his own parents. Then he stopped hunting, but the minute he started hunting again, he did kill his own parents.

I really wanted to write a story about hunting and human behavior, and asked Svetlana if I could use Bojana's typewriter. "Of course," she said, as if it were the most natural thing in the world. She set everything up for me on a little table. I had learned touch-typing in grade school on an electric Smith Corona. Comparing those huge Smith Coronas with Bojana's cute Olivetti was like comparing the All-Soviet Bread Factory to a toaster oven. Microsoft Word was for kids, but the typewriter was God, the desk shook with each keystroke.

To practice the AZERTY keyboard, I tried typing out the sentence with the hedgehog from *Madame Bovary*. I kept slipping up.

Often some prozling nocturnal animal; a hedgehog or a zeasel; would rustle through the foliage; and occasionally they heard the sound of a ripe peach dropping from one of the trees along the zall.

On my last day in Paris, Svetlana and I went to the gay pride parade. High above a sea of bobbing heads, gilded people glided by on floats. Soon we got elbowed off the sidewalk into the street, where the crowd was no longer a sea of heads but a solid jostling wall that reminded me of the phrase "a wall hewn out of living rock." The wall hewn from living rock pushed us toward the center of the street. We were right up next to the float, eye level with stiletto heels. The drag queens' feet were enormous, way bigger than my feet. I wondered where they had gotten such large-sized women's shoes.

When I turned, Svetlana was gone. No matter where I looked I saw only men. I remembered Svetlana was wearing a pink cardigan over a white T-shirt. I saw a flash of pink, but it turned out to be a shirtless baby riding on a man's shoulders.

After what felt like years, a small hand grabbed mine. "Selin! I thought I lost you."

"I thought I lost *you*."

Hand in hand, Svetlana and I fought our way back up to the sidewalk. Sailors glided by, distributing condoms with pictures of anchors, followed by ten Jackie Kennedys on a floating stage, and then by a papier-mâché penis the size of a missile launcher. The penis float was playing the Macarena and at "Hey Macarena" it discharged white paper streamers.

Finally, we got to a side street and Svetlana let go of my hand. "I guess there's no point in flaunting gay pride that we don't even have," she said. My hand felt bereft.

We went back to the apartment so I could pack. I felt nervous because Ivan and I had been out of contact for two weeks. I didn't understand the Internet. I didn't understand that it was possible to check university email from a computer outside the university.

"If you're worried, you should just call him," Svetlana said.

"But I'm not worried."

"Yes, you are."

Svetlana and I sat on the edge of Bojana's bed. I held the receiver and read the number from my Van Gogh mini address book, and Svetlana dialed it on the rotary phone.

There was a foreign-sounding ringtone, and then a lady robot spoke rapidly in Hungarian. "Respected something! Something something something," she said. Then she recited some numbers. I understood the numbers. They were Ivan's phone number. Filled with horror, I slammed down the receiver.

"Please tell me you did not just hang up on his mom," Svetlana said.

"I think he gave me a disconnected number. It was a robot."

"What did the robot say?"

"I don't know—she spoke Hungarian. But she said his phone number."

"And then what?"

"Then I hung up."

"You didn't even listen to the whole message?"

"Why should I listen? It's in Hungarian."

"I really wonder sometimes how you manage." Svetlana picked up the phone, redialed the number, and listened. After a minute, she handed me the receiver. "She's speaking English now."

". . . has been changed," the robot said, in a British accent. "The new number is . . ." I wrote the new number in my address book and then hung up and we dialed it.

"Hal-loo?" said a man.

"Hello," I said. "May I speak to Ivan, please?"

"Eh. Just a minute," he said.

"Hello?" said Ivan.

"Hi," I said.

"Where are you?"

"I'm in Paris."

"In Paris, still? But your plane is from Brussels?"

"Yeah, there's a connection in Brussels."

"Aha, okay."

There was a pause.

"Well," I said. "I just wanted to make sure that we're still on."

"You wanted to make sure that we're still . . . what?"

"On."

"Are we still *on?*"

"Right."

"In other words, did I forget you're coming?"

"Well, or if something came up."

There was a pause. "I didn't forget you're coming," he said. "I may forget lots of things, but I didn't forget that."

The flight the next morning was at seven, so I reserved a car for five. I called the car service myself without asking Svetlana. Then, even though I wasn't done packing yet, Svetlana and I went running by the river. It was ten-thirty at night, the sky was pinkish gray. We saw a Ferris wheel all in lights, and it reminded Svetlana of a childhood friend she used to torment. She used to write about it in her journal: *Sanja is coming over in twenty minutes. I wonder how long it will take to make her cry.* And then later: *It took exactly three minutes and forty-three seconds.* "I was conducting a scientific experiment to see how much Sanja could take," she explained.

It was the last time we could run together along the Seine. Svetlana said we could try running along the Danube at the same time, when she was in Belgrade.

Svetlana kept reminding me to finish packing, but then we would think of something we hadn't talked about yet. Soon it was two in the morning. "You should really pack," Svetlana said. "Wake me up before you go."

It took me until four to get everything into the suitcase. I went onto the balcony, lit a cigarette, and looked at the museum, wondering whether it would still be there in a thousand years. When would it not be there anymore? I took a last bath in Bojana's claw-foot tub, put on a new navy-blue button-down dress that my mother had given me, drank a cup of Nescafé, and ate some bread. At ten to five, I patted Svetlana on the shoulder.

Within ten seconds of getting out of bed, Svetlana had noticed a sweatshirt and a book I'd forgotten. "Just think of all the other things you must have left here," she said.

"If you find anything, just throw it out," I said. "Don't carry anything to Italy."

"Don't forget to call me in Belgrade."

She helped me into the elevator with my suitcase and I pulled the accordion gate between us. The elevator started to sink and sink.

Outside, it smelled of early morning. A green street-cleaning truck drove by, spraying water and brushing the sidewalks.

The car, a white Renault, pulled up almost immediately.

"Selin!" someone called from the sky. Svetlana was standing on the balcony in Bojana's kimono. "You forgot your slippers!" She threw my flip-flops, wrapped in a Monoprix bag, over the balcony. They almost hit the head of the driver, who was opening the trunk. Svetlana was still waving from the balcony when the taxi pulled away. "Farewell!" she called in Russian. "Farewell!"

On the plane, a flight attendant came around with newspapers. All the adults were reading them. I took one, too. From the *International Herald Tribune*, I learned that a ninety-five-hundred-pound elephant called Kika had been artificially inseminated in Berlin. The sperm had been taken from two male elephants and there was no way of knowing for certain which was the real father, but zoologists favored Jumbo of Cleveland. Jumbo's sperm had been flown to Berlin in a tiny cooler that was "hand-checked" at airport security, because X-rays would have killed the sperm. So, that's what newspapers were about.

The crossword puzzle was called "Zooropa." "Asiatic mammal visits the Bois de Boulogne?" *But that's me.* I felt a hand on my shoulder, and looked up to see a man with eyeglasses tied to his head with pink string. "If you need any help with that, ask me," he said. "I just finished it."

It can be really exasperating to look back at your past. *What's the matter with you?* I want to ask her, my younger self, shaking her shoulder. If I did that, she would probably cry. Maybe I would cry, too. It would be like one of those Marguerite Duras books I tried to read in Svetlana's aunt's apartment.

Elle pleure.

Il pleure.

Ils pleurent, tous les deux.

. . .

I spent most of the Brussels stopover in the duty-free store, liquidating my last French francs. I thought about buying a gift for Ivan, but what? They were giving out free samples of Campari. I tried one. I couldn't understand why anyone would want to drink something that tasted like that. For a while, the thought of buying Ivan a necktie was incredibly funny to me. I looked at the ties, trying to tell which was the most tasteful.

At the gate, I sat in front of the windows and tried to read Flaubert's story "Hérodias." I couldn't get past the first sentence: "The citadel of Machaerus stood to the east of the Dead Sea, on a cone-shaped basalt peak." I read it again and again, but it didn't seem to mean anything. Outside the window, porters were tossing suitcases like bales of hay. I knew I should have been thinking of things to say to Ivan. But where were the things supposed to come from—from *outside* my head?

Almost all the passengers on the Budapest flight were men in suits, except for a Hungarian-speaking mother and daughter with matching dour mouths, and a guy with a guitar case who seemed to be asleep standing up, and who had a scruffy, brooding expression that was somehow familiar. I saw him again on the plane as I was looking for my row. He was seated now, but still asleep.

Minutes after takeoff we were already crossing the German border. On the video map the white airplane was simultaneously in Belgium, Holland, and Germany, the first-class cabin nosing toward Cologne, while economy lingered in Liège and one wing grazed Heerlen. Europe was so small. It seemed weird that people took it so seriously.

I took out *Teach Yourself Hungarian,* read a text about someone called Auntie Mariska, and memorized the phrases "My head hurts," "It hurts a lot," and "It hurts terribly." The text was followed by true-false questions, which Hungarians called *igaz-nem* questions. It was true that Auntie Mariska had rheumatism, that she considered Budapest to be beautiful but noisy, and that she preferred cognac to winter salami.

"Hey," said an American voice. I looked up. It was the brooding narcoleptic. "Aren't you from Peter's program?" I recognized him then, from the orientation. His name was Owen. He asked how I was getting to Peter's apartment.

"A friend is meeting me," I said.

"A friend from Peter's program?"

"Not really."

"I just feel like Peter isn't going to show at the airport. He said he might, but I don't have a good feeling."

"Yeah," I said, nodding.

"Would you be interested in splitting a taxi?" asked Owen.

"I think I'm going with my friend," I said. There was a silence. "Maybe he can give you a ride, too," I said, because there didn't seem to be any other option. The captain announced our descent to the Budapest area. Owen went back to his seat. I didn't see him again until the line to passport control. It turned out that Owen also studied Russian, and had spent a year teaching English in Siberia. I asked what it had been like. He said it had been cold.

"I don't see Peter," Owen said, coming out of the turnstile behind me. But Ivan was there, reading a paperback novel. The book looked so small in his hands, almost unstable, like it might crumble to dust. He had a tan and looked at once different from my memory and unmistakably himself. I was so happy that the first thing I said to him instead of hello was "Thank you."

"What are you reading?" I asked, patting his arm. He looked up and smiled. He was reading *The Joke* by Kundera. "I got you a book, too," he said. "It's in the car."

"This is Owen," I said. "He's in Peter's program."

"Ivan," said Ivan. The two of them clapped hands in a masculine, almost angry way.

Ivan took my shoulder bag and Owen's internal-frame backpack and strode ahead of us, pulling my suitcase along on its wheels. His car, a gray Opel, was parked on a windswept roof. Owen and the guitar went in the back. Ivan presented me with a tiny book called *Just Enough HUNGARIAN*. The cover illustration showed three women or dolls, with long skirts and no feet, balancing beakers of red wine on their heads. Ivan started the car and backed out of the space, his arm across the back of my seat.

I leafed through the phrase book. If a Martian read it, the Martian would probably decide to avoid Hungary.

"I'd like something for (snake bites, dog bites, burns, sore gums, bee stings). I'd like some (antiseptic, gauze, bandages, inhalant). It's a (sharp pain, dull ache, nagging pain). I feel (sick, dizzy, weak, fever-ish). I have (a heart condition, rheumatism, hemorrhoids). It hurts. It hurts a lot. The pain occurs (every day, every hour, every half hour, every quarter of an hour). It hurts all the time. I'm ill. My child is ill. It's urgent. It's serious.

"The toilet is blocked. The gas is leaking. The boiler is not work-ing. I have a toothache. I have broken my dentures. I have lost (my contact lenses, a filling, my bag, my car keys, my car, everything). Someone has stolen (my car, my passport, my money, my tickets, my wallet, everything). I've had an accident. I've run out of gas. My car has broken down. My car won't start. My car is (one kilometer away, three kilometers away). I have (a puncture, a broken windscreen). I think the problem is here.

"Don't hang up. There's a delay. I'm sorry I'm late. I don't under-stand you. I think this is wrong. No, not that. That's enough, thank you. I won't take it, thank you. Please stop."

"Oh, thanks!" I remembered to say.

"I hope it's useful," Ivan said. "I looked at a lot of books and this was the best one. It doesn't tell you a lot of useless grammar and the pronunciation guide is really good."

I looked at the pronunciation guide. "Meg-kairem, hodj vaagh-yoh le aw feyait aish aw for-kaat," it said.

"May I take a look?" asked Owen. I passed the book back to him. "This is great," he said. "Really useful. I have to get myself one of these."

Ivan told Owen where he could find such a book. His right thigh swayed in the space between our seats. He was too tall for the car. Was it only to me that he seemed so much more present than other people, or was it an objective fact? He was wearing shorts now, and evidently had been for a while, because his legs were the same even tan as his arms.

At the highway entrance ramp, my left knee and his right leg came into contact. I shifted my knees to face the door. Ivan glanced at me, then back at the road.

"I'm sorry it's such shitty weather," he said. "I wanted there to be decent weather when I show you my city."

"I think your city looks nice," I said. Ivan laughed. I noticed then that the sky was almost black and we were passing through a wasteland of warehouses and factories.

"My uncle designed that factory," Ivan said.

"Which one?"

"The largest and ugliest one."

Ivan asked Owen questions about his life. A doctoral student in history, Owen was writing a dissertation with "hegemonic" in the title, about the Ukraine. He said we had to start calling it just "Ukraine," without the definite article, because in Russian "Ukraine" meant "borderland," and to call a whole country "The Borderland" was insulting. Apparently if you called it simply "Borderland," people would think it was a proper name, semantically unrelated to its other instances.

Ivan pointed out a blue-gray car that was being pursued noisily by a blue car-sized cloud of smoke: this, he said, was a Trabant, powered by the same motor as a chain saw, manufactured in East Germany out of cardboard.

"Well, not cardboard," Ivan conceded a moment later, though nobody had challenged him. "But the body is made of plastic."

"Doesn't it melt?"

"No, and that's the problem. You can't even burn it. Well, you can burn it, but the fumes are toxic. So it was indestructible, until . . ." He started to laugh. "Until the West Germans developed a bacterium to eat it!"

. . .

We walked along an open-air passageway in a suburban apartment building. The sun came out, and it suddenly got really hot. Then the sun went back behind the clouds. "I think this is where Peter's grandmother lives," Ivan said, stopping in front of one of the doors and ringing the bell. An old man opened the door. He and Ivan talked in Hungarian. Ivan knew so many words that he never used with me! I was used to seeing people have to decipher what he was saying, but the old man laughed immediately and shot back some remark.

"It's number eleven," Ivan told us, after the man had gone back inside.

We rang the bell at apartment eleven. The door opened. There was Peter. We followed him to a dim living room with drawn velvet curtains, a grand piano, houseplants. There were two women there: Cheryl, one of the other English teachers whom I remembered from orientation, and a Hungarian woman about Peter's age.

We all sat, Owen and I on an overstuffed sofa, Peter and Ivan in facing armchairs, and the Hungarian woman, Andrea, on a wooden chair with a lot of angles. Cheryl sat on the carpet under the piano.

"Hey, you—are you sure you wouldn't prefer a chair?" Peter asked. Cheryl shook her head. "I have my bag here," she said softly.

Andrea had just moved back to Budapest and was giving English lessons. Peter's grandmother was out playing canasta. Daniel, another teacher in the program, had a Hungarian mother, but didn't speak Hungarian.

"Why doesn't he speak Hungarian?" asked Ivan.

"I suppose it's because there's nobody for him to speak Hungarian with in Vermont," said Peter.

"He could speak with his mother," Ivan said. I felt implicated when he said that, because I usually talked to my mother in English. This now seemed childish—like everything American.

"How is *Eunice?*" asked Peter, who had a way of fiercely enunciating people's names, as if correcting a mispronunciation.

"She's fine," Ivan said, sounding both proud and rueful. "She's the same."

"Did she stay at all in Budapest?"

"No, we met in Paris and hitchhiked for a while in Italy and Switzerland, and then she went home. She's spending the summer in Cambridge, studying with Vogel."

"The 'stern old tyrant'?"

"They seem to get along."

"Oh, they get along, do they? Well, I'm sure she's learning a lot."

Ivan frowned. "I don't know how long she will keep hiding like this, before she can become a scholar. She's always hiding behind these obstacles, behind Harvard."

"She *likes* Harvard."

"She likes it, she likes it. She never wants to leave. She already knows classical Chinese, Korean, and Japanese, but still she found another reason to put off starting her own work."

"Classical Chinese is very different from modern Chinese, no?"

"Completely different."

"But her Japanese should come in handy."

"Why do you say that?"

"She'll already know some of the Chinese characters."

"Kanji are a small part of Japanese," said Ivan. "The whole grammar is with katakana."

"Yes, I know they have a phonetic alphabet for foreign words, but the roots are basically Chinese characters."

"No, there are *two* phonetic alphabets. One is just for foreign words."

As they talked, Ivan sounded grouchier and grouchier, while Peter smiled more and more blandly. The doorbell rang. Two boys came in: Frank, whom I remembered from orientation, and Gábor, a person unknown to me, who had dense eyebrows and was carrying a plastic bag full of shoes. "I'm trying to sell some shoes," Gábor snapped.

"Well, let's put those by the door for now," Peter said.

Ivan and Gábor nodded at each other—they were already acquainted. "How about you, *Frank?*" said Peter. "Do you know *Ivan?*"

Frank and Ivan had been in a Dostoevsky class together. They
started criticizing the professor—the same one who taught the class
I'd taken on the nineteenth-century novel. Gábor sat next to me,
stared into my face, and made a sneezelike, four-syllable utterance. I
wondered for a moment if it was about the shoes. But when he said it
again, I realized it was "Hi, how are you?" in Hungarian.

"Good, thanks," I said.

"Gábor! Don't overwhelm my teachers!" said Peter.

"They have to learn sooner or later," Gábor said. "To *survive.*"

When the other teachers had arrived, we all headed to the hostel
where we would be staying. Peter and the others took the tram, while
I, and the luggage, went with Ivan in his car. The river came into view
with its array of bridges, and the Gothic façade of the parliament rose
up from the shore, looking as intricate and organic as a coral formation, or something that had been elaborately eaten by termites. A
bronze woman seemed to hover over the distant treetops, holding a
leaf over her head: a monument, Ivan said, to the Soviet "liberators."

The hostel was a dormitory during the school year. In the gloomy
lobby, an old man sat in a booth with a lamp. He lugged a logbook
from under the counter. Ivan leaned over and pointed at one of the
pages. The man said something gruff. Ivan replied in a charming
voice. It didn't work—the old man shut the book and folded his arms.

"He won't give us the room keys until Peter comes," Ivan told me.

Together we carried all the bags from the car up the half flight of
stairs that led to the elevator, in a dark hallway near a cafeteria. It
smelled of life—of some people's whole life. Ivan leaned against the
wall. I sat on my suitcase. Ivan looked at his watch. "I wonder what's

taking them so long," he said. "I'm supposed to meet my high school friends on the Danube."

"Oh," I said.

"They're having a barbecue, with a bonfire. They grow cherries there, and plums. One of my friends, his girlfriend speaks Russian. At least, she supposedly studies Russian literature, so she should speak Russian. We can find out. And all of them at least sort of speak English. My friend Imre will be there, from Harvard, so of course he speaks English just like I do."

"Cool," I said, mystified by why he was telling me these things. I was really surprised when he asked if I wanted to come. "Sure," I said.

"You *do?*" he said.

"Only if it wouldn't be inconvenient."

"No, don't be crazy. I'm really happy."

Ivan said we might as well leave the bags there and go: the others couldn't be lost because Peter was with them. I asked if I should leave my suitcase with the others.

"Somehow I don't think the others will be so happy about carrying your suitcase upstairs," Ivan said. "I'll take it back to the car."

Outside, the sun had reappeared. The air was hot, bright, and motionless.

"So," Ivan said as we drove out of the city. "How was Paris?"

"It was okay," I said. "Parts of it were kind of tense." I explained how I had been supposed to keep Svetlana from feeling like a third wheel with Bill and Robin, which Bill hadn't always seemed to appreciate.

"Bill is the one she was with on the airplane? I thought he was her boyfriend, the way they were asleep."

"No, he's Robin's boyfriend."

"And where was she?"

"She was in the row ahead."

"She was on the plane, also?"

"Yeah, in the next row."

Ivan frowned. "Was this Bill kind of an ass?" he said.

I felt glad when he said that, because it surely meant that Ivan wasn't like Bill, that he wasn't behaving with me as Bill did with Svetlana. "We didn't really get along," I said. "Then Svetlana's aunt came and started saying how when she was our age she was throwing parties for Marina Tsvetaeva's doctor's niece. Then she made Svetlana get a six-hundred-dollar haircut and a two-thousand-dollar dress. So Svetlana was having anxieties about femininity and dresses."

"Uh-huh. Were you also having anxieties about femininity and dresses?"

I flushed and became unable to speak. He waited awhile, then gave up. "So tell me about Svetlana," he said. "I suppose she's incredibly smart."

"Yeah," I said. "She thinks really differently from me. She never sees anything as an isolated event—she always puts it into a framework. Anything you do is a symptom of your whole personality and a result of the history of Western civilization, or a metaphor for Western civilization, or something related to Western civilization. Whereas, to me, everything seems so much like an individual case, and I have a hard time thinking about Western civilization. Sometimes I'm really impressed by how she makes all the parts fit together. But other times it doesn't seem true."

Ivan nodded, as if he knew just what I meant. "My best friend in high school, Dávid, he's like that," he said.

I tried to think of something to ask him about Dávid, to prolong the feeling that we were actually talking to each other. But I couldn't think of enough questions, and the moment quickly passed. Outside the window was a lot of white light, and some billboards, one with a picture of a giant Magnum bar, and another, a Benetton ad, that showed a gaunt blond woman and a gorgeous African man wrapped in a blanket together. I couldn't imagine what their lives were like.

"What was your favorite part of Paris?" asked Ivan.

I thought over what I had and hadn't liked in Paris. I said I had liked going running by the river with Svetlana. "We went almost every night," I said.

"You went running while you were in Paris? That was your favorite thing?"

I nodded. "I liked to see the lights."

"Hmm. Okay."

"What was your favorite thing in Paris?"

"Montmartre," he said immediately. "It seemed like the most intense part of the city. Did you like Montmartre?"

"I liked it. But, I don't know. We went to Sacré-Coeur at night, and I got spooked."

"What was spooky?"

"I guess the crypt . . ." I was thinking about the boy we had seen crying.

"The sacred heart? You were spooked by the sacred heart?"

"I guess I was spooked by the sacred heart."

Some distance outside the city, the engine stopped running right in the middle of the road. Ivan pulled over to the shoulder and the car dipped into a sandy ditch.

"This happens a lot," he said. "I have to get some water. Do you think the Chinese restaurant has water?"

He was looking at a red building with a pagodalike roof. Yellow brushstroke letters on a red sign spelled out CHINESE RESTAURANT in Hungarian.

"I think even in China they drink water," I said. I had been hoping that this would sound funny, but it didn't.

"What?" said Ivan.

"Never mind," I said.

"No, tell me."

"Nothing."

"But what did you say?"

"I think the Chinese restaurant will have water," I said.

"Uh-huh," Ivan said. "We'll see."

Taking a jug from the trunk, he crossed the street, which shimmered in the heat. Just ahead of us was a square with a commuter rail station, a newspaper stand, pay phones, and a yellow abstract statue, the kind Svetlana and I now called a modern-day sundial. The sun glared off the windows of the Chinese restaurant, but inside you could make out red vinyl booths and bottles of soy sauce like tiny women, one on each table. Ivan disappeared into the building and reappeared in the window. He talked for a while to a Chinese woman, who eventually took the jug from him, went to the back of the restaurant, then returned, now carrying the jug with both hands.

"They had water," Ivan said, popping the hood. "At first I thought she didn't want to give it to me, but it turned out she didn't know Hungarian. She knew German, though, for some reason." There was something tolerant and amused about how he said "she."

He unscrewed something and poured in the water. Steam hissed angrily. He got back in the car and turned the key. The engine growled three times, then started running. But when Ivan tried to pull back up onto the road, there was an awful impotent enraged sound, and the car didn't move—it was stuck in the sand. The wheels were turning and turning.

"Should I get out?" I said, getting out. I felt sure that my weight was holding down the car. But still the wheels spun with no resistance. Ivan shifted the car to neutral and got out to push it.

"I can push, too," I said.

"It's more helpful if you go back in the car and steer."

I sat in the driver's seat and reflexively put on the seat belt. Then I took it off again, blushing. I put my right arm on the passenger seat and looked out the back windshield. Ivan stepped back and threw his weight against the rear bumper. The car rocked forward. Ivan braced his arms against the trunk. His muscles stood out, sweat formed a triangle on his shirt, and the car pitched to and fro, until finally with a scraping noise the tires engaged. I steered toward the road. The car had manual steering, like my mother's old Volkswagen. In the rearview mirror I saw Ivan half running behind the car, and I felt despair and envy. Of course he couldn't love me, not when I lived through so many layers, when I was spooked by Montmartre, and wore a seat belt in order to steer a car out of a ditch.

The car lurched onto the asphalt and I straightened the wheel. Ivan stood up straight, so his head disappeared from the mirror.

I considered climbing over the gearshift box to the passenger seat, but instead got out of the car and walked around. Ivan sat in the driver's seat, rubbed his oil-streaked hands, and looked around, maybe for a napkin. I opened my bag and took out one of the alcohol swabs my mother had given me from the hospital. Ivan's frown intensified.

"Wow," he said darkly. "Thanks."

I registered this information with an inward sigh: so, you weren't supposed to carry around alcohol swabs.

Ivan stuffed the wrapper and the blackened tissue into the ashtray, started the car, turned on the blinkers. "I was watching you steer," he said. "I could tell you drive really well. You probably drive a lot."

"I've had a license for almost two years," I said.

"There must be a lot of other things you do really well that I don't know about," he said. I didn't say anything.

. . . .

We parked in an unpaved lot in front of a grocery store. "It's a barbecue, so we'd better bring something," Ivan said. The word "we" gave me a sinking feeling, as if I had already done something wrong—like I was already freeloading. I started to get out of the car. "You can wait here if you like," Ivan said. I watched him go into the store, and turned over in my mind why he had said that. Why would I *want* to wait in the car? I got out, but couldn't make up my mind to go into the store. I saw a phone booth and remembered I'd promised to call my mother from Budapest. I went in and tried to dial AT&T, but you needed a coin deposit.

I got back in the car, sitting sideways with the door open. *Just Enough HUNGARIAN* was on the dashboard. I looked at the chapter about food shopping, at some of the phrases Ivan might have been using at that moment. The "butcher" vocabulary included a drawing of a cow divided into thirteen numbered sectors. How remarkable that you were supposed to be able to name thirteen cuts of beef, after you had been bitten by a snake and your car was stolen.

"Did you learn anything useful?" Ivan had returned with a heavy-looking plastic bag.

"Tenderloin," I said in Hungarian, showing him the book.

"Hm?" He looked at the picture. "Ah, you could work in a meat-packing factory." One of his friends was dating a Slovenian girl who didn't speak any Hungarian, who had moved to Hungary just to be with him, and had gotten a job in a meat-packing factory. Ivan had mentioned her more than once. In Slovenia she had been an engineering student.

We were walking through a swamp, among ferns and skimpy trees. Ivan was eating coil-shaped cookies from a plastic box.

"Are you sure you wouldn't like some cookies?" he said.

"No, thanks," I said.

A stray dog showed up. Its shaggy and vigorous tail reminded me of the palm frond of an Egyptian slave in a movie, fast-forwarded.

"This looks like a pretty fun dog," said Ivan. He held the cookie box at arm's length over the dog's head. The dog danced on its hind legs and cried.

"You don't like to tease the dog," Ivan observed, looking at me. He tossed the dog a cookie. The dog snapped it up. Ivan was trying to get something out of his pocket. "Could you hold this for a second?" he asked, handing me the cookie box. The minute I accepted it, the fun dog jumped up on me, scrabbling with its paws on my dress.

I held the box farther from my body and threw one of the cookies a few feet away. The dog ran off to get it.

"Ah!" Ivan exclaimed with chagrin. At first I thought he was upset I had wasted another cookie on the dog. Then I looked down and realized that my dress was covered with mud. "I'm sorry," he said.

"It's okay," I said. "It's washable."

Ivan frowned at the ground, then looked up. "You know, I didn't do that on purpose."

"Sorry?"

"I didn't give you the cookies to hold on purpose."

The sense of hurt took my breath away. It would never have occurred to me that he had done it on purpose.

"You'd better take it off," he said. "The dress."

"Take it *off*?"

"I'll wash it for you at my house. They might not have washing machines in the villages. I'll bring it to you tomorrow."

"That's really not necessary."

"It's the least I should do. Anyway, your stuff is in my car, you can change your clothes."

We had already turned back toward the car. The dog followed. Ivan ate the last cookies, stuffed the box in the plastic bag, and pretended to kick the dog. The dog ran away.

Ivan opened the trunk, walked around the car, and stood with his back to me, leaning against the hood. I opened my suitcase. All my clothes were there, where I had put them in Paris. I stepped out of my sandals and pulled on a pair of jeans under the dress. Then I took out a T-shirt. As fast as I could, I took off the dress and pulled on the shirt.

"Are you decent?" asked Ivan.

"I don't know," I said.

Ivan handed me a plastic bag, for the dirty dress. I would rather have thrown it in the river, but I wadded it up and put it in the bag. "I'll give it back to you tomorrow," he said. We walked back through the swamp and came out on the edge of a damp beach, where a group of boys and girls were playing volleyball. Ivan called something. The players waved and one of them came over. Wiry and cherubic, with bright blue eyes, he wore white shorts and a stained white shirt.

"Imre, have you met Selin?" Ivan asked.

"No," said Imre, looking at me with his bright blue eyes. "But I think I know all about her."

Imre said something to Ivan in Hungarian, and Ivan said something back.

"So," Imre said to me. "You came to visit."

"Right," I said.

"How long are you staying?"

"Five weeks."

"Five *weeks?*"

"Not in Budapest. It's a program, to teach English in villages."

"You mean you're in *Peter's* program? Have you ever been to a Hungarian village?"

"No."

"There will be a lot of sheep. Do you like sheep?"

I shrugged. "Sheep are okay."

"What I should have asked is, do you like shepherds? That's the

goal of the program, to teach English to shepherds. Do you like shepherds? Have you ever taught English to shepherds? Have you?" he
demanded when I didn't answer. "Have you ever taught English to
shepherds?"

"There is a first time for everything," I said. A girl with curly black
hair called something to Imre, who rejoined the game.

"Do you like volleyball?" Ivan asked.

"No," I said. "But you can play, I have a book."

"Nah, I don't really like volleyball, either." Ivan sat on the ground,
placing beside him the long-sleeved shirt he had been carrying. I
sat next to him, automatically picking up the shirt. The ground was
damp. I realized that I had probably been supposed to sit *on* the shirt.
It was a soft wine-colored shirt—I remembered it from school. I held
it in my hands and we watched the volleyball game. Imre dove on
the sand, but the ball flew off in the wrong direction, nearly into
the water.

"What the hell is he doing?" said Ivan.

"I don't know," I said.

He laughed. "Hey, do you want to run along this river?"

"What?"

"We could run along this river. Like you did on the Seine."

"Oh. No, that's okay."

"Why don't we just go for a walk then?"

We stood up. I handed him back his shirt, then regretted it. Why
hadn't I held on to it a little longer?

We walked some distance to a pier. Ivan told me about his high
school friend who explored Neolithic caves and collected rocks, only
one day it turned out he had collected some radioactive rocks, and his
parents made him throw them out. Another friend liked scuba diving
and visited a Viking shipwreck in Finland. The day before the under-
water archaeologists did their inventory, he dove down and put a
statue of some Hungarian gymnast inside the ship, and it was listed in

the inventory. Then there was a story involving a taxidermy closet at
their school.

Feeling that I had to say something, I told him about the time my
biology teacher had woken me up by throwing a dead sea lamprey at
my head.

"A what?"

"A sea lamprey."

"What's that?"

"Sort of an eel. They swim upstream, like salmon."

"Oh," he said.

That seemed to do it for zoology.

"Everyone says Paris is so expensive," Ivan said. "I didn't think it
was so expensive. Did you?"

"I guess not."

"The wine is cheap, bread is cheap. Cheese is cheap."

"Bread is cheap," I agreed. I hadn't bought wine or cheese. "Once,
there was a sale on kumquats."

"Speaking of cheese: one day we fell asleep on a bench and somebody stole our camera case . . ." Ivan started to cough.

"Oh no," I said.

". . . but inside it," he said, and I saw it wasn't coughing but nascent
laughter, "was only some cheese! Ha!"

"Aha," I said. "Funny."

"We laughed for a long time, thinking of the thief who will open
the camera case, and inside is only some cheese." After a moment,
Ivan stopped laughing and cleared his throat. "Here is that dog again."

He was right. It was the dog.

"It has such soulful eyes," he said. "They're somehow Dostoev-
skian."

"Are they?"

"I think so. Do you like Dostoevsky?"

"So-so." I glanced at him. "*You* like Dostoevsky."

"Yes," he said.

I started petting the dog, stroking its brow and its silky ears. It sat, closed its eyes, and swept the ground with its tail. I turned its ears inside out. It shook its head and turned them the right way again. "He doesn't like his ears to be inside out," I said.

"Is it so strange?" Ivan brushed against my ear with the back of his hand. I felt my body stiffen, I was filled with dread. And yet, I knew I wanted him to touch me—didn't I? Wasn't that my general policy?

"Would you like it if someone decided to turn *your* ear inside out?" he asked, lightly pulling at my ear. The horror intensified and sank into my gut. I knew from Shakespeare class that ears were sexual. Was he making fun of me—of my general policy? And wasn't he right, that I had been tormenting the dog?

"No," I said.

He withdrew his hand. The floor seemed to drop, and was actually dropping—the pier we were sitting on wasn't a pier at all but a wooden float bobbing on the water. The dog took a little step to steady itself and wagged its tail.

"Should I throw the dog into the river?" Ivan asked.

"Why do you want to throw the dog into the river?"

"Seeing a river makes me want to throw something into it. And I can't throw *you* into the river."

Though I could tell this was meant to sound playful, I felt insulted and humiliated. "Oh," I said.

He sighed. "I think you don't like to throw the dog into the river."

Ivan was telling another story. He and his girlfriend were trying to get to Verona, but when they got in a car and said, "Verona," the Italians said, "Ah, Roma!" and they had to repeat, "Verona, Verona." That was the whole story.

"Did you ever get to Verona?" I asked.

"We got there," he said. He didn't seem to want to talk about Verona. "So what don't you like about Dostoevsky?"

I thought it over. "He makes me embarrassed and tired."

"Why?"

"I don't know."

"Why do you think?"

"He invents these supposedly complicated problems and then gets so worked up about them—like, it's hell, it's intolerable humiliation, it's the mathematically highest point of abasement. But to me, none of those things seem particularly hellish or humiliating or complicated. When I can't get worked up myself, I feel embarrassed. And tired."

"Wow. Even *Crime and Punishment* makes you feel this way?"

I nodded. "It's like he does this shoddy, depressing thing, killing an old lady—and instead of shoddy and depressing, it's supposed to be an earthshaking philosophical crisis."

"But don't you think there is a philosophical conflict? Don't you think in some sense Raskolnikov is justified to kill her? If it was the only way he could study?"

"I guess so," I said. "But how could that be the only way? Why couldn't he do something else?"

"But then there would be no story."

"I guess."

"Isn't it a real question—what's so bad, *practically,* about killing an old woman who nobody likes? Personally, that old woman makes me really mad. I see women like that on the tram all the time. They always expect you to give them your seat. Sometimes I'm reading, and it really makes me mad that I have to give her my seat so she can just sit there and think nothing."

I wondered why he had told me something so terrible about himself.

"Did you feel a raindrop?" I asked.

Ivan frowned. "Yes."

We went back to the car and sat inside to wait out the rain. "What were we talking about?" asked Ivan.

"How it's okay to sacrifice old women if it enables your intellectual development," I said.

He laughed. "I'm not saying I would kill anyone. I just have violent thoughts on the tram, and it helps me relate to Dostoevsky. You never have such thoughts?"

"I don't know," I said. "Definitely there are times when I'm tired and don't want to give up my seat on the bus to an old person. But I get depressed, not angry—like about how I'll be an old woman some-day, and even more tired than I am now. I never think I deserve the seat more because I'm reading a book." Worried this might sound self-righteous, I added, "Maybe it's just because I don't read on the bus, it makes me carsick."

Ivan's classmates, now grown more numerous, were sitting around a bonfire, stripping the bark off of sticks and using them to skewer pieces of bacon fat. They held the fat over the fire, then dripped it onto bread, and ate the bread. They never actually ate the bacon, just dripped it on the bread. Ivan sharpened a stick for me. When the raw bacon fat came my way in a Styrofoam tray, I took a piece and made some effort to impale it on the stick. The thing is, I didn't really want a piece of bacon impaled on a stick.

"You're being too gentle," Ivan said. He took the bacon and im-paled it on the stick. I held it over the flames for a while, but I couldn't imagine eating it or dripping it onto anything, so I gave it back.

"I think you have to eat this from earliest childhood to like it," he said apologetically, cutting a slice of bread.

Some of Ivan's friends asked about where I was from. They perked up when I said my name was Turkish but immediately lost interest when I said I had grown up in America. Soon they gave up talking to me and switched to Hungarian. I could actually understand a lot of the words they said, because so many of them were numbers. They would make these utterances full of Hungarian numbers and laugh riotously. They had all gone to a special math high school.

"They're talking about how much ballast to throw from the hot-air balloon," Ivan explained. "Are you sure you wouldn't like some bread? At least have a tomato."

It had gotten dark. I stared into the fire and counted the different colors: orange, yellow, white, blue. I ate a tomato.

Someone nearby was repeating a word that sounded like "Sonya." "Sonya, Sonya!" I wondered what it meant. "Sonya—Selin!" I realized it was Imre, calling me Sonya, and I felt so betrayed I could barely talk.

"Yes?" I managed.

"The bread," said Imre.

I looked at him. "What?"

"Behind you, in the bag."

I turned. Sure enough, there was a bag of bread. I handed it to him. He didn't take it.

"You have to apply a knife," he said, smiling.

"Excuse me?"

"You have to apply a knife to the bread."

"He means, to cut it," Ivan said. "You have the knife."

They weren't wrong; the bread knife was right next to me. I looked from the knife to Ivan to Imre and back to Ivan. After a moment, Ivan took the bread and the knife, cut a slice, and handed it to Imre.

"Thanks," Imre said.

I stood up.

"Are you going somewhere?" asked Ivan.

"I'd better call my mom," I said. "To tell her I got here okay."

"Now? I don't know if there's a telephone around here."

"I saw a pay phone, near where you parked. Outside the store."

"You did? Why didn't you call her when we were there?"

"I didn't have any coins."

He frowned. "You could have asked me for a coin."

I didn't reply.

"So now you still don't have any coins, right?"

"Right."

"So how are you going to call?"

"I'll buy something from the store and get change."

"The store might not be open anymore. Do you have any forints?"

"I have traveler's checks."

"Traveler's checks? Why do you have traveler's checks?"

I felt very miserable. Why did anyone have anything? "Because I'm traveling," I said. My mother had gotten me the traveler's checks. I had signed them at our dining table.

"It's much better to use your ATM card. You can go right to a bank and you get a better exchange rate."

"I didn't bring an ATM card. I didn't know it would work here."

"It would work better than traveler's checks." Ivan dug through his pocket. "I don't have change, either. I'll go with you to the store."

I sat back down. "Never mind, I'll just call tomorrow."

"But does your mother expect you to call today?"

"Well . . . she might have forgotten the exact day."

"Uh-huh. And if she didn't forget, it seems to me she will be worried. Right?"

I didn't say anything.

Ivan cleared his throat and said something to his friends, nodding in my direction. I recognized the word for mother, which was echoed around the campfire in different diminutives: *anya, anyu, anyus, anyuska.*

· · ·

The store was still open. "I'm sorry about the food," Ivan said. "Would you like anything to eat? Some cookies?"

"No, thanks," I said.

He bought some cookies anyway and gave me a coin. "But you need some kind of an access number," he said. "Do you know what it is?"

"Yeah."

"You do? Oh, okay, then." He stood in front of the phone booth, with his back to me. I went inside and dialed the number.

I glanced at my watch while the phone rang. It was four in the afternoon in New Jersey. My mother picked up. "Did you arrive? Where are you?" she said in Turkish.

"I'm in Budapest," I said. "I just got here."

"Is everything okay? Your friend met you? Is he behaving like a human being?"

"Everything is okay. Everyone is behaving like a human being."

"But your voice isn't excellent. Where are you calling from? Is the Hungarian friend there?"

"I'm at a phone booth. The Hungarian friend is waiting outside."

"He's waiting outside? Well, I won't keep you. But let me not forget to tell you: someone called you. Did you apply for a job this summer in Turkey as a researcher?"

"No," I said. "Oh, I mean yes—for *Let's Go*, for a travel guide."

"*Let's Go*, exactly. They called from there. They want you to go to Turkey now, for eight weeks. I told them I didn't think you could do it, but I would ask you anyway."

"No, I can't just leave here now. I could go in August."

"August, right? That's what I said. But they said you would have to leave immediately and spend eight weeks."

"Then it won't work."

"They sounded upset—it sounded like they really want you to go."

"But I applied for a job with them ages ago and they turned me down."

"They turned you down? Well, I hope they're happy now. They said the kid who went had *emotional problems* and had to go back to Boston." She said "emotional problems" in English. "I didn't think you could go. I just couldn't help thinking how nice if you were nicely in Turkey now, instead of dragging yourself around God's Hungarian villages."

"But I'm very necessary to God's Hungarian villages."

"Oh, of course, you are the only thing that was lacking from the Hungarian villages!"

"How is your mother?" asked Ivan as we walked back to the bonfire. "Was she happy you called?"

"Yes." I told him about *Let's Go* and the kid with emotional problems. "Maybe it's true that all the researchers in Turkey get a nervous breakdown," I said. "I wonder if I would have had a nervous breakdown."

"In Turkey? You wouldn't have a nervous breakdown. You'd give *them* a nervous breakdown." I forgave him for a lot when he said that. I forgave him for almost everything.

The bonfire was burning lower. Periodically a branch would disintegrate into embers and the whole structure of the fire would be knocked down a few degrees. Ivan handed me a piece of watermelon.

Finally, they were putting out the fire, getting up, collecting bottles and trash. Ivan was talking with Dávid, Imre, and a boy in a leather jacket.

"We're leaving now," Ivan told me. "We're taking some people with us."

"Hello," everyone started saying to each other. "Hello, hello." "Hello" meant both hello and goodbye. I never got tired of seeing Hungarians say hello to each other in serious voices, and then turn in opposite directions and walk away.

The little store was closed when we got back to the Opel. The three boys got in the back and I sat in the front with Ivan. The car smelled intensely of bacon and bonfire. I fell asleep almost immediately.

"Did you catch that, Sonya?" Imre asked at some point.

"No," I said.

"Too bad," he said. "It was funny."

That actually made me laugh. What an asshole, I thought, and fell back asleep.

The car stopped, and Imre and the boy with the leather jacket got out at the deserted corner of two unlit streets.

"We got rid of two," Ivan told me, backing up in an alley. "You're next."

We drove through the center of the city, past all the illuminated bridges and the international hotels, where adults were staying for reasons unrelated to barbecues, and then up Castle Hill, where Ivan left Dávid on a narrow street lined by Gothic buildings. "I decided it's actually faster to come this way first, and leave you at the hostel on the way back," he said.

It was nearly one when we got to the hostel. All the lights were out. "I forgot about the curfew," Ivan said, parking the car. "I'll have to talk to the concierge."

In the dark lobby, the same old man was sitting in the same booth with the yellow lamp. He and Ivan had an argument. The old man repeated the word "time."

"Let's get out of here," Ivan said finally. We went back to the car. He said the concierge wasn't letting me in. "There's probably room for you to stay at my house tonight," Ivan said, starting the engine. "You can meet some of my sisters."

Soon we were driving on an unmarked road with infrequent streetlights and infrequent cars. The headlights picked out four or five skinny girls standing in the dark by the side of the road—their bare legs, short skirts, and pale faces. They looked about my age, maybe younger.

"I can't believe the number of prostitutes," Ivan said. "Every time I come, it's worse. Now they made it all the way out here." He didn't sound like he wasn't sorry for the prostitutes, but he also sounded like he was criticizing them.

We turned onto a narrower, darker road. Ivan turned on the bright beams. There was a sudden jerk and his right arm flew out in front of me. A little animal had run out in front of the car. It was frozen right there in the headlights, its eyes flashing, like a little piece of its will was flashing out at us from inside its head. Then it scurried away.

"Could you tell what it was?" asked Ivan.

"No," I said.

"Maybe it was a cat," he said. "Or a rat."

"Oh."

"Look at these horrible places I'm bringing you. You must really trust me."

I felt a pang. "Of course I trust you."

He frowned. "Well, I didn't bring you anywhere horrible. This is where I live."

The gravel path, overrun by bushes, ended in a circular drive before two modern-looking houses with a lot of big dark windows and a shadowy black garden. The headlights sparkled off of some kind of pool. Ivan carried my suitcase to the door of one of the houses. We went inside, into a little hallway.

"I think my youngest sister is asleep in the living room," he said in a low voice. "We should leave our shoes here." I heard footsteps hurrying down a staircase, and a pale thin girl rushed in. She wore wire-rimmed glasses, a flannel nightgown, knitted socks, and an expression of demented joy, and she rubbed Ivan's arm, beaming from him to me.

"This is my sister Edit," Ivan said. I held out my hand, which she shook in both of hers, so then I held her hands with both of mine, too, and we both started to laugh. She and Ivan exchanged a few words and she left the room. I heard her running up the stairs.

"She's in a really good mood," Ivan said.

"So I noticed," I said.

"She just had her first date," he said. At the word "date" I could feel my face fall—I could feel myself losing the cheerfulness I had felt to see such a joyful and dear-looking person, and there was nothing I could do to disguise it.

We went up half a flight of stairs to an open floor with steel book-cases. "We designed the house ourselves," Ivan said. We continued up a narrow spiral staircase, which led to some large dark space. Through a long window resembling a bus window, lights glimmered on a distant hill. Ivan came up behind me with the suitcase, and turned on a lamp. We were standing in a long attic with a sloped ceiling and a skylight. A huge bed stood like an island on a raised platform.

"I used to sleep here in my last year of high school," Ivan said. "Now my youngest sister uses it. On this visit she said she'll give me my old room, she will sleep in the living room. I said no, of course—but it turns out she really likes to sleep on the sofa! Only my father doesn't like it. When he leaves for work in the morning, there are sleeping people in the living room."

Edit's head appeared through the top of the staircase. "I found some little linen only, I'm sorry!" she said, climbing up into the room. She started to shake the pillows out of their cases. The pillows were square and at least twice as big as any pillow I had ever seen on any bed.

"I'll show you the bathroom," Ivan said. I followed him downstairs to the kitchen, and then down some more stairs to a landing with red walls. The toilet was in one room, the bathtub in another. "My parents are sleeping on the other side," Ivan said. "Try to be careful about noise."

I nodded.

"I want to talk with my sister now," he said. "And you probably want to sleep."

"I do."

"I'll wake you up tomorrow morning."

"Okay," I said. "Thank you."

"Good night," he said.

"Good night," I said.

When I left the bathroom, Ivan and Edit were sitting in the dark kitchen and we all had to say good night again. Edit asked if I would like a bath. I said I could wait till the morning.

"But you will feel better *now*," said Edit.

"Yes, take a shower," Ivan said. "You had a long day."

Indeed, it had been not just long but malodorous. I went upstairs to get my shampoo and a change of clothes, then back down to the bath. The bath reminded me of Turkey—it had a handheld showerhead, a plastic stool, lemon Fa, and no curtain. A draft came from a window near the ceiling. The hot tap barely ran warm. It cost some effort to undress. I didn't look in the mirror.

With the most circumscribed motions, terrified that I would splash the floor or make a noise, I washed my hair twice with the apricot-scented children's shampoo that Svetlana and I had bought on sale at Monoprix. The water started running cold. I still smelled like a barbecue. I washed my hair a third time in cold water and finally couldn't smell smoke anymore.

The kitchen was as black and still as if it had been empty for years.

Back in the attic, where I had left on the light, I noticed a girl's short-sleeved blouse and denim skirt lying on the floor, and a telescope standing on a long wooden table under the window. I wanted to look through the telescope, but felt embarrassed—it felt like looking in someone's medicine cabinet. The medicine cabinet of God. Well, and what would change if I saw some stars?

I couldn't get over the enormity of the bed and the pillows. I wondered what would have happened if Edit hadn't been there to change the pillowcases. Would Ivan have done it, or would he simply have handed me the clean pillowcases, or would there have been no changing of the pillowcases?

The sheets hadn't been changed, and there was all kinds of stuff inside the bed. Straight off, I found a sock, a clock, and a Paris Métro ticket. Gradually, other items emerged: a pencil, a second Métro ticket, two yellow tickets from the Paris commuter rail, and a copy of *Let's Go Thailand* with a marker at "Bangkok: Places to Stay." Thinking about all the other people who must have slept here, I turned off the lamp, and then the only light was from the hilltops far away on the other side of the window.

At breakfast I met Ivan's mother, who looked just like Edit. I was surprised at first by how young she seemed, then realized that, even though Ivan seemed so much older than me, we were basically the same age—our mothers were probably the same age. I met Ivan's youngest sister, Ilona, who was wearing a faded calf-length sundress. "Ilona," she said in a serious voice as we shook hands. She didn't smile at all, but looked into my eyes with an open, serious expression. Ivan's mother said it was wonderful that I was there to meet everyone. She said that only two of Ivan's sisters were missing: one was in Transylvania at a folklore camp, while the eldest was at the hospital in Pest, with her boyfriend's father. "I'm afraid he's dying," Ivan's mother said, about the sister's boyfriend's father. "But it means you must come back, to meet everyone else."

Ivan carried my suitcase downstairs. I understood that the rest of my life would consist of causing Ivan to lug that suitcase in and out of his mother's old car, for all our days. Before heading to Peter's grandmother's apartment, we were going to drop off Edit at the commuter train. While we were waiting for her to get her things, Ivan showed me the garden. It had rained again and the ground was springy underfoot. We walked among the baby watermelons and burned-out roses of late June, under the fruit trees. Ivan told me the Hungarian words for cherry and sour cherry, and asked if Turkish also had two separate words, and which of the two I preferred. I liked the sweeter ones, but I knew it would sound childish to say so.

"Do you prefer the sour ones?" I asked.

"Yeah, the sour ones are more interesting. The sweet ones don't taste so distinctive. But they're ripe now." He picked two of the dark, almost black cherries and handed one to me.

A plastic-lined canal was full of fat sleek orange carp, with gauzy fins and plaintive round mouths opening and closing. They wanted, and wanted. "They're beautiful," I said.

"They're a pain in the ass," Ivan said. In the winter they had to be caught and transferred indoors. He indicated, through the dusty glass of an annex, the carps' winter tub.

Edit came out wearing a long skirt and boots—just as if it were already fall, and time for things to happen, and not the summer anymore.

Back in Peter's grandmother's apartment, Cheryl was sitting under the piano again, and Andrea was teaching everyone how to say "please" in Hungarian. "So, you were locked out?" Peter said.

"The concierge wouldn't give us the key," said Ivan.

"Why didn't you tell your roommate you were going to be late?" Peter asked me. "She could have left the key for you downstairs."

"I didn't know who my roommate was," I said.

"Your roommate is *Dawn*."

"Hey," beamed a plump red-haired girl wearing a T-shirt that read ESCHEW OBFUSCATION.

"Hi," I said.

"You could have asked me," Peter said.

"I didn't think of it," I told him. "I'm sorry."

"You shouldn't be sorry," Ivan intervened. "The concierge definitely had a spare key, he just didn't want to be helpful. We were probably supposed to bribe him."

"Did you give him *Andrea's* name?" Peter asked Ivan.

"I gave him *your* name."

"But I told you that *Andrea* made the reservations."

"No, I don't think you told me that."

Peter smiled at Ivan, then patted my shoulder: "Well, the important thing is that you're here. Let's put those bags where my grandmother won't trip over them and break her neck. Excellent. Are we ready to go?"

"Peter is taking you guys sightseeing," Ivan told me, as the others stood up. "I have some stuff to do."

"Okay," I said.

"You have my number," he said.

We all filed out of the apartment and along the balcony toward the stairs. Ivan hung back from the group. "You should go ahead," he told me. "You should make friends with those kids. After all, they're the ones you'll have to call if you have any problem in the villages." When he said that, the world seemed to stop. "I mean," he added, glancing at my expression, "after I'm in Tokyo."

"Right," I said, opening my eyes wide to keep tears from overflowing.

. . .

Talking with Dawn felt so different from talking with Ivan that Ivan
seemed almost not to exist anymore. Dawn asked how I knew Peter. I
said he was a friend of a friend. Dawn had met Peter earlier that year
at the London School of Economics. London was great, especially the
cider. The downside was that your snot turned black. It was totally
democratic—even Princess Diana's snot was black. Luckily it was a
temporary condition.

"This is just my second day in Budapest, and already when I blow
my nose it's hardly black at all. The air here must be really unpolluted.
Speaking of nose blowing, I hope Peter takes us somewhere where we
can buy tissue, because there's no toilet paper in the hostel. I think
they use newspaper instead. There were stacks of old newspaper in the
toilet stalls. You can so tell that only boys live here most of the time.
I haven't asked Peter, but I'm sure they sell toilet paper in Budapest.
Don't you think?"

"Yes," I said.

"Yeah, Budapest is a totally modern city. I bet it's just the college
boys who use newspaper. And college boys are slobs in every country.
Still, I'm going to stock up here, in case they don't have toilet paper in
the villages."

When I looked back at the parking lot, I didn't see Ivan. I didn't
see his car.

Peter took us first to the American Express. Everyone was exchanging either traveler's checks or dollars, just like I was—nobody was
using an ATM card. The next stop was a bookstore, where people
bought phrase books. There was one shelf of English books. I picked
up a book called *Favorite Hungarian One-Minute Tales*. The first tale,
"On the triviality of conversations," was written in dialogue form:

"How are you?"

"I'm wonderful, thanks, and you?"

"I'm okay, but why are you dragging that rope after you?"

"That's not a rope—those are my intestines."

That was it—that was the whole story. I was dumbfounded. Was it possible that the concern over the triviality-dungeon of conversations, which I had taken to be one of Ivan's particularities, was actually part of the Hungarian national character? How did you separate where someone was from, from who they were?

I leafed through a book called *The ESL Miscellany*. It was full of awful-sounding advice. If you had a particularly shy and nonparticipatory student, it said, you should have the other students move their desks in a circle around the "nonplayer" and conduct the whole rest of the class that way. Any time anyone raised their hand to ask or answer a question or make a comment, they should address the question or comment not to you, the teacher, but to the nonplayer, who should do his best to answer.

"This book looks pretty useful," said Owen, leafing through another copy. "It has a lot of good exercises."

I turned to the exercises. "*The dog kicked by the boy is red*. Circle the picture that applies." The pictures showed a red dog kicking a boy, a dog kicking a red boy, a red boy kicking a dog, and a boy kicking a red dog. It was the kind of test used to diagnose Wernicke's aphasia.

"I think I'm going to buy it," Owen decided. "Do you want to split the cost? One of us can read it here in Budapest, and the other can take it to the village and leave it there as a gift."

I didn't want to read the book, not in Budapest and not in a village, but I didn't want to seem snotty so I said okay and paid for half of it. It wasn't expensive. It was, however, big, and Owen didn't have a bag, so I ended up carrying it all day.

We spent the afternoon sightseeing. We saw a church with an

eight-hundred-year-old king and queen in its crypt. It had been a mosque under the Turks. A stained glass window represented various scenes from the life of Saint István, including the death of István's son in a bear hunt.

"The geometric patterned tiles are supposedly based on Islamic designs," Peter told me. "Do you see a resemblance?"

"I guess so," I said doubtfully.

"Oh, you guess so?"

We visited a theater that had once been a Carmelite monastery and had been renovated by Kempelen Farkas, a.k.a. Wolfgang van Kempelen, inventor of the chess-playing Turk. We saw a colossal Incredible Hulk–colored monument representing seven Hungarian conquerors riding bionic-looking horses. One horse had antlers. Saint István's right hand was in a box somewhere. The Chain Bridge had been reconstructed after each world war. The sculptor of the lion statues was said to have drowned himself out of shame because the lions didn't have tongues—though others said that if you looked closely in their mouths, you could see the tongues right there.

Margit Island used to be called Rabbit Island, either because the Turks who built a harem there used to screw like rabbits, or because the early Hungarian kings, who loved hunting but didn't have any forests near the city, sent all the rabbits to this island and hunted them. During the Tatar invasion, Béla IV promised that if the Tatars were vanquished he would give his daughter Margit to God. Then the Tatars were vanquished. Béla built a convent on the island and sent Margit there. She was nine. She became a nun, never washed herself above the ankles, and died at twenty-eight.

"Nobody really knows why it's called the Fisherman's Bastion," Andrea said at the Fisherman's Bastion. "Some say because the guild of fishermen defended the castle. Some say because here used to be a fishermen's village. Some say because here used to be a medieval fish market."

"Those don't sound mutually exclusive," Owen said. "I mean, couldn't they all be true?"

Andrea gave him a mysterious look. "Who knows?"

"The square isn't named for a blanket, is it?" I asked Andrea in Batthyány Square. *Battaniye* was Turkish for blanket.

"The square is named for Count Batthyány," Andrea said.

"Owen tells me you two bought an interesting book," Peter said. I took *The ESL Miscellany* out of my bag.

"Selin saw it first," Owen said.

"Can I borrow it?" Cheryl asked.

"Of course," I said. "Would you like to take it now?"

"Oh, no—I'll let you read it first."

I was surprised to learn that Cheryl was twenty-three, she looked so young, with her curly hair and tiny peaked face. She was wearing a little striped shirt, white shorts, and white sandals, like Piglet, and carried a tiny purse with the strap across her chest. At first I felt an affinity toward Cheryl because she was the only one other than me who was really trying to learn Hungarian—she carried under her arm the very same edition of *Teach Yourself Hungarian* that I kept hidden in my suitcase. Whereas I shrouded my studies in secrecy and pretended not to understand anything, Cheryl did exercises in restaurants and constantly asked Peter questions. Sometimes she asked about inconsistencies in the book that had puzzled me, too, and then I felt very close to her.

It came as a blow to realize that, just as I was interested in Hungarian because of Ivan, Cheryl was interested because of Peter. We were just the same, except that we were also different, because when Ivan said idyllic things about plum and cherry trees I felt tense and mistrustful, whereas Cheryl seemed really into the bucolic stuff. She kept asking about the village where she would live—whether there would be mountains, a lake, and animals. Peter said that Hungary was full of beautiful mountains, ice-cold lakes, and frolicsome horses, and that maybe she would be able to borrow her host family's bike, wear her bathing suit under her clothes, and ride to the lake to swim under the mountains among the rabbits and the deer.

Cheryl really wanted to be placed in a host family with lots of non-English-speaking children, so she could learn Hungarian. The third or fourth time she mentioned how she didn't want anyone in her family to speak English, Peter said that there would likely be at least one English speaker in every household. The villagers would probably arrange it that way because they wanted to practice English, just as she wanted to practice Hungarian. Cheryl said they could surely change her assignment—they could find her a family with lots of children who didn't know any English at all. "As long as there are beginning-English students and a lake and I can see a mountain, I will be perfectly happy," she said, reminding me of how my grandfather used to say he was a simple man with simple tastes: "All I need is a little milk from a goat that has been fed for a month on wild green pears."

We were all supposed to go to a jazz club to meet Gábor, the one who was trying to sell shoes. I had to drop my suitcase at the hostel first—it was still at Peter's grandmother's apartment. Peter said it was getting late, so I would have to go by myself and meet them later with a taxi. I wrote down the name of the club, and Peter carried my suitcase to the tram stop. Andrea came, too. The sun was setting and everything was mauve and gold and beautiful.

"I'm curious why you didn't leave your luggage at the hostel yesterday, with everyone else's," Peter said.

"We did wait a bit for everyone else," I said, thinking longingly about the future day when I would cease to be accountable for that suitcase. "But Ivan was in a rush. He had to meet his friends."

"Yes, okay, but your things. Why didn't you leave them at the hostel?"

"Ivan said I shouldn't, because then other people would have to carry them upstairs."

"It would have been less trouble than this, don't you think? I mean, people still have to carry your things."

I didn't say anything.

"Oh, well," Peter said, "I suppose it worked out for the best, since you ended up sleeping over at Ivan's house, and this way you had your things with you. It would have been inconvenient if your bags were in the hostel."

"Peti, I've been thinking," Andrea said. "Why don't I take her in my car? Then we'll meet you at the club."

"Oh, do you have a car?" Peter asked.

"Of course I have a car!"

"And does this car work?"

"Yes!" Then, derisively, "No, you have to push it."

"Well, you used to!"

"That was a year ago!"

"Oh, naturally. I expect it couldn't *possibly* be the same."

"No!" she exclaimed.

"No," he said.

"Don't hurt my little car!"

"I won't hurt your little car."

Andrea took the top handle, I took the side handle, and we lugged the suitcase between us.

My room was on the fourth floor of the hostel. It had three beds, three desks, a washbasin, a wardrobe, and some math equations penciled on the wall. This was not the work of Dawn, eschewer of obfuscation. We deposited the suitcase and left.

The jazz club was in a basement. The saxophonist was doubled over, face contorted, gasping between phrases. The sounds seemed to come from outside of life. You felt not just sorry, but also afraid. I wondered where Ivan was.

Peter handed me a glass with a lime in it. "This is a gin and tonic," he said.

They didn't have cider, but the bartender mixed Dawn a drink with apple juice, Sprite, and vodka, and she said it was even better.

In a black room with orange lights and pounding Spanish music we stood in a big circle dancing. It reminded me of preschool, when you also had to stand in a circle and clap your hands. I began to intuit dimly why people drank when they went dancing, and it occurred to me that maybe the reason preschool had felt the way it had was that one had had to go through the whole thing sober.

When nobody was looking, I went back to the table where we'd left our things. I found my bag and lit a cigarette. After the first drag, a weak but perceptible energy gathered behind my eyes. Suddenly I noticed Cheryl sitting among the jackets and bags, her head drooping under its fluffy mane. When I said hi, she raised her melancholy eyes. She looked like a sick lapdog. "I don't feel well," she said. "I wish Peter would take us back."

Feeling a wave of pity for us both, I suggested we split a cab back. "I saw some cabs outside before," I said.

"You can go," she said eventually, after a long silence. "I don't think it would be polite to leave before Peter."

There didn't seem to be anything to say to that. I took another drag from the cigarette. "Peter tells me you're from Turkey," snapped a familiar voice.

"Oh—hi, Gábor," I said.

"I'm very curious about the attitude of Turks regarding the collapse of the Ottoman Empire," Gábor said. "One day you're the largest empire in the world; the next, you're a republic the size of Texas."

"Ha, funny," I said, looking for an ashtray.

"I'd be interested to learn the standard Turkish attitude," he said.

I saw an ashtray a few tables over. When I got back to the table, Gábor was still looking at me expectantly. "It's probably like the Hungarian attitude about being a republic the size of South Carolina."

"Ha!" shouted Gábor. "Trianon! Touché!"

We got back to the hostel at three. Dawn talked nonstop, even while brushing her teeth. The pillows were the same size as the ones in Ivan's attic. Dawn was testing her clock radio, causing a Hungarian woman to talk in our room. I fell asleep in the middle of trying to figure out how to position my body with relation to the enormous pillow.

The next thing I knew, Louis Armstrong was singing "What a Wonderful World." "I see friends shaking hands, saying, 'How do you do?' / They're really saying, 'I love you . . .'" I thought of the times Ivan and I had shaken hands, and tears welled in my eyes.

The women's shower room in the dormitory was a big tiled box with no stalls—just a row of showerheads. "It looks just like in a movie about a concentration camp!" Dawn exclaimed, pulling her shirt over her head and stepping out of her panties. I swallowed back a sigh. The hits never stopped coming in adult life. I took off my clothes and hung them on a metal hook.

"I hope it's really water that comes out!" Dawn said cheerily, turning on the shower. I turned to look at her, then remembered we weren't wearing any clothes and looked away.

The shower was marvelous—forceful and almost unbearably hot. "The water's really hot," Dawn said. "The floor is slanted. I don't know why I waste time shaving my legs." After a minute, a cascade of foam rushed from Dawn's shower to the drain. A similar cascade rushed down my shoulders.

"Isn't it sad that girls are so much more self-conscious about their bodies, compared with boys?" Dawn said. I agreed that it was sad.

. . .

At eight we met at the commuter rail station to take a day trip to Szentendre, which Peter said was a picturesque historic town on the Danube. Andrea had brought *kifli:* crescent-shaped rolls first baked by Hungarians to commemorate the Turks' defeat in Vienna, and later introduced by Marie Antoinette in Paris, where they became known as croissants. At the station in Szentendre we climbed two broken escalators through a concrete chute covered with graffiti. I read my first complete handwritten indigenous sentence in Hungarian. It read: *János was here.*

We came out into a sunny, strangely familiar plaza. In the next moment I recognized the modern-day sundial, the Chinese restaurant, and the sandy place where Ivan's car had overheated. So this was Szentendre. This time, instead of continuing along the river, we took a winding road up to the old town, which was full of Serbian churches. We passed a Marzipan Museum with a marzipan Elvis in the window, and listened to a blind accordionist. Peter clapped along, making eye contact with each of us and smiling. The Orthodox cross incorporated an impaled crescent, to symbolize victory over the Turks. Owen could read the Old Slavonic inscriptions. Some Serbian merchants had thanked God for the end of the plague.

The church interior smelled unmistakably of church interior. An artists' colony had painted frescoes in the choir. Christ and the apostles were sitting in rows, staring straight ahead, with highly specific, human-looking faces. They looked like some guys you might see while returning to your seat from the airplane lavatory. The cathedral had been "built by Dalmatians."

At the top of the hill was a paved square with a parapet, filled with artists' stalls. At one stall, a German couple was yelling at a painting of some cowboys. They were just pointing at the painting and shouting. The artist, looking bored, leaned on the parapet and lit a cigarette. He had his back to the view—the whole town spread out like some fantastic salad.

One painting showed a family with vivacious smiles; in my mind I titled it: *Now We Will Tear Each Other Limb from Limb.*

The three other girls in the program, Cheryl, Dawn, and Vivie, kept taking group photographs. The problem of a group photograph was who was going to take it. Andrea and I always volunteered, but the rules of etiquette dictated that the camera owner had to try to get a stranger to take the picture so everyone would be in it.

While posing with the others next to a cannon, I wondered when I would see Ivan again. He had said, "You should give me a call." Had that been yesterday, or long ago? How close were Ivan and Peter—how often did they talk? Did Ivan know we were here? I looked at my watch. Practically no time had passed for the last twenty minutes.

The German woman was holding another canvas at arm's length, glaring at it over her glasses. The painting showed sheep, a herdsman, and some kind of autonomous mop.

Peter went somewhere for some reason. We were waiting for him on a parapet overlooking the Danube, across from a traffic circle with a statue of a bear.

"Is that the bear who ate István's son?" I asked Andrea. I had meant it to be a polite question, but it came out somehow abruptly.

"I don't think so," she said.

"It just reminded me of the story you told us about how István's son was eaten by bears."

"Oh! I suppose it's possible that it is one of those bears. But I don't think that the sculptor planned it to be any particular bear."

"How do you say bear in Hungarian?" asked Cheryl.

"*Medve*," said Andrea.

"That's similar to the Russian word," said Owen.

Andrea explained that in olden times, when Hungary was shamanistic, the bear had been a sacred animal. Over the centuries the original Hungarian word became taboo and a Slavic word was adopted in its place.

"Wow! What's the real, taboo word?" asked Vivie.

Andrea laughed. "Who knows?"

Vivie's eyes widened. "Ohhh—you're not allowed to say it."

It was cold for swimming, but there were two people in the water: a barrel-chested man and a tiny little girl in a blue bikini. The girl was almost exploding with delight. The man stood awkwardly, like the first guest at a party, shifting his weight in the knee-deep water and rubbing his arms. Then he squatted so that only his head stuck out of the water. Then he vanished altogether, reappearing nearly a minute later with a perplexed expression. The girl clapped and shrieked, turned the man around by his shoulders, and climbed onto his back. The man stood up, his torso plastered with leaves. Overwhelmed by happiness, the little girl began to sing. She was so happy—but she didn't know what anything really was. She didn't know what anything meant. She knew even less than we did.

The ferry back to Budapest was full of reveling women in their fifties. Elbows linked, they danced, stomped, sang, and coughed. In the bar, they banged bottles against the counter. The few men in their party were slumped at the tables, heads buried in their arms. Only two were sitting upright, addressing a salami of durable appearance with a pocketknife.

There were no free seats. No matter where we stood, we were blocking the access from the bar to the women's bathroom. Owen, Dawn, and I climbed up a ladder and found ourselves on an empty upper deck. We sat on some piles of rope. Owen fell asleep. I hugged my knees and watched the scenery slip by behind the white-painted metal cables.

The sun had disappeared behind a flat gray sky. The trees that scrolled past were a vivid, almost plastic green.

"Southern Comfort," Dawn was saying. "Do you think they'll be offended?"

"I don't see why," I said, wondering what Southern Comfort was.

"Peter told us to bring gifts, right? And he said Hungarians like to drink. I wanted to bring something representative of where I come from. My mom got mad when I told her. She said I might as well bring them a shotgun."

"I wish we had some Southern Comfort right now," I said.

"Me, too." She propped her feet on a crate of life jackets. "What did you bring your host family?"

"Chocolate."

"Chocolate." She sighed.

"I'm afraid I'll accidentally eat it all before I get there," I said, following the rule that you had to pretend to have this problem where you couldn't resist chocolate.

"What if I accidentally drink the bottle of Southern Comfort before I get there?"

The sky was a creamy gray, but if you looked at it without blinking it started to sparkle and prick your eyes. Dawn fell uncharacteristically silent. She was asleep.

An elegant house of modern design glided by, almost close enough to touch. I wondered who lived there, and whether they had a daughter.

I took *Dracula* out of my bag. In the first paragraph, the hero, a real estate lawyer, arrived in Budapest. Crossing a splendid Western bridge over the Danube, he found himself "among the traditions of Turkish rule." The lawyer had to get to Transylvania to help Dracula buy some property in London. Dracula, who had taught himself English from books, asked the lawyer to correct his pronunciation. "But, Count, you know and speak English thoroughly!" protested the lawyer.

The real estate lawyer started having a lot of problems. There was an incubus, a succubus, wolves. Dracula was intercepting his mail. I saw right away where he had gone wrong: he hadn't made enough friends. Of *course* he had problems in his village.

We glided into Budapest at twilight, the city poured over with a viscous glowing blue, lights already blazing on the splendid Western bridges. Upside-down electronic billboards were reflected in the river, advertising Tuborg beer and Minolta cameras.

We spent the rest of the evening at an outdoor performance of Donizetti's *The Elixir of Love*. The singers looked imploringly at the audience as if we could somehow help them. An elixir of love—what an idea. You loved *that* one, the one who didn't love you, so what good was an elixir that turned her into someone else? I kept looking around the bleachers at the audience, middle-aged people in practical clothes. Every single one of them cared about love, but how much? A lot, or only a little bit? The opera went on for a long time. Eventually the two youngest people onstage got married, so we could all go home.

The next day, Sunday, we were supposed to go to Mass at a famous cathedral, and then to the baths at a famous hotel, where you didn't wear any clothes and someone scrubbed you with some wonderful something. Dawn's clock radio went off at seven-thirty. Burying my head under the enormous pillow, I condemned all organized religions, especially Islam and Catholicism. If it wasn't for the Islamic obsession with baths, then there might not be a public bath tradition in Budapest, it might have just expired with the Romans, and maybe the Otto-mans wouldn't even have invaded Europe, and Ivan wouldn't have had to read those books as a kid. If not for Catholicism, there would be no morning Mass, and Ivan would never have written me such convo-luted messages about freedom and hell and innocence and seduction. By this point I was really mad. There was no way I was going to go listen to those guys talk in Latin.

The clock radio was playing Louis Armstrong again—"Blueberry Hill," this time. The moment Dawn woke up, she was full of ques-tions about what she should wear and whether she should shave her legs, having previously shaved them the day before yesterday. Then she tried to shave in the sink and cut her leg. Then there was a worse prob-lem: she had gotten her period. Dawn sat on the edge of the bed with her head in her hands. "Do you think I can wear a tampon in the baths?"

I had no idea what kind of evidence would support or contradict the conclusion that you could wear a tampon in the baths. "Yes," I said.

"You do?" She sat up. "I'll just wear a bathing suit, right? Do you think other people will wear bathing suits?"

I said I did. She cheered up. It was so easy to cheer her up.

Dawn carried her passport, plane tickets, and traveler's checks strapped to her body in a zippered wallet. Her cash rode around in a smaller patented pouch clipped onto her bra. It was called a Bra Stash. When she saw that I was planning to leave my passport and checks in the room, Dawn insisted that I lock them in the wooden wardrobe together with our other valuables: my Walkman, the Southern Com-fort, and her clock radio. I didn't see how the wardrobe was any harder to break into than the room.

"I'm looking forward to getting to the village," Dawn said, "just for security reasons. I mean, in a little village I can leave all my things in my suitcase—and if I come back in the evening and notice that something is missing, I'll *know* who took it." I imagined Dawn going from door to door in the village like Miss Marple, solving the mystery of who stole her clock radio.

"I think I'll have to take a rain check," I told Peter in the lobby.

"A rain check?" He looked amused.

"Well, maybe not a rain check exactly . . ."

"What is this rain check?" asked Andrea.

"A rain check means you promise to do something another time," said Peter. "Let's say you have a ticket to an outdoor opera, and it rains. They might give you a *rain check*, which would be a ticket good for another performance. So it's a metaphor. If you and I have arranged to go to a movie and I take a *rain check*, it means I can't make it today but I promise to go another time."

"I see," said Andrea, sounding a little sad that they didn't get to go to the movie.

"So I'm not going to go to Mass," I said.

"But it's not really a rain check," Peter said.

"That's true. I misused the expression 'rain check.' But I feel more confident now about the right usage. I can teach it to the village children."

"Excellent," said Peter. "That's what I like to hear."

I went back to bed and woke at eleven-thirty. I parted the curtains and looked outside at the tree-lined street, the tram, the pale candy-colored buildings. After taking a long shower in the empty shower room, I went downstairs to the canteen and bought a package of hazelnut wafers. I spent the rest of the morning on the sunniest part of the bed, eating hazelnut wafers and reading *Dracula*. *Dracula* had turned into a fragmented multivoiced narrative, which was my least favorite kind of book. A cowboy turned up from somewhere and said things like, "Miss Lucy, I know I ain't good enough to regulate the fixin's of your little shoes." Well, I knew perfectly well that fixin's were what you served with a turkey, and I didn't appreciate that cowboy implying otherwise.

The author hadn't been able to make up his mind about Dracula's powers and limitations—whether there were circumstances under which he could sometimes venture from his coffin during the day, or harm somebody wearing a crucifix; whether his control extended to all animals, or only some of them; whether every person he bit automatically became a vampire.

Van Helsing showed up from Amsterdam to explain everything: "Thus, whereas he can do as he will within his limit, when he have his earth-home, his coffin-home, his hell-home . . . still at other time he can only change when the time come." I had never met a Dutch person who talked like that. They always spoke amazing English.

I flipped to the author biography. "A student of pure mathematics, Stoker was also an active speaker with the Philosophical Society," it said. I thought it was weird that a mathematician had created such an internally inconsistent world.

In the afternoon, I got on a random tram to see where it went. The tram passed Peter's grandmother's apartment and veered onto an unfamiliar, increasingly residential street. A few people got off at each stop, and nobody got on. Soon there was no one left but old people. Chain-link fences gradually outnumbered the wooden ones and sand replaced the gravel under the rails. After another five minutes even all the old people had left, except for one man who was either passed out or dead.

I disembarked on a narrow tree-lined street in front of a chain-link fence. A Doberman pinscher started barking its head off on the other side of the fence. A sign read HARAPÓS KUTYA. I looked it up in the dictionary. It meant "biting dog."

Nearly every house on that street had a BITING DOG sign, and the dog to back it up. I walked around the block. The barking didn't let up for one minute. I saw only two humans, elderly women, sitting in lawn chairs. They swiveled their heads as I approached. "Good day," I said as I passed. "Good day," they said. When I looked over my shoulder, they were still watching me.

I took the tram back and walked in a straight line until I came to a phone booth. All around the booth were stone buildings with plaster façades in every different kind of yellow. I took out my Van Gogh address book and thought about calling Ivan. Instead, I called Svetlana in Belgrade. Aunt Bojana answered. She said Svetlana had come back from Italy that morning, and was still asleep.

"I think that boy exhausted her," she said. "She will be sorry she missed your call. Is there a number where she can find you?"

There was no such number.

I looked at my watch and realized it was already morning in New Jersey. My mother answered the phone on the second ring. "Yes?" she said coldly.

"It's me. Selin."

There was a pause. "Selin—sweetie! Where are you? You sound like you're in the next room."

"I'm still in Budapest," I said. "It's a very good connection."

"Are you calling from the hotel?"

"No, from a pay phone. Just a phone on the street."

"Is anybody with you?"

"No."

"You're all alone on the street? What time is it?"

"It's broad daylight. It's three in the afternoon."

"Oh, okay." She sighed. "I just can't imagine it. I can't imagine you on the other side of the world, at a pay phone on the street." She asked what the street looked like. I told her about the yellow buildings. I said there were begonias in a flower box.

"It sounds lovely," she said. She asked about Ivan. I told her I had met his mother.

"He has a mother? I can't believe it. What was she like?"

"She was nice," I said. "She gave me a book."

"What kind of a book?"

"A book about Hungary. Everyone here is obsessed with being Hungarian."

"What about the rest of the family? Did you meet them, too?"

I explained that I had met everyone except the sister in Transylvania and the sister at the hospital.

My mother sighed. "He will want to marry you," she said. "I'm very concerned. That's what it means when men want you to meet their sisters."

"Don't worry, nobody wants to marry me," I said. But somewhere inside, a tiny part of me felt a thrill.

In the evening we went to the opera house to see *Rigoletto*. *Rigoletto* turned out to be about a poor girl being dishonored and then murdered. It was supposed to be really sad for her father.

We got back to the hostel at midnight. The TV was on in the lobby—the summer Olympics were starting soon. We were leaving for the villages early the next morning.

After we had packed our bags, Dawn said she was going to write in her journal. She took out a three-ring binder, a pile of brochures and tickets, a pair of scissors, and a glue stick. I got out my notebook. A clock somewhere tolled two. Dawn decided to call her parents in Texas, where it was still only seven. I thought of calling Ivan, except that at his parents' house it was two.

Dawn paused on the threshold. "Look—there's a note for you!"

She handed me a folded paper, a worksheet, with answers in milli-
liters. Kovács Csaba had gotten them all right. I turned it over. *Dear
Selin,* I read. *Maybe this is the last one of the long series of missing you. I'm
going back home now. I was trying to locate you the whole day. If you want
you can call me till late tonight. Iván.*

The door closed behind Dawn. I imagined the stairs to the lobby,
the pay phones in the dark, the coins against my thumb, his voice.
The scramble to think of things to say, with only little reprieves, during which I would have to listen to whatever things he had thought up
to say. Then the dial tone again, higher-pitched than in America—it
was always there, like the sea inside a shell—and the empty dull feeling in my chest, like now, only worse.

At the same time, it seemed certain to me that someday I would
really want to hear his voice and wouldn't be able to, and I would
think back to the time that he had invited me to call him, and it
would seem as incomprehensible as an invitation to speak to the dead.

Dawn came in and said the phones were out of order. I was pretty sure
she had used the wrong coins.

There was a knock on the door. It was Peter, carrying a plastic library bag—the kind that said A WET BOOK IS NOT A DEAD DUCK. He
was locked out of his grandmother's and needed a place to crash, and
had remembered that we had an extra bed. "Is it okay?" he asked.

"Of course," said Dawn.

Peter looked at me. "Sure," I said.

Peter's plastic bag turned out to contain a toothbrush, which didn't
really support his story about having been locked out. But I was glad
he was there. Even though he was Ivan's friend, he somehow stood for
a world in which all that uncertainty and anguish wasn't real.

JULY

Someone somewhere was eating raw garlic from a bag. We had our own compartment. Raindrops sat on the windowpane. Every now and then the fattest drop would trickle down like an insuppressible tear. The train started moving. Gradually the drops went rigid and started charting jagged lines across the panes, like a graph of some unknown process.

Everyone fell asleep. Peter looked smaller than usual, a doll of himself, but Andrea's head on his shoulder looked life-sized. Cheryl slept sitting upright, her pale hands on the armrests and her eyelids fluttering. Vivie, who had a gift for comfort, made a pillow out of her jacket and snuggled up against the window. Dawn's head bobbed closer and closer to my shoulder, finally coming to rest and becoming heavy. The train went underground. I closed my eyes.

The second train was more crowded, and smelled of the human condition. A man was lurching up and down the aisles with a shopping cart full of alcohol. It wasn't yet eight in the morning, but he was doing a lively business by both the bottle and the glass. The glass was a clouded tumbler attached to the cart with duct tape and string.

When we passed an uneven stretch of rails, the man and his cart cap-
sized in one of the compartments, breaking several bottles, which
added their vapors to the already robust bouquet.

I looked out the window at the unfurling ribbon of sunflower
fields and yellow churches, trying to prepare myself for different sce-
narios that might arise in the villages, like what if a child ran at me
wearing antlers. I thought about it a lot, but didn't make any headway.

The mayor of the central village picked us up at the station and
brought us to a municipal building. In the conference room, posters
represented various aspects of rural Hungarian life: a medieval castle,
a grape arbor, a guy roasting an ox. The mayor gave a speech, and
Peter translated. The mayor thanked us for coming to share our culture and language, and hoped that we would take something away in
return. Then he asked whether any of us knew HTML, because his
village needed a Web page. Owen knew HTML. The mayor shook
his hand and said that he, Owen, would live with him in his home.

The mayor's teenage son, Béla, took us sightseeing. He was wearing bright yellow headphones around his neck, the cord disappearing
into his puffy jacket. When Vivie asked what he was listening to, he
took a Sports Discman out of his pocket and passed it around, so we
could listen to Hungarian rap music. I had never actually listened to a
Discman before. There was a faint hissing sound, and then some boys
were yelling in Hungarian with perfect clarity. They were right there,
yelling in your ear.

We followed Béla down a muddy gravel road, past pink wooden
houses and little plots sown with corn and sunflowers, to a twelfth-
century church. The church was locked. In the back, by the graveyard,
stood a cottage with a sign that read CARETAKER, SZEKERES JÁNOS.
Béla banged on the door and windows, until Szekeres János came out,

rubbing his eyes. Unlocking the church, he proceeded to talk for an hour about pillars and naves and Cain and Abel.

Part of a great king's body might have been buried in the crypt at some point. The king had originally been buried in Budapest, then canonized, then exhumed and dispatched, in pieces, to reliquaries across the country. The remains of the remains were reinterred. During the Ottoman invasion, they were dug up again and sent away for safekeeping—maybe to this very crypt, although then again maybe not; the caretaker meticulously weighed the evidence pro and con. In any case, nothing was here now, it had all been sent back to Budapest after the Ottomans left. I expected the crypt to be dark and gloomy, but it was pale and light, with yellow vaulted ceilings and archways, so maybe death would be that way, too.

We visited a folklore museum. János was there again, as in some tiresome dream, describing the different ways of turning cotton into string. In the back room of the museum a woman served us pork chops. I had never eaten a pork chop. My parents rarely ate pork. Almost nobody in Turkey did, not even atheists. At first, tears came to my eyes and swallowing took a lot of effort. But eventually it was just like eating anything else.

Everyone kept asking Béla questions. I listened carefully, so I would learn how to talk to Hungarian village teenagers. I didn't learn anything useful. At some point, Owen asked Béla if he had ever been to Budapest: a city two hours away by train.

"To Budapest?" repeated Béla.

"You see, we just came from there," Owen said.

"Sometimes my friends and I go to Pest on the weekends," Béla said. He gazed at Owen with unconcealed wonder, and said that they would be brothers.

When Vivie apologized for eating slowly, Béla said that eating slowly was good: "If you eat slowly, you can feel the food."

"You don't *feel* food," Owen said, "you *taste* it."

"Yes," Béla said. "But I also mean *more* than to taste it."

"You *enjoy* it," suggested Daniel. "If you eat slowly, you *enjoy* the food."

"You enjoy," repeated Béla.

"You *relish* it," said Owen. "You *savor* it."

"Savior?"

"Not savior—*savor.* It's like enjoying something, but more slowly."

"I don't know this word," Béla said, his eyes shining.

I realized that I would never have corrected somebody who said "you can feel the food." That was how Owen would end up with students who said "savor," while I would end up with students who said "papel iss blonk."

After lunch we went back to the conference room. Representatives from each village came to collect their new English teachers. First a weary-looking doctor came from the village where a kid had tried to impale Sandy with antlers. "We need athletic boy," said the doctor. Frank went to the antler village.

The other village representatives were English teachers, all women. They approached Cheryl first, but Cheryl just shook her head and said that she was waiting for a family that spoke no English.

After Owen and Frank, the next to be chosen were Dawn and Vivie, then Daniel. That left me and Cheryl. There was only one village representative left, a woman with feathered hair and a kind expression.

"Hello, I'm Margit, the English teacher from Kál," she told Cheryl. "I think you are Cheryl."

Cheryl nodded. "But I'm waiting for a family that speaks no English," she said.

"Oh. Well, this is awkward, because I'm an English teacher." Margit smiled at me. "Is it you who will be coming with me, then?"

"Are we waiting for another family?" Peter asked the mayor.

"Nobody is here from Apafalva." The mayor glanced at his watch. "We must wait."

"Is Apafalva near the mountains?" Cheryl was asking, as we left the room.

"Poor Cheryl," said Margit, as we maneuvered my suitcase into her Ford Fiesta. "I don't like to leave her there. I don't understand why she is so particular that her family should not speak English."

"She really wants to learn Hungarian. She thinks she'll learn better if the family doesn't speak English."

"It's a pity, because I don't think she will find such a family. You see, a family that doesn't speak English would be shy to host an American student. We want you to be comfortable."

"Cheryl has unconventional ideas about comfort," I said.

"I think your friend Peter also has unconventional ideas. Is it true he put you on a train from Pest at six in the morning?"

"Well, it was more like six-thirty."

"This is unusual and difficult to understand, because there are many later trains. What were you doing here all morning?"

"Sightseeing."

"Now, this is very interesting. You came from Budapest to Feldebrő at six-thirty in the morning to go sightseeing."

"I think Peter wanted us to visit the crypt."

"Oh, I see. Well, the crypt is interesting. It's very old. Did you find it interesting?"

"Very interesting," I said. "Only I think we stayed there a little too long."

She asked how long we had spent in the crypt. When I told her, she almost died laughing. "You came from Budapest at six-thirty in the morning, to sit in a crypt for more than an hour! Now look at you! You have dark circles under your eyes."

"I do?"

"You do. What would your mother think? She would think we are torturing you."

"Oh, no, she would think I'm building up stamina."

"Stamina! Two hours in the crypt!"

Margit turned off the rural highway onto a dirt road. The telephone and electric poles seemed unusually tall, maybe because the houses were so small—white plaster boxes with dark red roofs. Small plots of land had been given over to the cultivation of various tall leafy plants. As we approached in the car, the plants looked like a chaotic thicket, but at a certain angle they miraculously aligned themselves in rows. For an instant you could see all the way down, clear to the next house, before they dissolved again into disorder.

I would be staying with Margit and her family for only the first week of the program. There were so many people in the village who wanted an English teacher living with them that I would live with three different families. I would teach for nearly four weeks, and would spend one week with the children at a camp near Szentendre.

Margit's household comprised Margit's husband, Gyula, their children, Nóra and Feri, and Barka, a dog. There were a lot of cats, who weren't allowed inside. Nóra had given them all names, which only she knew. Margit's physical type was familiar to me, but Gyula didn't look like anyone I had seen before. Sinewy, tan, with a golden mustache, he wore a long-sleeved plaid shirt tucked into denim short shorts and a blue cap with a visor. "*Wilkommen!*" he said, lifting my suitcase out of the trunk and carrying it upstairs.

The second floor of the house was a recent addition; the walls of the front room were still crisscrossed with wooden beams and pink insulation fluff, and a plastic sheet was taped over the window frame. But the back room was finished and beautiful, with a yellow carpet, a green sofa bed, a glass-topped desk with a vase of goldenrods, and, standing in the corner, a little snarling stuffed weasel. When Margit saw the weasel, her expression grew strained and she said something to Gyula, who replied at length.

"My husband thought that your room is very empty, so you might like a little weasel," Margit said, turning to me. "We can move it downstairs now. He won't be hurt." It wasn't clear to me who it was that wouldn't be hurt—her husband or the weasel. In either case, it seemed clear to me that if you really wanted to be a writer, you didn't send away the weasel.

"Are you sure you won't be frightened when you wake up?" Margit asked.

"Oh, no," I said.

I was frightened when I woke up.

Razor-sharp cucumber slices floated in ice-cold vinaigrette. The beets didn't correspond to any ideas I had previously held. In the middle of dinner, Gyula went out the front door, returning with a 1.5-liter Coke bottle full of a kind of inky homemade wine that they kept in the toolshed. Gyula filled three heavy tumblers and raised one, and Margit translated what he was saying: that I should consider their house to be my house, and if I woke up hungry in the middle of the night, I should help myself to whatever they had.

Margit's manner of speech reminded me of Ivan's—the way she pronounced my name, and the questions she asked, like what languages I spoke and what other countries I had visited. Americans didn't ask such questions. Margit had been to Paris and Vienna, and Petersburg when it had been Leningrad. She had studied Russian for twelve years under the Soviets, but had forgotten everything. "It's a pity," she said, "since it's such a beautiful language."

Every two years, Margit traveled to London with a group of her English students. On their last trip it had rained every single day and they had spent an entire afternoon drinking scotch in her hotel room. They couldn't drink in the bar, because most of the students hadn't turned eighteen yet. It was strange to Margit, because in Hungary there was no drinking age, and weren't the students just as much her responsibility, whether they were in a bar or in a private room? The scotch in London was very good.

Margit asked what I thought of the television show *ER*, which had just come to Hungary. Margit thought it was less stupid than *Dallas*.

After dinner, it was time to check the fields. The whole family piled into the car. When Gyula opened the trunk, Barka jumped right in and lay down, like she rode there all the time. Margit climbed into the back with the children, and I got in the front and put on my seat belt. Gyula started shouting and waving his arms.

"He says you can trust his driving," Margit said, laughing. "He's a very safe driver and we're not going far."

I immediately took off the seat belt. More hilarity ensued. "No, no," Margit said, "keep the belt and feel safe!" I said that wearing a seat belt didn't reflect a judgment about safety, it was automatic, because at home it was against the law to not wear a seat belt. This, too, they found hilarious. "If we are driving to the fields and a policeman catches us, he might put you in jail!"

The fields were a few minutes' drive away. Gyula took a shotgun out of the trunk and disappeared into the corn. A female scarecrow lolled on a tall stake, her dress flapping in the wind. Margit said it was her own old dress. "It shrank, so Nóra and I made a scarecrow. For some reason, Nóra gave it a cat's face." Sure enough, the scarecrow had a little cat nose and whiskers.

"That should be scary for the birds," I said.

"Unfortunately, our birds are very brave." We walked around the fields and Margit pointed out the different crops: tobacco, wheat, chickpeas, watermelons, other melons, poppies, grapes, cherries, apples.

Back at the house, Margit put the children to bed, and then brought out an apple cake she had made. Gyula set a bottle of whiskey on the table. I felt embarrassed to eat cake without the children. Margit, who seemed to guess what I was thinking, said that Feri didn't like cake, and Nóra had to cut down on sweets, though she was only seven. Did anyone ever get as much of anything as they wanted?

"Now," said Margit, when Gyula had poured the whiskey. "Tell us all about yourself."

"But I have," I said. "You already know everything about me."

"Now you will tell us the long version," she said, sitting back in her chair. "We have so much time. We have all night."

It made such a strong impression on me when she said that. Just for a moment, as if in a flash of lightning, I seemed to glimpse some unseen vista stretching out before me and opening in all directions before it went dark again.

Margit asked what I wanted to become after the university. I told her what I wanted to become. "You'll write a novel about us," she exclaimed.

"Maybe someday," I said.

I was surprised when she asked if I had a boyfriend. I thought it was clear that I wasn't someone who had boyfriends. But when I said I didn't, she seemed disbelieving. "I thought maybe you had a Hungarian boyfriend," she said, "and that's why you came to Hungary."

"No," I said. "What gave you that idea?"

"I don't know," she said. "I suppose it's just something I thought of."

The alarm went off at a quarter to eight. I lay in bed a few minutes puzzling over why exactly I had to get up and teach English to school-children now—whether I had made some mistake and, if so, where.

Nóra was already at the table with her little backpack, eating a roll with butter and jam. Why did the children have to learn English over the summer? Margit made me a really strong Nescafé, and we all got in the Ford Fiesta. I fell asleep and woke only as the tires were crunching over the gravel behind the school building.

The classroom was completely devoid of antlers, indeed of anything more weaponizable than a potted fern, some children's drawings, and a map of Hungary. The students sat at three long tables arranged in a U shape. Margit sat at the lowest table with the smallest children and smiled expectantly. I hadn't realized she would stay. I felt so relieved.

I asked the kids to say their names and ages, and how long they had studied English. Ádám, who was fifteen, had taken three years and was really good—he could really talk to you. Róbert, who was the same age, had never studied any English at all. Neither had many of the younger children, including Nóra. The smallest boy, Miklós, was four and could barely say anything in any language.

Katalin, who was seventeen, was beautiful, with waist-length flaxen hair and a perfectly plain face. Why was "plain" a euphemism for "ugly," when the very hallmark of human beauty was its plainness, the symmetry and simplicity that always seemed so young and so innocent. It was impossible not to think that her beauty was one of the most important things about her—something having to do with who she really was.

Miklós's mother, Tünde, worked in the school. Thin, with mousy hair, big glasses, and a beseeching smile, she often lingered in the classroom and hovered over Miklós, who was incredibly small, even for a four-year-old. Feeble, pink, he resembled an infant squirrel. If you asked him anything, he twisted in his seat in paroxysms of shyness. Tünde would actually prod him with her finger, and then he would squirm more. She gave him a lot of advice, all of it wrong, insisting with particular tenacity that he pronounce all silent *e*'s. If he ever managed to say "one" or "five," she corrected him. "*Oh*-neh. *Fee*-veh."

"*Five*," I said loudly.

"*Fee*-veh," she repeated, with her obsequious smile.

"Is there any way to make her stop doing that?" I asked Margit.

Margit thought about it. "We will ask her to bring an eraser." There was no eraser at the board, just a chalk-saturated rag. Tünde disappeared for the rest of the morning. The next day she was back, sitting at the teacher's desk with a big pink heart-shaped sponge and a tub of water. Every time I looked in her direction she held up the dripping heart. She continued to urge her son to say "*Fee*-neh" when asked, "How are you?" Róbert, who was suggestible, also said "fee-neh" and "fee-veh." Nóra, who never took sides, mumbled something in between. Whenever Miklós made any utterance, no matter what, Nóra clapped her hands and stroked his head and shoulders.

At noon every day, everyone went home except for me and Róbert, whose mother was the school principal. Róbert and I went into a large supply closet where, at a wooden desk surrounded by rolled-up maps and projector screens, we were served an elaborate lunch by the school cook, Vilmos, who wore a white apron and chef's hat. First was soup, then either chicken paprika, beef stew, fried cutlets, or cabbage rolls, and finally fruit preserves artistically laid out on dessert plates. We addressed these meals with dedication, industry, and few words. Sometimes I asked how he was, and he said he was "fee-neh." Then he asked how I was, and I said I was *fine*. At first it seemed strange to go into a supply closet every day and eat a three-course meal with a fifteen-year-old boy, but soon I came to view it as part of the natural course of things.

After lunch, I tutored Ádám and two other fifteen-year-old boys for the English entrance exam to a special computer school. It was easier than the morning session, because the three boys already knew a lot and worked hard, and also because Tünde didn't sit in—she dropped by only to bring a two-liter bottle of flat Pepsi and one glass on a silver tray. I would pour myself a glass, then give the bottle to the boys. Usually they took only polite sips, but one day they spent their lunch break playing soccer and then they swigged down the entire two liters. It disappeared into their bodies, soaked up by their cells.

Before that summer, I knew almost nothing about the Beatles. I didn't know why it was important to be a mop-top, or what a mop-top was. Whenever I heard older people talking about them, I just tuned it out. There were never any bad consequences. I really thought I could go through my whole life that way. But the Beatles turned out to be one of the things you couldn't avoid, like alcohol, or death. "Wouldn't it be fun to teach the children some Beatles songs?" Margit asked, on the very first day. When I said I didn't know any, she got one of the girls in the class to loan me a greatest hits compilation: two ninety-minute Maxell cassettes with the song titles carefully written on the liner in ballpoint pen.

I was troubled by the Beatles, by the contradiction between their jaunty, harmoniously innocent warbling, and the calculating cynical worldview that seemed to underlie it. All the time they had been pleasing that girl, the Beatles had been keeping tally, resenting her for making them show her the way, waiting to be pleased in return. They went on about how they worked like a dog to make money to buy her things, and in exchange she had to give them everything. What if she didn't? What if she didn't know how?

"Seventeen" was daunting because of the line that I expected to go "And the way she looked was way beyond her age," but which instead went, or so it seemed to me, "And the way she looked was way beyond her man." I was deeply struck by the inequity between the girl and her man—the way it made her vulnerable to the Beatles, even as it indicated that she had already been defeated and humiliated, suckered into going with someone so far below her. At the same time, the fact that she was just seventeen, and had a man at all, meant that youth was no excuse for me, for how I was incapable of making anyone drive my car, or of telling the Beatles things they wanted to know, or of evoking in them or anyone else the feelings they described, the feelings that Ivan must have felt for his girlfriend, eight days a week.

Margit took me to visit her former student Judit, who now spoke English as well as Margit, but persisted in asking for lessons. "Judit is a very clever girl," Margit said, looking discontented. "She has read very much—in English, in German, in many languages. She is too advanced for me. I have nothing more to say to her."

"That's a success story," I said. It was what my mother would have said.

"Yes," Margit said uncertainly. "She has a real appetite for learning. She will enjoy talking to you. But I will not stay."

We found Judit reading on a sofa, next to a window that overlooked the vacant lot separating her parents' house from the train tracks, right at the edge of the village. There were books everywhere—stacked on the coffee table in front of the sofa, on top of the TV, in the bay window, on the floor between the sofa and the wall.

Judit stood when we came in. She was taller than me, over six feet, wearing a baggy jogging suit that hid her body but exposed her extremely thin wrists and ankles. Her remarkable eyes—pink-rimmed, gray, almost quivering—were magnified by thick glasses.

Judit's mother, who somehow strongly resembled Judit, though she was ordinary-looking and Judit wasn't, brought lemonade on a tray. Judit moved aside some books, including the one she had just been reading: *The Mill on the Floss.*

"Is it good?" I asked.

"Yes, it's interesting. But I have to look many words up in the dictionary." She picked up a glass of lemonade with a strikingly long, thin hand.

"Are you reading it for school?"

"Indirectly. You see, I dropped out of my program in the spring."

Judit had been studying at a flight academy, because her childhood dream had been to be a pilot, though in fact this was impossible, because she was one centimeter too tall—even for a man, she was too tall. I made an expression of sympathy. She turned her huge, watery eyes toward me. "It's the way cockpits are designed," she said.

"Is that why you left the program?"

"No. I was not in the pilot training program. I was studying to become an air-traffic controller."

"Was it . . . it wasn't fun?"

"Fun?" She frowned slightly. "I left because of my eyesight. I have always had problems with my eyes. Every few years I need a surgery. Since my surgery last winter, even with glasses on it's very difficult for me to pass the eyesight tests."

I wondered what to say to someone whose situation was so different from mine, and seemed so much more difficult. The phrase that came to my mind was "rotten luck," like people in English novels said about war tragedies. "That's unlucky," I said aloud.

"I don't look at it that way," said Judit. "It's better I should drop out of the program now than that I should graduate, become a flight controller, and crash a plane because I didn't see it in the fog." I acknowledged that, when viewed in this light, things had indeed worked out for the best. "In the fall," she continued, "I will begin working for my uncle's import-export business. My languages may be useful then." In addition to English, she knew French and German, and was studying Italian.

"Have you been to any other European countries besides Hungary?" she asked.

I said that I went to Turkey every year to see family, and that I had just been in Paris.

"Do you have family there, too?"

"No, I went with a friend."

"Was it your boyfriend?" she asked. Again with the boyfriends.

"No," I said. I told her about Svetlana, about Robin and Bill. It seemed to me as I spoke that I was alienating her, and in fact this turned out to be the case. "I don't understand why your friend was invited on this trip," she said. "If my boyfriend was interested in somebody else, or if another girl was interested in my boyfriend, I would not invite this girl to join us on our vacation."

"But Svetlana and Robin are friends. They were friends for years, before they knew Bill."

"I don't agree. If she had really been a friend, she would not have gone to Paris, and she would not have told you these things." When she said that, I felt ashamed and wondered where I had made my mistake. Had it been by going to Paris, or knowing the story, or telling it to a stranger?

I was relieved when I heard Gyula's car outside. Margit had had to take the children somewhere, and he had come to pick me up.

The house was empty when we got back. I started to head upstairs, but Gyula led me to the table and pulled out a chair, and the next thing I knew he'd brought out the whiskey again. "Marlboro?" he suggested, taking a pack from his pocket. But the idea of smoking cigarettes with an adult was too strange, and I declined the Marlboro as well as the whiskey. Gyula looked thoughtful, then went outside to the shed and came back with an orange tackle box and removed two stacked trays from the upper compartment. They were full of ammunition, bullets and cartridges and birdshot, neatly arranged in compartments.

He took out several cartridges and stood them upright on the table. "German," he said. "American—like you." Even the bullets here had nationalities. There were Czech, Finnish, Yugoslavian, and Chinese bullets. "Soviet bullet," he said in Russian, tapping a domed cartridge with a red band.

Holding up one of the German cartridges, Gyula twitched his nose and made scampering motions with his hands. Then he beat his palms against his legs in a way that sounded just like wings, and expelled a stream of air, *ffff,* through his teeth. From these gestures I understood, eventually, that the little German cartridge was for shooting rabbits and pheasants.

Standing a larger, American cartridge on the table, Gyula closed his eyes for a moment, then placed his index fingers, pointing upward, against his temples, opened his eyes wide, and turned his head sharply from side to side. "*Özbak,*" he said. That turned out to be a roebuck.

He took out a third cartridge, really different from the other two, brass-plated, reminiscent of a pen. He looked at me for a moment. "*Mensch,*" he said, lowering his voice. Then, in Hungarian: "Man."

Gyula told a hunting story. There was a roebuck in it, and Barka, and the police, and a confrontation, and barking. He repeatedly praised Barka, and said she was a vizsla, and imitated the way she pointed with her foot. He produced some papers from the bottom compartment of the box. "*Biztosítás,*" he said. "Do you understand? *Biztosítás.*"

I looked up *biztosítás.* It meant insurance. When he saw I had a dictionary, Gyula told me some other words, for gun registration, hunting license, and gun license. The most important point seemed to be that you needed two licenses—one for you and one for the gun.

"Two licenses," I repeated.

He nodded and said that I was clever.

The Ford Fiesta pulled up outside, and the children ran in, followed a moment later by Margit. "Oh dear," Margit said, taking in the bottle of whiskey, the open tackle box, and the array of bullets and licenses. "It seems there has been a lecture."

· · ·

The next afternoon, Margit and Gyula were both busy, so the school principal gave me a ride home. When we got to the house, Gyula was running out the door wearing a powder-blue suit. He waved in passing, shouting something about the bus. The principal tried to offer him a ride, but he was already halfway to the main road. He was a really fast runner, even in that suit, which was reserved, I later learned, for his weekly German lessons in the city.

I found myself alone for the first time in days. Remembering that they had said I could eat whatever I wanted, I cut a big slice of apple cake and ate it while reading *Dracula*. It felt amazing to eat anything without having to listen, nod, smile, or do anything with my eyebrows. Dracula visited the Wolf Department at the Zoological Gardens. "These wolves seem upset at something," he observed. The next morning the cage was all twisted out of shape and the gray wolf Berserker was missing. Dracula had temporarily inhabited its body. Dracula had a totally different experience at the zoo from that of other people.

Someone was knocking on the glass door. The main door was open, and behind the glass stood a small blond girl.

"Hello," I said.

"Hello," she said. "I am Reni. We will go on an excursion."

I opened the door. She came in but wouldn't sit down, and only glanced at her tiny watch, its face no bigger than a nickel. She didn't seem interested in cake, either. She just kept saying we would go on an excursion.

"Okay," I said. I got up and started to clear the table.

"We will go on an excursion now."

"Now? Like, right now?"

"Yes, of course!" I noticed then that she was wearing a tiny backpack with both straps on. I suppressed a sigh. Hungary felt increasingly like reading *War and Peace:* new characters came up every five minutes, with their unusual names and distinctive locutions, and you had to pay attention to them for a time, even though you might never see them again for the whole rest of the book. I would rather have talked to Ivan, the love interest, but somehow I didn't get to decide. At the same time, I also felt that these superabundant personages weren't irrelevant at all, but somehow the opposite, and that when Ivan had told me to make friends with the other kids, he had been telling me something important about the world, about how the fateful character in your life wasn't the one who buried you in a rock, but the one who led you out to more people.

As soon as we left the house and reached the main road, Reni's expression brightened.

"After ten minutes, the bus," Reni said happily, when we reached the main road. "We sit."

We sat on the edge of the asphalt, facing the forest. Reni tilted her head and looked at the clear sun-filled sky. "I love outdoors!" she said, then added, "I don't like Margit's house."

"No?"

"No. It's many animals."

"You mean Barka?"

"No. The kill animals, that Margit's husband, with the gun. I hate hunters. Of course, I don't talk this to Margit's husband."

The bus came, a high coach bus with plush seats and tinted windows. We climbed up the stairs and sat near the middle. Reni explained that she had been one of Margit's students—the worst one. Now she studied agricultural engineering, and had a boyfriend. Reni was twenty, and her boyfriend was only sixteen, but he was usually very adult. Only now they were having a fight, and he was behaving like sixteen.

"What's the fight about?" I asked.

"Many things," she said. "He is not lovely."

"Not lovely?"

"Not at all."

I glanced over at her—hearing about her boyfriend made me curious about her appearance. She looked cute and businesslike, with chin-length blond hair, a plain white T-shirt, and wire-rimmed glasses. We talked about crop rotation. The bus left us in Gyöngyös, the second-largest city in the county. In an hour, another bus would take us to a Christmas fortress in the mountains. (This later turned out to be a spruce and fir forest. "Christmas trees," Reni said, pointing out the window.) Meanwhile, in Gyöngyös, we would visit Reni's favorite place, the natural history museum, where they had a very special animal. The animal was large, and didn't exist.

"You mean it's imaginary? Like a unicorn?"

"No, no, it's very old. We look at bones."

"Oh, a dinosaur."

"No, not a dinosaur."

"What's it called in Hungarian?" She seemed reluctant to tell me at first but I kept asking, and eventually she met my eye and said, slowly and loudly, *"MAMMUT."*

The mammut lived in a long yellow mansion formerly inhabited by Hungarian nobles. All the lights were off. Elderly women in historical black skirts and white aprons were folding sheets by a dusty window. When we came in, two women put down their sheet and walked us through the museum, one leading the way with an electric lantern and switching on the lights, the other trailing behind and switching them back off again. Every now and then, one or the other of them would urge us to buy one of the Latin-titled monographs that they carried in their apron pockets. Reni declined, first politely, then in an angry outburst that surprised me, though it didn't seem to offend the women.

We didn't linger over the geological, petrological, and minerologi-
cal history of the Gyöngyös region—they evidently annoyed Reni in
some way, and she walked through in a hurry. But as soon as we got
to the ferns, her face lit up, and by the insect room she was in a trance.
"I *love* nature!" she sighed, looking at an ancient dung beetle. She
knew all the insects' Latin names, and asked me the names in English. The only one I knew was "ladybug."

We came to the vertebrates. "Oh, it's *lovely!*" Reni breathed, when
we came to the hedgehog. The hedgehog was indeed nice, though it
was no less dead or killed than any of the animals in Margit's house.

Standing in the shadowy doorway of an unlit room, the woman
raised her electric lantern, and we made out the gleam of huge pale
arching bones. Then she switched on the light and there was the
mammoth, standing before a green velvet curtain on an elevated platform with no railing, so you could walk right under the curved
human-sized tusks. Unencumbered by flesh or fur, each rib looked so
elegant—high, vaulted, marble-white, like the most graceful bridge.
O Mahmut Bey, you must know that I am always still expecting you,
even now, after so many years.

On the way back to the village, we got off the bus too early, finding
ourselves at an intersection with a restaurant, a gas station, and a sign
that read KÁL, 6 KM. I suggested that we walk, but Reni said that six
kilometers was very far and that I would be tired.

"I've an idea," she said. "My boyfriend's telephone."

"Your boyfriend's telephone?"

"That is only one kilometer. Come."

We left the highway, walking down a narrow paved road that
turned into a dirt road. After about half an hour, we arrived at an
orange and brown house with a BITING DOG sign. Reni knocked at the

gate. An ugly fist-faced black dog leaped out of a shed, bolted across the yard, and threw itself slavering at the fence.

"Oh, Milord!" Reni thrust her hands through the gate and seized the dog's head in such a way that it became incapable—though not, I thought, undesirous—of sinking its teeth in her person. Its hindquarters thrashed in the air. "Milord is a very nice dog," Reni said. Slobber dripped down her wrist.

A woman came out with a plastic basket full of laundry, noticed Reni, frowned, and went back inside.

"That is my boyfriend's mother," Reni said. "She does not love me." I nodded.

"But she is helpless," Reni continued. "Her son loves me. Now she will call him."

"Wouldn't your boyfriend's mother let us use the telephone?" I asked, some minutes later.

"Oh, no!" said Reni. "She thinks I am . . . a very bad girl. I don't know in English." She was still holding the dog's head, which emitted a low growling sound. I offered to knock on the door and ask if I could use the telephone, but Reni said the mother was very suspecting and would think I was also bad.

After we had been standing outside the house for some ten minutes, Reni's mood underwent a transformation, even though our external circumstances hadn't changed in any way I could see.

"My boyfriend knows we are here," she said, squinting at the upstairs windows. She released the dog, sending it into a conniption, and aimed a handful of gravel at the windows. One pebble hit Milord. He reacted in a manner consonant with his personality. Reni reached over the gate and began to open the latch from the inside, then glanced at the foam flying out of Milord's mouth. "Laci! *Laci!*" she shouted, turning to me. "You call, too."

"Laci," I called.

"We must make a *more* sound," she said. "Together. One, two, three."

"LACI!" we bellowed. "LACI!"

The boy who came out onto the porch looked older than sixteen, with olive skin, full lips, and gelled hair. His low-cut white undershirt revealed a golden cross in a nest of chest hair. Reni explained about the bus and the telephone. Laci leaned on the porch rail, making no move to come to the gate. Laci's mother came back out. She and Reni yelled at each other. Then Laci said something, and the mother went inside. Reni and Laci exchanged some remarks. Laci didn't change his relaxed posture or lazy tone of voice.

"He says that we may not use the phone." Reni's voice was trembling.

"Is there a pay phone near here?" I asked. "I have a phone card." I had bought one at the grocery store with Margit but hadn't used it yet.

"Oh—a phone card!" Reni exclaimed, and called something to Laci. Laci sighed and disappeared into the house, then ambled over and handed Reni a telephone card over the fence.

"We don't use your card," Reni told me, "because you are the guest!"

We walked five minutes up the road to a pay phone, and Reni dialed Margit's number, to ask her to come get us.

"It was Margit's husband," she said, after she had hung up. "It's not comfortable. We have very much arguments, because I hate hunters." She sighed. "Well, I go now. You wait here."

I asked where she was going. She said she had to give Laci back his phone card because it actually belonged to his mother. She started walking back up the long straight road to the house. When she was about a hundred yards away, I noticed a figure approaching from the distance. As the figure came closer I saw it was Laci, running. Reni stopped. He jogged the rest of the way to meet her. On the other side of the road, a grassy slope descended to what I could now recognize as a tobacco field. Reni rejoined me at the telephone box, beaming. Laci was lovely again.

Gyula didn't seem mad about having to get us, or troubled by Reni's views on his way of life. In the car he asked her lots of questions, roaring with laughter at her responses.

"We all like Reni very much," Margit told me when we got home.

"I really like her, too," I said.

"But none of us likes her boyfriend. He is not clever or serious or kind. Unfortunately, he is very handsome. Did you meet him?"

"I saw him."

"And you found him handsome?" As I was thinking about how to answer, Margit burst into laughter. "You did not find him handsome!" she cried, clapping her hands.

In the evening we rode on bicycles to Gyula's parents' house. Nóra had her own little bike. Feri rode in a sling attached to Gyula's back. I was perched on a giant men's ten-speed.

"I was worried that you would be cramped, with your long legs," Margit said. "But luckily our neighbors' son is just as tall as you are."

Gyula's father, an agricultural engineer, had become famous by crossbreeding chickpeas and wheat, though not with each other. Gyula was also an agricultural engineer but had lost his job when the Soviets stopped funding the village research center. We rode past the center: three long buildings, one corrugated metal, one rose-colored stucco, the third candy-pink. The surrounding sea of corn and tobacco was reflected so clearly in the windows, it almost seemed to be inside the building.

Gyula's parents' street had a suburban look, with sidewalks, lawns, and nonedible shrubs. Gyula's mother, wearing a silk zebra-print skirt and blouse, ushered us into a living room and showed me her husband's monographs, in Hungarian, German, and Russian. There was a trilingual pamphlet about winter precipitation and beets, and an English translation of the proceedings of a forum on irrigation. On the first page was a list of participants:

ÁBEL, GY., *assistant manager*, Szarvas State Model Farm, Szarvas.

ÁDÁNY, N., *deputy director*, National Meteorological Service, Central Institute for Atmospheric Physics, Budapest.

BALOGH, ZS., *academician, university professor*, Eötvös Loránd University, Department of Plant Physiology, Budapest.

BÁRDOS, A. S., *chief engineer*, Borsod Chemical Works, Agrochemical Section, Kazincbarcika.

BÖDÖR, J., *scientific head of department*, Research Institute for Viti- and Viniculture, Kecskemét.

CSAPÓ, J., *retired director*, Research Station for Beet Growing, Sopronhorpács.

CSORNAI, SZ., *production vice president*, Lenin Cooperative Farm, Tiszaföldvár.

DEÁK, B., *research worker*, Agricultural Research Institute of the Hungarian Academy of Sciences, Martonvásár.

DUDÁS, E., *deputy minister*, Ministry of Agriculture and Food, Budapest.

The questions, in boldface, were followed by the participants' responses in alphabetical order of last name. It was impossible not to admire the clear, concise manner in which Gyula's father differentiated between the irrigation needs of winter versus summer barley, questioned the neglect of rice in the Great Plain, and summarized the advantages of flooding irrigation for alkali pastures.

Gyula's mother brought out an old yearbook. Gyula's father and twenty other young men with combed hair and intent expressions looked out from the glossy black-and-white pages, and I thought about how, long before I was born, they had been memorizing the Krebs cycle, eating winter salami, and contemplating the future—their own, and that of Hungarian agriculture. "I brought you here because Gyula's mother makes a very nice *paprikás* chicken with homemade noodles," Margit whispered.

Conversation at dinner circled around the ambiguous nomenclature of seasonal barleys. Gyula's mother brought out an apple strudel and poured us all brandy. I drank the brandy because it was less trouble than explaining about not drinking it. On the way out, she pressed something warm, heavy, and yielding into my hands. It was wrapped in foil but it felt alive. It was another strudel.

On the way back, I couldn't keep the handlebars completely straight, and yet, coasting in arcs down the empty moonlit road, I realized that falling off a bicycle was far more difficult than I had previously imagined.

In class we worked on the conditional tense. "If I were Picasso," said Katalin, "I would love many women." A less beautiful girl wouldn't have said that, I thought. Beautiful people lived in a different world, had different relations with people. From the beginning they were raised for love.

For the lesson on directions, I drew maps of American towns. Take a left onto Main Street, and then your second right onto Elm Street. The firehouse will be on your right.

"*On* your right, Selin, or *to* your right?"

"Either is fine."

"But which is more polite?"

Nóra and I went for a walk. She told me the Hungarian names of things, and I wrote them down. I hadn't brought the dictionary, so it was what the language philosopher Donald Davidson called "radical interpretation." The street looked empty but was full of words: "puddle," "mud," "bottle," "chocolate wrapper," "gum," "gum wrapper." Nóra pointed sorrowfully at a dead bird and said, *"Madár,"* which I thought meant "dead," but then she pointed at the sky and said *"Madár,"* again, and I realized it was "bird." The grass was sometimes *"gaz,"* and other times *"fü."*

"What's this, *gaz* or *fü?"* she demanded.

"Gaz?"

"No, Selin—*fü!"*

We came to the main road, with telephone and electric lines. *"Telefon oszlop,"* said Nóra. *"Telefon oszlop, telefon oszlop, telefon oszlop. Elektromos oszlop."* I wasn't sure what *oszlop* was, the pole or the line, until we came to a waist-height concrete column sticking out of the ground: *"Beton oszlop,"* Nóra said. I knew *beton* was concrete—Turkish used the same word. It seemed so funny to me that you could have a telephone *oszlop*, an electric *oszlop*, or a concrete *oszlop*. The whole world could be redescribed in terms of *oszlop*. I tried to tell Nóra that she was a Nóra *oszlop*. She listened with a serious expression. "Now we run," she said, and took off for the hills. "Run, Selin," she yelled. Despite her sturdy build, she could run really fast. We ran and ran, through increasingly suburban streets, arriving in the end at Gyula's parents' house. Gyula's mother came out with a weary expression and gave us cake. Ten minutes later, Margit came with the car to get us. It turned out that Nóra's tendency to run to her grandparents' house was well-known. It was because of the cake.

. . .

On Friday, I stood in front of the class singing "Hello, Goodbye" by the Beatles. It was like falling off a cliff: time stretched, there was so much time to think different thoughts. "You say yes, I say no," I sang. "You say stop, and I say go, go, go." I remembered a Turkish expression: "I say *bayram haftası* [holiday week], he says *mangal tahtası* [the wooden base of a brazier]." I thought about holiday week, and how today was Friday, and Ivan had said we could see each other on the weekends.

"Hello, hello!" I sang. "I don't know why you say goodbye, I say hello."

"Hello, hello!" sang the younger kids. "Hello, hello, hello, hello, hello, hello!"

By the time I got back to Margit's house, I had been thinking for hours about calling Ivan, trying to figure out the best way to get down the road to the pay phone. But as soon as I had put down my backpack, Margit said that someone called Mrs. Nagy would be coming to see me in half an hour. Exactly thirty minutes later, Mrs. Nagy arrived with her son Zoltán.

We sat at the table. Margit and Mrs. Nagy chatted in Hungarian. Zoltán, whose pallor, small head, and straight black hair made him resemble an Edward Gorey drawing, stared at the floor. I mechanically ate all the pretzel sticks Margit had set out, like it was a job someone had given me. Margit said that Mrs. Nagy said that I should talk to Zoltán in English, because he knew no English at all, only German. That didn't strike me as such a great reason to talk to him in English. "She says that you must talk to him and that you mustn't be shy," Margit said. Mrs. Nagy herself spoke no English, though she taught German now, and had taught Russian in the past.

I glanced over at Zoltán. He was looking at the floor. "Should I talk to him *now?*"

Margit also looked at Zoltán. "Well, maybe later," she said.

. . .

I ended up having dinner with the Nagys. Everything was covered in sour cream. "EAT," Mrs. Nagy said, in both Hungarian and Russian, gazing into my eyes. "EAT." I tried, but I had always disliked sour cream. To my relief, Mrs. Nagy eventually took my plate away and put it in front of Zoltán's little brother, Csaba—a pudgy, pale child who looked just like their father, and who ate everything. I felt great relief to see the food disappearing into his little body.

Over cream puffs, Mrs. Nagy interrogated me in Russian about higher education in America, asking whether only rich people were allowed to go to the university, how much money my parents made, and whether it was difficult to become a stomatologist. Then she said I should see some of the buildings her husband had built.

"AR, CHI, TECT," she shouted, handing me a folder of brochures.

Mr. Nagy leaned over to point out various features of the buildings, all of which were long two-story structures made of reddish wood. I nodded and pretended to understand, because I was scared Mrs. Nagy would start translating again.

After we had looked at the buildings, Zoltán and Csaba recited poetry in German. Fortunately, they didn't know a lot of poetry in German. Then Csaba took out a plastic recorder and played an incredibly repetitive song about a cuckoo.

"Enough," said the father. Smirking, Csaba launched into the refrain for the fifth time.

"Enough," repeated Mr. Nagy. The boy giggled. His teeth clicked against the plastic, and the exhalations of laughter passing through the recorder made a whistling sound.

"ENOUGH!" shouted the father, and punched Csaba in the stomach. The boy sat down. It had happened so fast that the smirk was still hovering around the corners of his mouth. My mother had once told

me that whenever she saw a kid being struck in public, she always tried
to show some solidarity, by either saying something to the child or
making eye contact. But I couldn't think of how to show solidarity with
Csaba from where I was sitting, and also it seemed hypocritical, because I didn't want him to start playing the recorder again.

I tried to imagine describing this dinner to Ivan, in case he ever
asked me why I hadn't called him. I couldn't imagine it. I thought
about telling Svetlana. *Only you would end up in such a situation*, she
would say, as she often did. I wondered if it was true that different
people gravitated toward different kinds of situations. On the one
hand, it seemed to me that I hadn't done anything special to end up
here—that it could have happened to anyone. On the other hand, I
couldn't imagine Svetlana sitting at the Nagys' dinner table. Was that
what was meant by fate?

I found myself thinking about a girl from school, Meredith Wittman, who had lived on the same floor as me and Hannah and Angela,
though the few times I said hi to her, she murmured something without looking at me or moving her mouth. A graduate of Andover, she
carried her books in a Christian Dior bag and had once written a
feature for the student newspaper's weekly magazine about Boston's
salsa and merengue scene. I happened to know, because I had over-
heard her telling her friend Bridey, that Meredith Wittman was doing
a summer internship at *New York* magazine, and for a moment now I
reflected on the fact that, although Meredith Wittman and I both
wanted to be writers, she was going about it by interning at a magazine, whereas I was sitting at this table in a Hungarian village trying
to formulate the phrase "musically talented" in Russian, so I could say
something encouraging by proxy to an off-putting child whose father
had just punched him in the stomach. I couldn't help thinking that
Meredith Wittman's approach seemed more direct.

At ten, Mrs. Nagy finally stood up and said something to Zoltán, who put on his jacket. Mrs. Nagy put her hands on my shoulders. "UNTIL TOMORROW," she intoned in Russian. "SEE YOU TO-MORROW. AT SEVEN IN THE MORNING."

"Tomorrow?"

"TOMORROW WE GO TO THE GREAT PLAIN."

This to me seemed excessive. "Unfortunately, I'm not free tomorrow," I said.

Mrs. Nagy laughed delightedly and said it wasn't true—she had checked with Margit and I was free. In parting, she urged me to speak English to Zoltán on the way home, because sometimes he seemed stupid, but really he was only quiet.

"He doesn't seem stupid!" I said.

Mrs. Nagy patted my shoulder and said I was a good girl.

Zoltán and I were walking along a dirt road between shadowy green fields. A low bluish cloudbank was rapidly encroaching over the starry black vault of the sky.

"You should say something," Zoltán said abruptly in English, a language I had been told he didn't speak. I was scared half to death. I said the sky was beautiful. He nodded. "It's blue," he said. We turned onto a wider road, with telephone wires. "There's a telephone box," I said.

"We could call somebody," he said.

"We could call any telephone in the world," I said.

Two figures were coming toward us through the darkness: Reni and her boyfriend.

"Hello, Reni," I said.

"Hello," said Reni.

"Zoltán, this is Reni. Reni, this is Zoltán."

"Hello," said Reni.

"Hello," said Zoltán.

"Laci," said the boyfriend.

"Zoltán," said Zoltán.

We stood a moment in silence.

"Hello," Reni said finally.

"Hello," said Zoltán.

"Hello," said Laci.

"Hello," said Reni.

"Hello," I said. Reni and her boyfriend continued on their way.

"You should say something," Zoltán told me, after a minute.

"I think it's raining," I said.

"It's raining," he said, nodding. He looked at me expectantly.

"Why don't *you* talk a little?" I said. "Tell me something about yourself."

There was a long silence. "I am bored," he said.

"Bored?"

"Sorry, it's a mistake. Not bored—*boring.*"

The rain started coming down in earnest when we reached the drive. A flash of lightning illuminated the fields and the yard. Nonetheless, Zoltán refused to come inside.

"There's lightning," I said.

"It's okay. I'm used."

"Well, see you tomorrow."

"Bright and early," he said gloomily. He lurked in the shadows next to the shed while I knocked on the door. Margit let me in.

"Is that an animal?" she asked, peering into the storm.

"No, it's Zoltán."

"Zoltán!" Margit called, stepping onto the porch. But he was gone.

A bolt of lightning lit up the whole bedroom, as if the gauzy curtains didn't even exist, illuminating every cubic inch, unto the weasel.

.   .   .

I had told Margit not to get up early with me the next morning, but was happy when she did anyway. "The rings under your eyes are worse than ever," she said. "Try to sleep in the car."

In the car, sleep was out of the question. Mr. Nagy drove, Zoltán sat in the front, and Csaba and I sat in the back with Mrs. Nagy between us.

"COW, Selin," she said urgently, shaking my shoulder. "COW. COW. COW. In Hungarian we say COW."

Zoltán asked if he could turn on the radio.

"I love the radio!" I said.

A disco beat filled the car. "Trust me, and I will never ever let you down," a man sang unconvincingly.

"BRIDGE," shrieked Mrs. Nagy, gripping my leg.

Sunflowers filled the window, stretching to the horizon. I pre-emptively shouted the Hungarian word for sunflower. It didn't work. "SUNFLOWER. SUNFLOWER. SUNFLOWER," Mrs. Nagy repeated piercingly, patting my knee and pointing out the window.

It took a long time to even get to the Great Plain, and once we got there it was still a long drive to our destination: an open-air market, crowded, yellow, dusty, and already hot. Mr. Nagy needed new pants. We strolled through the stalls of tracksuits, rayon dresses, and night-gowns. Mrs. Nagy picked out various pairs of pants, and Mr. Nagy would go into a corner, take off his existing pants, and try on the new ones. Then Mrs. Nagy would tug at the waist and the crotch and make him walk in circles. The pair she liked best was bright green.

"What do you think?" she asked me in Russian.

"Remarkable," I said.

They bought the green pants. Mr. Nagy put them on immediately and carried his old gray pants bunched up under his arm.

Next we shopped for a plastic gun for Csaba and a soccer jersey for Zoltán. Zoltán tried on several of the jerseys over his shirt, and his mother yanked at the hems, stood at a distance, knelt on the ground, and asked my opinion. Sweat streamed down Zoltán's temples. They ended up not buying a jersey.

Mrs. Nagy said it was time to buy me a gift. "A GIFT. A GIFT. A GIFT." Every time we passed a floor-length dress, she pulled it off the hanger and held it in front of me and asked Zoltán if he thought it looked nice. The sun climbed higher in the sky. We were all drenched in sweat. Csaba was shooting everyone with his gun. Suddenly Mrs. Nagy decided to buy me a hat.

"A HAT, A HAT, A BEAUTIFUL HAT," she said, pulling me to the stands that sold baskets and other straw goods.

I felt some irrational primal resistance toward letting her buy me a hat, even though it was clear, or should have been clear, that this was the only way we would ever be able to move on with our lives. She picked up a wide-brimmed child's hat with a ribbon, set it on my head, and started yanking down on the brim, trying to make it fit. "Hat," she murmured under her breath in Hungarian.

Panic mounted in my body. "I DON'T NEED A HAT!" I shouted in Russian. Everyone turned to look at me. "You know what I like very much, is this," I said, picking up a tiny misshapen basket.

"I didn't know you liked baskets," she said, a bit accusingly. She bought me the basket, and then a little stuffed basset hound that fit inside. The basset hound wore a tragic expression; a plastic heart glued to its front legs read I LOVE YOU in white script.

"Did you like the market?" Zoltán asked on the way back to the car.

"It was interesting," I said. "Do you guys come here often?"

"No," he said. "This is the first time."

On Sunday morning, I took the bus to the nearby city of Eger, to meet with Peter and the other English teachers. The bus was like paradise.

For an entire hour, nobody taught me anything or wanted to be taught anything, and I listened to "All My Loving" and thought about Ivan. I got to Eger almost an hour early for the meeting, and immediately ran into Dawn. "Thank God you're here," she said. "I really need a drink, and I didn't want to go to a bar alone."

We went into the first bar we saw. There were already a few guys inside drinking. Dawn ordered apple juice, vodka, and Sprite; I got a Diet Coke. We sat in the back by the pool table. Dawn explained that she had been assigned to a family of non-English-speaking tee-totalers, and hadn't spoken to anyone or had a drink all week. "I wish I'd known before I gave them the Southern Comfort," she said. "They locked it in a cabinet and I don't know how to ask for it back."

When we had finished our drinks, we walked to the designated meeting point: a monument representing the sixteenth-century battle in which István Dobó led two thousand Hungarians to victory over a hundred thousand Ottomans. When Peter came into view I felt a terrible jolt, and realized it was because Ivan wasn't with him.

There were a lot of weddings in Eger that day, unless it was one huge wedding snaking through the city. You kept catching glimpses between the buildings: a band, a table heaped with flowers, a stern family assembled for a photograph. Statues and yellow-gray buildings stood out against an overcast sky. Peter took us to climb Eger's famous minaret: the northernmost Ottoman building in Europe. The mosque had been destroyed in 1841. Standing alone, the minaret looked hopelessly skinny and out of place, like it had wandered out there on a dare and gotten lost.

The dungeons of the Eger fortress had been converted into a torture museum. It was sort of an architectural embodiment of the triviality-dungeon of conversation. You could have your picture taken with a turbaned and mustached man wearing pajamas and a scimitar.

Whenever I tried to tell Hungarian people about the amazing similarities between Turkish and Hungarian, they refused to believe that the grammars had anything in common, and invariably brought up the presence in Hungarian of Turkish loan words, like those for whip and handcuffs. In fact, although the words for whip really were similar—*kırbaç* and *korbács*—the Turkish word for handcuffs (*kelepçe*) was actually the Hungarian word for trap, whereas the Hungarian word for handcuffs (*bilincs*) was the Turkish word for consciousness. I didn't really know what to make of this, though it was certainly true that consciousness could be a trap.

Cheryl's sad tale: for three nights she had camped on the mayor's sofa. On Wednesday she had been sent to a more remote village two hours to the south, to live with the local handyman.

"He treats me like an idiot," she said softly. "He thought I didn't know how to turn on a light switch or a faucet. I tried to say that we have electricity and plumbing in America, but he wouldn't listen. He kept turning the switch on and off. To show me how the toilet worked, he flushed it seven times in a row. Now the toilet doesn't work."

"Isn't he a handyman?" asked Owen.

"I don't think he's very good at his job," Cheryl replied.

"We're doing our best to get you out of there," Peter said.

Cheryl didn't say anything.

We took turns meeting with Peter, who was leaving for Mongolia in two days; we wouldn't see him again until September 12 at noon in front of the Science Center. Cheryl went first. The rest of us sat by a

fountain watching part of a wedding procession between two buildings, exchanging tales of village life. Daniel's whole class consisted of
teenage girls, some of them really hot. Their fathers all made the same
joke, he heard it at least once a day: "If you ever touch my daughter,
you will have to marry her!" Then they laughed and laughed.

Everyone wanted to take a trip together at the end of the program.
They wanted to go to Romania to see the beautiful forests. Brigands
lived in the forests, and if you didn't know what you were doing you
would get yourself killed, but Peter had some Romanian friends who
would drive us around in their car. The whole setup sounded totally
unappealing to me, what with nobody but Peter's friends to protect
you from the brigands, and nobody but the brigands to protect you
from Peter's friends, but I didn't say anything. I would be in Turkey,
anyway.

When it was my turn to talk with Peter, he asked me if I had spoken to Ivan. I said I hadn't.

"Why not?"

I thought about it. "They keep sending me on excursions."

He laughed. "You should call him," he said. "You should call
Ivan."

"I guess so." I realized I had pulled a fistful of grass out of the
ground. "I don't know why I'm pulling out Eger's grass."

"Oh, don't pull out the grass," said Peter.

"It's a destructive habit," I agreed.

"Well, all right then. Don't pull out any grass, and call Ivan. That's
our plan for you."

Vivie, Owen, and I were on the same return bus—our villages were in
the same direction. At a newsstand, Owen read a German newspaper
while Vivie and I paged through the Hungarian fashion magazines,

and discussed how the models looked less tormented than models in American magazines.

"Maybe it's like how, in cultures where everyone is starving, the standard of beauty is less skinny," Vivie said. We both looked for a moment at the confident Hungarian women, each of whom knew tens of thousands of the words closest to Ivan.

On the bus, Vivie said that her host father referred to sunflowers as "the five fingers of God."

"What does that mean?" I asked.

"I have no idea."

In the shower that night, after I had rinsed the shampoo from my hair, I trained the jet of water between my legs, which was something you could do with a handheld showerhead, though it had never occurred to me before. The sensation was both new and familiar, like a song I'd heard incompletely a long time ago. As I felt my whole body contract and tighten around something that wasn't there, I felt like I understood for the first time what the point of sex would be, and I thought about all the ungrounded longing I had felt around Ivan, and it seemed to me that I couldn't live another moment without feeling him inside me, filling that terrible emptiness. And yet apparently I could live, and had to live, and did live. Upstairs, the goldenrod and the weasel were waiting. I thought for the thousandth time of calling Ivan, and for the thousandth time was unable to think my way around the problems of how to get to the phone and of what to say. Nonetheless, the fact that I could theoretically call him continued to torment me until I fell asleep, and dreamed that I went to a little house where I was supposed to live, and Ivan was inside and shouted at me to go away; then he changed his mind and showed me how to turn the faucets on and off.

Nóra was sobbing with the terrifying abandon of children, as if she would never be consoled. One of the cats had had kittens.

"We have at least fifteen cats now," Margit said. "There may be others. Nóra says they will eat the mice, but I don't think there are fifteen mice left here."

"Couldn't they eat the neighbors' mice?"

"They have already eaten the neighbors' mice."

I was packing my suitcase, though I didn't know where I was going. Nóra followed me from room to room, weeping, a kitten in her arms. She leaned her body against me, warm and damp and snuffling. Even the top of her head felt damp and tearful when I patted it. The kitten was really wet. It looked mildly surprised. So that's what life is, it seemed to be thinking.

When Gyula came back from his German lesson, Nóra set the kitten on the table and jumped into his arms. Gyula lifted her up and dried her eyes. The kitten approached the edge of the table, looked at the floor, and mewed. Then it jumped off and skirted the corner, disappearing in the direction of the bedrooms.

Gyula deposited Nóra on the sofa so he could carry my suitcase to the car. Margit and I got in. Nóra was sitting at the round table on the porch, head buried in her arms. Gyula picked up some kind of a scythe and started sharpening it on a stone with a grinding, whining sound. Margit put the car in reverse. In the mirror I watched Nóra zoom farther away, then closer, then farther again. Her face was still cradled in one arm; with the other arm, she was waving tragically.

A red bus was speeding toward us from the left, a blue bus from the right. "We have a choice," said Margit. "We can be killed either by a red bus or by a blue one." We crossed the train tracks, then drove alongside them for a few minutes, stopping at a small pink house that faced the station. Margit said I was going to spend the next week there with a girl named Rózsa, who was my age and was in training to be an English teacher. She said she wasn't going to stay long because Rózsa didn't care for her.

Rózsa came to the door with her aunt Piri. We were staying at Piri's house, which was bigger than Rózsa's parents'. Rózsa and Piri were small-boned, with fair skin and black hair, but Rózsa was taller and thinner. Piri wore a yellow sweat suit; Rózsa, a turquoise plaid shirt and turquoise sweatpants. Rózsa was silent and severe. Piri, a piano tuner who spoke fluent Esperanto, stroked my hair and uttered mysterious exhortations. "*Saluton!*" she said. "*Bonvenon!*"

Margit left right away. Rózsa showed me my room. We carried the suitcase upstairs. Then we sat in silence. Having noticed a washing machine in the bathroom, I asked if I could do laundry. It turned out that the machine was broken. Rózsa proceeded to wash all my clothes herself in the bathtub, scrubbing every item, even the underwear, with a little brush.

"What's this?" She held up a dripping white T-shirt—it looked huge in her hands, like a flag—and pointed at a yellow stain. "There, under the arm."

"Well, I think it's from deodorant," I said.

"I don't like that," she said darkly. "I don't like it at all."

I repeatedly proposed washing the clothes myself, but she said that since I was used to a machine, I wouldn't be able to manage.

We loaded the wet clothes into a plastic basket, took them outside, and started pinning them to a clothesline that hung between two trees. After I had pinned up two of my sodden flaglike T-shirts, there was a cracking sound, one of the trees split in half, and the line fell down.

We collected the wet clothes and went inside to Emese's bedroom—Emese was Piri's daughter, who worked in a store. A length of fishing line ran across the wall, for hanging posters. One poster hung from the line: a portrait of Beethoven, mounted on foam board.

"I think it's a nice surprise for Emese, to find your clothes on the wall," said Rózsa, climbing on the bed and pinning up my jean shorts.

"Couldn't we hang the clothes in my room?" I asked.

"Why? Are you frightened of Emese?" She looked searchingly into my face, as if for signs of fear.

"What? I've never met Emese."

"You mustn't be afraid of her, you know," she said. Her face was so close to mine that she couldn't see both of my eyes at once, and kept looking from one eye to the other.

"Okay, but I still don't want to get her bed all wet."

In response, Rózsa pinned a pair of my panties next to Beethoven.

We went back to the bathroom to dry our hands. The towel rack came off in a cloud of plaster dust. Detached from the wall, it resembled a prehistoric bone.

Piri brought out the pieces of a white plastic table and said we should reassemble it; then we could have dinner on the patio. Rózsa and I unfolded the legs and screwed them in, but when we stood the table up, the legs buckled and collapsed. Piri mirthfully brought out a roll of duct tape. We taped the legs straight. The minute we got the table to stand, there was a clap of thunder and rain started pouring from the sky like from a giant overturned bucket. We didn't have dinner on the patio.

Rózsa and I sat in the mustard-colored living room, where four incredibly loud clocks each told a different time. Crashing noises came from the kitchen.

"Piri is cooking," Rózsa said in a voice heavy with significance.

"Should we help?"

"No. Piri does not know how to cook. And she puts medicines in the food."

"Medicines?"

Rózsa checked her dictionary. "Laxatives," she said. "She puts laxatives in the food."

"Why?"

She consulted the dictionary again. "Because she believes that everyone has a constipation."

Next to each place setting at the dinner table lay a square paper cocktail napkin. When I unfolded mine and put it on my lap, Piri jumped from her seat, whisked away the napkin, and rushed to the kitchen.

"Why did you do that?" asked Rózsa. "Why did you do that with the napkin?"

"I don't know. In America, people put napkins in their laps."

"Why? Do Americans always spill food onto their clothes, like little babies?"

I thought it over. "I suppose they do."

Piri came back with a large checkered cloth, probably a tablecloth, which she handed to me with a flourish. "She says this will protect your clothes better than a little napkin," Rózsa explained. I tried to decline, but Piri was too excited about the tablecloth. I thanked her and covered my lap with the cloth.

Emese came home in the middle of dinner. She was tall, with a beauty mark on one cheek, and a gap between her front teeth that gave her a sheepish expression when she smiled. Kicking off her high-heeled boots, she sank into a seat with a luxurious sigh, rubbing the back of her neck.

Emese noticed that I liked the summer cucumber pickles, and kept moving them near my plate. I could have eaten a bucket of those cucumbers, which had been pickled in the sun, without vinegar. I saw that she liked the corn, and slid the bowl closer to her.

"I do not understand people who gorge themselves," Rózsa said.

After dinner, Emese changed into a miniskirt and went out. Rózsa and Piri and I put on our nightclothes and sat in the living room, talking about Esperanto.

Esperanto had words from every language in the world. However, the only Hungarian words were *papriko* and *gulašo*. Reaching for her phrase book, Piri knocked over a silver mirror and it broke into three pieces. She and Rózsa dissolved into helpless laughter, and Piri went to get the glue.

She returned with a phrase book, published in the eighties, which translated between Russian, Esperanto, Hungarian, German, and English. "We would like to know more about the rest cures (sanatoriums) of your country," I read. "We would like to talk to the workers." "I am a Communist (Socialist, Democrat, Liberal)." "I am an atheist (Catholic, Protestant, Jew, Muslim)." "I would like to see this lathe more closely."

The list of frequently used nouns included: struggle for peace, woman, love, constitution, deputy, congress, delegation, friend, mother, little girl, salmon, sturgeon, red (black) caviar, champagne, vodka, watermelon, cherry, sour cherry, horseradish, and beefsteak.

"*Fini!*" exclaimed Piri happily: she was done gluing the mirror.

On the way to bed, I almost fell down the stairs; the carpet on the staircase was attached only to the top step. In the middle of the night, when I got up to use the bathroom, I saw a tall figure looming near the top of the stairs. It was a young man with a carving knife. He looked me over from head to toe. "Hullo," he said moodily, and stumped downstairs. I hurried to the bathroom and locked the door.

Piri had made croquettes for breakfast, which I was supposed to eat with jam. Nobody else was eating jam.

"We know that you like jams," said Rózsa, handing me a soupspoon and a big jar of jam. "No, you can take more than that. We made a lot." Piri handed me the checkered cloth. "Here is Selin's towel," said Rózsa. "Because you're a little baby!"

"Oh, thanks," I said.

As we ate, I asked Rózsa about the young man I had seen wandering around with a carving knife. She said he was Emese's boyfriend, András, and had come to cut a watermelon. "He is very usual. He comes at midnight or one o'clock, with a watermelon. But he gets up very early and goes to work. You must eat more jam."

"Where does he work?"

"At the discotheque. He gets up very early, and works very hard." I had seen the discotheque—it was called the Elefánt Diszkó—across from the train tracks. I wondered what work was done there early in the morning. "He is not interesting for me," Rózsa said. "But it's okay. Emese loves. I don't love. I don't split hairs."

Piri's house was so close that we could walk to school. Rózsa was carrying a cake she had baked, for Tünde. It was part of a plot to induce Tünde, who turned out to have influence in the matter, to let Rózsa come to Szentendre with me the following week.

Margit came to drop off Nóra, but she wouldn't stay for class anymore; she said Rózsa wouldn't like it. With Margit gone, Tünde was constantly underfoot, ordering the children to pronounce silent vowels and telling Rózsa to tell me that I ought to talk more myself, instead of making the children talk.

"She says your job is to speak very much," said Rózsa, "so they hear an American."

"I *do* speak very much," I said.

Rózsa shrugged. "I do not say this. Tünde *néni* says this. She loves to split hairs."

The new class was bigger and met in both the morning and the afternoon. Rózsa had made really detailed lesson plans in Hungarian; if I didn't interrupt her, she was ready to talk for the whole time, without giving the children a word edgewise. For most of the first day I sat in the window and listened to her, while eating the peanuts that Tünde had brought on a silver tray. On the second day I suggested to Rózsa that she could teach her plan in the morning and I could do my own plan in the afternoon.

"No, this is Selin's class," said Rózsa. "You must teach all of it. I'm just your translator."

"That's not true, you should get to do your plan."

"I made it for both of us!"

"Well, I think since it's your plan, you should get to teach it. And I'll teach my plan."

"Oh, have you a plan? Then I needn't translate. From now on, I am quiet. I sit in the corner." She really went off to a corner, sat on one of the tiny chairs, and glared at me for the rest of the day.

We were supposed to be learning body parts, so I drew a person on the board and we talked about her body parts. Then we played Simon Says. After I had been Simon for a long time, I said that one of the kids should be Simon, and whoever did it would get a Blow

Pop. A boy named Attila raised his hand. He did a good job at first, but then he must have run out of ideas, because he kept saying, "Simon says touch your knees. Touch your knees. Simon says touch your knees. Touch your knees." We played Hangman. I gave Blow Pops to the winners.

"This is your plan?" Rózsa asked afterward in a voice full of outrage. "Candies and games?"

"That's basically the American way."

"I think that you are very . . ." She consulted her dictionary. "Inexperienced."

"We have different systems."

"Yes—I am serious, and you are not!"

As we were walking back to Piri's house, we ran into Reni, who was wearing canvas gloves and an oversized sweatshirt that hid her shorts. She said she had been gardening.

"Do you know Rózsa?" I asked.

"Yes," she said, just as Rózsa said, "Of course."

We stood there for a while, and then Reni kept walking.

"I am not popular here," Rózsa said.

"No?"

"No. Somebody a little more clever than most has said that I am special."

"Special how?"

She checked the dictionary. "Conceited," she said. "Particular, fussy. Fastidious."

"They think that you split hairs."

"Yes."

We went to Tünde's house, so that Rózsa could ingratiate herself some more. Tünde gave us Coke and Reese's Pieces, then she sat her

son, Miki, on her knee and had a long talk with Rózsa. I ate almost
the entire bowl of candy, and made faces at Miki, who squirmed and
smiled at the floor.

"What's the matter with you?" Rózsa snapped at me.

"Nothing," I said.

"Selin likes children," Tünde said in Hungarian.

"Selin *is* a child," said Rózsa.

"Oh, no, she's a teacher," said Tünde, with her obsequious smile.

Afterward I asked Rózsa how it had gone, and what Tünde had
said.

Rózsa looked into the distance. "She said many stupid things," she
said. "But I am a persevering girl. Steadfast."

Emese was playing something by Liszt on the piano, bending over the
keyboard to coax out the quiet passages, and pouncing on the loud
ones like a cat on a mouse. Her white tracksuit rustled. The piano, a
stained upright, was amazingly out of tune, considering that Piri was
a piano tuner.

András came for dinner with his knife and a yellow melon. I asked
about the melon's Hungarian name. Its Hungarian name was "yellow
melon." Piri made batter-fried meatballs, rice with raisins, stewed
apples, and a cucumber salad. A full day of near-continuous eating
had left my appetite strangely undiminished.

Piri urged Rózsa to eat more. Rózsa said she didn't see the point
of eating when one wasn't hungry. I offered to do the dishes. András,
who had been silent all evening, said that I was different from
Emese—I was a house-loving woman.

"Is it true?" Rózsa asked, looking into my face. "Are you a house-
loving woman?"

I started to wash the dishes. Rózsa stood over my shoulder and
said I was using too much water and soap. I tried to be more sparing,

but still she poked my arm and complained. Finally I told her to do the dishes herself, so I could learn how to use less water.

"I see that I am the only real house-loving woman here," Rózsa said, pulling on the rubber gloves.

Instead of soaping and rinsing each dish individually, Rózsa put them all in a tub of soapy water, then replaced the soapy water with regular water. She really did use less soap and water.

We went outside to give the leftover rice to the neighbors' dog. The dog, a little spaniel, stood on its back legs and yelped. I knelt to pet it between the slats of the fence. Its eyes shone with emotion—with desire and what looked like love. Rózsa let me put the rice in its dish. The dog gobbled it up. I stroked its little brow. When we went back to the house, the dog yelped piteously behind us. Looking back, I saw its head bobbing urgently over the fence.

"It would not be sad if you did not love it," Rózsa said testily.

I always tried to go to bed early, so I could read in English—real, dense English, with lots of sentences back-to-back, totally unlike "Simon says touch your knee to your elbow," or "I would like to see this lathe more closely," or "Somebody a little more clever than most has said that I am special." I finished *Dracula*, and started *The Magic Mountain*. I found a lot to relate to in *The Magic Mountain*, particularly how they ate breakfast twice a day. Sometimes, after a whole day of eating, I would rush upstairs and devour a few squares of the chocolate I had brought from Paris to give as gifts.

Sooner or later, Rózsa's footsteps creaked up the stairs and stopped outside my door. "You said you were tired, but I see your light on."

Rózsa wanted to sit up late in the living room, having meaningful conversations.

"There isn't *anything* you want to know about me?" Rózsa asked, when we were sitting in the living room. "I'm so boring?"

The ocherness and clock-ticking seemed to intensify with each passing second.

"It's not that I don't want to know about you," I said. "I just can't think of the questions."

Rózsa gave me a burning look. "You can't ask me questions," she said. "But I could ask you many questions."

I didn't ask what the questions were, but she told me anyway. First she wanted to know what I thought about Hungarian people. I said I thought they were friendly and hospitable. She said I had to tell her my true thought.

"That is my true thought. Everyone I've met has been really friendly and hospitable."

"They only try to seem this way with you because you're the guest!"

I sighed. "Why do you want me to say something negative?"

"I want an honest confession," she said. "I want the whole truth, both good and negative."

I tried to think of a confession. "Tünde gets on my nerves," I said.

Rózsa snorted. "Of course you don't like Tünde. Who likes Tünde?"

"You don't like her, either?"

"Of course not! She is proud. I don't know why, since she is neither beautiful nor clever. But I asked about all Hungarians. Not just Tünde."

"I've been here like two weeks. I'm only ready to talk about Tünde."

"Tünde is *not* interesting! What about *me*? What do you think about me?"

She looked so much like Lucy from *Peanuts* that I felt a wave of tenderness toward her. "I think you have a passion for truth."

"And you are different? You do not love truth?"

I thought about it. "Truth is okay," I said.

"I hate lies. This is what I hate most about Hungarians: they say one thing but think something else."

"I'm pretty sure everyone does that—not just Hungarians," I said.

"*I* don't," she said. "I say what I am thinking or I say nothing. I don't lie."

"But civilization is based on lies."

Piri came in with a plate of cylindrical wafers and asked what we were talking about. Rózsa told her that I'd said civilization was based on lies.

"But that's true, Rózsa," Piri said. She set the plate on the table and left the room, nodding to herself and saying, "*Igaz, igaz.*"

"I have another question," Rózsa said. "How old is your Hungarian friend?"

"What friend? Reni?"

"No, not Reni! Your boyfriend. The Hungarian boy from America."

"He's not my boyfriend. He's twenty-two."

"Oh, gracious! He's very young. *My* friend is twenty-five. But he is like your friend. He is separate. He is not anymore my boyfriend."

"I'm sorry to hear that," I said.

"*You?*" Her eyes flashed. "Why are *you* sorry?"

"Because you . . . had a disagreement."

"We had a disagreement." She tilted back her head. "Hungarian men are very interesting. They know how to say what you want to hear. They are very clever. But they do not mean these words. Five or six months later, when it is enough, then they will say the really awful things."

Those words, "when it is enough," stayed with me for a long time.

Rózsa and Piri took me on an excursion to the primitive man's cave.

"The primitive man's cave?"

"The cave of the primitive man."

"What is he, like a hermit or something?"

"Maaaybe," said Rózsa.

On the narrow-gauge railway, Rózsa and Piri sat with the picnic basket. I stood at the railing, watching the forest.

"Do you see the loco?" Rózsa pointed at the engine.

"I do."

"We call it the coffee machine."

"Why?"

"Because it's small and makes steam!"

I waited what I hoped was a decorous interval, then put on my headphones. All I wanted was to stand there, listen to the Beatles, watch the trees go by, and think about Ivan. Speaking more loudly, Rózsa said I couldn't stand by the railing because I might fall. I pretended not to hear. "Selin," she said. "Selin."

"What?"

"Why don't you sit?"

"I like the view."

"What view? There is nothing. The primitive man's cave is not here yet. Here are only the trees. You don't have to stand up to see them."

"But you can see more of them if you stand up."

"But you aren't really looking!" she exclaimed. "You are—" She flipped through her dictionary. "Wool, gathering!"

"That's true," I said. "I am woolgathering."

"You are thinking about your friend," she said. "That's why you don't want to listen to me."

"But Rózsa. Don't you ever like to . . . to do woolgathering?"

"No! I am not a dreamer."

The primitive man's cave was at the top of a steep hill. I was wearing men's Birkenstocks, which were so ugly that I thought they would be good for hiking, but they weren't.

"Why are you wearing your slippers?" Rózsa asked.

"I don't know," I said.

The primitive man didn't live in the cave anymore. His presence had been established by the things he had left behind, like some hundred-thousand-year-old flint spearheads. Bones had been found, from animals that lived before the last Ice Age: cave bear, cave hyena, tundra deer.

Rózsa took my hand and led me into the blackness. It was my first time in a cave. It smelled terrible. The farther we went, the colder, darker, and more malodorous it became. Spiderwebs attached themselves, like long trails of agglutinative suffixes, onto our arms and faces. When our eyes got used to the dark, we could see the spiders. "They're tired," Rózsa said. Indeed, I had never seen a more sluggish lot of spiders.

I tried to think about the primitive man—to picture him getting up in the morning. How did the primitive man know it was the morning? I wondered whether Ivan had been here. It didn't seem like a highly trafficked cave.

It was harder to walk down the hill than it had been to climb up. The Birkenstocks kept slipping.

"You must take small steps," Rózsa said. "You needn't hurry, or you will fall."

But small steps seemed to present more opportunities for slipping, so I took big steps and ended up running, gaining so much momentum that it took a lot of effort to stop at the bottom without trampling any picnickers.

"I know why you did that," Rózsa said, when she had caught up with me. "It's because you were afraid."

In the evening, when nobody was looking, I crossed the street to the train station. Rózsa had said I must never go there: the café was frequented by Gypsies.

Pale fibrous clouds lay on the surface of the sky, which resembled a dark blue inverted bowl. The moon was a perfect white disk. In the window of the café, the men, tables, bottles, and a piano stood out as sharply as a scene in a movie. Some distance away, on the other side of the station entrance, stood a glowing phone booth.

I went inside and pulled the door shut. The overhead light came on. I started to dial Ivan's number, but couldn't go through with it, and instead called Svetlana in Belgrade. She answered on the second ring and almost immediately launched into a description of the Italian trip with Bill.

"We were each overwhelmed by the ecstasy of the other's presence," she said.

"That's a great sentence," I said.

"I admit I prepared it beforehand. I've been waiting for somebody I could use it on."

"Oh—I thought you made it up just for me."

"Well, probably I did, on some level. I can't imagine who else I would say it to. Maybe my shrink, but he gets crotchety when I talk about Bill. But I knew you would understand. When you think about all the infinitely many galaxies and combinations of DNA, and against all those odds you met this person—it's a *miracle*. I wanted to prostrate myself in every church."

"Right," I said. I couldn't imagine viewing Bill's presence on Earth as any kind of a miracle, but wasn't that itself the miracle—that love really was an obscure and unfathomable connection between individuals, and not an economic contest where everyone was matched up according to how quantifiably lovable they were?

I told Svetlana about Piri's house. "I *know* that living room," she said. "There's always one fly buzzing around, and nobody can catch it. Why hasn't Ivan rescued you yet?"

"I haven't called him."

"Why not? Wasn't that the whole point of going to Hungary?"

"I don't want him to think I'm complaining. Anyway, I should probably be solving my problems myself." I told her how he had told me to make friends with the other kids.

"Do you even realize how crazy you sound? You should call him, before those ticking clocks make you even crazier."

Svetlana had had coffee with her friend Sanja—the one she used to torture when they were little girls. Sanja was having an affair with the married thirty-five-year-old father of two young children. He was a news announcer on the national radio station. Svetlana knew his voice intimately—all Serbs did. "I learned about Radovan Karadžić's resignation from the married man who is sleeping with my old school friend Sanja," Svetlana reflected.

"He must have a pleasant voice," I said.

"Actually, he speaks in a really irritating monotone. Sanja says his voice is totally different in bed. I hope for her sake it is. Can you imagine hearing sweet nothings in the voice of a newscaster?"

"Did you make her cry?"

There was a pause. "I did, actually. Not on purpose. I was just trying to figure out, from scientific interest, whether she had any ethical problem with having an affair with a married man."

"Did she?"

"No! Not at all! First she joked about it, and then she became defensive, and then she started to cry. But not out of remorse—just to make me feel sorry for her, and change the subject. My father says that surviving a war makes you either very bitter or very frivolous. I think it made Sanja frivolous."

"But it made you bitter?"

"You bet. But I'd rather be bitter than frivolous. Okay, my sexual experience might be limited to kissing my cousin's boyfriend in the Belgrade zoo at age thirteen, whereas Sanja is having an affair with a thirty-five-year-old married newscaster. But even so, I think I have a deeper understanding of love than she does."

At that point our conversation was interrupted by a terrific crashing sound. Looking up, I saw a man straddling the broken window of the station café, one leg inside, the other in some bushes. He was shouting at another guy who was still inside the café, and then they both jumped out the window and started rolling on the ground.

"I thought Rózsa was being racist about the Gypsies," I said.

"No, Hungary has a Roma problem," said Svetlana. "I can't believe you're there, watching them throw each other out of windows."

"I can't believe you're *there*, driving people's mistresses to tears."

"I know. I thought about making an anonymous call to his wife, but I figured it wasn't really my business. I *feel* like it's my business, though, because it's part of the story of my trip to Belgrade. I've been thinking about that a lot lately. Do you know what I mean?"

"About what's part of the story of your trip?"

"Yeah, exactly. Talking to you on the phone now is part of the story of my trip to Belgrade, and so is the fight in the café. And when *you* tell yourself the story of *your* trip to Hungary, Sanja will be part of it."

"That's true," I said.

"For a while now I've been conscious of a tension in my relationship with you," Svetlana said. "And I think that's the reason. It's because we both make up narratives about our own lives. I think that's why we decided not to live together next year. Although obviously it's also why we're so attracted to each other."

"Everyone makes up narratives about their own lives."

"But not to the same extent. Think about my roommates. Fern, for example. I don't mean that she doesn't have an inner life, or that she doesn't think about the past or make plans for the future. But she doesn't compulsively rehash everything that happens to her in the form of a story. She's in my story—I'm not in hers. That makes her and me unequal, but it also gives our relationship a kind of stability, and safeness. We each have our different roles. It's like an unspoken contract.

With you, there's more instability and tension, because I know you're making up a story, too, and in your story *I'm* just a character."

"I don't know," I said. "I still think everyone experiences their own life as a narrative. If you didn't have some kind of ongoing story in mind, how would you know who you were when you woke up in the morning?"

"That's a weak definition of narrative. That's saying that narrative is just memory plus causality. But, for us, the narrative has aesthetics, too."

"But I don't think that's because of our personalities," I said. "Isn't it more about how much money our parents have? You and I can afford to pursue some narrative just because it's interesting. You could go to Belgrade to come to terms with your life before the war, and I could go to Hungary to learn about Ivan. But Fern has to work over the summer."

"*You're* working."

"But my mom paid for my plane ticket. I'm not going to *make* money, to like give to my family."

"I don't think that's the point. Fern is just an example. Valerie's parents are engineers, she doesn't have to work, but she's still more like Fern than she is like us."

"I don't know," I said. "I guess it feels elitist to look at it that way."

"Don't you think *you* pretending not to be elitist is disingenuous?" Svetlana said. "If you really think about who you are, and what you value?"

Back at the house, Rózsa was waiting for me. "Now *we* will have our talk," she said, pulling me to the living room. "How is your friend—what was his name? Was it *Iván?*"

I didn't know who had told her Ivan's name. "I don't know how he is."

"Why not?"

"Because I didn't talk to him! I talked to someone else."

Rózsa fell silent. "I am sorry," she said. "I am sorry, and I am ready."

"For what?"

"I am sorry," she repeated, "and I am ready."

"What are you ready for?"

"*Őrület,*" she said, pointing to the entry in her dictionary: "mania, frenzy, madness."

"You're ready for madness? What does that even mean?"

"While you were at the station, I also talked on the telephone. Tünde called. I can come with you to the camp."

The bus to Szentendre left early in the morning. Piri gave me a pill at breakfast that she said would prevent me from getting sick. When I said I would prefer to wait until I was actually sick to take any pills, both Rózsa and Piri started talking heatedly at the same time. "*Malsano!*" Piri shouted in Esperanto, mime-vomiting. "*Malsano, blechhh!*" Eventually I put the pill under my tongue and pretended to swallow.

When the bus passed the station, I saw that the window of the Gypsy café was crisscrossed with duct tape. I fell asleep with my head against the window, and woke up just as we came to the intersection where Ivan's car had overheated. There it was again: the Chinese restaurant, the commuter train station, the modern-day sundial.

Rózsa and I were stalled at the gate of the campground. She was holding our bags and I couldn't figure out how to work the latch. The caretaker's dog bounded slavering in our direction, then stopped short

as if a ghostly hand had grabbed its collar. The caretaker came out of
his cottage and started yelling at us. Rózsa and I stood there, watching him.

"He said you're stupid," Rózsa told me after a moment.

"I see," I said.

The caretaker was still yelling.

"Not stupid," Rózsa said thoughtfully. "Idiotic."

The children were being organized to walk to the cafeteria for lunch.
One of the gym teachers brought me a can of corn and most of a watermelon. I came to understand that I wasn't going to the cafeteria
with the others, but would remain at the campground, eating corn and
watermelon. It seemed like an odd arrangement—I think it seemed
odd to all of us—but we went along with it. Safety concerns were
hinted at. "You can open the can yourself, nobody else has touched it,"
Rózsa said.

A delegation of gym teachers brought me a glass of tap water, then
immediately took it away and poured it in the sink. One teacher went
outside and seized a can of Coke from a small child who had been
about to open it, and gave it to me. I tried to return it, but everyone
protested vehemently, including the child.

I sat on a bench, drinking the Coke and watching the children being
corralled out of the campground. Once everyone had left, I decided, I
would go to the train station and call Ivan. While I waited, I ended up
eating the whole can of corn, as well as most of the watermelon.

Ivan picked up on the third ring. "Hallo?"

"Ivan?"

The silence at his end was so long that I thought we'd been disconnected. "Where are you?" he said finally.

"I'm in Szentendre. I'm at the modern-day sundial."

There was another silence. "Do you want me to come get you?"

I nodded, then remembered he couldn't see me. "Yes."

"Okay," he said, and something seemed to relax between us. "What the hell are you doing there anyway?"

I tried to describe the camp. I thought it might be the kind of institution that would make sense to him as a Hungarian, but as I spoke I could tell it didn't.

"Is it an English camp, do they study English?"

"No."

"So what are you doing there?"

"I don't know," I said. "I think I'm on vacation."

Ivan said that if they didn't need me to teach English, I should bring a toothbrush and stay the night at his parents' house. He said he could pick me up in an hour—we could meet at a restaurant he knew. The restaurant was on a boat. "It's easy to recognize," he said, "because it's the only restaurant that's on a boat."

Even for him, it seemed a diabolical choice of landmark. "How will I find it, if it's on a boat?"

"The boat is stationary. You know," he added, "I think you owe me some kind of a present."

It was true that I had never given him anything, and he had given me two books and a cassette tape. After we hung up, I stopped by the newsstand. They sold cigarettes, flowers, newspapers, and lottery tickets. But Ivan didn't smoke, girls didn't give boys flowers, hideous photographs of politicians were plastered on all the newspapers, and it didn't seem right to get a lottery ticket for someone doing a Ph.D. in probability.

. . .

Back at the campground, I put a toothbrush, contact lens case, and change of underwear in my backpack. I could wear the same jeans tomorrow, but I would need an extra T-shirt. I couldn't decide between two shirts: the one with the most flattering neckline or the one that was cleanest. The clean shirt, actually unworn, featured an ample smocklike body, a tight crew collar, and a picture of Dr. Seuss's Sam-I-Am balancing a plate of green eggs and ham on a pole. It was a gift from my five-year-old half-brother—he had chosen it himself. Some part of me felt that it wasn't what the occasion called for. And yet I knew, I held it on principle, that I couldn't change Ivan's feelings for me by appearing before him in one shirt rather than another, and so I brought the one that was clean and that had been a gift from my brother, who was innocent.

I looked among my belongings to see if I had anything that could be construed as a gift. All I found was an agricultural journal with an article by Gyula's father. At first it seemed inappropriate, but then I noticed that the whole issue was about winter barley. It seemed to me that Ivan would understand this allusion to our correspondence about cereal crops—about grains that slept in the ground and were awoken. I put the journal in my backpack.

When the camp director, Ildi, returned from lunch, I told her that I was going to visit a friend and would be back the following day. This news wasn't received calmly—not by Ildi, and not by any of the gym teachers. "Who is this friend?" one teacher asked, and then everyone started talking at once. Some teachers seemed to be advancing one point of view; others, another. It would have been interesting to see how it turned out, but when I checked my watch I saw that it had been forty-five minutes since I had called Ivan. When nobody was looking at me, I shouldered my backpack and ducked out the gate.

. . .

Walking along the riverbank, I examined every boat for signs that it could be a restaurant. A guy on one boat was eating a sandwich, but it looked like just his own personal sandwich.

"Restaurant on a boat?" I eventually asked a cheerful-looking man with a fishing kit.

"Restaurant on a boat," he said. "One kilometer."

I recognized it right away—it was almost comical how much it looked like both a boat and a restaurant. Compact, blue, it had a bar downstairs and a restaurant on the upper deck. Ivan wasn't in either the bar or the restaurant. I sat on a bench in the entryway, rising and falling gently with the current.

From where I was sitting, below the level of the ground, all I saw at first were Ivan's legs. I recognized them immediately and ran out of the boat. "What happiness," I said.

"What happiness," he said, and we beamed at each other. I noticed then that Ivan's mother was there, and also their car, the Opel, with a canoe tied to the roof. It took me a while to understand the plan, which was that Ivan and I would paddle the canoe back to Budapest while his mother drove back in the car. First, we all went into the boat restaurant to get something to drink.

"Would you like a beer?" asked Ivan's mother.

"She doesn't drink beer," Ivan said.

"Really? Is there a reason?"

"I guess I'm not used to it," I said, adding that America had a drinking age and it was a pain to get a fake ID.

"Oh, then it's because of the American law," she said.

"Well, I don't know if it's because of the *law*."

"Of course it is!" She sounded so sure that I wondered if she was right. "Soda water for me, I suppose," she told the waiter, sounding a bit regretful, when I had asked for Coke and Ivan had ordered lemonade.

Ivan's mother asked about the village. I told her about Margit and Gyula and Rózsa. The parts about Rózsa were supposed to be funny, but neither Ivan nor his mother laughed, and his mother looked a little concerned. When I tried to pay for the soft drinks, she touched my hand and said it was her pleasure. "It's not every day I get to spend time with Ivan and meet his friends."

The idea that I was Ivan's friend, or that meeting me would tell her anything about his life, was so outlandish that I burst out laughing. She laughed, too. She asked whether the people at the camp knew I would be staying out overnight. I said that when I left they had been discussing the subject in a lively fashion.

"Good, so they know," Ivan said. But I felt relieved when his mother said we should go back to the camp so he could talk to them himself.

Ivan's mother got into the back of the car, Ivan drove, and I sat in the front and pointed out the way. When we pulled up in front of the gate, the caretaker's dog started barking its head off. The caretaker glared at us, grabbed the dog's collar, and went into his house, slamming the door. A second later we saw the curtains of the front window jerk angrily together.

"That guy thinks I'm idiotic," I explained, a little proudly.

Rózsa came out of the main cabin, wearing a sailor tunic. I introduced her to Ivan, who towered over her, and whom she addressed in a courteous and reserved manner, strikingly different from the baleful aphoristic tone she used with me in English.

Ivan's mother and I waited by the car. "You're not very lucky, going straight from Rózsa to Ivan," she said, putting her arm around my waist. "It seems you are always under some captain."

It took me a while to process this novel grouping of ideas—Rózsa, Ivan, and my luck.

Ildi came out of the cabin. Her glance passed over Ivan, Rózsa, me, Ivan's mother, the parked car, and the canoe on the roof, before returning to Ivan. "This must be Selin's friend," she said. Ivan talked to her in his warm voice, the one that hadn't worked on the concierge at the hostel. Soon he and Ildi were both laughing. "See you tomorrow," she told me, and waved to Ivan's mother, who waved back.

I stepped first into the canoe, which was shaking and felt like life. Ivan waded into the water, pushed the canoe off the shore, and climbed in behind me. He demonstrated how to hold the paddle, the angle to put it in the water. Because I was in the front, I didn't have to steer, or set the rhythm. I just had to row at the pace that he set, to keep us from going in circles. As he spoke, I felt how I liked following instructions, and it made me ashamed. Following instructions was what had led to the Holocaust. And yet it turned out that shame was a separate thing. If you enjoyed something, you enjoyed it, whether or not you were also ashamed.

At first it bothered me that I couldn't see Ivan. But gradually he felt more and more present to me, just as if I were facing him. It was amazing to be so close to the water, to see the world rising up all around us like some crazy plant. Sixteen-wheel trucks glided by on barges, looming over us, temporarily blocking the sun. Ivan explained that trucks weren't allowed on the streets on Sundays, and so were transported by barge. We bobbed in the wake of a motorboat, gently but vigorously, and all at once.

Ivan was working really hard, as usual. He talked almost the whole time. He told me the story of Saint George. He said there were two versions: one truer, the other less true. In the truer version, they killed Saint George eight times, once by hammering nails into his skull in a prison in Palestine, but he always came back to life. The less true version was the one about the dragon.

Once upon a time, Ivan said, a town was invaded by a dragon. For years, the townspeople were able to placate the dragon by giving it two goats per month. Then they ran out of goats, and had to switch to humans. The governor organized a lottery, "a sort of raffle," to choose the victim. One day, the lot fell to his own daughter. The governor was beside himself. But the daughter said that rules were rules.

"Why the long faces?" asked Saint George, who happened to be passing by. They explained the situation. He said he knew just what to do: he would kill the dragon.

The daughter, who had been having a long day, said, "Oh, go away, Saint George"—though in fact he wasn't a saint yet, so what she really said was, "Go away, George. You'll just get eaten, too. Your plan is shitty."

Just then, along came the dragon. George raised the wooden spade he had for some reason, instead of a sword ("something just like this," Ivan said, holding up his canoe paddle), and the dragon fell. George put his belt around the dragon's neck—I was somehow interested by the part where he took off his belt—and led it into the town.

"Look," George told the townspeople. "I've tamed your dragon, and now if you all convert to Christianity, I'll kill it."

That was the punch line—the part when Ivan, who had started laughing at "Go away, George," completely lost his shit, so I thought the canoe would tip over. I laughed too, but I didn't understand. I didn't see why George had to kill the dragon, once it was already tame, or why he had tamed it by hitting it, and not by love. As I moved the canoe paddle again and again, in the same motion every time, it began to seem to me that I was the dragon, and that Ivan had tamed me, for reasons having nothing to do with me at all. The sun bore down on us—it was the hottest part of the afternoon. I didn't identify at all with the governor's daughter. I didn't identify with any of the girls in the stories that Ivan told. Their sassiness, their spirit, felt wholly alien to me.

• • •

Another canoe slowly overtook us. Ivan greeted the rowers—a cheer-ful, tanned, wiry couple in their sixties—and they chatted for a minute.

"They just retired," Ivan told me, when the couple had passed us. "For the first time ever, they can canoe as much as they want. They went from Budapest to Visegrád this morning, and now they're going back. This is the easy part because now it's downstream." For a mo-ment it felt like we weren't in the Danube at all but in the river of time, and everyone was at a different point, though in another sense we were all here at once.

We reached the city limits, passing under the first of the six bridges. The second bridge seemed to come almost immediately. Ivan pointed out the bridge between his house and his high school. "I used to cross it every day. Twice a day."

We passed a boat called *СОНЯ*—that was Sonya—and another called *STEAUA*, which was Romanian for star, or something like star. "Basically, every Romanian ship has 'star' in its name," Ivan said.

The plan was to land near the sixth and last bridge, find a pay phone, and call Ivan's father to pick us up. It seemed like a weird plan to me, but apparently Hungarian people had a high tolerance for last-minute arrangements and driving around the countryside. But as we neared the sixth bridge, Ivan suddenly said that he wasn't sure where exactly we would be if we landed there—he wasn't sure if his father would know where we were. He said there was actually a seventh bridge, a new one, built for a World's Fair that hadn't actually taken place. Near the bridge to the nonexistent fair was a village that his father definitely knew.

"What do you think?" he said. "Should we keep going to the sev-enth bridge?"

We kept going to the seventh bridge. The traffic and city noises fell away, and for a few minutes we stopped rowing and drifted. The only sounds were the splashing of water against the canoe, the distant chirping and whirring of tiny animals, and the even more distant roar of an airplane. The sun sank toward the water. The air was soft and golden.

Soon the seventh bridge appeared above us, modern and strange, with some kind of red steel pylons. But there had been a lot of rain lately, and the landing place Ivan had been thinking of was flooded. You could see the tops of young trees and bushes sticking out of the water. It was impossible to reach the shore. We kept going until we came to a little promontory. Ivan got out first and dragged the canoe aground. I handed him our bags and shoes. He helped me out.

"I'm so hungry I could eat the first thing I see," he said.

"That sounds like a curse in a story—like, you say that and then the first thing you see is your favorite sheep."

"I don't have a favorite sheep. When I'm hungry, it's just sheep and non-sheep. Food and non food. By the way, are you food?"

I thought about it. "I don't know."

"Don't worry, I wouldn't eat you. You're my favorite sheep."

We came to a footpath running alongside an embankment. Ivan said he would go find a phone and would be back in twenty minutes. He said I should stay behind and watch the canoe.

I sat on a log and watched the canoe. The leaves on the plants looked big and prehistoric. The whole world slowly turned blue. I heard footsteps—a lot of them. A man came into view leading two goats. The goats had gentle, foolish expressions. They didn't seem interested in the canoe.

It grew harder to make out the numbers on my watch. I shivered and wished I had brought a jacket. After a minute, I unzipped Ivan's backpack. It was bigger and more masculine than mine, black with red trim. He hadn't brought a jacket, either. I heard a motor, and worried that the brigands had finally come for the canoe. Instead, two policemen rode up on motorbikes. I stood perfectly still and hoped they wouldn't notice me, but they did. They got off their bikes and started asking me questions. The only question I understood was whether I was homeless. "Do you have a *house?*" they said loudly, and one of them put his hands over his head in the shape of a pointed roof.

"House, yes," I said. The police looked relieved, said some more things, and looked at me expectantly, apparently waiting for an account of my situation.

I thought for a moment about how best to summarize the circumstances. "My friend," I said, "went to the telephone."

This explanation seemed to completely satisfy the police. "Good, good," they said, then got back on their bikes and drove off. After they had left, I felt a tiny bit abandoned.

I couldn't stay there one more minute. I decided to start walking in the direction Ivan had gone, and to continue until I found either him or a phone. It was already almost impossible to make out the canoe, but I dragged a couple of leafy branches in front of it, just to be safe. Then I took out my notebook and sat on the embankment to write a note, in the dark, explaining to Ivan that I was incapable of further watching the canoe.

Dear Ivan, I had written, when I heard the approach of pounding footsteps. They grew louder and louder and then Ivan flopped onto the ground beside me, out of breath, his shirt torn and muddy.

"I thought I wouldn't be able to find you," he said. "I never feel like I'll be able to find you."

I wanted to touch him, to hold him somehow, but I just touched his sleeve. "I was writing you a note," I said. "I was about to go look for you."

Ivan recounted his experiences. He had been chased for several kilometers by a wild dog. At some point he had lost the dog, and then the dog had reappeared with a giant dead rabbit in its mouth. Eventually Ivan climbed over a fence—that's how he lost the dog. But then he had to find a phone on the other side of the fence.

"I really wanted to not screw up," he said. "After last time."

"Last time?"

"The food was bad, it started raining . . ."

He passed me a two-liter bottle of Sprite—the store hadn't sold water. For a while we sat there talking about the dog, taking long gulps of lukewarm, highly carbonated Sprite, until Ivan said we should head to the highway exit, where his parents were going to pick us up. Both of them were coming: his father, who knew the road, and his mother, who had had less wine at dinner.

I was surprised to discover how close the highway was—less than ten minutes' walk. We sat in a bus shelter overlooking a complicated interchange with an overpass, an underpass, and a roundabout. Everything looked brand-new. The letters on the signs and the lane markings on the road sparkled white. The asphalt seemed as smooth and puffy as a freshly baked meringue. There were no cars in sight. A gas station sign glowed in the distance.

Ivan started to think of different things that could have gone wrong with his parents. His mother might have let his father drive the car. Or his father might have fallen asleep in the passenger seat and been unable to navigate.

"I don't always get along with my father," he said.

"How come?" I asked.

A brightly lit coach bus sped over the overpass.

"He thinks I'm selfish."

The Opel came into view, advancing in a hesitant fashion. Ivan walked into the road, one arm raised, and the light from the headlights washed over and around him. Ivan's mother pulled the car over; Ivan's father was in the passenger seat. Ivan and I got into the back. The mood in the car was more cheerful than I had expected. Nobody seemed angry or particularly worried.

At first I thought it would be easy to find the canoe since it was so close by, but the car couldn't go back the way we had come. By the time we had circled around the embankment and come out on the other side, I had lost all sense of orientation.

"You were watching the canoe a long time," Ivan told me. "Do you remember where it is?"

It did seem very hard that I should have so little to show for all the time I had spent guarding the canoe.

It was Ivan who eventually recognized the landing place, because of a dead tree. Ivan and his father carried the canoe back and tied it onto the roof. "All my friends have missed me," observed Ivan's mother, swatting at the mosquitoes.

In the kitchen, Ivan's mother sliced cold meats, cheese, cucumbers, and tomatoes for sandwiches, and opened a bottle of red wine, which she and Ivan drank. When we had finished the sandwiches, Ivan's mother said she would show me where I could sleep. It was a little room down some stairs with a daybed, a TV, and a mahogany sideboard with a display of filigree teacups. The room's regular occupant, Böbe, who seemed to be either a housekeeper or a relation, I couldn't tell which, was away for the weekend.

Left alone, I washed up, changed into the Dr. Seuss shirt, got in bed, and started writing in my notebook. I kept thinking about the uneven quality of time—the way it was almost always so empty, and then with no warning came a few days that felt so dense and alive and real that it seemed indisputable that *that* was what life was, that its real nature had finally been revealed. But then time passed and unthinkably grew dead again, and it turned out that that fullness had been an aberration and might never come back. I wanted to write about it while I could still feel it and see it around me, while the teacups still seemed to be trembling. Suddenly it occurred to me that maybe the point of writing wasn't just to record something past but also to prolong the present, like in *One Thousand and One Nights*, to stretch out the time until the next thing happened and, just as I had that thought, I saw a dark shape behind the frosted glass and heard a knock on the door.

"Come in."

"I almost expected for you not to be here," Ivan said. "I never feel like I can count on you to be somewhere." He was glaring at the sideboard.

"I feel like that, too," I said. "Cool teacups."

"Böbe brought them from England. She arranged them like this. She decorated the whole room herself, that's why it looks this way." The cups' gilded handles all faced right. Ivan turned one to face left. He said Böbe would think ghosts had done it—the ghosts of Jesus Christ and Winston Churchill. Finally he looked at me. "What are you writing?"

"Nothing." I put the notebook in my backpack. "Oh, do you want an agricultural journal about winter cereal?"

"Not really. Can I sit down?" I nodded. He hesitated between the bed and the chair, then sat on the chair. "I thought you weren't going to call me," he said. "This Rózsa must be really horrible."

I said I had wanted to call earlier but things had been complicated. I said that Rózsa wasn't so bad—just intense. Ivan asked in what way she was intense. I told him about the living room with the four clocks, and how she wanted me to ask her questions about herself, and make honest confessions.

"That could be fun," Ivan said.

"I'm really bad at it."

"You and I are both bad. But we could practice. We might get better."

"Practice how?"

"We could ask each other questions, like a game, with rules. They would have to be real questions, and then the other person would have to really answer. Do you want to try?"

"Right now?"

"I can go first. I can ask the first question." He was looking at the floor. I was always surprised by his profile, by how delicate it was.

"Okay," I said.

He looked up. "Why did you call me today?"

"I—" I cleared my throat. "I wanted to leave on a better note." Where had that sentence come from? Almost every word was wrong. Everything after "I wanted" was wrong.

"On a better 'note'?"

"With a better ending than before."

"So it isn't a good note when you just disappear? When you leave me cold?"

I looked at his face to see if he was serious.

"No," I said. "It's not."

Something changed in the atmosphere. "Okay," he said. "Now it's your turn."

But nothing would come, neither the thoughts nor the words.

Ivan said he would go again to give me time. "Why did you write to me? The first time?"

I felt my face light up. "I've wondered that so many times. I was just so curious about you. You had such a different energy from any-one else. I wanted to talk to you, but I didn't know how."

"I think I understand," he said. "Anyway, I'm glad you did."

"I'm glad you wrote back. I wasn't sure that you would."

"You thought there was a chance I wouldn't write back to you? No way. Your message was so refreshing, so different from all the things that people usually say."

"That's how I felt about you."

"That's good."

"I know." Neither of us said anything for a while.

"I think I'm going to get a heart attack from this," he said eventually. "I think it would help if we were at least drinking wine. But I guess you don't want to."

"You can, though."

"What if I bring the bottle, and maybe you'll have some, too?"

"Okay."

The moment he left, the room felt different, drained. I looked around. Something was moving—a moth, fluttering around the ceiling lamp. The lamp had three bulbs, each in its own glass lily, all blossoming out of a ceiling fan.

Ivan came back with a bottle of beer. "I think my mother finished the wine," he said. "We drank most of it before. She was telling me I should have entertained you better. She said I should have taken you out."

"You did take me out."

He took a swig and proffered the bottle. I shook my head. "I can't believe you want to go through this sober. Well, I think it's your turn."

I took a deep breath and tried to steady my voice. "Why did you tell me to get over you?" I asked.

He fixed his eyes on a point some five feet ahead of him on the carpet, as if the answer might be written there. "I always knew this thing between us was really delicate," he said after a moment. When he said "this thing between us," my chest constricted. "I always thought a time would come when you'd get fed up. I decided from the beginning that, when that happened, I'd let you go and not keep calling you. When I wrote that to you, I thought you'd decided to get over me."

I didn't say anything.

"I *had* to think that, from the way you were acting."

"But if I'd already decided, why did you have to tell me?"

There was a pause. "That's a good question," he said. I felt proud. Then I felt ashamed for feeling proud. "I guess I meant it for myself," he said. "*I* had to get over *you*. I felt really heroic doing it. I decided it was time to let you go, and then I did it."

"It really hurt," I said.

"I know that now," he said. "I'm sorry. But you know, when I called and you wouldn't talk to me, I was hurt. So when I wrote that to you—partly also it was a power thing."

The breath caught in my throat. It had never occurred to me that power was something he would actually *use*, on me of all people. "Want me to ask another one now? So we'll be caught up?"

"Go ahead."

"Why were you so sure there was a time when I'd get fed up? Why did you think from the beginning that eventually you would have to let me go?"

"Well . . . partly it was because I knew I was leaving. I knew I was probably going to go to California, and I was definitely going to leave Boston. But also, I always felt that this thing is really hard for you. I always felt like it was harder for you than for me."

"Why would it be harder for me?"

"Because you're alone."

It felt like being hit, like finding out that the worst thing I had ever thought was true. "What?"

"I mean, you grew up alone, you were an only child for a long time. This thing with talking, for example, is easier for me. I have a lot of sisters, I'm used to talking to them."

It seemed to me that that wasn't what he had meant. But I didn't want to ask or know any more. "Your turn," I said.

He nodded and took a swig of beer. "Why did you write what you wrote to me, when I was in California?"

I felt a shock, like when he had mentioned power, but this time the feeling was intoxicating. I felt it, his power—but like he was going to use it delicately—but not like he wasn't going to use it. I undid the clip that had been holding back my hair, and it all fell into my face, so I clipped it back again.

"I had to get your attention," I said. "First you had your thesis, and you didn't write to me for weeks. And then when you finally did write, you were already leaving to go somewhere else. You were going away and I had to get your attention."

"Well, you definitely got my attention."

"I know."

He laughed. "But you know, I still don't understand whether you meant what you wrote—or whether you were just trying, like you said, to get my attention."

I nodded. "I don't know, either."

He raised the bottle as if in salute, drank from it again, and then held it toward me over the bed. After a moment I took it. I liked the weight, the rough coolness of the foil-wrapped neck. The beer itself was bitter and watery, same as always. It was comical how exactly the same it was as all the other times it was beer.

"Your turn," he said.

"Well—I don't understand why you . . ." I took a deep breath. "Why do you . . ."

"Why do I what?"

"Why do you take the trouble?"

"Trouble?" He sounded annoyed.

"Why do you go through so much effort?"

"What effort? Are you asking why I go through the effort to spend time with you? Because I enjoy spending time with you. Is that what you want to hear?"

"You do?"

"Yeah, I do. Now it's my turn, right?"

"Yeah."

"So why didn't you call me after you went to the village? Why didn't you call me for more than two weeks?"

I didn't say anything.

"You can't not answer."

"Because sometimes after I see you, I feel really bad," I said. "It's almost physically painful." I touched my sternum.

He averted his face. "Now, this sounds like something I'm not used to hearing from you," he said, and I could hear from his voice that he was smiling. He was happy that I hurt like that. And I knew I had felt the same happiness, anytime he mentioned feeling hurt by me. Why was it fun for us to make each other suffer? Did that mean it wasn't love? Surely that wasn't what love *was*?

In any case, once I had admitted that I felt physical pain, things went easier between us, time itself seemed to move more smoothly. Ivan asked what I thought about Hungary, just like Rózsa had. I said it was interesting. I said that some things seemed to tell me more about him, but other things seemed not related to him at all.

"That's how I felt in New Jersey," he said. "I wanted to learn something about you. But I didn't learn anything. It was just suburbs." Ivan asked whether New Jersey was an intense place, and how long I had known I wanted to be a writer. I asked why he had left Hungary to study abroad, and why his father thought he was selfish. He took off his glasses, and looked so weary and handsome.

Ivan asked why I thought it was so hard for us to have a conversation: we had avoided it all this time, and once we had forced ourselves, it had almost killed us.

I said maybe it was specific to talking. "We could do it over email."

"I don't know," he said. "We took turns, but basically you wrote something, and I wrote something else, and then you wrote something else. It was never really a conversation."

"It was never really a conversation," I repeated, thinking it over.

"It was *better*," he said.

The moth, which had fallen asleep on the lamp, woke up and started zooming around the room. "You probably don't want me to kill it," he said.

"Go right ahead," I said.

But he caught the moth and cupped it in his hands and said to open the window. I jumped out of bed and raised the sash, and he stood beside me and let the moth fly away. I remembered that I was wearing only a T-shirt and underwear, and got back into bed.

Ivan stood at the foot of the bed, casting a long shadow. "It's past five," he said. "It might not be a bad idea for us to get some sleep."

"It's probably not a bad idea," I said.

He stood there another moment, then picked up the beer bottle, turned out the light, and left.

I dreamed I was sitting in a tiled bathhouse. Late afternoon light poured through a high window, and water was seeping under the door, slowly filling the room, mounting higher and higher. Then the door opened and a wall of water gushed in, and through the same door my brother also came, but it wasn't my real-life brother, it was Ivan, and I stood up and we embraced. The water was up to our knees. We held on to each other really, really tightly.

"I love you so much," I said.

"I know—so do I," he said.

I woke up with tears in my eyes. Sunlight streamed through the window, sparkling off the gilded teacups. I found a disposable camera in a side pocket of my backpack, and snapped a photograph of the teacups, with one handle facing left. At least I would know I hadn't dreamed the thing about the teacups.

· · ·

At breakfast there was ham. You read those rhymes as a child, and they seemed so abstract—and then you grew up and there they were, the eggs and the ham, the goats and the boats, the logs and the dogs, and the cars and the bars. We would not, could not, on a plane. We would not, could not, in the rain. We would not, could not, here or there. We would not, could not, anywhere.

I met the last two sisters: the one who had been at a folklore camp in Transylvania, and the one who had been in the hospital with her boyfriend's father. Ivan's mother showed me a chart they used to use when everyone still lived at home—a grid with the days of the week and the different chores, cocoa and dishes and setting the table, with markers for each of the five kids. You could see how much those days meant to Ivan's mother.

"It's very rare now that we're all together again," she said. "Luckily, tomorrow will be one of those occasions." The older sister explained that they were all going on a canoeing trip in western Hungary.

Before Ivan could drop me off in Szentendre, we had to stop at the Thai embassy in Budapest. He explained in the car that today was the last day he could pick up his Thai visa: "We're going away tomorrow, we get back Friday, and I leave for Bangkok on Saturday morning."

"I see," I said.

"So you picked a good time to call." That was when I realized that I wouldn't see him again—not for a long time, and maybe not ever.

The Thai embassy was on a leafy side street with unmarked lanes and no sidewalk. Ivan parked on the shoulder, almost in a bed of ivy, and walked up to the gate. I sat in the sun-filled car listening to the birds. When he got back, Ivan apologized for taking so long. But I would have liked to stay there all day.

The Thai visa took up a whole page in his passport. Printed on rainbow-colored paper, it incorporated a hologram, a red eagle-man in a flaming circle, and a xeroxed passport photo. Unsmiling, underexposed, Ivan looked as sooty and grim as a coal miner from ancient times.

When we got back to Szentendre, the campground was deserted. Rózsa had told Ivan that if we were late we could find them at the beach. Ivan drove to a big white hotel at the end of the street. He said it had the biggest beach. The beach wasn't visible from the parking lot—it was downhill behind some trees.

"Do you want to go down and make sure they're there?" he asked.

I shook my head. "I bet they're there," I said. We got out of the car and stood facing each other.

"So," he said. "You're going away."

I felt my eyebrows tense. "You are," I said.

"My email account will be active a little while longer," he said. "And yours will be active for a long time. So we could be in touch." Everything hurt, especially "could," and "a little while longer." "You should try to have a nice time," he continued. "Even here."

I nodded.

"You should visit me in California."

"Okay."

"Come here." I stepped forward and he drew me toward him, holding me so close that I had difficulty breathing. Standing on my toes, my face pressed sideways against his chest, I was unable to see over his shoulder and found myself instead looking down, toward the gravel path that led to the beach. I patted his back, which felt so solid and present under his T-shirt. I felt at a loss—for words, breath, thought, everything.

I said bye first, to be brave. I still thought bravery would be somehow rewarded.

"Bye," he replied.

It seemed to take hours just to reach the beginning of the gravel path. Then I started downhill toward the shore. After a few steps, I stopped. I hadn't heard the car door close. I hadn't heard the motor start. I thought about turning back. Was that one of the things that could be done? Well, of course it was. Here I was in this world, with the same rights as anyone else—I could turn, walk in circles, stamp my foot. But none of these things would change the fact that he was going clear around the Earth, with no plan and no reason to come back to where I was.

I kept walking toward the river. I could *hear* the tears welling up. They made a creaking sound. I felt too worn out to blink them back, and anyway there was nobody there to see. I felt my face changing, my cheeks getting soft and hot. I came to a tennis court. Two couples my parents' age were playing doubles. One of the men, who had a beard and was standing very close to the net, let out a yell—"*És!*"—with every volley. Nobody seemed to notice or care that there was a weeping person there in a Dr. Seuss shirt. Invisibility felt like a blessing.

Behind the court lay a few green-tinged tennis balls among some green gravel. The beach came into view. I felt a flood of relief and realized it was because the beach was empty and the campers were elsewhere. I wasn't ready to join them. I went back to the tennis court and watched the game for a few minutes, to give Ivan time to clear out. Then I climbed back up the hill. He was gone.

I lit a cigarette as I started walking along the main road. The cigarette magically and unequivocally stopped the flow of tears. It was impossible not to feel that it was a benevolent force, the way it protected you like that. Passing the restaurant in a boat, I followed the shady path along the river to the ferry dock. White fluff resembling milkweed fell from the trees, silently and in great quantities. It hadn't been there last time. I had never seen anything like it before. The whiteness kept falling and falling, like in a sentence from linguistics or the philosophy of language. I thought about the winter—how I used to run into Ivan sometimes walking through the snow-covered quad, a satchel strap crossing the front of his black puffy jacket. I remembered how we'd had so much time ahead of us.

At the dock I sat on a bench under a willow tree, trying to make a plan. The first, main thing was not to start crying again—to be a good sport. That thought itself made my throat ache, because hadn't I *been* a good sport, the way I had listened to all those stories about bullets, and sung the Beatles, and guarded the canoe? I ate so much pork, I thought, and blinked back a tear.

I found a phone booth and tried to call Svetlana. "All the lines to this country are busy," said the operator. I didn't understand how that was possible. After some hesitation, I called my mother. She wasn't at home, but I found her at her lab. I didn't know at first how to explain the situation, but then I just told her that Ivan was going to Thailand, and she seemed to understand just how I felt. She told me to go see some beautiful things. Beauty encouraged the production of endorphins, which helped make you feel better and prevented inflammation. I was in the phone booth for a long time. An Italian woman kept yelling *"Telefono!"* and banging on the glass. I pretended not to notice.

I walked around looking for beauty. I saw a ruined bridge, crumbling towers, sunlight, a garden, closetlike buildings, buildings inside other buildings, plaques with skulls and crossbones, and a ceramic Madonna in the shape of a pound cake. I sat in a church for a long time writing in my notebook.

Five nuns were chanting in the back. People kept coming into the church, seeing the nuns, and leaving respectfully. Nobody made me leave. I spent the whole day alternately walking around and writing.

At sundown, I headed back to the campground. Rózsa met me at the gate.

"Where have you been?"

I told her about the Thai embassy, and about how I'd gone looking for them at the beach. I tried to make these things sound complicated enough to have taken the whole day.

"You have been *loafing,*" she said. Rózsa was no dummy.

I made friends with the children. Two little girls, Zsófi and Cica, followed me everywhere. Zsófi perched on the arm of my chair and smiled down at me, while Cica sat in my lap smiling up. "Your hair clip is beautiful," they said softly. "Your bag is beautiful. You speak Hungarian very well." They loved to hit the badminton bird back and forth. Sometimes they asked me to brush their hair. I was their favorite and I was proud.

There was another little girl, Erzsébet, who also always tried to sit on people's laps and make eye contact. She was slightly older, lumpen, potatolike. Nobody wanted her to sit on their lap. At first, I felt sorry and tried to pet her. "You needn't pretend to love Erzsébet," Rózsa said testily. And in fact I soon found Erzsébet unbearable, and would go to great lengths to avoid her. I was scared by how repulsed I felt, by her simpering and coyness, by her abjectness that seemed somehow aggressive, by the way she repeated my name and tried to climb onto my shoulders.

The boys also wanted to interact, though they went about it differently. They liked to run up, say something, and run away fast. Sometimes they asked about song lyrics that they didn't understand. "'I would never break your heart,'" Ádám read from a paper folded up in his pocket—he wanted to know what it was to break someone's heart.

"What is 'Tokyo ghetto pussy'?" asked another boy. A few of them nodded—they had all wondered this.

Fábián, who was fourteen, was always up on the roof, or jumping out of a tree. I saw a lot of him because the first aid kit was in our cabin. One afternoon, when I was sitting on the cot reading and Rózsa was putting ointment on his bee sting, he looked right at me and said something I didn't understand. Rózsa spoke to him sharply. I figured he had been making fun of me. But after he left, Rózsa gave me a significant look. "He wants something from you," she said. "I told him that you already have a friend and you're too old."

Did it never end? Where did it end? The next time Fábián came running into the cabin like a crazed revolutionary, a bloodstained T-shirt wrapped around his arm, I felt a little jolt.

"Can't the American girl understand anything I'm saying?" he asked Rózsa as she got out the iodine.

"Nothing," said Rózsa.

"But I've heard her speak Hungarian."

"She imitates like a parrot."

"Parrot," I echoed.

Fábián's eyes widened. He lingered another moment, staring at me, then ran outside.

Rózsa told the cafeteria server not to give me too much of anything because I wasn't hungry. This was untrue. It turned out to be a ploy to get me to go to the supermarket with her, which I would have done anyway.

The supermarket had everything. I had never felt so happy to see Whiskas, the cat food. I bought almond cookies and Rózsa bought sanitary pads. I had my period, too—we had ended up synchronized. In the beauty aisle, Rózsa gazed at boxes of hair dye. "I want to paint my hair, but oh, it is expensive," she announced in a mechanical tone, like someone reading a teleprompter. Outside, I offered her a cookie, but she said she was on a diet.

"You don't need to be on a diet," I said, which I thought was both truthful and polite. But she gave me a passionate look and said,

"Needless eating is horrible—I can't understand it. When you eat needless things, you will get fat."

We walked for a while in silence.

"I'm not happy," Rózsa said.

"Why not?"

"I don't know."

"Are you worried about school?"

"No."

"Then why?"

"Because I'm alone."

I felt a wave of exasperation and despair. Was that what all of life was going to be like—you had to be sad when you didn't have a boyfriend?

"We have each other," I said tensely.

At the train station, Rózsa started haggling with one of the old women who sold flowers. She picked up a twenty-forint bouquet of carnations and wildflowers with one red rose in it, all tied tightly together with a rubber band. Rózsa wanted to buy just the rose. She got it in the end, for five forints. "This is your rose," she said. "You will put it in your glass and then we are not alone."

She said we didn't have to be back at the camp yet—we could take a walk, wherever I wanted. There wasn't anywhere I especially wanted to go. I suggested we go where *she* wanted. "No," she said. "Where you want."

"But I want to go where you want."

"No, I must suffer. We must go somewhere I don't want."

I thought it over. "Why don't you think of somewhere that will make you suffer and we can go there?"

"Selin doesn't want *anything*," Rózsa said in a mocking voice. "Is it true?"

"I wish."

"Why?"

"There is no suffering if you don't want anything."

Rózsa's look got even more smoldering. "That's balderdash," she said.

We sat on a parapet. A cool wind rushed under the blackening sky, a baby somewhere was crying, and a big yellow umbrella with a beer logo tumbled down a hill.

"I was there—where you want to go," Rózsa said. "I was there on Monday."

"Where?"

"I was there," Rózsa repeated. And it seemed to me that she meant the dock, where the white stuff had been falling from the trees, though I wasn't sure why, or what she would have been doing there.

"Do you think it's going to rain?" I asked.

"Yes. Why?"

My heart quickened. "I don't know," I said. Then I realized I wanted it to rain because maybe Ivan and his family would come back to Budapest a day early and Ivan might call me. I knew there were a lot of flaws in this reasoning. But my body didn't know.

A whole ocean of rain seemed to be pouring out of the sky. We sat under an awning near a hotel parking lot and ate yellow plums. Eventually Rózsa ate one of the cookies I had bought, and I felt happy and proud, like I had successfully fed a shy and proud animal.

Within minutes the sun was blazing as if it didn't remember a thing.

One evening, the children were in a pageant arranged by Ildi and the gym teachers. There was an outdoor stage, with folding chairs for the adults. The older boys were in one program, the girls in another. The younger boys weren't in any program at all, and were sitting on blankets under the teachers' watchful eyes.

For the older boys' program, a canvas screen had been hung from the ceiling, ending a few feet from the ground. German techno music started playing. One by one, the boys marched across the stage in time to the music. The screen hid their bodies from the waist up. All you could see were their legs. Numbers had been pinned to their shorts.

"The American girl will judge the boys' legs," announced one of the gym teachers, handing me a clipboard with a mimeographed form on which to rate all the legs on a scale from one to ten.

I looked from the form to the adolescent boys' legs. I knew that the legs were going in a circuit, because the numbers kept repeating. But other than the numbers, they all looked the same. They all looked like legs. The whole point of people having faces was that that was how you told them apart.

"I can't," I said when the music stopped, and tried to give back the form. They wouldn't take it back.

"She needs to see them again!" called Ildi.

The music started up again. The legs resumed their circuit. I started to notice differences between them. Some were longer, others shorter, some skinnier, others more muscular. Some were freckled and several had skinned knees. I understood that number eleven was Fábián, because he had a cut on his thigh, and also because of the way he walked—it was a kind of stamping dance. Whether despite or because of the fact that all you could see were his legs, the dance was both comical and highly characteristic of his personality.

Nonetheless, when I tried to put the legs in any kind of order, either ascending or descending, I felt panic rise in my chest. The gym teachers kept pointing at the clipboard and urging me to write. Or did I need to see the legs a third time, one of them asked, and everyone laughed.

"Do you want me to help you?" Rózsa whispered. I nodded.

"She wants to see numbers seven, eleven, two, fourteen, and ten," Rózsa called. Numbers seven, eleven, two, fourteen, and ten came out again and pranced across the stage. Rózsa looked at them carefully and whispered her scores to me. Then the boys came out from behind the screen, and I awarded cardboard medals to the winners. First place went to a dark, muscular boy who was fifteen and reminded me of Reni's boyfriend. Fábián was the runner-up.

Madonna's "Vogue" started playing. It was time for the girls' program: a fashion contest. The girls sashayed onto the stage two at a time, one from each side. They struck a pose at the middle, then strode off in opposite directions. Wearing lip gloss, eye shadow, and hair clips shaped like flowers or shells, they looked so groomed, groomed to please. There was no screen hiding their faces, and you could see the many different things they were feeling.

Zsófi and Cica came out together: Cica in a tiny gold-spangled off-the-shoulder shirt, Zsófi in a green polka-dotted dress. Pert, dimply Cica strode around confidently to the music and posed with her hand on one hip. Taller and coltish, with long trembling eyelashes, Zsófi mostly just stood there, occasionally dancing in place in a private, thoughtful way.

I thought the first prize would go to Ági, who was fifteen and punkish, with boy-short hair. She marched out wearing ankle boots, short shorts, and a little leather jacket, and when she took off the jacket and twirled it on one finger, everyone clapped and whistled. Ági shared the stage with her friend Éva, who looked paralyzed by shyness. When Ági took off her jacket, Éva tentatively shrugged off her brown cardigan. "You'll get cold!" yelled a male gym teacher. She put the cardigan back on.

The judges were three grown men: the gym teacher, Ildi's visiting husband, and a sort of repairman who was always hanging around tightening things. They did several rounds of callbacks, while the girls who weren't called sat awkwardly to one side. Finally, the repairman announced the winner and runner-up: Zsófi and Éva—of all the girls in the pageant, the two who had seemed the most confused and uncomfortable. I didn't understand right away. But then I saw that, when you looked past their demeanor, clothes, and hairstyles, Zsófi and Éva really did have the most raw physical beauty. Éva's face was so worried you could barely look at her, but she had a lovely body and long legs.

Zsófi accepted her bouquet with a placid Bambilike expression. Éva started to take off her cardigan again, then stopped, then went through with it after all. This time I noticed her cute, optimistic breasts. The repairman kissed her cheeks. Then all the girls came back onstage, and the men kissed all of them. What had men ever done, to deserve so much beauty and grace?

I spent the last evening of camp in the cabin, writing. I was sure that Ivan would call, because it was his last night in Hungary. He would be back from his family trip tonight, and would be leaving for Bangkok in the morning. He knew the number of the camp. He had asked me how long I was staying. Why would he have asked, if he wasn't going to call?

For some reason, nearly everyone left me alone that night. Nobody wanted me to sing songs with the children, or play badminton. There was only one interruption, around nine. Fábián came crashing through the door, his prizewinning left leg covered in blood.

"Can you help me?" he asked.

I had just identified the iodine bottle in the first aid kit when two of the gym teachers came in. "Lukács Fábián, you leave the American girl alone!" they shouted and, leading him away, bandaged his leg in a visibly efficient fashion. I kept writing until ten.

Ivan didn't call.

AUGUST

We were supposed to return to the village at eight in the morning. By 7:40, all the children were lined up outside the bus. Nonetheless, the bus didn't leave until 8:40. It wasn't clear to me what was happening between 7:40 and 8:40—why we weren't just getting in the bus, which was sitting right there, as was the driver. Fábián stared at me for almost the whole time. At one point I met his eyes, and immediately looked away.

Fábián and his friends spent the whole bus ride scuffling, singing, and thinking of different ways to exploit the fact that the bus had an emergency exit in the roof. Now it was the bus driver who stared at Rózsa and me, by means of a mirror over his seat.

Rózsa looked in the dictionary for words that she thought described her, and wrote them on a paper: *uncharitable, unquestionable, unforgettable.* I told her I agreed with "unforgettable."

"Me?" she gasped. "Why?" Her eyes, gazing into mine, looked frightened. I wanted to tell her: *You're doing it right now.*

I watched the scenery go by, wondering whether Ivan was already at the airport, whether he felt sad to leave Hungary or only excited to go to Thailand. It seemed weird how he cared so much what country he was from, but also cared so much about going to other countries. Or no, that wasn't weird—he just cared about countries. He thought they were meaningful concepts, and that it really mattered which one you were from and which ones you visited.

After leaving everyone else at the school, the bus driver drove Rózsa and me home, and even carried our bags to Piri's door. We had dinner at Rózsa's parents' house. Her parents were unwell and didn't eat with us. We ate from trays in her bedroom, which she shared with her sister: a person she had never mentioned to me ever, not once.

On Sunday, I went to a horse show with Juli, the girl with whom I would be living for the last week of the program. I wasn't sure what a horse show was going to be. Even once we got there I wasn't sure what it was. There was a lot of dust. Some of the horses were pulling carriages. Then there was a raffle. Juli, who was in training to be an English teacher, was convinced that she was going to win a horse. Juli's father repeatedly offered to buy me a piglet. At first I thought he was joking, but he wasn't laughing, and there really was a man selling piglets.

Juli said there was a beautiful horse we had to see. She led me to a wooden stall. Inside was the most delicate-boned horse with crazed eyes, completely surrounded by flies. It smelled terrible. Exactly one week ago, Ivan and I had been on a canoe. The raffle winners were announced. Juli was unshakably confident that she would win a horse—right up to the minute that they called her name and she won a goat. She tried to give it back. The raffle people laughed, then became menacing. That goat caused Juli no end of trouble. In the end, she had to hire a man with a pickup truck to drive it to a nearby village and put it up for several days, as a sort of guest, until she could find it a more permanent position with some different people.

· · · ·

"Did you like the horse show?" Rózsa demanded when I came back for dinner, covered with dust and sweat.

"It was stressful," I said. Rózsa couldn't conceal how happy she was that I had been stressed out by the horse show.

"I know you saw the horses, but what about the gorilla?" asked Piri's daughter, Emese. "The gorilla" turned out to be what they called Juli's boyfriend.

Things seemed to be going okay until dinner, when I didn't finish my potato puree. "How many ice creams have you had with Juli?" Rózsa asked, slamming down her fork. According to Rózsa, Juli hadn't wanted to host me but had had no choice: they all had to put up with me and take their turn.

It was strange to keep meeting people after Ivan left. I had come to Hungary because of him, and now that he was gone, my reasons for being there felt increasingly unclear. The reasons had been unclear even before, but now it was somehow more glaring.

Juli and her family lived in a six-room apartment upstairs from the Elefánt Diszkó, which Juli's father managed. A figure corresponding in both appearance and demeanor to my idea of "a broken man," Juli's father slept in the spare room; his work at the disco often kept him busy till four in the morning. I stayed in Juli's sister Bernadett's room, while Bernadett slept in the living room, on a water-sofa. The water-sofa had a dead fox draped over it.

Juli's mother, a beautician, was very thin, with unusually bright eyes. For dinner she made a soup called "boy-catching soup" and a cake called "mother-in-law cake." These two dishes seemed to sum up a whole worldview of entrapment and placation.

Bernadett, who was also going to be a beautician when she grew up, never did any beauty treatments at all, and thought they were stupid. She spent hours in the bath and often walked around the house wearing no clothes. "*Béna*," Juli hissed. When I asked what this word meant, Juli read from the dictionary: "A paralytic—ungainly, awkward, unsightly, misshapen."

"Don't compliment me!" shouted Bernadett.

Juli's dog, Blanka, a silvery pale-eyed husky, walked around the living room, dining room, and kitchen, bumping into the walls and furniture. Sometimes she climbed onto the water-sofa and sat there looking disinterested and confused, like a visitor from another planet.

Every night, Juli and Bernadett filled their pockets with rocks, and we all went out to walk Blanka. "Wolf! Wolf!" boys shouted as we approached, and they would throw rocks—not directly at the girls or the dog, but a few inches in front of them. Then Juli and Bernadett would throw rocks straight at the boys' heads.

It was interesting: Rózsa always said that people hated her, but I never saw any sign of it, whereas Juli and Bernadett, who really lived in this state of warfare with the local boys, barely seemed to notice anything unusual, and didn't even interrupt their conversation when they were throwing rocks at people's heads.

When we got to the fields past the train station, Juli took off the leash and let Blanka run. Blanka was utterly transformed, her elongated body hurtling across the field, close to the ground, her tail puffed out behind her like a plume of smoke.

We went back to the apartment through the empty disco. A mirrored ball glinted in the near-darkness. Juli poured out three tiny glasses of her favorite liquor: Charleston Follies. Bernadett lay on her back on the pool table and rolled around with her legs in the air. Juli looked at her. "Mexican bean," she said disdainfully.

"Did you just call her a Mexican bean?" I asked.

"Yes," she said. "There is a worm inside." Juli said that Bernadett loved "to jump like goat shit on a boat." She said this was a Hungarian expression.

"Juli, the strobe," Bernadett said, sitting up.

There really was a strobe light in the corner, on a tripod. Juli turned it on. Bernadett lay back on the pool table and resumed her wallowing. Blanka trotted in circles under the strobe light, flickering in the empty dark disco, like a living silent movie. This was an amazing sight. And yet, I didn't know where to put it. It just seemed to sit there, like a fur hat whose apparatchik had been airbrushed away.

I felt in a panic to pay attention to everything, to figure out what the deal was, to retroactively earn the right to even be in Hungary— because after all I hadn't applied to the program, Ivan had just talked to Peter, and probably I had climbed over the heads of countless more deserving English teachers. I knew there had to be something important left to do or learn, if only I could figure out how not to squander my time and opportunities.

I sat up late at Bernadett's desk, under a poster for a German band called Mr. President, making a list of the potential uses of my time and opportunities.

1. Learning Hungarian. (How? Studying in this room, talking to Juli, trying to befriend the Gypsies?)
2. Having universal and meaningful human experiences (in English).
3. Understanding regional history ("Ottomans," "communism," "Habsburgs").
4. Changing children's lives? Some of them (Ádám, maybe Csilla) do seem like they want their lives changed.

I stared at the list for a long time. The longer I stared, the less sense it made.

On the way to the bathroom, I glanced involuntarily through the open door of the spare room—why was it so hard not to glance through an open door, even when you didn't want to see inside?—and saw Juli's father sitting on the edge of the bed, watching Olympic weightlifting. The lifters' bodies looked almost green. They trembled, bulged, and strained, like they were going to explode.

In my last week at the school, I helped the children put on a play. I wasn't allowed to choose the play. It was like Epictetus said about life: "Remember that you are an actor in a play, the nature of which is up to the director to decide." The play Tünde chose was called *Chicken Licken*. The action was identical to that of the story I knew as "Chicken Little." In the past, I had only ever seen the phrase "chicken licken" used to designate the chicken fingers plate at Friendly's. As a name for a dramatic protagonist, it seemed sinister, grotesque. I proposed that we change it to "Chicken Little." Tünde said no. "If it's Turkey Lurkey, it's also Chicken Licken," she said grimly.

Turkey Lurkey, Ducky Lucky, and Goosey Loosey were played by the three biggest boys in the class. Wearing cardboard masks with beaks, hunching their shoulders to resemble wings, they hulked around in single file, like a row of totem poles.

"Ah, here he comes now," said the Narrator. "The stupidest chicken in all the world."

The dialogue in the play wasn't very challenging, so I told the advanced students to write soliloquies where they said what they were thinking.

Turkey Lurkey talked about what it was going to be like when the sky fell. "There won't be any more space," he said. "The sky will lie on the earth, like a book on a table. I don't know who or what is a king, but we must find one."

Bernadett was Foxy Loxy. "I'm hungry all the time," she said. "I've never been full—not once. Eating is more important than having friends." She said she hated cowardice and stupidity. She could never feel sorry for anyone who wasn't clever, brave, and strong.

On the last Saturday of the program, all the English classes gathered at the auditorium in Feldebrő, and each one performed a play. Daniel's students staged a Wild West adaptation of *Romeo and Juliet,* with gunfights and cowboy hats. The script, props, and costumes were more sophisticated than ours, and I worried that my students would feel bad. But when I saw the boys troop onto the stage in their bird costumes, with their hooliganlike energy and weird asides, I understood that everything was okay, and I was filled with affection and pride.

On my last night in the village, there was a party at the school. The English students came, and their parents, and the other teachers. Rózsa had said she wouldn't come, but she did, wearing little bows in her hair. She gave me two doilies she had embroidered herself, with scalloped edges, purple roses, and purple script; one read TO DEAR SELIN, the other FROM UNFORGETTABLE ROSE. Juli gave me a potted cactus plant with googly eyes, and the school principal presented me with a leather hair clip and a decorative miniature shoe.

Vilmos, the cook, was there in his white hat. He had made a marvelous soup, tiny meatballs, apple pastries, and punch. Later he followed me to the bathroom and lurched toward me and put his hand on my waist, and I saw he was really drunk. I didn't feel scared. "You're a very good cook," I said, patting his shoulder, and detached myself. He didn't follow me—he wandered back down the hall.

The sun was setting and turned the school's pink façade a blazing molten liquid color. At the same time, rainclouds were gathering over part of the sky. The sunflowers glowed in the golden light, standing out with superfine clarity against the blackening clouds. Someone had built a bonfire. Margit gave me a match. Everyone held hands around the fire and sang a song about beautiful blue eyes. At the one line about black eyes, Margit, who had black eyes like me, took my hand and sang with extra energy.

When it got dark, Ádám brought out a boom box and there was dancing. Vilmos turned up again, no longer wearing his white hat. When the music changed to a slow song and all the boyfriends and girlfriends paired off, Goosey Loosey asked me to dance. He put his hands on my waist and I put my hands on his shoulders. I had never really looked at him before, because he was so quiet and not that good at English, but I saw now that he was taller than me, with hazel eyes. He said a few things in English. They were all things I had taught him how to say.

At seven-thirty in the morning, Juli and Bernadett walked with me to the train station. They kept saying I mustn't fall asleep or I would wind up in Prague. Various mothers had given me provisions for the trip: several peaches, a bag of yellow plums, a kilogram of cookies, and six rum chocolate bars. At the station platform, I heard my name and turned to see Nóra galloping toward me, followed by Margit with Feri. Margit handed me something in a plastic bag. I hugged each of them again and again. The train came into sight, rumbling closer, bringing the feeling of aliveness and plenitude inherent to incoming trains. Just then, Gyula came running across the vacant lot waving his arms. He made it to the platform just in time to heave my suitcase up after me onto the train. "Goodbye, Selin! Goodbye!" they all shouted, and I shouted, "Goodbye," and the doors closed.

As the train accelerated out of the station, the doors flew open again, like a hole in the world. They couldn't be pulled shut until the next stop. I looked in the bag Margit had given me. It had the kind of sandwiches I liked best, with thin slices of meatball and green pepper. I stood in the corridor the whole way so I wouldn't fall asleep and wake up in Prague. A friendly gay guy was walking up and down the corridor, waving an unlit cigarette in a comic manner. I gave him a book of matches. He put his hands together and bowed. Then he stood next to me smoking out the window until his stop, at a tiny station in the middle of nowhere. There was only one person waiting there, a man with a crew cut standing in the shade. The two friends looked so happy to see each other. The first thing the guy with the crew cut did was offer his friend a light.

In the airport check-in line a girl smiled at me and I smiled back, and then she came over and told me the story of her life. Her name was Teodora, she was Romanian, and was going to meet her husband, who was third in command on a cargo ship the size of a small town. Her husband's ship normally circled nonstop between Denmark and China, but now it had broken and would be docked for three days in Istanbul, so she had a chance to visit. "I haven't seen my husband in two months," she said. For a moment the words "husband," and "two months," with all they implied, seemed to open an abyss between us.

This was Teodora's first time on an airplane, though of course she had spent a lot of time on ships. She had never been to Turkey. "Are there lots of people like you?" she asked, with a hopeful expression.

"Definitely," I said, wondering what aspect of me she was referring to.

She asked my age. Something flickered across her face. "I'm

twenty-six," she said, as if it were bad news she had received only recently. "It isn't the age I feel like."

"What age do you feel like?"

"Nineteen—like you."

But, to me, nineteen still felt old and somehow alien to who I was. It occurred to me that it might take more than a year—maybe as many as seven years—to learn to feel nineteen.

When we reached the check-in counter, Teodora started to explain something really complicated to the airline workers. There was something special about either her ticket or the way her baggage was to be handled, because of the international status held by her husband's ship. The workers were not familiar with this status. Teodora seemed to think that they doubted her husband's credentials.

"How can I prove my husband is third in command on a ship?" she mused. "I have anchors on my shirt!" The airline employees were only moderately impressed by her shirt.

Most of the passengers on our flight were middle-aged Turks with ravaged faces, heading home from a package tour of Mallorca.

"You can't believe what we've lived through," one man told me in Turkish at the gate. At first I thought he might have mistaken me for someone he knew, but then I saw from his abstracted expression that he neither knew nor cared whether he knew me.

"It wasn't nice?" I said.

"What was nice about it? Nobody spoke Turkish there. We had a guide, if you can call him a guide—a sadist, in the clinical sense. What can you say about a man like that; he searched in life for his foothold and he found this one." He shook his head, apparently reviewing the places in the world where clinical sadists could find their footholds.

. . .

All the way to Istanbul, the tiny plane rolled and pitched to and fro. From one side, all you could see was the crazily zooming and retreating ground; from the other, only sky. Overhead bins flew open. A giant cheese went tumbling down the aisle. Then the plane lost altitude so suddenly that several people hit their heads on the ceiling. Each new violent movement was met by groans, cries, and laughter. Some of the older passengers were praying. One guy threw up in his airsick bag, and then everyone started doing it.

The worst part was the descent. Every second was more sickening. You could feel your soul sloshing around in your body, bouncing around in there like goat shit on a boat. Teodora gripped my hand, and I squeezed hers back. Then suddenly the last clouds fell away behind us, and there was the Sea of Marmara and the Bosphorus, as shimmery and living and inscrutable as the flank of some gigantic fish. Teodora leaned raptly toward the window. "It's my husband's ship," she said, pointing at the freighters far below. "Somewhere, one of them." I looked at the nape of her neck, at the downy hair that had escaped from her ponytail, at a delicate gold chain with an S-shaped clasp lying on her freckled skin—all things that her husband must have known so well.

I was going to stay the night with my aunt Belgin and cousin Defne before we all went to Antalya, on the Mediterranean, to meet my mother and other aunts. Belgin and Defne were my only relatives in Istanbul, a city I hadn't visited since childhood. I had spent more time in Ankara, my mother's hometown—the city Atatürk founded, the capital of the secular republic. My mother thought Istanbul was sad, with its narrow streets and run-down buildings. But I wanted to see it, because Ivan had talked about wanting to go there, because it sounded like the cities in nineteenth-century novels: sprawling, multi-layered, heterogeneous, aswarm with parvenus, monomaniacs, and dealers in used furniture.

My aunt Belgin worked at a national laboratory chain that processed medical tests. They had said they would send a driver to the airport. I couldn't find the driver. I tried to call the lab, but the AT&T code didn't work—you had to buy phone tokens. I didn't have Turkish money, and the currency exchange wouldn't take either Hungarian money or traveler's checks.

I went back to the pay phones and was trying to figure out how to make a collect call when a neatly dressed young man appeared at my elbow. "The phones are operated by means of tokens," he said. He went on to explain the concept of a token—"It's like a coin, but it works only in the telephone"—and offered to buy me one, if I gave him the money. I explained that I had only Hungarian money.

"Let it be Hungarian, then," he said tolerantly.

"How much should I give you?"

"Whatever you think is fitting."

I handed him a bill. He dashed off at an incredible speed, then came back holding the same bill. "The exchange doesn't take Hungarian money," he said.

"They don't take it," I agreed.

"Oh, well, give me the Hungarian money," the young man said after a moment. "Who knows, maybe I'll use it someday. I might come across some Hungarian tourists on their way back to Hungary. Then they can give me their last Turkish liras, and I'll give them my Hungarian money. They'll say, 'Thank you,' and I'll say, 'Goodbye, safe travels.'" Seemingly cheered by his future exchange, he handed me a token and I called the lab. I got transferred four times. The fifth person I talked to said that the driver had left, and would be here soon.

The young man carried my suitcase from the phones to the customs exit. Periodically a wave of devastated-looking air passengers would pour out of the gate. Some of them had people waiting for them; others trudged on alone.

I tried to give the young man some more forints, but he said he had enough. "After all, maybe I'll never come across any Hungarian tourists." He didn't want any cookies, either. He said he didn't have good relations with sweets. Then he offered to buy me a beer. Beer again! I wondered if Ivan would have accepted—if he and this guy would have ended up friends, through their shared love of beer. In parting, the young man gave me another telephone token. "You might need it," he said. "If not, it will be a memento."

The only person who had been standing at the customs exit as long as I had was a man holding a sign that read ROYAL EMIRATES TOURISM WELCOMES MR. AHIB SADEEN. At various points, two different women also rushed up to me and asked if I had seen Ahib Sadeen yet.

"Not yet," I said.

A man came out of the gate in a blindingly white shirt and jacket accompanied by four women in black burkas. It was Ahib Sadeen. For some reason, his arrival was the decisive event that made me feel I had been waiting too long. I went to the information booth and asked them to page "the driver from Güven Laboratories." They said it wasn't possible to page a person unless you knew their name. I pointed out that I knew the name of the laboratory. They said you couldn't page a laboratory—it wasn't done.

"Couldn't you just do it as a kindness?" I asked. My mother often talked about kindnesses in her conversations with Turkish service employees. Compared with Hungarian, Turkish *sounded* clear as water, but speaking was really difficult. To say anything, I felt like I had to search my brain for every phrase I had ever heard before and then redeploy the one that best matched the circumstances.

They eventually agreed to page "Güven Bey"—Mr. Güven—

which obviously wasn't going to accomplish anything, because Güven
was a common given name, it meant trust, and it wouldn't be used on
its own, without a surname, to page someone at the airport. I waited
around awhile anyway. Nobody showed up.

I used the second token to call the lab again. "What—you mean
Yusuf Bey hasn't come yet?" a secretary said.

A wave of hilarity rose in my chest. I *knew* Yusuf Bey. He had
been my grandfather's driver in Ankara for years. He was never on
time anywhere. Once, he broke a car by driving over an enormous
boulder that was sitting right in the middle of the road. When my
grandfather asked, "Yusuf, why didn't you drive *around* the boulder?"
he said, "I thought it was paper."

Once I knew it was Yusuf Bey, I found him right away. He was
standing in a corner eating sunflower seeds.

"Oh, so *you're* Selin Hanım," he marveled, brushing off his hands.
"The last time we met, you were shorter."

"I was ten years old."

"Ah, so that's why."

Everything in Belgin and Defne's house was tiny—the chairs, the
plates, the notepads. My toes barely fit in the slippers. Belgin had
made a beautiful dinner with stuffed grape leaves, battered mullet
that you ate whole, and cranberry beans stewed in olive oil.

After dinner, Defne's and my cousin Ayhan came to visit. In the
years since I had seen him, he had become sinisterly handsome, with
tousled chestnut hair and penetrating blue eyes. He had just started a
new job in an office run by his father, having been fired from his previous position for biting a man's ear.

The four of us watched the evening news. A bomb had gone off in
Atlanta, harming nobody. A forest fire had been raging for weeks in
Marmaris; it was now thirty fires, and nobody knew how to put them

out. In Valencia, a matador had been gored to death. They showed his body being tossed around by the bull, so lightly, it seemed, and then his coffin was borne away on a sea of shoulders. Aunt Belgin changed the channel. African men in loincloths were bounding across a field of tall yellow grass.

"Ah, the Japanese Dracula," said my cousin Ayhan. "How they can jump." He repeated the phrase "Japanese Dracula" several times.

"How can they be Japanese, it's Africa," said Defne.

"The Japanese Dracula may also be found in Africa. If only I could jump like that. Can you imagine? I'd come home from work in the evening and jump, like this." He stood up to demonstrate, capsizing a little table but catching it before it hit the floor. "So, kids," he said. "Are we going to a bar or what?"

"To a bar, now? Are you crazy?" Defne said. "Selin just got off an airplane, she's tired."

"Anyway, don't you have work tomorrow?" Aunt Belgin said.

"Not until eight-thirty. That means I have to get up at seven-thirty. I sleep for three hours a night—four hours, maximum. So there are five hours to go to a bar."

"Jump home to bed, Japanese Dracula," Aunt Belgin said.

"If only!" said Ayhan sadly, picking up his jacket.

The rim of the bathtub and the top of the mirrored cabinet were crowded with products for dry or damaged hair. I saw a deep recovery healing shampoo for deep damage repair, a dry remedy moisturizing mask for damaged curly hair, a total repair conditioner for hair damaged and dried by styling products, an ultimate moisture conditioner for very stressed hair, and a bottle that just read EMERGENCY TREATMENT: HAIR DAMAGED BY DRYNESS. I stood under the shower, luxuriating in the hot water yet troubled by a mounting sense of unease about my relatives' hair.

The sofa bed was designed for someone different from me—not just smaller but also, it seemed to me, with a different personality.

In the morning, Defne took me to see the famous university where she studied business management; it stood on a hilltop overlooking the Bosphorus, just above a fifteenth-century fortress that had figured in the siege of Constantinople. Even though it was the summer, the university had an atmosphere of late nights and intense relationships, of the oldest and the newest books, and for the first time I felt a flicker of excitement about going back to school in the fall.

We visited Topkapı Palace, where we paid extra to go inside the harem: an exquisitely tiled labyrinth formerly known as "the golden cage." The harem was beautiful, but I felt relieved when it was time to leave for our next destination, a giant shopping mall, where we sat in a courtyard and ate Belgian waffles. All around us, women and teenagers were also eating Belgian waffles. The mall had a Japanese stationery store, where I bought a new spiral notebook. It had the most supple and creamy paper, and a pink cover decorated with a maroon anthropomorphic bean. The bean had one hand on its hip, and was waving with the other hand. It was a marvelous notebook.

Our plane got to Antalya at ten at night. My mother had arrived some hours earlier. As usual, she had elegant new things I had never seen or thought of before: eyeglasses with extra-thin lenses and thick frames, the palest taupe sandals with kitten heels, a wine-colored leather overnight bag. Her toenails were painted almost the same taupe as the sandals but even paler, a color I had never before seen on nails. The sandals were mesmerizing, they themselves looked like two well-turned women.

My mother couldn't understand how I had so much energy after a plane trip. "It isn't normal," she said. "Have you taken something?" I said that maybe it was because I *hadn't* taken anything. The worried expression on her face didn't change. "Take this," she said, and gave me half a Valium.

My mother herself had taken half a Valium on the plane from New York a few days earlier, and had subsequently lost her passport and entered the country in some way that she said it would be better if I didn't know about. Later, in Ankara, my mother had been walking down a street and had fallen down because the pavement was so uneven. A grocer's helper ran out of a grocery, picked her up, called her "sister," and offered her a cigarette. Well, that was Turkey: the roads were crap, but people were respectful to their elders.

"This came for you in Ankara," my mother said, handing me a postcard with a picture of the Bridge of Sighs. The back was covered with compact, curly handwriting.

> *Hi, Selin,*
> *Well, I made it to the birthplace of your literary hero,*
> *Casanova (ha, ha). The atmosphere is very decadent, almost*
> *unreal. I keep feeling like I'm in "Death in Venice" and about*
> *to succumb to the plague on my way to trying to ravish a*
> *small boy or something. Bill just left. We had an extremely*
> *intense time, with even more ups and downs than usual, not*
> *to mention our standard "debate" about art in every single*
> *cathedral. Also, I've been having really freaky dreams here. I*
> *think I might be subconsciously affected by the fact that Venice*
> *has no classical history. It was only founded in the fifth*
> *century (by refugees from Attila the Hun). I guess with my*

classical sensibility it makes sense that I felt more integrated in
Rome. Then again, who knows, maybe I'm just freaked out
about going back to Belgrade. Anyway. Speaking of Attila, I
hope you're faring well in the land of the "devil incarnate"
and nobody is chasing you with antlers. I really wish we could
have one of our long talks. I wanted to tell you about a dream
I had involving an orgiastic carnival with nuns, but I'm out
of room as you can see.

Love, Svetlana

. . .

There was something unnerving about the Antalya hotel—the constant hissing of sprinklers in the undergrowth, the startled expressions of the staff members in their gold-braided uniforms, the shrubs on which huge orange-red blossoms gaped like demented lions with rigid sticklike tongues. I heard Russian everywhere: the beginning of my course of study in the Russian language had coincided with a boom in Russian tourism to the Turkish Mediterranean. Though it was August, the leather stores were full of Russian people buying enormous sheepskin coats. They were planning for the future.

There was a dinner buffet, with a kebab station and a swan made of butter sweating in a tub of ice. We all sat at a long table—me, my mother, Defne, Aunt Belgin, aunts Seda, Şenay, and Arzu, Arzu's son Murat, and Murat's new girlfriend, Yudum. Whenever Yudum stepped away for a minute, everyone started criticizing her. Defne took exception to her name, which meant "sip." "Who has a name like that?" asked Defne, whose name meant "laurel."

Yudum had to share a room with Murat's mother, Arzu, who worked for the secret service, had a mania for cleanliness, and was always climbing on chairs to dust the invisible tops of things. Murat got his own room, but Yudum wasn't allowed to stay with him—she had to stay with Arzu. Together they dusted the top of the wardrobe.

. . .

I tried to hang out with my peer group, Defne, Murat, and Yudum, but was unable to assimilate myself to their mode of being. They seemed always to be waiting for something, for the removal of some obstacle— for a business to open, for the sun to move, or for someone to come back from going to get something. Whenever they actually did anything, like go in the water, eat lunch, or walk somewhere, they did it in an abstracted, halfhearted way, as if to show that this was just a side diversion from the main business of waiting. All they talked about was when the thing they were waiting for was going to happen. But whenever that thing did happen, nothing seemed to change. The sense of provisionality was the same, it just gradually found a new object.

In the end I spent most of my time alone, reading or swimming. I was more into swimming than anyone else in my family—that came from being an American. I also walked around more. "She goes from there to here, from here to there, from there to here again," Aunt Arzu observed more than once.

"She's been like that since she was a child," my mother said proudly.

My mother swam for half an hour a day, holding her head very upright. Sometimes I joined her. Once when we were swimming along like that together we came upon a gigantic turd floating at eye level. Thinking it might be some kind of a stick or small log, I pointed it out to my mother. "It's shit," she said with a pained expression.

None of my aunts believed what we had seen. They kept trying to refute us on theoretical grounds. "Shit would have fallen apart into small pieces," Aunt Arzu said.

"It would never float intact like that," Şenay agreed.

"Who heard of shit floating? Does shit float? I've never heard of such a thing," Seda chimed in.

"I say this as a doctor," said my mother. "Go swim over there and you'll see shit floating."

. . .

Every day near sunset, I swam out to the plastic raft that was tethered near the buoys about a hundred meters from the shore. I lay flat on my back on the warm blue plastic, listening to the sloshing of the waves and to all the inner noises one's head made after swimming. The sun dipped toward the horizon, a little earlier every day. I lay with my feet facing the shore and thought about how five thousand miles *that* way, toward the sun, was Boston; whereas Tokyo, where Ivan was, lay five thousand miles in the direction of the encroaching darkness. Five thousand miles farther in the same direction—clockwise, from the North Pole—was California.

I was usually the only person on the raft, but one afternoon I became aware of a man headed in my direction. He was swimming the crawl, unhurriedly and somehow inexorably, turning his face to breathe every four strokes. On reaching the raft, he treaded water for a minute, squinting—he was in his forties or fifties, with a shaved head—and pulled himself up on the metal ladder.

"Is okay?" he asked, pointing at the raft. I nodded. He lay on his back a couple of feet away from me, propped on his elbows, water glinting on his arms and his rising and falling chest. You could tell from looking at him that he was Russian. The raft continued to rock and splash for a while, then slowly settled down.

I decided to try to talk to the man. Outside of school, I had never spoken Russian to anyone who was actually from there. I told him I was studying Russian in the university.

"Is that so," he said. Sounding only slightly bored, he asked where the university was, where I was from, where my parents were from, where I was born, and what I studied: all questions I knew how to answer. I asked what he did by profession. He said he was a businessman.

"Is it interesting?" I asked.

"The point isn't whether it's interesting," he said after a moment, and rubbed his thumb and index finger together. I felt a jolt of sexual current, and I was appalled. What was so attractive? His indifference to boredom? The way he had invoked money? What did I care about his money? I remembered how alienated I had felt in the Hungarian villages, listening to the Beatles sing about money and women—I'd thought it was some weird 1950s thing. But what if my body also responded in some way to money? What if that was the way women were?

"So," said the Russian man. "Are you here alone?"

I shook my head. "My mother and four aunts are here."

"Four aunts," he said. "That's a lot." He squinted at the shore, possibly looking for aunts. "And in the evenings?"

"In the evenings?"

"Do you spend the evenings with your four aunts?"

I immediately felt the same sense of insult and injury I had felt at times with Ivan—as if he were making fun of me or trying to trick me. "I don't know," I said.

"And what don't you know?"

I looked over at him—at his arm, which had a brown birthmark and a smallpox vaccination, and at his mouth, which was so clearly, though for reasons I couldn't articulate, not an American person's mouth.

"It was very pleasant to meet you," I said, and slid to the edge of the raft and back into the cool water, which seized me all at once, all over my body, not forgetting a single inch.

For the first five or six days I didn't suffer at all, carried along by the change of scene and the sense of a progression. This was the next step in the story. Ivan was in Tokyo and I was here. It was like when two characters in a movie went to two different places.

Then something changed. My life no longer seemed like a movie to me. Ivan was still in the movie, but had left me behind. Nothing extraordinary was happening anymore, or would ever happen again. I was just there with my relatives, living pointless, shapeless days that weren't bringing me any closer to anything. It seemed to me that this state of affairs was a relief to my mother. From her perspective, I thought, the past weeks had been a perilous, temporary adventure, something to be endured, and now things were back to normal. It was painful to feel at such cross-purposes with her. Almost everything that was interesting or meaningful in my story was, in her story, a pointless hazard or annoyance. This was even more true with my aunts. They didn't take anything I did seriously; it was all some trivial, mildly annoying side activity that I insisted on for some reason, having nothing to do with real life. I couldn't challenge or contradict this view, even to myself, because I really didn't know how to do anything real. I didn't know how to move to a new city, or have sex, or have a real job, or make someone fall in love with me, or do any kind of study that wasn't just a self-improvement project.

For the first time in my life, I couldn't think of anything I particularly wanted to study or to do. I still had the old idea of being a writer, but that was being, not doing. It didn't say what you were supposed to do.

I got physically sick. My stomach hurt, I felt nauseated all the time and especially when I tried to read, my legs and shoulders ached, I lost the strength to go anywhere or do anything, or smile, or hold my mouth up in a normal position when people talked to me. My face just fell like a cake. My aunts thought I was sulking or angry, and teased me. I wasn't sulking—I just couldn't move my face. I couldn't eat, or think about eating. I couldn't begin to think about sitting through the dinner buffet—about listening to everyone say passive-aggressive stuff to Yudum, to Yudum trying to accrue social capital by mocking me and Defne, to Aunt Seda plying me with lamb and teasing me about how I used to be a vegetarian, and to Murat saying the béchamel needed more butter. My mother told everyone I had an upset stomach, and ordered tea and toast from room service. The toast came lined up on a silver rack, like outgoing mail, with quince jam—a kind of jam I had always made fun of in the past.

After a few days, the physical symptoms passed. Inside my soul, I still felt like I had fallen off the end of the conveyor belt, but I was able to eat, read, swim, and hold my face together such that I wasn't constantly staring at people with the stricken eyes of death.

My mother and I took a day trip to visit my grandmother's half-brother Şükrü, who had recently bought an interest in a hotel in the Antalya region. It was a long, disorienting taxi ride over winding inland roads. The hotel had no beachfront—it just seemed to be an empty luxury hotel built for no reason on a swamp. Şükrü met us at a circular drive. Stocky, unctuous, bald, with fleshy lips and pale eyes, he was nothing like my grandmother—my skinny, black-eyed grandmother, with her deep voice and booming laugh.

Şükrü received us in a gazebo, where a waiter brought tea and petits fours. He explained to us that we were sitting in Turkey's first golf hotel. There was a new mania among wealthy American and Scottish people to play golf in exotic locations, for example in Malaysia. In Turkey, people were still backward, and didn't know about golf hotels. His partners had bought this land for pennies, because it didn't have a beachfront, and all Turkish people knew about was beaches. Well, the golfers didn't care about beaches. You gave them a pool and a first-rate golf course and they were happy.

In truth, the land here was a little swampier than was totally con-sistent with a pleasant golf experience; basically it was impossible to strike a ball in such a way that it would go anywhere, and a lot of the property would have to be drained. But the main building was fin-ished, for all practical purposes, and Şükrü was living there himself, along with his daughter—Seda had briefed us on the daughter, a social-ite who featured regularly in the tabloids—and his grandson Alp. Alp, he said, was really thriving here, in the empty hotel on a swamp.

Alp drove up in a mud-splattered golf cart. Though he was only eight years old, his barrel-shaped body, paunch, and humorous eyes gave him the aspect of a miniature adult.

"Get in, get in," Şükrü told us. "He'll give you the tour."

My mother and I looked at each other. After a moment we got in the golf cart. My mother sat in the back, next to and partially under a large metal rake. I sat in the front next to Alp, around whose neck glinted a tiny golden roller skate on a gold chain. Shifting gears with a professional flourish, he backed into some shrubs and careened onto the main drive.

We drove past a fleet of parked golf carts, a rolling hill, and a mound of sand, then veered into the future golf green. The ground was so swampy that the tires left indentations in the mud. The thing that really struck you, directly, in the face, was the amount of life. Members of God's creation kept flying into your arms and face. The landscape quivered and whirred, the tall grass and palm fronds trem-bled, the mud seemed to wriggle. Frogs plopped into ponds and un-known creatures rustled among the leaves. Something buzzed loudly past my ear and something or somebody flew into my eye.

Alp gunned the motor to get over a small hill. The tires briefly lost their purchase. "Don't worry—I'm here," Alp said.

"Gently, dear Alp, my child," my mother said.

"I'm going to show you everywhere," Alp said.

"You already showed us so much," said my mother.

"You haven't seen anything yet."

At some point he braked abruptly, leaped out, grabbed the enormous rake, and started to bludgeon the earth. It turned out he was killing a snake. He snapped its spine and then beat it till it stopped moving, reminding me of Saint George.

"Filthy," he explained, looking back at us and winking.

I wasn't sure how things were going for Alp out there, at the deserted golf resort in the snake-rich swamp. It was by no means clear that everything was going well. And yet, the encounter with him made me feel a glimmer of optimism. I thought I might write something about it, about the golf hotel. But when I tried to think of a plot that led to that swamp, I couldn't face it—not another hotel, no, I couldn't.

When I got back to school in the fall, I changed my major from linguistics and didn't take any more classes in the philosophy or psychology of language. They had let me down. I hadn't learned what I had wanted to about how language worked. I hadn't learned anything at all.

Acknowledgments

Working on this book has made me increasingly conscious of the debt I owe all my teachers, particularly those I encountered in my first year of college. I didn't always believe them at the time, but they were basically right about everything. I would also like to express my affection and gratitude toward my former classmates from the same period, many of whom I haven't spoken to in years, though their earlier selves still feel very present and dear to me.

"Nina in Siberia" is based on a real text, "The Story of Vera," which I first encountered in 1995, and which was coauthored over the years by some number of Russian-language instructors working, so far as I have been able to determine, under a shroud of secrecy. I thank the Harvard Russian Language Program, and particularly Patricia Chaput and Natalia Chirkova, for introducing me to it.

A first draft of this book was written in 2000–1 with support from Eric Hsu. Beatrice Monti della Corte and the Santa Maddalena Foundation provided the idyllic, pug-saturated atmosphere in which I eventually revisited it, and discovered that time had turned it into a historical novel. I am also grateful for the generosity of the Rona Jaffe Foundation, the Whiting Foundation, Koç University, and the Cullman Center for Scholars and Writers.

My agent, Sarah Chalfant, and my editor, Ann Godoff, have supported *The Idiot* and its author in every way. Will Heyward contributed insights on topics ranging from Stendhal to the fauna of New Zealand. Casey Rasch is destined for great things. Lorin Stein gave me amazing notes, as always. Dimiter Kenarov was far more useful than a bald man's comb. I wrote the end of this book at the desk of Rajesh Parameswaran. My beloved parents, Olcay Ayanlar Batuman and Vecihi Batuman, always put my education first. Lindsay Nordell's readership has been like a splendid shining jewel that I still can't believe I get to hold in my hand.

Fyodor Mikhailovich: when it came to titles, and not just titles, what writer could ever touch the hem of your lofty garment?